THE
ISLE OF BATTLE

Also by Sean Russell

THE ONE KINGDOM
Book One of the Swans' War

THE
ISLE OF BATTLE

Book Two of the Swans' War

SEAN RUSSELL

An Imprint of HarperCollins Publishers

EOS

EOS
An Imprint of HarperCollins*Publishers*
10 East 53rd Street
New York, New York 10022-5299

Library of Congress Cataloging-in-Publication Data

Russell, Sean.
The isle of battle / Sean Russell.
p. cm. — (Swans' war ; bk. 2)
ISBN 0-380-97490-8
I. Title.

PR9199.3.R84 I87 2002
813'.54—dc21   2002024269

First Eos hardcover printing: August 2002

Eos Trademark Reg. U.S. Pat. Off. and in Other Countries,
Marca Registrada, Hecho en U.S.A.
HarperCollins® is a trademark of HarperCollins Publishers Inc.

Printed in the U. S. A.

FIRST EDITION

10 9 8 7 6 5 4 3 2 1

www.eosbooks.com

This book is dedicated to two fine gentlemen:

Stephen Donaldson, and my agent Howard Morhaim.

Their friendship, support, and wisdom have

been indispensable.

Acknowledgments

As usual I have a long list of people to thank, starting with my wonderful editors, Jennifer Hershey and Diana Gill. Sean Stewart, Tim Holman at Orbit, Kate Elliott, and Ian Dennis. My wife, Karen, who does everything to give me time to work. A special thanks to Rose Klinkenberg, who kept telling me I needed the character who later became Theason Hollyoak (and even suggested the name). And Jill and Walter at White Dwarf Books, of course.

THE
ISLE OF BATTLE

❧❧

What Went Before

It was said that the Wynnd was a haunted river—a river of many mysteries and many branches that took men places none had seen before. A sorcerer was said to sleep in the deep, cool waters, dreaming of an ancient kingdom divided and brought to ruin. Wyrr was the sorcerer's name, and his token had been the double swan.

A thousand years after the sorcerer gave himself to the river, two families went to war for the throne of the Kingdom of Ayr. They warred until there was no kingdom and no throne, but only their abiding enmity, which they passed down from one generation to the next, like a disease. These families were the Renné and the Wills, and their banners bore the double swan.

The Swans' War persisted for generations, driving many from the heart of the old kingdom to the farthest reaches of the land between the mountains. There they hoped to find peace and forget their pasts. A small number even reached the Vale of Lakes in the most distant north, but the Vale lay at the headwaters of the River Wynnd, and from time to time the currents drew the unwary away on strange journeys.

Tam, Fynnol, and Baore were three young Valemen of uncommon curiosity and unexpected tenacity. Unlike most of their kin, who wished to forget the past, these young men dug through an ancient battlefield searching for artifacts which they hoped to carry down the River Wynnd and trade for horses. But as they delved into the old meadows by Telanon Bridge, a traveler came and spent the evening by their campfire, charming them with stories of distant places.

That night, as they slept, armed men found them in the dark and would have murdered them had not the stranger, Alaan, led them to safety, holding the bridge so they could escape, but at the cost of his life.

The three young men from the Vale spent the night hidden among rocks in the river, and when the sun rose, they found the boat with their artifacts in it had been cut free and sent down the river. The men-at-arms who had attacked them were not to be found, but instead a caravan of "black wanderers" appeared: the dark-haired, dark-eyed Fáel on their spring pilgrimage to the north.

The Fáel were a mystery to the other peoples of the land between the mountains, believing in vision weavers and story finders and all manner of ghosts and spirits. This band of Fáel had brought Cynddl, a story finder, with them, and he offered to pay the Valemen to take him down the river so that he might "listen" to its tales, that they not be lost. Seeing a chance to recover their hoped-for adventure, Tam, Fynnol, Baore, and Cynddl set off into the wildlands down a haunted river.

They did not know that the men-at-arms who had tried to murder them at Telanon Bridge were seeking them still. To their horror, they were hunted down the length of the Wynnd and were forced to fight desperately to preserve their lives. By night an apparition haunted them, watching Baore as though he drew the thing to him, though he feared it like Death itself.

The River Wynnd lived up to its reputation, and carried the travelers along secret branchings, into strange landscapes where they found long-extinct animals and peculiar people.

Far to the south, the Renné and the Wills prepared for war again, and an arranged marriage between Elise Wills, heir presumptive to a nonexistent throne, and Prince Michael of Innes would give the Wills the wealth and the armies they needed.

But Lady Elise had a mind of her own, and she went to her father, the blind minstrel, Carral Wills, and told him she would not marry this prince and see the war begin again. With the help of a group of minstrels, she slipped out of her family's castle and fled, taking a boat on the River Wynnd.

Traveling south by night, the Valemen ran ashore upon an island that appeared on no map of the river. There they met an old scholar who called himself Eber son of Eiresit. He dwelt in the uninhabited wildlands with his servants and young son, Llya, who had not the power of speech. Eber told them that the river tried to speak to him but he could not understand it.

Days later, as they continued their journey, a messenger from Eber, a traveler named Theason Hollyoak, caught up with them and told them that the river spirit that followed them was a nagar, and to escape it they must leave the Greensprings—as the Fáel called the wildlands—with all speed. Pursued by men-at-arms and a nagar, the Valemen and their Fáel story finder pushed south.

But nothing could be predicted when traveling on the River Wynnd, and the Valemen saved three minstrels whose boat was sinking. One of these minstrels was Elise Wills, traveling under another name and putting her father's musical training to good use in her bid to escape Prince Neit of Innes—Prince Michael's father—and his counselor.

All were going to the tournament at the Westbrook Fair, where the Valemen had learned that Alaan, the stranger they met by Telanon Bridge, was still alive and planning to sell their artifacts.

The fair was the focus of many plans that summer, for the cousins of Toren Renné conspired to end his life there and cast the blame on the Wills. Samul, Arden, Beldor, and Dease believed that Toren's attempts to reconcile with their enemy, the Wills, had to be stopped or they would bring the family to ruin.

Cynddl and his companions from the Vale took Elise Wills to a Fáel encampment near the fair, but her presence became known to Sir Eremon, a knight rumored to have once gone by the name of Hafydd . . . though Hafydd had been dead for years. Sir Eremon, who was a counselor to Prince Neit, sent his guards to steal Elise away.

Alaan appeared and convinced the Valemen to aid him in rescuing Elise Wills at the Renné costume ball that would end the fair. He also recruited Elise's betrothed, Prince Michael, and a champion of the tournament named Pwyll Stagshanks, a man-at-arms who had proven himself equal to the best knights in the land.

Sir Eremon, however, thwarted Alaan's attempt and chased him into the hidden lands. The Valemen escaped with their lives, but learned that Elise Wills had thrown herself into the river, in despair at ever escaping.

The Renné conspirators tried to murder Toren but instead killed one of their own—Arden, who had gone to Toren to admit his part in the planned murder. Everything appeared to have gone awry with the most tragic results.

And so begins our story, on that night of the Renné Ball, beneath a full moon, in the land between the mountains.

One

Torches guttered and flared, haloed in the mist that boiled above the river. No body had surfaced, though that was of little comfort to Prince Michael of Innes. He walked knee deep in the slow-moving river, feeling the mud give softly beneath his boots, half afraid that he would stumble over Elise Wills motionless on the bottom.

"What a foolish act!" he whispered to himself. Foolish and desperate, but had he not considered the same thing himself? Escape from Hafydd—escape at all costs.

He found the whole evening strange and unreal. Even his feelings seemed veiled, as though this same cold mist was all that moved within his heart. Elise was gone . . . yet he didn't believe it. Her own father had said she couldn't swim. She'd gone into the river rather than let their marriage serve Hafydd and his ambitions. *Rather than marry* me, the Prince reminded himself.

Voices sounded along the shore, muffled in the murk, but there was no elation in those calls, no sudden joyful discovery to blow the clinging mist from his heart.

The Prince set one foot down in the ooze, then the other. A ghost of anger made itself felt, though distant and unformed. He cursed Hafydd under his breath, the words swirling out in a fine mist.

A blunt-ended punt loomed out of the fog, its masked and costumed inhabitants drawing quick breaths of surprise as the prince appeared in the haze: a man, strangely costumed walking on water. A ghost. After all the madness at the Renné Ball, a ghost should have been expected.

One of Hafydd's revenant honor guard hurried by along the bank, a torch held high, forcing back the night and illuminating the wraiths of mist that swirled around them. Prince Michael prayed that they would find Elise alive—and prayed that they would not. Such a courageous act should not end with being dragged from the river, drenched in failure. She deserved better than that. It was selfishness alone that made him hope she would be found, still among the living.

The party that had come with the Wills family were desperately searching, running this way and that, even the men-at-arms choking back tears. They had known Elise all her short, sweet life, he reminded himself. They wouldn't feel this numbness that penetrated his heart.

Torches wavered above him suddenly, and he realized he'd come back to the bridge. A small knot of dark-robed men gathered on the bank, their whispers barely distinguishable from the river's voice. They glanced up as the Prince appeared, but then ignored him, as they did habitually. Hafydd was there, at the center, tall and proud. He moved down to the river's edge and crouched—the motion giving the lie to his years. He glanced at Michael, then away. A gray man, Michael thought, dressed in black, grim and hard as stone.

For a moment he didn't move, his men arrayed about him, silent and intimidated. But then he stood, drawing out his sword. Prince Michael felt himself step back, though he hadn't willed his limbs to do so. Hafydd slid down the small bank into the water. He plunged the blade into the smooth back of the river and held it still, his eyes closed. None of his minions dared speak.

"She's gone," Hafydd said, but then his arm jerked as if the river had shuddered. His eyes opened. "*Sianon*," he whispered. He seemed about to collapse, crumpling over the blade he still held in the river. Two of his guards stepped forward to support him but the knight shook them off and drew himself up.

Hafydd turned and strode up the bank, disappearing into the fog, his minions following after like so many shadows.

"Lady Elise . . . ?" Baore said, but could not finish the sentence. The look of fear and concern on his face said more than Elise needed to hear. He kept glancing at the bank, looking for a place to land—somewhere up the Westbrook, Elise thought, far from the bridge where she had given herself to the river.

"It is all right, Baore," she managed. But it was a lie. She could not even sit up. Her head seemed to be in a whirl, her thoughts a crazed jumble. Memories came flooding in. War she saw, endless years of war and battle and blood. And with these visions came a terrible sense of excitement and anticipation that sent a wave of dread through her, drying her mouth and causing her limbs to tremble. What had she done? What kind of a monster had she made her bargain with?

The boat slid to a halt in soft mud, and Baore leapt nimbly over the side to haul the craft high up the bank. He tried to help her out but in the end reached in and lifted her in his arms, setting her down by the coals of a smoldering fire. He disappeared a moment and returned with a blanket wrapped around a bundle of clothes. This he held out to her awkwardly.

"They're my cousin Fynnol's," he said, "but I think they'll fit."

Elise glanced up from where she crouched by the fire. Baore was a shadow presence in the darkness and mist. "Thank you," she said, but could not move to begin to put them on.

She began to tremble again, not from the cold. *She had drowned in the river! Drowned!*

"You must get out of that wet costume," Baore said, mistaking her trembling for cold. But she could not, and in the end Baore helped her, dressing her like a child, averting his eyes as he did so, which would have made her smile if she had been capable of it.

He rekindled the fire but the flames did not warm her.

"They will be looking for me," she managed, her head perhaps spinning a little less.

"We came a distance upstream, my lady," Baore said. "They will look downstream toward the Wynnd."

She nodded. It made sense, surprisingly. The trembling in her limbs was fading slowly, and the visions that had swum in her head were receding. Though she still felt as though the world spun beneath her, and her feelings were not her own, she closed her eyes and saw the wraith, the nagar Sianon, hovering before her in the water, luring her, deceiving her.

"I must find Alaan," she said. "He—He might be able to help me find my way through this."

Baore was crouched down across from her, shifting the wood in the fire. He glanced up. "You struck a bargain with . . . her," he whispered.

She looked up at him, but his gaze dropped to the fire.

Then very softly she said, "How resolute you were to refuse her, Baore Talon."

Elise took a long deep breath. She was regaining something like control but even her senses seemed wrong—contradictory. She was dressed in the clothing of a man and it felt strangely familiar. Sianon had shunned women's dress, she realized, the memory coming unbidden.

Elise took up the whetstone Baore had given her—Sianon's whetstone—and held it a moment. Stone endured when all else wore away. It seemed at once familiar and unknown to her—as though she could almost remember it. She had a memory of hands honing a dagger edge on this very stone, so very long ago.

She tucked it securely into a pocket. With an effort she stood. If Hafydd found her thus, she knew she would not survive a moment.

Hafydd had long ago made his bargain with Caibre and was more dangerous than her.

I must find a place of safety to gain control of this transformation, she thought. She glanced over at Baore, who looked like a man who had lost a brother in battle. He had met Sianon. He knew.

"I must find Alaan," she said. "Will Tam know where he is?"

She could see the big Valeman shrug in the firelight. "We were, all of us from the Vale, to help Alaan in his plot against Hafydd—"

"Hafydd lives," she said. "Alaan failed."

Baore put a callused hand to his brow. "Who—Who knows what's become of the others, then? They've not returned here, where we were to meet."

"Alaan will not let them come to harm if he can help it. Don't be concerned. We will wait here, but not too long. When Elise's body is not found, Hafydd will become suspicious. Best not to be near the river then." She looked out at the passing stream. "Best we draw the boat up, Baore. I don't want to be found just yet. When Caibre learns that I've come back, let it be too late."

Prince Michael climbed up the embankment, which was slick with dew. Costumed onlookers still stood about gawking at the river hidden in fog. At the height of the road the mist thinned, as though a river of haze flowed beneath the bridge that arked over the Westbrook. The onlookers—nobles returning from the Renné Ball—were being told that Lady Elise had been thrown from her horse over the bridge rail. Prince Michael wondered if any believed it.

One thing was certain: there had seldom been a Renné Ball that provided gossips with more fodder.

The Prince found Lord Carral, wrapped now in a heavy wool cloak but still sitting upon a horse, his mask discarded, replaced with a look so wretched and pitiable that it tore at Michael's heart.

"Is there any news, sir?" the servant who held the lead to Carral's horse asked as the Prince emerged from the fog—like a man walking ashore, Prince Michael thought.

Michael shook his head, and then remembering Lord Carral's affliction, said, "Neither good news nor bad." He remembered Hafydd's odd reaction when he put his blade in the river, but as he had no idea what it meant, he said nothing.

"Prince Michael?" Lord Carral said, as though there could be some doubt. The Prince knew that Carral Wills never forgot a voice.

"At your service," Prince Michael said.

The slightest hesitation. "Do you mean that or are you merely being polite?"

"Of course I mean it, sir."

"That's good, for I'm about to ask a favor. Can you find your horse and ride with me a short distance down the road?"

"Certainly. I shall escort you all the way to the Wills encampment, if you wish."

The habitually blank face seemed suddenly overwhelmed by sadness. The sightless eyes closed tightly, distorting the handsome face. "I shall take the other direction," he said very quietly.

"Toward Castle Renné?" Without thinking, the Prince held up his hand. "No. It is none of my business where you go. Let me find my squire."

In a few moments he was on his horse and accompanying Lord Carral across the bridge. Among the onlookers, nobles of both Prince Michael's family and Lord Carral's waited. A few guards remained among them, but no one saw anything odd in Prince Michael and the father of the drowned girl crossing the bridge. It was thought that perhaps they went to seek news on the other shore.

In a moment they had passed beyond the retinue of both families, and were on a shadowed road, populated only by staggering stragglers. The pale light of stars and moon shivered among the trees of the wood, and washed over the road as the wind moved the branches.

"You needn't go farther than this," Lord Carral said.

"But it is late and you have only one unarmed servant to guard you."

"That will be enough. After what I have lost this night, anyone may have my purse."

They drew their horses up in a patch of clear moonlight, and just as they did so, the drumming of galloping horses reached them. Six riders appeared out of the shadow. Prince Michael thought they would be Hafydd's guards sent to retrieve Lord Carral, but they were neither knights in black nor retainers of the Wills family or of his father.

The riders thundered by, spraying them with detritus and sand.

"They wore Renné blue, I think," Prince Michael said. "Though why in such a hurry I cannot guess." He found the riders' sudden appearance unsettling.

For a moment Lord Carral said nothing, then unexpectedly, "You tried, Prince Michael. We all tried, but we failed her. . . ." Again the minstrel shut his eyes tight, squeezing back the tears. "Don't blame yourself," he said after a moment. "Hafydd is formidable."

"But what will you do now?" the prince blurted out.

"Better you not ask," Carral said, then softly to his servant, "Take me on."

Prince Michael sat on his mount for a moment watching the famed minstrel disappear into the shadows of the trees. Carral's gray was a pale mass in the dark, as though the nobleman rode a cloud, and then it too was gone. The Prince spurred his horse and turned back the way he'd come.

At the bridgehead he found one of his father's knights, torch in hand. "Who were those riders who sped by?" Prince Michael asked.

"Did you not hear?" the man said. "Arden Renné is dead: killed by an assassin's arrow this very night."

★   ★   ★

A strand of mist snaked along the valley bottom, curling in the moonlight. Tam and the others crossed an open meadow, which tumbled down toward the river. Below them dark trees stood silhouetted against the haze. They were back in the land between the mountains, their scheme to bring an end to Hafydd, in ruins—Alaan on the run, chased by Hafydd's minions.

They went slowly, the moon throwing their shadows down in a jumble beneath their feet. Tam wondered if the others felt as exhausted as he. All that had happened that evening seemed suddenly to drain his emotions away, leaving nothing behind—like a retreating wave. Tam only wanted to lie down and sleep, to bury his head beneath blankets and be left in peace.

"But what is that, Cousin?" Fynnol asked Tom, and pointed.

As they crossed over the shoulder of the hill another artery of mist appeared, weaving its way among the trees.

"It must be the Westbrook," Pwyll said, looking around to find the moon. He pointed off. "The two rivers must meet there beyond the wood."

"Then our camp is not so far off," Cynddl said.

"Let us make some haste," Pwyll said, starting off, "and see if Alaan has returned."

But Fynnol slumped down hard upon a stone. "Give me a moment's rest. We've been caught up in madness all this night and I for one am exhausted and still frightened. I admit it. Even the climb down from that place left me shaking, and once again the lackeys of this man Hafydd tried to murder us." He put his head in his hands for a moment, and Tam stepped nearer and patted him gently on the back.

"What *has* become of Baore?" Fynnol asked loudly.

"I don't know," Tam answered, "but I suspect he's come to no harm."

"Then why didn't he meet us in the garden as we'd arranged?"

"Much occurred within Castle Renné," Tam said softly. "Likely the explanation is innocent enough. He was protecting some grandmother in the chaos. It would be like him. With a little luck the woman will adopt him and leave Baore her vast estates."

But the jest fell flat. Tam knew he should leave such things to Fynnol.

Pwyll was trying hard to be still, but he kept glancing down toward the Westbrook—there in the ribbons of mist.

"Come along, Fynnol," Tam said, again patting his cousin on the back, "we'll go down to our encampment and find food and drink. That will help more than rest."

"Nothing will help but to be out of this madness." But Fynnol rose up resolutely and they went off down the hill. At the bottom they found a rutted cart track worming into a small wood. Here they stumbled forward in the blackness where the moonlight would not enter. As they came out of the trees into the pale light again, they found a road that ran alongside the fog-bound river and followed it through the tendrils of mist that reached out to catch them.

There were people camped here and there along the roadside or not far off, sitting around campfires, often playing or listening to music. Tam thought the music more moody and sad than he would have expected, but perhaps that was fitting for the end of the fair. It certainly suited his own mood.

Two riders came toward them, and they all hesitated a moment as though they might slip off the moonlit road. Then Cynddl waved them all forward.

"These are Fáel," he said.

In a moment they reached the companions.

"Cynddl!" said one of them, surprised. "Nann has sent riders out seeking you."

It occurred to Tam that they must look an odd bunch in their costumes, the fine fabrics stained and torn to ruins.

"And you have found me," the story finder said. "What is it Nann wants that cannot wait?"

The two wanderers glanced at each other.

"We bear sad news, good Cynddl," one of them said softly. "Rath passed over this night. A great wind blew out of the west, and when it had passed he was gone."

Cynddl stood, unmoving for a moment, and then raised a hand to his mouth.

"Take my horse," one of the riders said, slipping down to the ground.

But the story finder shook his head. "No, two of our company have not yet been found this night. Mourning Rath will have to wait."

"But Cynddl," Tam said. "Certainly we will find Baore and Alaan. You needn't concern yourself with this. We know Rath was your friend and your teacher."

Cynddl turned to Tam, his eyes glistening in the moonlight. "I will be among my friends at this time," the story finder said, and then turned to the rider. "Tell Nann I will come when I can. The living have need of me yet."

The man who had dismounted glanced up at his companion, then nodded. Tam did not understand the customs of the Fáel well enough to know for sure, but this was certainly not the response the men expected.

As the riders departed, the companions went on, without speaking. No one sure what to say. Cynddl kept his eyes fixed on the shadowy road, leaving the others to watch out for their safety on the notoriously perilous roads.

"Let me tell you this," Cynddl said as they passed beyond the singing of a group camped by the roadside. "It is the story I would tell at Rath's funeral. Rath found this tale, though it came to him slowly, a few words at a time, for it was barely a whisper when Rath heard the first phrases." Cynddl took a long breath, paused a moment, and then, in his ancient voice, began. "A young maiden whose name was Ninal dwelt on the shores of the great river. Her parents had crossed over when she was young, and then her only brother had died as well. She was left alone in their home, tending their gardens and their few animals. The land about her was beautiful, and she lived the passing of the seasons, the apples ripening on the trees in the fall, the cherry blossoms in the spring. Her days were filled with her labors and walks along the river, for she was a steward of the woods and shores around her. Sometimes at night she would wake, thinking that she heard voices, but when she would go to her window and listen, she heard only the river muttering and the trees whispering each to the other.

"One evening she went to the bank of the river to draw out her net and found a black swan tangled in the web. With great care she unraveled the snarl, and let the frightened bird swim free. But when it had gone a dozen feet into the gloom, it stopped and turned back, regarding her with an intelligent eye.

" 'Why did you free me?' it asked.

" 'Because you are too beautiful to die,' she said, wondering what manner of magical creature the river had brought her.

" 'So are many, but death finds them all the same.' It began to swim away, but then stopped. 'But I am in your debt,' it said. 'Come to this place and each night I will tell you a story until summer's end.' "

"And so she did. Each night at dusk she would wait on the riverbank, and just as the darkness fell and the stars appeared, the swan would come and paddle about just at the edge of her vision and it would tell her a wondrous story. To hear a voice after so many years alone was the greatest relief to Ninal and she found that her daily labors were of little consequence now. She lived to hear the swan's story at day's end.

"All through the summer she heard her nightly tale, but as autumn set in she realized that there would be only a few stories more and then the silence and the solitude would return. The night of the last story, she hid a net in a small bag and took it with her to the river. As the swan neared the end of this last story, the maiden slipped the net from the bag, but then found she could not cast it. She couldn't bear the idea of enslaving this creature of the river and sky.

"And so the swan finished its tale and swam away. In her despair and loneliness Ninal threw the net into the river and then lay on the cold bank and wept beneath the stars.

"In the morning she went down to the river, and to her horror found the swan entangled again in the net, but this time it was still and cold. Gently, she freed the drowned bird and carried it up onto the bank where she made a pyre. When the pyre had burned to nothing, Ninal took the ashes and poured them into the winter river.

"That night at dusk she came down to the bank and told a story to the night. And the next night she did the same, and the next, until a hundred nights had passed. On the hundredth night she paced along the bank telling her tale, but just as she finished the bank beneath her feet crumbled and she was swept into the cold river.

"She struggled to reach the shore but the current was too swift and the bank crumbled and fell wherever she touched. As she began to grow cold and weak she realized a black swan swam just out of reach.

" 'Now you have had your revenge!' she wailed as she sank lower in the water.

" 'Revenge? I am but a spirit now, and have no influence on your world.'

" 'Can you not save me?' the maiden cried. 'I am not ready to cross over the river.'

" 'Few are,' the swan said. 'I am unable to help you even if I wanted to. But I will do this. I will tell you a story about a sad, lonely maiden who lived on the banks of the great river. . . .' "

Two

Alaan went down, too quickly, slipped and slammed his knee on the worn stone, tearing his fine costume. For a moment he slowed, his throbbing knee forcing him to take more weight on his hands as he slid and scrambled over the rock.

The wind funneled up the gorge with an agonizing moan. Alaan clung to his place while it shoved and tore at him, flailing his costume about his face. His arms trembled and his knee throbbed. Above, he could hear voices, the words shattered and swept up into a violent sky.

Is he among them? Alaan wondered. Had Hafydd come seeking him? Had he been lured here away from the armies of the Prince of Innes?

The wind dropped away, growling down the slope, and Alaan followed it, his knee stiff but bearing weight now. An arrow sparked off the stone by his hand and he jumped, letting himself fall and slide a dozen feet to a ledge. Pulling his own bow over his head, he nocked an arrow and shot the first man to appear above. The next he thought he might have missed, though narrowly.

He pulled his bow back over his head and shoulder and went on, the way widening and becoming easier. The advantage here was his, for he had been this way before and, as much as he could, had committed the path to memory, though by moonlight everything seemed steeper and more dangerous.

A ledge should slope off to the right not far below—though when it didn't, he was possessed by a sudden fear that he'd passed it when he let himself drop down to avoid the arrows.

But no, there it was, much as he'd remembered, though appearing narrower now. He swung himself onto the ledge around a buttress of stone and paused there a moment, gazing up. He didn't have to wait long. The men-at-arms followed behind, climbing down quickly, searching for holds and trying to watch for him at the same time. How the lead men must be expecting an arrow at any second.

Alaan knew that Hafydd, if he were here, would not be among these. He would be safely behind, letting his guards suffer the risks. Alaan barely had the heart to use his bow, but he didn't want to make their pursuit seem too easy. Hafydd was suspicious by nature. So Alaan stayed there awhile, and drove the men back up the draw, repelling two of their attempts to rush him. And then he went on, trotting quickly along the ledge, his battered knee having stiffened up again as he stood.

To his left the night world stretched away—shadows like shale, mountains of jagged moonlight. A cloud passed over the face of the moon, and Alaan was forced to grope forward, barely able to discern the ledge. It would be easy to misstep in such light, to be fooled and find oneself suddenly a creature of the air—for a brief moment.

The cloud passed and he hurried on. Where the rock bent around a corner, he stopped to look back. There they were, following quickly along, their costumes lending a macabre air to the scene in the stark light; like a madman's painting. Alaan pressed himself on. There was some distance yet to go, even to one who could find hidden shortcuts.

The ledge led to another gully, though not so steep, with a slop-

ing floor of loose rock, some of it large, most not. Alaan could almost run now, his knee loosening up a little. The trick was to keep
his speed under control. The rock slid beneath his feet, and he
stood upon its moving back like a trick rider at a fair. When it
slowed, he went on, leaping knee-high boulders, falling once to
bloody his knuckles. Twice he paused to fire arrows back up at the
men behind—keeping them at a distance.

The path he took offered them few branchings or even other
passable tracks to take. Alaan did not want to lose Hafydd's
guards—or Hafydd. Not yet.

Is he there? he wondered. *Does that aspect of Caibre survive in this
stern knight?*

Alaan knew what miscalculation now would mean. Hafydd had
made a bargain with the nagar, ancient soul of the sorcerer Caibre.
Only Alaan still had memories of Caibre from an age ago when he
had overrun kingdoms, putting man, woman, and child to the
sword. Of spells that had thrown down mountains, toppled castles,
and shattered the bones of the earth. Caibre was a monster whose
air was the smoke of war, whose wine was the blood of his enemies—
and it was always difficult to predict who Caibre would decide was
his enemy. Difficult to predict, one day to the next.

He pressed on until he was down from the high cliffs and under
the trees of a wooded gully. This place did not match with any view
that could be seen from above, but Hafydd would not be much
bothered by that. He had chased Alaan before.

Beneath the trees the air was moist and cool, and the ground was
soft beneath his feet. A little stream curled out of the dark to
bounce and burble along the gully bottom, as though it had come
to keep him company.

This should allay Hafydd's worst fears, Alaan thought: *water.* He
could not die where there was water.

Streaks of moonlight swarmed over the ground as the wind
whipped the trees to and fro, and Alaan went forward haltingly, trying to make sense of the frantic landscape.

The air rasped cruelly in and out of his lungs now, and his mind seemed numbed, the sound of his breathing loud in his ears, punctuated by the dull thuds of his footfalls.

There was a shout from behind, and an arrow buried itself in the ground near his boot. Alaan pushed himself on, dodging into shadow, the trees throwing stains of moonlight at his feet then stealing them away.

On the wind he thought he heard a distant baying like hounds, but he paid it no mind.

The slope began to level, and Alaan leapt the moon-silvered stream, which only whispered now. He stopped in the shadow of a tree, bent double, listening. The moonlight chased madly across the clearing. When the silhouettes of men appeared, he showed himself, waited until he was seen, then slipped into shadow and ran on.

He knew how dangerous this was, keeping the men so close, but on the paths he traveled, if he lost his hunters they would never find him again—and he didn't want that; not yet.

The slope went steeply down again, and the smell of rotting vegetation wafted up on a falling breeze. By the time he found the shore of the swamp, he was out of breath, and stopped again, standing with one foot in the tepid water.

A man shot out of the shadow, sword raised. Alaan barely had time to pull his own blade and dodge a vertical stroke. He slipped on the wet bottom, having stepped back without thinking, and fought to regain his balance, barely parrying a thrust at his heart. Alaan's own blade sank into the man's throat as he felt steel drive deep into his thigh above the injured knee.

The man, dressed as a toy soldier, reached up and grabbed Alaan's blade, choking as he did. In the pale light dark fluid ran down his hand, and he fell to his knees. Alaan yanked his blade free and wallowed into the water, limping terribly. Across a few yards of open water he forced his way into the reeds, looking back to see his track plainly marked where he'd stirred up the bottom. The man lay at the swamp's edge, still gurgling and choking.

Alaan pulled his bow free, ducked down and nocked an arrow. Others appeared, catching up to the magnificent runner who now lay choking on the bank. Alaan shot the first man and just missed another as they retreated up the bank into the protection of the trees and the shadows.

Not waiting to see what the men would do, Alaan plunged into the reeds. His pursuers were too close now, and he was wounded. He bulled through the rushes, trying to balance on one leg, the sharp-edged reeds lacerating his hands. As his shoulders began to ache, he pulled free of the cattails into open water.

"A staff," he muttered, barely able to go on. "I need a staff."

If anyone was close behind him now he would be caught out in the open, vulnerable. He slipped down into the water and crossed the pool, half swimming, half pulling himself along the bottom. His bowstring would be wet and useless now, but there was nothing for it. He had to put some distance between himself and his hunters.

In the sky, goatsuckers dove and wheeled, crying forlornly, and frogs sang of their night of love. A snake slid silently by. Alaan knew his hunters would be difficult to hear in this place, but then he need not be so quiet himself, which had advantages when one was in a hurry.

He reached a shallows and tried to stand on the soft bottom, lost his balance and toppled into the water with a splash. He crawled on, dragging his injured leg, cursing under his breath. A channel opened up to his left and he followed it, able to pull himself forward now, letting his body half float, the weight of his sword and quiver dragging him down.

Alaan glanced up at the sky, hoping for clouds, but the moon, perfectly full, floated in a clear, star-filled sky. He dragged himself into the rushes again, forcing his way through, taking many turns and doing as little damage as he could. His bow was impeding his progress and should have been cast aside, but he wanted to leave no markers of where he'd been—and he might have use for it yet. Again he found open water and went back down to his half-swimming pose, digging his fingers into the soft muck of the bottom and propelling himself forward. He glanced over his shoulder often, afraid that he'd been found. Without the use of his bow he wouldn't have a chance. He wouldn't last long in a sword fight, hobbled as he was.

Alaan felt like a hunted beast paddling through the swamp with tall, armed men in pursuit. Again he pulled himself into the reeds and forced himself through. The bulrush stands were dense and stood high above his head, offering perfect cover. Another snake slithered, frightened, into the reeds almost beneath his feet.

"Yes," he whispered, "I am a son of Wyrr. You should fear me."

He came to another channel but crouched down, having thought he heard some sound above the singing of the frogs. For a moment he stayed very still.

"If Welloh stuck him, he didn't get him anywhere that mattered," a voice said. "He's kept on like a frightened hare." Three men came into view then, wading down the center of the channel, swords drawn. Two archers followed behind.

"Oh, Welloh stuck him all right. The point of his blade was bloody. He'll slow down, by and by, our whist; that's what I say—"

"Keep your voices down!" another hissed. Two more men brought up the rear, swords in hand.

Alaan let them pass by. Seven men he'd counted. There seemed to have been many more than that. How did Hafydd slip so many into the ball?

When the troop of men were out of sight, Alaan paddled across the channel, slipping through a narrow opening in the rushes. Something snagged his good ankle and he was forced to stop and cut himself free. *Tanglevine.* He'd have to be more wary. The telltale blossoms, blood red by day, closed at night and were difficult to see.

He slunk on, stopping now and then to listen for men above the sounds of the swamp. He found a low island of soggy ground and lay down in the reeds. He'd rest here a bit, but not long. Alaan knew that if Hafydd was among these men, he'd be able to track him no matter how cunning he was. Sorcerers had their means.

Taking out his dagger, Alaan slit his pant leg to above the knee. There was not much blood from the wound, which was already swollen and terribly painful. He pulled some rushes aside so the moonlight illuminated the injury. He'd had worse—much worse—but he'd been near the healing waters of the Wyrr then. He cut some fabric from his now filthy costume and bound it over the wound. These stagnant waters were foul and not healthful, but there was nothing he could do. Escape was suddenly much more difficult.

A man shouted off in the distance, too far away for the words to carry, but the tone was clear—desperation. Someone had met one of the swamp's serpents, or perhaps a swamp cat. There were any number of dangerous beasts in this place.

Another call, in answer this time.

Hafydd, however, would survive. Beasts were wary of the children of Wyrr—they were smarter than humans in this regard. He hadn't gone far when he heard calling again, not so far off and not so desperate now. More muffled and despairing.

He followed the cries, which were separated by long periods of silence. It took him some time in the pale moonlight to locate the source. He parted the reeds and found a man, dressed in a magistrate's costume, lying a few yards away. His head barely out of the water, he was hopelessly entangled in a web of fine cord. A judge who'd met his judgement.

The two regarded each other a moment.

"You've not heard of tanglevine, I take it?" Alaan said after a moment.

The man was tiring fast. He wouldn't be able to keep his head above water much longer.

"Gloat if you must," the man said, "but my fellows will do for you yet."

"They can't even find you when you're calling. How will they ever find me? No, your friends have fallen to the same fate as you. Or have met with some of the swamp's other perils. Or have wandered off into farther reaches and will not find their way here again." Alaan reached out with his sword and tugged at a loop of vine. "I once tried to count all the little spines in a short length of tanglevine but soon gave it up. They're sharp as glass, as you've no doubt learned, and once they tighten cannot be made loose again." With the tip of his sword Alaan pointed toward a closed blossom, black in the moonlight. "Do you see these flowers? They are like those plants that devour the flesh of unwary insects. At dawn they will open and slowly search about until they have found you, alerted already by the tugging of the vines. Their kiss burns like no passion you've ever known. They digest their prey a bit at a time, alive at first, and then the carcass. They don't seem to care much if their food is alive and screaming or dead and rotting. They haven't much refinement in this regard."

"They say you are brother to that bloody Eremon, and now I believe it."

Alaan tried to smile. "You shouldn't talk so to the man who will set you free."

Hope flashed in the man's eyes. "Why would you do that?"

"You don't look like one of Hafydd's guards. I assume you serve Hafydd's nominal master, Prince Neit of Innes?"

The man nodded.

"I have no argument with Prince Neit, though I think he's an ass. You've been hunting me, but I'll forgive you that. You are a man-at-arms and have no say in who will be your foe, who your friend."

The man gazed at him now, wondering, hardly daring to hope. Did this stranger torment him?

"I will have your oath, though. If I set you free, you will do me no harm and do as I say. You cannot survive this swamp without me, I will tell you that. It is more fierce than you."

The man continued to watch him closely but said nothing. Then he asked, "What will you have of me?"

"Have of you? What have you to offer?" Alaan paused. "I want to know if Sir Eremon has come after me. Is he here in the swamp?"

The man said nothing, watching him.

"You will not keep your head up much longer," Alaan said.

"He is not here," the man said.

Alaan felt a wave of relief and disappointment. "You are certain?"

"Yes."

"Then give me your word that you will harm me not, and I will set you free."

The man's head began to tremble. "You have it," he said, his tone saying that he still believed Alaan toyed with him.

Alaan raised his sword, and when he brought it down, the man turned his head and closed his eyes. But when he felt some of his bonds loosen he looked back again.

"Who are you, then?" he almost whispered. "Who are you who sets his enemies free?"

"You? You aren't my enemy, man-at-arms. Hafydd, whom you call Sir Eremon, is my enemy. But you . . . you are but a sword with a man attached. There are ten thousand like you. But I will spare your life—out of pity for you, who have no thoughts of your own."

Alaan continued to slash away at the vines that held the man until he could move again, though his arms were still pinned to his sides. With some difficulty Alaan hauled the man up and cut free his legs and feet.

"What about my sword?"

Alaan poked around in the water and rushes until he felt something solid, then fished out a sword. He assured himself that the man's arms and hands were immobilized by the tanglevine and then slid the man's sword back into his scabbard.

"Why did you ask for my word if you were to keep me bound?"

"Because I take no more risks than I must, man-at-arms. This way. . . ." He pointed with his sword. "Let me put a hand on your shoulder."

"Welloh did wound you, then . . . before you cut his throat out."

"He would have murdered me on the spot—me, who had never done him harm or even known his name. Any man would have done what I did. Even *you*." Alaan waved his sword. "This channel."

They turned down a narrow, open waterway, the man's gait awkward from his bound arms, and Alaan leaning on him and hobbling like a cripple.

They did not talk as they went, Alaan silent from the pain, the other still suspicious and harboring his words, Alaan guessed. They staggered down an open channel in thigh-deep water, bubbles rising where they disturbed the soft bottom. A breeze set the reeds to hissing.

It was a long hour of going and stopping to rest Alaan's wounded leg. Twice he sat down in the water, overcome by pain, the man-at-arms standing docilely by.

"Your wound must be deep," the man-at-arms said, gazing at him.

"To the bone," Alaan answered between clenched teeth.

"I am a man of my word," the other said. "Free my hands and I will do what I can to help you."

"Perhaps you are, but I will not take that chance." Alaan reached down and touched his leg. "I wonder why Hafydd did not venture forth with you," he said, the pain in his leg subsiding a little with immobility. He forced himself up, stiff-legged and dripping.

"Hafydd; that's what you call Sir Eremon?" the man said. "There were some among my fellow men-at-arms who said that he was Hafydd and had once served the Renné."

"To say that he served the Renné is less than true, I would think, but he was their ally—as much as he was any man's." Alaan put his hand on the man's shoulder and they set off again.

"But it is said that Hafydd died upon a battlefield, murdered by his own allies."

"He did not die. Not there. Though there was barely life left in him; only a tiny spark that was fanned back to a flame. A flame of hatred. And how do you and your fellows like to serve this man?"

The man was silent for a moment. "We like it not," he said quietly, his voice bitter. "He is a dark presence in our master's halls. At night, some have seen him walk out beneath the stars to speak with shadows—*the servants of Death,* men whisper. Hours he spends alone in his chambers, reviving arcane arts, long lost. I have seen the whole castle awake, every soul filled with dread as though Death himself were about to sweep down upon us, but it is the work of Sir Eremon, alone in his rooms. He is a sorcerer come back from the dead, that's what many say—though they say it low for none would face him with such accusations. None of the men who say he should be burned would dare stand before him and draw a sword. He is feared. I have never known a man to be so feared."

"Yes, he is feared: a strange gift to ask of one's father. What will you do when I let you go? Will you strike out on your own—they will certainly believe you dead after tonight, for I would guess most of your fellows are."

The man looked at him in the moonlight, then shook his head. "I have taken an oath to Prince Neit of Innes. My father served his father, my grandfather his."

"But now you fraternize with his enemy. Does your oath allow that?"

The man shook his head. "I'm your prisoner. My duties to my lord change when that is so."

Alaan snorted. "We are almost at the swamp's edge. You will be on your own from there. If you are foolish enough to go back to serving the Prince of Innes, that is your business."

The shore rose up out of a thin mist, dark and overshadowing. Alaan cast the man's blade up on the hard ground and then cut him free with the tip of his own sword.

"Carry on along the bank for about an hour in that direction. You'll find a dry stream going up the hillside. Follow it over the crest and then make your way down the other side. You will come out somewhere near Westbrook. I can't say exactly where."

The man turned to look at him, incongruous in his elaborate costume. "And what of you?" he asked. "What will become of you? Your wound is septic. You should come with me."

"No, it is safer for me here, until I've healed. But before you go, cut me a staff from that tree."

The knight looked at him a moment, then found his sword and cut a heavy staff with it, hesitating only an instant before applying his perfectly honed blade to wood.

Alaan took the staff, leaned his weight on it and grunted his approval. "Beware, man-at-arms. There is a war coming and your oath binds you to the wrong side. Hafydd is more than just a sorcerer, he is ruthless and without principles. War is like food to him: he must have it to live. And war he will have unless I stop him. Do you want to do your duty to the House of Innes? Kill Hafydd. That would be an act of heroism—none greater."

The man cocked his head and looked at Alaan. "I am almost convinced that what you say is true. That is what Sir Eremon says about you, that you are a sorcerer of words."

"It is better than being a servant of Death, which Hafydd certainly has become."

The man saluted Alaan once with his blade, then set off along the embankment, working his stiff shoulders as he went, a victim of his own loyalties, and the loyalties of his father, and his father before him.

Alaan hobbled back into the swamp, bitterly disappointed that his plan had not worked. Hafydd had not chased him, making a lie of all Alaan knew of the man—or thought he knew. And now what would he do? Heal, and begin again, with new knowledge to consider.

He was an hour into his painful journey when, above the sounds of the swamp and the wind, he heard a long drawn out howl. *Hounds!*

He stumbled on, his injured leg barely bearing weight. Any hounds that Hafydd sent would not be the common variety, but would have some enchantment upon them to allow them to track him anywhere, and when they finally found him . . . He did not like to think what would happen.

He fell and dragged himself up out of the water. For a moment he stopped to listen. Yes, they were there, though from where the sound came he could not tell in this mist.

They are coming closer, he thought. And he drove himself on. He limped painfully, making more noise than he wanted. The baying grew louder. He must have a bow. In the state he was in he knew he could not hope to stand against men and hounds—not if the men numbered more than one.

He limped stiff-legged through the mist, his legs pushing the fetid waters aside. Around him the reeds grew up, waist high and higher. Perfect for hiding an ambush if the mist were not cover enough. The baying was near now. He could hear men shouting, hear the splash of their footsteps.

Alaan had only one hope. He had cached some food and supplies on one of the very few islands this forsaken swamp contained. If he could reach there before the hounds got him . . .

He tried to run, but could only hobble, his wounded leg growing weaker with each step. It started to give way beneath him and he was forced to take more weight on his staff so that his shoulder began to ache.

"Come on now," he whispered. "They'll be on top of you in a minute."

He could make out the words the men were shouting. Sensing his nearness, the baying of the hounds grew frenzied. Alaan kept glancing back and almost fell on the shore of the island as he did so. Up onto dry land, taking his whole weight on the staff now, his leg too weak to bear him. He was into trees and reached out to steady himself on them, to pull himself up.

"Thank the stars it's still here!"

He dropped to his knees and grabbed up the bow he'd left here, stringing it quickly. He nocked an arrow and gazed into the wafting mist, moonlight playing tricks on his eyes. The howling of the hounds was loud in his ears, their handlers urging them on. He could hear them splashing through the waters.

And then they were at the shore of the island, two massive beasts surging up the slope, almost dragging a large man behind them.

Alaan let the first arrow fly and two more. One dog went down and the other broke free of its master as the man took an arrow in the shoulder. Alaan had a brief impression of others running, and then the dog was upon him.

He swept up his blade and forced himself to his feet, swaying, his leg about to give way. He saw the beast lunging and dropped down to his knees, under the diving jaws. He drove the point of his sword into the breast of the beast and was bowled backward, his sword torn from his hands.

Up in a second, he snatched his bow and shot two men as they came up the slope, the last not ten feet away. The others turned and ran, unnerved perhaps by the death of the great dogs.

Alaan shot two of the retreating men in the back, hearing one plunge into the waters and then crawl on; not long for this world, he was sure.

He knelt, gasping, trying to calm his pounding heart. A brief glance told him that the dog that lay near was all but dead, his blade deep in its heart. And then he swayed, the world tilting beneath him. The fog seemed to grow thicker, and then darkness. . . .

When he opened his eyes again, the moon had washed into the west. His leg throbbed as though being pounded by a hammer. A fire crackled a few feet away.

"Look who's back with us," a voice said.

A man costumed as an executioner crouched down before him, and Alaan realized his hands were bound behind.

"Beware of him," another said. "Sir Eremon warned that he is always dangerous while he lives. Have no speech with him."

The man stared at Alaan a moment, a sweaty face in the firelight, and then rose to his feet.

Alaan cursed under his breath. He had lost consciousness. They would never have taken him otherwise. He wondered about his wound. The foul waters had corrupted it, or there would not be so much pain. Of course his powers of healing were greater than most men's—many times greater—but he was not beyond illness or injury. He could certainly die of a disease were it virulent enough. He would need to return to the River Wynnd.

He glanced around. There seemed to be three men. Not insurmountable odds—if only his hands were free.

Three

The great gate to Castle Renné stood closed, though Lord Carral's servant assured him that lights still burned in windows high up in the stone walls.

The servant hailed the gatemen, his voice strangely loud—almost offensive—in the quiet.

"Who comes to our gate at such an hour?" a guard responded.

"Lord Carral Wills," the servant said, with only a second's hesitation. This revelation brought no answer, but from above whispers floated down like feathers.

"What business could Lord Carral Wills have here so late, on this night of all nights?" someone called from above.

"I shall discuss that with Lady Beatrice Renné, or Lord Toren, and no other," Carral cried out in frustration.

"Did you hear my lord?" Carral's servant called.

"Wait and we'll ask what should be done," came the judgment from above.

Perhaps silence is a kind of darkness, Lord Carral thought, his horse shifting impatiently beneath him.

They waited without speech, lord and servant, an understanding arrived at by long association. Doubt seemed to grow inside Lord

Carral, feeding on the silence. But this doubt was immediately followed by the memory of Elise—he would never forget the sound as she had entered the water. Immediately he had known what that sound had meant.

Because I have shirked my duty, he reminded himself bitterly. The easy excuse of my blindness and my love of my art were all I needed to let my brother Menwyn shoulder my responsibilities. If I had taken them up myself it would never have happened. Menwyn merely sat upon the empty throne.

A dull thud came from beyond the gate, followed by a terrible creaking.

Death's gate could sound no worse, Lord Carral thought.

"Lady Beatrice will see you, Lord Carral," an educated voice said a few feet in front of them, "but please be aware, Lady Beatrice has suffered a tragedy this night; as you well might know."

"What tragedy is this?" Carral asked quickly.

"Her nephew, Lord Arden Renné, was murdered but an hour ago."

"I did not know," Lord Carral said.

Into the embarrassed silence his servant said softly, "Lord Carral's own daughter, Lady Elise, was lost this night. Drowned in the Westbrook."

"It is a loathsome night!" the man cried. "Misfortune has struck everywhere!" He spoke low to someone near him, and the gate creaked horribly again. Carral actually pulled back on his reins when he heard his servant start forward, a sudden chill running through him at the thought of going through this gate.

You've spent your life in darkness, he chided himself, *the darkness beyond shall be no different.*

He spurred his horse forward, hearing its hooves clatter down on hard stone. There were a few men around him; he could hear them breathing and moving quietly. His horse jerked its head slightly and then was still.

"I have him, sir," his servant said.

Lord Carral dismounted unassisted.

"If Lord Carral would follow me . . ."

Carral's servant handed him his walking stick and put his lord's hand on his shoulder. In a moment they were inside, the air growing warm and more moist. Sounds also changed as walls closed in.

They ascended a long stair, and then went quietly along a hall. The man who led them did not offer to make small talk, though when he did break his silence he was both respectful and gracious.

They were left sitting in chairs in what Carral was certain was a hallway. People—servants, he was sure—passed in procession, silent even for their kind.

This house is in mourning, Carral reminded himself. As was he, though his own grief had led him here; to what would be seen as treachery. Elise, however, would have approved. He tried to push aside thoughts of his daughter. There would be time enough to mourn her—an entire lifetime.

A door opened and the servant led them inside.

A warm, female voice spoke. "This can't be true!" the voice said. "Your lovely daughter cannot be lost on this same night that has seen my nephew's passing!"

"But it is true," Lord Carral said, struggling to speak. The genuine dismay in Lady Beatrice's voice touched him and he felt tears threaten.

Small, cold hands took his and lifted them up. Lady Beatrice stood so close that he could smell her perfume and the powder in her hair, mixed with smoke and the bitter scent of burning tapers. "To lose a nephew who was a man-at-arms is tragic but not completely unexpected. To lose a daughter of such grace and promise . . . How could such a thing happen?"

"She leapt from a bridge into the Westbrook, drowning rather than allowing herself to become a brood mare in the plans of my brother Menwyn and his ally, the Prince of Innes . . . and his servant, who calls himself Eremon."

"*Hafydd,*" Lady Beatrice whispered.

"Yes."

"How I have come to hate the sound of that name, harsh and bitter as it is," she said. Lady Beatrice took his arm. "Come, speak with me. We have much to grieve us. Who else could understand our hearts now?"

She led him across a room, to an open window. Carral could feel the night pouring in. "What is it that I might do for you, Lord Carral? It seems no accident that you have come here immediately after your daughter's loss."

"It is no accident, Lady Beatrice," Lord Carral said. He took a deep breath. "I have come to declare myself head of the House of Wills, and my brother Menwyn a usurper. I refute his claims, his policies, and his alliance with the Prince of Innes, who has ambitions of his own. The Prince wanted a grandson who would bear the blood of the Wills heir, which will not come to be now, alas— and yet for the good of all. That is the gift of my daughter's sacrifice. I would not see this sacrifice made in vain."

He stopped, wondering if he sounded like a father, mad from grief. But he knew it was too late now, he must go on. "Lord Toren Renné had planned to return the Isle of Battle to the Wills. That was before the spectacle Menwyn and Prince Neit staged at the ball. Your family have no choice now—they cannot return the Isle to an alliance that plans to make war against them. But if you do not return it, the Isle will become the justification for the war. I can solve this dilemma for you. Recognize my claim and return the Isle to me . . . and I will sign treaties of lasting peace with the Renné."

He listened to Lady Beatrice breathe, perhaps a little more quickly now that he had revealed the reason for his visit.

"What you offer, Lord Carral, is . . . worthy of our most careful consideration. It is also noble and good, for you are both honoring your daughter and her intentions and trying to avoid a war, for your own good reasons, I think. But I'm not sure what you propose will do much in the end. Menwyn and the Prince will use you as the excuse for war, saying we hold you against your will or some other ridiculous claim. Anything to legitimize their intentions. And their intentions are, as you say, war." He heard her try to calm her breathing.

"Is your answer no, then?"

"It is not my place to answer. It is my son, Lord Toren Renné, to whom you must speak."

"But you are his most valued counselor."

Her hand shifted where it still held his arm, as though he were a dear cousin come to call. "I am merely one of his counselors, and not the most valued, I must tell you. But I will speak with him, all the same. I will try to arrange that you meet him also."

There was a terrible creaking from below, like something inhuman screaming out in pain.

"That is the main gate, Lord Carral. Through it comes a bier bearing the body of my late nephew, Lord Arden Renné. Do you know who murdered him?"

"Please tell me it was not some minion of Menwyn or Hafydd."

"How I wish that were the case, surprisingly. No, he was murdered by his own cousins. Do you know why?"

"I know not."

"They mistook him for Lord Toren, who they hoped to kill, thus stopping the return of the Isle of Battle to the Wills." She drew a long uneven breath, and stooped a little, stiffening, clinging tightly to his arm.

"Should you take a chair, my lady?"

He felt her move and thought she shook her head. "It does not matter how often you've felt it," she whispered, "still it is unbearable."

"What?"

"One's own heart breaking."

Four

They found Baore hunched over, staring into the flames of a small fire.

No one spoke or greeted him. They had heard the news upon the road: Elise Wills had drowned that night, drowned in the Westbrook, and no one knew if she had intended this or been thrown from her horse.

Baore looked up as his companions appeared, and then went back to staring at the fire.

"There you are, Baore," Tam said, putting a hand on his friend's solid shoulder. "We were worried about you."

Baore nodded, his mow of blond hair bobbing as he did.

Fynnol sat down across the small fire from his cousin. Fynnol dark and quick, a crow among men. "We heard about Elise Wills," he said. "We're all terribly sad and sorry."

"She lives," Baore said, stirring a little.

"What are you saying?"

"At the ball she asked me to await her in our boat by the bridge. When she cast herself in, I was there to take her out."

Fynnol looked up at the others, quick as a bird. "But everyone said she drowned."

"The Westbrook was thick with fog. No one saw what I did."

"But where is she?" Cynddl asked.

"She has taken herself off. I expect her back soon—before morning."

The others threw themselves down by the fire, too shocked to be happy. And clearly Baore was not happy at all. He sat by the fire like a man ill and fevered, trying desperately to find some warmth.

"But Alaan has not appeared?" Pwyll asked. The Tourneyer had fetched a pail of water from the Westbrook and now doffed his shirt and began to wash his muscled torso—dark with bruises from the jousting.

Baore shook his head.

Tam stared at the big Valeman. What was wrong? Something had happened this night that had unsettled Baore—unsettled him deeply. He should be elated that Elise was alive. Tam glanced at the river. He knew there was only one thing that would disturb Baore so. The nagar must have appeared again.

"It has been the strangest of nights," Cynddl said. "Death has walked among us, and yet you tell us Elise has returned from Death's kingdom. Alaan put an arrow in the man we believed was Hafydd, but it was not him. We have been deceived on every side." But this neither prompted Baore to tell his story nor to ask theirs.

Cynddl looked at the big Valeman sadly. In the faint light the story finder looked both youthful and ancient, his gray hair and elder's voice contrasting with his vigor and smooth, pale skin, so uncommon for his race. His Fáel dark eyes were shadows that glittered when the flames blossomed.

"Morning is not far off," the big man said. "I for one need a little sleep."

He rose and went to his bag, taking out his bedding and rolling himself in it. He was immediately still, but Tam could tell by his breathing that he did not sleep, and Tam suspected he would not sleep this night.

Five

They carried the man in on a litter, his magistrate's costume torn to ruins, vivid tendrils of crimson, blue, and gold lying about him like fallen banners. He was trying not to cry out from the pain, but every now and then a moan would force its way through clenched teeth, no matter what he did. He was snake bitten and the healer stood by helplessly, his face a mask of neutrality; neither surprised, nor guilt ridden, nor despairing, nor hopeful.

Prince Michael had seen this look on the face of healers before. The patient would die—painfully and not as quickly as he might hope.

Death had been the victor these last days of the fair. Poor Elise, then the news of Arden Renné. Now none of the men Hafydd had sent in his relentless pursuit of his whist had returned: but one, he corrected himself, and that man was dying before his eyes.

"He was wounded, and the wound corrupted. Could hardly hobble a few steps when I left him. And the chills had him." The man-at-arms paused to take a few quick, shallow breaths. "I thought I'd escaped but was bitten by a snake on the very shore of that cursed place." He coughed. "I don't think your whist will have gone far." A spasm of pain tore through the man, and he whimpered despite all.

Hafydd and Michael's father, Prince Neit, stood mutely by, looking as though they thought the man should have the decency to hide his pain and die privately, and certainly not before they had asked all their questions.

When the man lay still again, panting desperately, Hafydd spoke. "Tell me again of this high place. Was there any water? Any at all? A spring, a trickle? The smallest puddle?"

"None that I saw, Sir Eremon," the man said, pushing the words out through the pain.

Hafydd shifted from one foot to the other. Michael had learned to spot the signs of the knight's anger, and they appeared now: the stiffness of the jaw and face, a paling of the skin. His guards would move away from him imperceptibly when these signs appeared. Prince Michael fought the urge to do so now.

"And he led you out the swamp? Why?"

"I don't know, sir." A quick shiver ran through the man. "He wanted only to know if you were with us. Nothing more."

Hafydd rubbed his fingers over his bearded chin. "He hoped to draw my attention there, but he could not." And then he was silent a moment. "He was not so clever as he thought," Hafydd continued, his voice even, and more unsettling for its lack of emotion, "not nearly so clever. This wound you say he had; are you sure of it? Could it have been a ruse?"

The man shook his head, his neck trembling a little from the effort. A general shivering coursed through him then. "His leg was bound up and the dressing bloody and stained. He could barely move for the pain. It was no act, I'm sure." He stopped again, convulsing horribly. The healer and a guard tried to restrain him so he didn't do himself harm or flop onto the floor. Hafydd and Prince Michael's father looked away.

The healer glanced up, the thrashing man jerking him this way and that. "I don't think you'll learn any more from him this night," the healer said.

Hafydd fixed him with a dark stare, and Prince Michael saw the healer cringe, turning his attention back to his patient, the color draining from his face.

"Then take him away," Hafydd said.

Prince Michael thought the healer might need someone to support him, so frightened was he, but he wobbled toward the door on his own.

"Healer," Hafydd called after him.

The man turned, unable to breathe suddenly.

"How long has he?" Hafydd asked.

"H-He won't s-see sunrise," the man stammered.

Hafydd nodded, turning away.

"Perhaps your whist will die in this swamp," Prince Neit said, "and we'll be done with him."

"Die? He'll not die where there is water. He will live, waiting. But he is of lesser concern now. There is another. . . ." Hafydd walked a few paces across the floor of the pavilion. "An enemy greater than my whist, or potentially so." He turned to look at Prince Neit. "I must ask leave to go deal with this matter. All of our plans hinge upon eliminating this person."

"And who might this be?" Neit asked.

"Her name is Sianon," Hafydd answered, "and she is a sorceress of great ability. Or will be very soon, when she comes back into her power."

Michael's father was suddenly still. Despite all the rumors, Hafydd had never spoken openly of sorcery or admitted any knowledge of it.

"She is a great threat to you, my Prince," Hafydd said, "for she will side with your enemies."

A little shiver ran through the Prince of Innes. "And you can deal with her—more successfully than you have this 'whist'?"

Hafydd became very still. He did not brook insults or even insinuation.

"It will take me but a few days," he said evenly.

Prince Michael felt his head shake involuntarily. His father did not realize the danger he was in from this man. Hafydd despised him. The knight hid it well, but now and then it appeared, like a fire burning beneath the forest floor. It would flare up and consume the forest in time.

"What troops will you require?" Michael's father asked.

"I will need only my own guard," Hafydd said.

"I will come with you as well," Prince Michael said.

Both men turned to look at him.

"I have always wanted to see a sorceress," he said.

Hafydd stared at him a moment, and Prince Michael struggled to control the trembling that began in his limbs. "If you wish."

Hafydd turned toward the door, but then stopped. "I will ride at first light. Be ready?"

Prince Michael nodded, unable to speak.

The knight swept out of the room, drawing all the tension and confused emotion and fear after him, like a sigh. The tent felt empty then, as though Prince Michael and his father didn't exist—at least not with the same vibrancy as Hafydd.

"Why do you retain him, Father?" Michael managed, dropping into a chair. His father walked to his writing table, lifted a paperweight and began flipping through some papers as though he searched for something. "Father?"

Prince Neit looked up at him; perhaps ashamed, Michael thought. "I need him for this war we are about to wage."

"But do we need the war?" Michael asked, even though he knew it would provoke his father's legendary temper. He fought to control his trembling breath.

"Do not bait me this night," Prince Neit said. "He is my general, and necessary until the war is over and won."

Prince Michael stretched out his legs. He was exhausted, suddenly. "And then what will become of him?"

"Then I will no longer need him."

"But he will no longer need you either, Father. That is what frightens me."

Prince Neit stared at his son in obvious incomprehension. "You have much to prepare if you are to leave at first light. Dawn is not far off."

But outside the tent it was still dark. It took a moment for Prince Michael's eyes to adjust, and then the moonlight, angling low over the trees, illuminated the world with a soft cool light. It seemed the longest night of the year—not the shortest.

He found his servant and ordered the preparations for his journey. He might have slept then, for an hour or two, but his thoughts were like a flight of frightened birds, fleeing this way and that.

He wandered through the encampment, avoiding the knots of people still awake, drinking and discussing the evening's happenings. His wandering led to the river, where he sat down on the grass embankment and watched the last strands of mist twist above the slow-moving waters—like wraiths that dissipated and died, going back into the river that spawned them.

He wondered if Elise's body would be found come daylight. Rivers weren't like lakes, they were shallow and the currents predictable. Bodies were recovered. Grief found him sitting there, and crept over him like twilight. He felt grief for poor Elise, but also for the marriage they might have had, the children—if not for Hafydd. And now he'd agreed to accompany the knight after yet another sorcerer—or sorceress, it seemed. *Sianon* . . . Was that not the name Hafydd had muttered beneath the bridge?

Someone has to observe him, he thought. *Someone has to find his weakness.* Is that why he went? Did the rat feel this when the snake's eye mesmerized?

Something broke the surface, causing him to jump. A fish, a big one, or perhaps an otter.

"Michael . . ." came a sound like a ripple.

Abruptly he was alert, his eyes darting over the moonlit bank and into the shadows of the river.

"Michael . . ." came the sound again, as though the river whispered his name.

A shiver ran up his back and he looked quickly behind him.

"I'm here, beneath the trees," came the sound again, strange and blending with the river voice.

He stood, backing away a step.

"Elise . . . ?"

"Yes, here, in the shadows. Come closer. I thought I should have to creep up into the camp to find you."

Prince Michael felt his limbs tremble as he went forward. In the pool of blackness beneath an overhanging tree something moved. He stood on the border of the shadow, afraid to go forward. Slowly his eyes adjusted to the dark, and there he saw Elise in the water, only her head and shoulders breaking the surface. His first thought was, *she's wearing nothing.*

"Elise," he said, his voice barely audible, but quavering even so. "Have you come to haunt me?"

"It is Hafydd I have come to haunt, but don't look so, Michael, I'm still among the living." She raised her arm, dripping, from the river. "Touch me if you don't believe it."

"No, I believe you," he said quickly.

"Come closer, then, I don't want any others to hear us."

He took a step, forcing himself forward. Elise might think she was among the living, but she did not look so. Her skin was paler than the moon, her hair stringy and strange. She looked like a wraith, and yet she was beautiful. *Hauntingly beautiful,* he thought.

"Closer," Elise said, and he felt a desire surge through him.

How can this be? he wondered. *She looks like the dead.*

Perhaps it was her nakedness, there just beneath the surface. Moonlight fell in between the branches, making a pattern on the water—leaves of moonlight.

"Your father said you could not swim," he said suddenly.

"He does not know everything about me. He is blind, after all." She moved her arms to stay afloat, the motion somehow seductive. Her face glistened in the fractured moonlight.

"Does Lord Carral know that you live? If his grief was an act, then he is an accomplished player."

"He does not know, and do not tell him. As cruel as it seems, it is better that he believe me dead. Trust that I know what I do in this."

Michael shrugged. He thought of poor Lord Carral: it *was* cruel to keep this knowledge from him.

"I trust you," he said, his eyes closing a moment. He could hardly bear the sight of her—so ghostly and so beautiful.

"What is it you want of me, Elise?" he asked.

"Will you spy on Hafydd for me? It is dangerous, even for you, so consider carefully before you answer."

"I spy on him anyway, for what purpose I have never clearly known. So now I will have a purpose. But what good will it do you, Elise? Hafydd thinks you're dead but I fail to see how that will profit you. He is as invulnerable as ever."

"Not so invulnerable. Have you spoken with Alaan since the ball? I seek him."

"I have not, but Hafydd tried very hard to kill him this night. He must have had two dozen armed men in costume at the ball. I don't know how he managed it. They went after Alaan when he appeared, and, as he did before, he led them through strange lands none of them had ever seen. Only one man returned, and he near to death. Alaan had killed many of them, and led them into a great marsh where they were lost or perished. Even the one man who returned was snake bitten." Elise was listening raptly, her glistening eyes on him. He felt his pulse increase. "It was Alaan who saved this man and set him free. But Alaan was wounded, grievously so, or so the man claimed. Alaan might be fevered himself by now." He paused. "But he is safe from Hafydd for a time, for now the knight will go seeking some sorceress named Sianon, or so he claims."

Elise's arms stopped moving for a second. "He said this? He said Sianon?"

"Yes, and it was not the first time I heard him say this name. Beneath the bridge, after you leapt, he stood with his sword in the water and then seemed almost to convulse. And then he said the name 'Sianon' with such astonishment."

Elise moved her arms a little, as at home in the river as an otter. Michael could see that what he'd said had unsettled her, and he felt suddenly worthless to be the bearer of bad news to this woman who had heard enough bad news.

"It is imperative that I find Alaan," Elise said.

Why did he feel he'd disappointed her? "He failed to rescue you at the ball," Michael said, a bit defensively. "Why do you seek him now?"

"He wasn't trying to rescue me," she replied, her voice like water lapping the shore. "He was trying to kill Hafydd. I realize that now. Which would have accomplished the same thing. With Hafydd dead, I don't think your father would be so quick to begin this war."

Laughter sounded not far off, and then voices reached them.

Elise was now alert, listening. "Watch Hafydd for me," she whispered. "We'll find the key to him yet." Suddenly, she stood up in the water, sliding her arms about his neck. She pressed herself close to him, wet lips finding his. And then she slipped back beneath the surface and was gone.

The Prince crouched by the river trying hard to catch his breath. That was not the kiss of an inexperienced young lady. It was passionate and knowing. Far too knowing.

He sat back on the grass, almost tumbling over. For a long moment he watched the water, listening to the revelers as they passed by. Then it was silent again.

"Are you there?" he whispered, but there was no answer. Elise was gone, beneath the surface like some river beast. Like a vision.

He stood and began removing his clothes, letting them fall in a heap on the grass. He slipped down the shallow embankment, his feet finding the soft river bottom. In the cool evening air the water seemed warm. A step took him in up to his chest.

He found it hard to breathe suddenly. Was Elise nearby? Did she watch him still?

Prince Michael had a strange sense that he was doing something forbidden. More forbidden than entering a lady's boudoir. He closed his eyes and let the warm water embrace him. Laying his head back, he heard his own breathing, ragged and loud in his ears.

He opened his eyes and looked up at the fading stars. A pale light, almost imperceptible, seemed to rise from somewhere down-river, like a body floating to the surface.

Hafydd awaited him.

Tam had volunteered to stand watch while the others slept. He let the fire burn down to coals, and put his back against a stump where he could see everyone, watch the path up from the river, and yet not be too out in the open himself. He looked up at the westering moon, the night black and bright with stars. The air was summer warm, still as sleep, and laden with the scents of new-cut hay and the passing river.

Pwyll was worried about Alaan and had said he might have to go looking for him. What they would all do now that they had performed their promised service to Alaan, Tam didn't know. They should go north, certainly. North to quiet and safety—at least for the time being.

A low splashing sound came from the river, as though some animal came out onto the banks. Tam took up his sword and crept through the bushes to the bank.

He thought he'd found their nagar, but then realized it was Elise Wills, dripping wet, busy dressing in clothes that she pulled down from the branches of a tree. Tam stood dumbfounded for a moment, seeing her pale skin and thickly tangled hair.

Elise started when she saw him and then relaxed.

"When the nagar offered Baore a bargain for his life," Tam said, "he refused. What of you, Elise? What choice did you make?"

Elise stopped buttoning her shirt and regarded Tam, saying nothing for a moment.

"Few would have the strength to choose as Baore did."

"You were dressed in a costume so heavy that even a strong swimmer would have been dragged down by it."

Elise gazed up at the moon. "What is it you want of me, Tamlyn Loell?"

"Truth."

He saw Elise swallow. For a long moment she said nothing, and then finally: "I could not refuse her," she said softly. "When Death's gate grinds open, Tam, we learn the true depth of our courage."

"But why Baore?" he almost whispered. "Why Elise?"

"Baore found a whetstone on the battlefield at Telanon Bridge. Knights of the Vow had carried it there, though it once belonged to a sorceress . . . Sianon. It has drawn her since you passed through the Lion's Maw. I have the stone now."

Tam nodded once, not sure what to say. His suspicions had proven true, but he felt no satisfaction from that. "Are you . . . ?" He suddenly did not know what he'd meant to ask.

"I'm still Elise," she said evenly, but then her shoulders dropped a little. She shook her head and turned her gaze back to the river. "No . . . I'm not—not quite myself, Tam. It's as though I had lived all these years with the belief that I was Elise Wills, only to suddenly wake and find memories flooding in. Memories of another life, when I was named Sianon and fought a long and terrible war against my own brother. I can't explain. . . . I've heard of people receiving a blow to the head and losing their memories, and then, years later, having these memories return. It is like that. I have not given my life over to Sianon, but this sudden knowledge stands between me and who I was." A tear trembled on her lashes, and then fell away to make the smallest splash in the river; like a tiny eye opening, then winking shut.

"But my head is aswim, Tam. I can make no sense of all these memories, these feelings, some of them so overwhelming—I have never known such emotions before. I must find Alaan. Only he might help me find my way through this."

"Alaan has not returned."

"No, he is wounded and hiding somewhere in the hidden lands. And Hafydd is after me. At first light he will begin his search, and he is not far off. We must wake the others. We're in danger."

But Tam did not move. "I am most afraid for Baore," he said softly. "Even if we go north now, Baore will stay with you, won't he?"

"That is Baore's choice."

"But he will choose to stay with you, will he not?"

Elise considered a moment, then nodded.

Tam thought she looked very beautiful in the moonlight, but he remembered the story Cynddl had told them. Men loved Sianon and did her bidding—but she loved none in return.

She looked up at Tam, her eyes pale in the cold light. "If you go north now," Elise said softly, "and leave Pwyll and me to find Alaan, I'll send Baore away—for your sake, Tam." Elise paused. "It will be my last act of compassion for some time, I fear."

"Will there be a war, then?"

She still fixed him with her gaze. Ladies did not meet men's eyes so. "If I cannot find some way to stop Hafydd."

"How can you stop someone like that?"

"There is only one way. Send him through Death's gate, as should have been done so long ago—with all of the children of Wyrr. . . . But I am not yet strong enough to do this. I don't know if I will ever be."

Tam looked up and down the river as though suddenly conscious that they were not standing vigil. A thin mist still curled and spun in the middle of the stream. "Alaan told us that there was no place safe from Hafydd, not if he is triumphant on the battlefield." He glanced at Elise. "Perhaps there is no place safe from you, either."

"You need not fear me, Tam. You and Fynnol and Baore and Cynddl; you saved me from Hafydd's men on the river. I've not forgotten. But I can't promise you safety from Hafydd. If he can, he will bring war to the land between the mountains. War that will make the petty feud of the Renné and my family look like a children's squabble." She rose to her feet, still holding Tam's eye. "You said you wanted truth, Tam; there it is. War, and perhaps even longer and more terrible now that Sianon has returned."

Tam took a long breath and looked up at the moon, traveling into the west. "I cannot go north. Not now. I know too much. Fatal knowledge, perhaps. I'm good with a bow, and though not the equal of Pwyll, I can bear a lance, ride, and use a sword, if need be."

Elise turned toward him. "My army is so small that I can hardly refuse a skilled man-at-arms. But I must find Alaan as quickly as I can. Even so, Tam, I would rather see you go north."

"There is no safe place. Alaan spoke the truth when he said that. Better to fight Hafydd here, then to have him send his marauders north, to the Vale of Lakes."

Elise smiled at him warmly and came forward. She reached out and pressed his hand, but he brought her hand up to his lips. The look on Elise's face changed then, and she tilted her head to one side, gazing at him—in confusion, perhaps.

"Beware, Tam, there is a part of me that has not known a man's love in centuries, and part of me that has never known it at all." Gently she drew her hand away. As she stepped past him she left a soft kiss on his cheek.

Tam stood watching the mist perform a slow dance in the moonlight. He felt his cheek turn cold where Elise had kissed him.

Beware, he thought, *the nagar are among us.*

When Tam came back into the camp, Elise was already rousing the others. "Hafydd is coming," she said to each as she woke them. "Hafydd is coming."

There was a fever of activity as the boat was dragged down to the Westbrook and all their belongings piled in. Once launched, with all of them aboard, there was barely a hand'sbreadth of freeboard. Baore took up a pole and sent them down the stream, the lazy current aiding him but little.

"Where will we go?" Cynddl asked. He looked up at the sky, which was rapidly growing light. A fire spread itself over a low ridge of clouds on the eastern horizon.

"I must find Alaan," Elise said, "but he is wounded and lies in the hidden lands, and I cannot find my way there."

Pwyll sat on the gunwale, a sword across his knees. "How do you know he is wounded?"

Elise looked at the man-at-arms carefully a moment. "I spoke this night with Prince Michael of Innes, who learned this from Hafydd himself. One of the guards Hafydd sent after Alaan returned saying he'd seen Alaan and that he was gravely wounded."

Pwyll made a fist and smacked it against the boat's planking.

"Where would he go, Pwyll? Do you know?" Elise asked.

Pwyll ran his hand back into his hair. "I know where he planned to go, but Alaan's plans can change in a moment. He went into a great swamp, hoping to draw Hafydd there." He looked up at the sky a moment. "I know a way there," he said, "though I have never taken it before." He met Elise's anxious gaze. "I will go seeking him, though Alaan urged me only to do so at the most urgent need."

"My need is more than urgent," Elise said. "But all of you: it is me that Hafydd seeks. If you strike out on your own, I doubt he will follow."

"Or perhaps he will," Tam said, "hoping for news of you." The light was growing now, and the banks of the river appeared as the mist burned away. They passed any number of people making their camps on the banks. Most were sleeping, though some were still awake and quietly going about their business in the gray dawn.

"But how does Hafydd know you are alive?" Fynnol asked.

Elise shrugged. "Alaan said that he was a sorcerer. He must have his ways."

"I will go with you, Lady Elise," Baore said as he planted the pole and propelled them forward.

"As will I," said Tam, wondering if he'd fallen under the spell of

Sianon. "I can't forget that Alaan saved our lives at risk of his own. Nor can I abandon you, Lady Elise, with Hafydd after you. It appears to be my fate to fight Hafydd and his servants."

"I will go with you as well," the Fáel said. "It seems that we began something on the river that is not finished yet."

Fynnol threw up his hands. "Well, I shall not be left behind because I am the only one with common sense. And anyway, we must flee from Hafydd in some direction, into the hidden lands seems as safe as any other course—or as dangerous." The little Valeman tried to smile, but it was a bitter smile.

"I don't know if there is a safe course, now, Fynnol," Elise said. "And if there were, I'm not sure it would be the course to take." She turned to Pwyll. "Where is your path into the hidden lands?"

Pwyll almost smiled. "It is not quite a path, Lady Elise. You will see." He turned to Baore. "We go north on the Wynnd, Baore."

Six

Alaan woke to daylight and found himself not only alone but with his hands free. He sat up, reeling, and almost toppled over. For a moment he steadied himself, eyes closed, swallowing down bile that fountained up into his mouth. When he finally opened his eyes, he found the ropes that had held his hands had been cut with a knife.

He forced himself up, his wounded leg throbbing and unable to bear the least weight. He hopped one-legged to fetch his staff, then stood, pain shooting through his leg, his vision blurring. When the pain subsided a little, he bent to examine the ground. Here and there spatters of blood and the signs of something being dragged.

"Well, if it was a wild beast it bore a sharp blade," he said.

With some difficulty he followed the drag marks down to the water's edge, but found no bodies. Alaan leaned on his staff and gazed around: daylight illuminated a thin mist that undulated slowly over the swamp. His island was a small hummock of rock and grasses, bordered by green and crowned with a few stunted trees. He limped down the shore until he came to a waterwillow that leaned out over the waters. His knife had been taken from him, but with his fingers he was able to peel a few strips of bark away.

He had to sit and rest partway up the small hill to his camp, but managed the ascent on his second attempt. In the darkness, his captors had not found the miller's bag Alaan had hung up in one of the trees. He lowered this now and opened it, removing a pot, some basic supplies of food, and two jars of springwater that he had carried here at much cost in labor and pain.

He feared now that all of his careful planning would come to naught. Hafydd had not followed him. And here he was, wounded, and suffering mightily. If his injury did not soon begin to heal, he would have to somehow reach the Wynnd, but knowing the hidden paths would be of little use if he could not walk two dozen feet.

"Well, A'Bert," he said to himself, "you're in trouble this time."

He stoked his fire, put on water to boil, and made a tea of waterwillow bark. It should bring his fever down, for he could feel it now—one moment hot, the next cold, a dull ache in his head like a counterpoint to the throbbing in his leg.

Alaan looked up at the sky. It was impossible to tell what time it was. Had he slept an hour or half a day? He did not know.

And who had done him the favor of eliminating his Hafydd's minions? He could not even begin to guess, but it seemed that whoever it was wished him well—or at least no harm—and that was the one bright spot in his otherwise dismal situation.

He sipped his tea from the pot when it had cooled a little.

"Well, Pwyll," he muttered, "will you come looking for me, or assume I've gone off on some other errand, as I have too often in the past?"

He ate a little food and lay down again, covering himself in the damp blankets he'd stored in the miller's bag. He lay listening to the sounds of the swamp, and thought he heard the distant baying of hounds just as he fell into darkness.

Sometime later he woke to a muddy sunset, a blind night settling in beneath cataract clouds. His fire had burned to ash, forcing

Alaan to dig deep for coals to rekindle the flame. He swallowed a little of the food he'd cached and brewed himself more tea of waterwillow bark, which was bitter and reminded him of mud.

He tried to make a bed of moss near the fire, and then lay down again, his thoughts muddled and ranging. A light rain spattered down, and he pulled his blanket over him and began to shiver. If more of Hafydd's guards found him like this, he would have little chance of running and none of fighting. But then they were likely all dead or so lost that they would never find him.

The songs of the swamp dwellers seemed to grow louder, and he covered his ears and fell into a troubled sleep. He woke to whispering and found an old man seated across the fire from him.

"Ah, son of Wyrr, you wake at last," the old man said, his voice soft and insubstantial, as though it emanated from some other place. He wore a surcoat and a suit of mail, but no helm. He appeared to be all of one color in the poor light—gray from head to toe. His hair and beard were thick and long, in the ancient style, and his face tanned and hardened as though he lived out of doors. To Alaan, he looked as old and worn as the rocks themselves.

"Who are you, sir?" Alaan asked.

"I am the Herald of Aillyn, though few recognize my titles now."

"You killed the men who held me here?"

"That was not me." The head shook in the dim light. "But I think it was you who defied my master long ago, stealing away his subjects and guiding them into the lands beyond."

"Long ago? It was an age. Your master made war on his own people, Herald, or were you not there to see? I led but a few to safety, fewer than I would have liked. If that was defying your master, then I am proud of it. What is it you want of me?"

The old man seemed to be gazing at him steadily, though it was difficult to be sure in the dark. "My master has need of your aid, Lord Sainth."

"I am Alaan, old man. Sainth is but a memory among my memories."

He saw the head shake, the long beard scything the air. "I know of your bargain, son of Wyrr. Why have you come to the Stillwater?"

Alaan grimaced from a spasm of pain. "I was awaiting my brother, but it seems he has chosen not to come."

The man nodded as though this were not unexpected. "My master . . . he does not rest easily, for he is trapped in a nightmare from which he cannot wake."

"It is the price some pay for the lives they lived."

The old man curled his hand around the hilt of his sword. "I saw you lead the man-at-arms out of the Stillwater, though he was your enemy. You are a man of compassion. Will you not aid your own blood?"

"I'm not as compassionate as you might think. I might offer aid to my enemies, but not to monsters."

"Aillyn is not a man to displease, son of Wyrr," the man said sternly.

Alaan laughed despite the pain. "Aillyn? He has been dead for centuries."

"So have you."

The fire crackled and a shower of sparks sprayed up, fanned by a gust of wind. Smoke whirled round, clawing at Alaan's eyes, and when he opened them again the old man was gone. Lightning stabbed the sky. Rain sprayed down like gravel.

Had he not been sitting? Had he not risen when the old man appeared?

Alaan sat up then, and swayed, almost toppling into the fire which had burned down again. He fanned it back to life and fed it from his dwindling supply of firewood. Rain hissed as it struck the rocks ringing the fire. Alaan pulled the blanket up over his head but couldn't bear the heat, and tugged it down again, letting the rain run through his hair and beard, welcoming the coolness. And then he was shivering again, huddled by the hissing fire, battered by wind.

He must have slept because when he opened his eyes a moon stared down through a hole in fast moving cloud. A moan passed through his lips, unbidden. The pain in his leg had spread into his knee and up his thigh.

He raised his head and thought he saw some movement in the faint moonlight. It had not been a beast, he was sure of that. He cast about then and found his sword, which he had set nearby but not so near that he might roll on it in his sleep.

He lay there shivering, wondering what was out there in the dark, and then fell into a nightmare and found what was inside worse.

Seven

The ringing persisted above all else, like some aural manifestation of the pain in his head. Neither shaking his head nor covering his ears did anything to dim the constant pealing. Dease's mind wandered like a lost child. Images seemed to surface from some depth, float across the surface of his consciousness, then drift away or pull apart into other visions. It was impossible to concentrate for more than a few seconds on any one thing.

Watching the groom saddle a horse for him, Dease realized he hadn't the slightest idea of how to do it himself—an act he'd repeated a thousand times. He turned away from the groom and found Toren gazing at him measuringly.

"Are you sure you can to do this, Cousin?"

"And if I don't, who else will?"

"There are others."

Dease shook his throbbing head. "No. It is our task to finish. . . ." What were they talking about? The light in the corner caught his eye; first light of day finding its way through a chink in the boards.

"Dease?"

"What is it?" Dease saw the concern in his cousin's face. "Have

I wandered off again? Well, I'll be myself in a day or two. You said it yourself . . . didn't you?"

Toren nodded. "But what if we find Beld and Samul before then?"

"Oh, it is unlikely, I should think. They'll be traveling fast and have half a day's lead on us. . . . Isn't that so?"

"That's what we assume."

The marshals of the fair had sent out riders seeking word of Samul and Beldor, and had returned saying two knights of their description had been seen going northwest on the Lakes road.

"Then let us be off. We've time to make up."

Toren nodded. He signaled the grooms to take their horses out, and the two cousins followed. Dease remembered how to mount—or at least his body did. A small company of knights accompanied them—all chosen by Toren. He wasn't fool enough to go alone, not knowing how large Samul's conspiracy might be—and Dease could not tell him. Servants and squires would follow behind as they could. Toren was certain they'd soon outpace them. Wasn't that what he'd said?

They set out silently into the dawn, without the blowing of horns or crashing of cymbals. Those few who saw them go neither waved nor cheered. They knew there would be no glory in this pursuit, no matter what the outcome.

Dease bent over his pommel, closing his eyes against the pain, wondering what he was doing there and what he would do if they managed to catch their cousins.

Let them outrun us, he thought. *Let them go far away and die in obscurity. Let us never hear of them again.*

"Dease?"

Dease opened his eyes to find his cousin staring at him again.

"You might hold us up," Toren said.

All the better. "No. I will manage. Don't worry. It's only a little ache. I'll bear up. What did Lady Beatrice say?" Dease asked, remembering that Toren had been summoned by his mother.

"I told you once. Don't you remember?"

Dease shook his head.

Toren drew a long breath. "Lady Beatrice wants me to recognize Lord Carral Wills as the rightful head of the Wills family. If we do, he will renounce the actions and alliances of his brother, Lord Menwyn." He took his attention away from the road and gazed at Dease. "What is your opinion?"

"At the moment I don't have one, and you know it very well."

"At least your judgment is not completely impaired. I have agreed to acknowledge Lord Carral. We'll turn the Isle of Battle over to him and he'll sign documents guaranteeing peace between our families."

Dease heard himself snort.

"Lord Carral is not just any Wills, Dease. I trust him."

"Of course you do," Dease said. "You want to believe that every man is as honorable as you."

Toren did not look at him this time. "Are you suggesting that I should not have trusted my own cousins? Or are you saying that this should have taught me a lesson, though it apparently has not?"

Dease's mind was reeling just trying to follow the conversation. "I'm merely saying that you expect everyone to have the same sense of honor that you do yourself—and you will always be disappointed."

"Oh, certainly not always," Toren said. Dease could hear the smile in his tone.

"Often," Dease said.

"But look at you, Cousin," Toren said, doing just that. "You risked your life in an attempt to save me. My trust was not misplaced in you, at least."

Dease closed his eyes against the pain. He felt a hand touch his arm.

"I would be happier were you abed and under the care of a healer."

"No. They are my cousins, too. No one else should deal with them."

"You see. That is your sense of honor and duty. It is a terrible thing we do—hunting down our own blood—yet we cannot leave a task to others just because it is repugnant to us. No, Renné should deal with Renné. That is our way, and it is right."

"I've often wondered if it is not simply that we think ourselves above anyone else's justice."

Toren's mouth turned down. "I fear, Cousin Dease, that even in your present state you see things too clearly. It must be why Lady Llyn favors you so."

Samul slowly unwound the dressing, and found the wound beneath still red and swollen but without signs of corruption.

Beldor glanced over at his cousin. "I knew he would betray us," he growled.

"We are the traitors, Beld. Have you forgotten?"

"It was Toren began it all. . . . " Beld said, but his anger suddenly drained away, and he rose and walked a few paces to the stream. They had stopped to water their horses and eat a quick meal.

Samul replaced the dressing, careful not to wind it too tightly.

Beld glanced back at him again. "You were Arden's ally in this matter, Samul."

"And had I not been, he would likely have wounded me more gravely. How could you not have known it was Arden?"

Beld shrugged. "He was there where he should not have been, and you know how like to Toren he is. He deserved what happened."

"They will say the same about us if Toren catches us."

This gave Beld pause. "Toren will not come after us himself."

"Oh, but he will. He'll never leave another to do his dirty work."

Beld took up the reins of his horse and examined them closely. "And what will he do with Dease, do you think?" he mumbled.

"It depends on whether Toren understands what part he played in things. It wasn't clear from the rumors we heard. Only that Dease had been injured tying to stop the assassins. Perhaps Arden didn't have time to tell him."

"Lady Beatrice would never reveal Dease's part in things, even if it were known."

Samul nodded. Yes, the Renné would always preserve appearances. There was no dissension within the family. There never had been. What would Toren do if he did understand Dease's role in things? Had Arden told him? Or did Toren really think Dease a hero?

"Do you think he'll catch up with us?" Beld asked.

Samul considered a moment. "The roads are filled with knights returning home from the fair. Without our Renné blue we aren't so much different from the others. We might slip away."

"Not at this pace," Beld said.

"If we hurry we'll be noticed. No, better to go slowly, but change our direction often. The land between the mountains is large. We'll find a place in it."

"A place? To do what?" Beld wondered aloud. The question seemed to echo over the river, and then the clatter of hooves on the stone bridge silenced them.

Samul stepped quickly out onto a rock in the river so he could see who passed. "A troupe of Fáel," he said. "They won't care about us." He jumped back to shore. "It's minstrels we need to beware of. They might recognize us from Castle Renné."

"They might recognize *you*," Beld spat out.

Samul tossed the reins over his horse's head and was about to mount. "Come along, Beld. We've our ride into obscurity to finish."

But Beld did not move. "You can ride into obscurity if you like, but I've a different course in mind."

Samul stepped up into the saddle and gazed down on his cousin, who stood squinting at him in the bright sunlight. "And that would be?"

"To finish what we've begun."

Samul laughed. "Toren is almost certainly pursuing us—with a company of armed men, I would guess. If he catches us there will be no 'completing what we've begun.' If we're lucky, he'll let us take our own lives."

Beld shrugged. "Perhaps, but what we heard about Lord Carral Wills has me thinking. We could find allies."

Samul shook his head. "Beld, Beld. You are talking greater treachery then even I am capable of. You would not go to the Wills. . . ."

"No, but Prince Neit of Innes might welcome us. We've seen that his counselor little heeds the niceties of treaties."

Samul could only stare. "This is the man Toren claims is Hafydd. Hafydd who hates the Renné. The same man you were recommending we take by force from Prince Neit's encampment and make pay the price for his raid on the Fáel."

Beldor did not flinch, but only gazed up at his cousin, a clumsy hand laid over his sword's pommel—an awkward lump of a man, broad in the shoulders, narrow of mind. His jealousy and resentment produced his every movement, Samul thought. Without it he would lie down and never move again.

"Alliances shift and change," Beld said, "sometimes with the blink of an eye. They are not built out of love, you know, despite what Toren might think."

"Even he is not so naive. They are built on mutual interest and trust and honor."

"And who would not trust and honor us?" Beld swung awkwardly into the saddle. "Think on it, Samul. If not that, then I propose we lay a trap for Toren and do what we have failed to accomplish once."

Because of you, Samul thought, fighting to control anger that he knew would do them no good. "When it was an assassination staged to look like a Wills plot, I was in favor of Toren's murder."

"You were its champion, in fact."

Samul ignored this. "But if we succeed now it might mean a war within the Renné. Those who think as we do—that Toren's removal is necessary—and those who support his policies. We can't afford a feud within the family now; not with Menwyn Wills and the Prince of Innes preparing a war against us."

"We're no longer part of 'the family,' Samul," Beld said. "But if we were allies of Prince Neit—well, then there could be no better time for a feud among the Renné."

"You are talking madness," Samul said, and turned his horse up into the trees.

"I am the voice of sanity itself," Beld called after him. "If we don't finish what we began, what will you do, Samul? Become a man-at-arms to some coarse lord in the Wold of Forget? You'd never bear it, Samul. I know you. You'd never bear it."

Eight

Beldor crept clumsily through the bush, scaring any game away long before he could get within bow shot. Samul watched him go, a little horrified by the feelings this sight engendered. Here, alone in the wood with him, it was very hard to escape the truth: he despised his cousin. Samul thought him to be absolutely the worst of this generation of Renné, but when looking for allies, Samul had felt a need of numbers, as though this broad support would prove his actions right. It had been a mistake, though, in the case of both Beldor and Arden.

Arden.

Samul gently touched his wound. It still pained him.

How ironic to now find himself on the run with this . . . creature he had not the slightest liking or respect for. It occurred to him then that he could take out his sword and rid himself of Beld. But no, he hadn't quite come to that. The murder of Toren was called for, justified by political expedience. Toren was bringing the family to ruin. Murdering Beld would be murder without real justification, though much greater satisfaction.

What had Beldor said? *We are no longer part of the family.*

At least he was right about one thing.

A pheasant fluttered through the bush, alerted by Beldor's clumsy passing. It was too far off to be shot, but that didn't stop Beld from wasting an arrow. He'd never find that one!

Too bad it isn't Dease here instead of Beldor, Samul thought. At least the conversation would be absorbing. And what had become of Dease? Was he playing innocent with Toren? Samul realized that's what he would do in the same situation. Play the innocent and let the others shift for themselves. Samul didn't blame him. He liked Dease too much to wish him ill.

Beld, on the other hand, he hated, and yet he knew they had a better chance of survival together than they did singly. That was the hell of his situation.

A hare darted out of the underwood almost beneath their feet, startling Beldor and making him stumble. He tumbled forward, bringing his great fist down on the panicked animal. The hare lay writhing on the ground, its back broken. Two more loud punches and the hare lay still.

Beldor rose up out of the leaves, laughing. "Did you see, Samul? Bows are for men not quick enough with their fists. That's what I say."

"You fell on it, Beld! I saw you!"

"Fell! How can you call that perfectly aimed punch a fall?"

Samul was about to argue but decided to cede the field. Beld would be in a better mood if his dubious triumph were left unchallenged. As difficult as it was to accept, a boasting Beld was easier to stomach than a morose one.

Beld lifted his trophy up, dangling by its ears. "There is the dinner I promised you."

"You promised me pheasant."

"Ahh," Beld growled, "let's not split hairs. I promised you a fine dinner and here it is. *Let's not split hairs!*" Beld threw back his blunt-featured head and laughed. "Did you hear, Samul? Let's not split—"

"I heard! I heard. You'll no doubt claim that was intentional as well, as weak a jest as it was."

"What a mood you're in, Cousin. Your own situation is no worse than my own, and I have kept my spirits up."

"Have you, now?" Samul said. Was Beld really so unaware of his own moods? He'd been sullen and volatile ever since the night of Arden's death, which of course was nothing unusual for Beld.

"I've been deliberating our future, such as it is," Samul said, changing the course of the conversation.

"That would put even me in a foul mood," Beld said.

They were walking down a path that led back to the small clearing where they'd staked out their horses. The day had begun to cloud, and a cool wind blew in from the south—from the distant sea.

"I think we should sell our horses and buy a boat," Samul said.

"Sell our horses! Your mind is misshapen. Horses such as these aren't bought and sold at country inns. If Toren is really chasing us, he'll hear of it and he'll recognize our mounts, sure. Once you're in a boat you can be only one place—on the River Wynnd traveling south. Toren would be after us in a trice. Or is that your plan? Have you finally realized that Toren's death is still necessary?"

"You missed your chance, Beld. You shot Arden instead. Do not forget that." Samul watched as Beld began to gut and skin their dinner. "Of course, Toren will think we've gone south toward the sea, but I'm proposing we cross over to the eastern shore. No one will expect us to go there, and certainly Toren will not follow."

Beld looked up at him, narrowing his small eyes. "Across the river lie allies of the Prince of Innes—or so they're sure to be. Have you reconsidered what I said?"

"Beld, there is an obvious question you have not asked yourself. Why would Prince Neit want us for allies?"

"Because we are skilled men-at-arms and because we know much of the Renné—how soon they can be battle ready, the size of armies, which fortresses are weaker than they look, which alliances are not really so solid. Oh, we have much to offer."

"Yes, and it might all be false."

"And we did what?" Beld asked. "Murdered Arden to make our betrayal look real?"

"Perhaps Arden's death was feigned. Or perhaps it was real but we seized upon the opportunity to make our claim believable. 'We are the murderers—hunted now by our own family—please take us in and we will aid you.' You seem to have forgotten that we were attempting to murder Toren because his policies were making the Renné vulnerable to Menwyn Wills and the Prince of Innes. Hard to convince them that we'd changed sides so suddenly, don't you think?"

"Toren wants our lives. We hate him, that's why we tried to murder him in the first place—"

"You hate him, Beld."

He suddenly recalled their meeting on the Summer Hill. *I will do this thing for I love him best.* Isn't that what Dease had said? Samul shut his eyes at the memory, closing out his view of Beld's bloody hands.

"I am only proposing we go east because it is the direction we are least likely to go in," Samul said. "There are neutral duchies and principalities even there. Not all are under the thumb of the Prince of Innes. If we have any hope of escape, it is east, as far to the east as we can travel, right up beneath the very shoulder of the mountains."

Beld took a long stick and sharpened it with his dagger. He used this to spit the hare, driving it through the flesh with slick hands. "Well, I for one will give up my horse with difficulty. Wouldn't it be better to have a bargeman take us across, horses and all? After all, it is more than unlikely that Toren will follow."

"Unlikely, yes, but not impossible. And certainly the men he has with him will not hesitate to cross over. No, we need the boat to convince Toren we have escaped toward the sea."

"A boat will be best for you," a voice said, and they looked up to find a man standing a dozen feet away, sword in hand.

Both Beld and Samul pulled their swords free of their scabbards.

"Unless you are wearing mail that will turn arrows, I would stand very still."

The man whistled, and an arrow buried itself by Samul's feet, then a second appeared from another direction. The archers were in the trees.

"If you want to be rid of your horses, and your fine armor and pack animals as well, I will be happy to oblige."

Other men scurried out of the underwood. They took hold of the horses and swept up the saddles from the ground.

"And your purses, if you please," the man said, holding out a hand.

He was a fair-looking man, neither old nor young, with a purple scar cut across one cheek, a drooping mouth, and an eyelid that hung limply down. He'd once been a man-at-arms, Samul knew right away, and was no one to trifle with—not when he held the advantage, anyway.

"Beld . . . " he warned beneath his breath, sensing his cousin's rage building. "Do nothing foolish."

"Listen to your cousin," the robber said evenly, "no profit in being stuck full of arrows. Your purses."

Samul had to put his sword down to unfasten his pouch. He tossed the leather bag to the robber, and Beld did the same.

"I'll leave you your swords, out of respect for your calling, and because the woods here about are filled with the most unworthy villains." He smiled crookedly, then stepped quickly forward, snatching up the hare on its spit. He saluted them with it and backed into the trees. A few silent steps and he was gone.

Beld filled the air with curses. "What shall we do now? We haven't a copper coin between us! Oh, I will hunt this dastard down and roast him like a hare!"

Samul laughed. "But nothing better could have happened!" he said. "Better than any plan we could make ourselves. Those thieves will be selling our horses here, our armor there. It will be a trail spread all across the countryside and going in all directions. Let Toren follow that!"

"But what will we do? All we have to our names is our swords and bows."

"And a small fortune in gems sewn into my clothing."

Beld turned on him. "Is this a jest?"

"Not in the least. Be prepared for every eventuality. That is what I say. Now we'll buy a boat and cross over the river. Who knows if Toren will ever realize that we traveled that way? The only thing I regret, Beld, is the loss of our dinner."

Nine

The bruised face of the moon gazed down into Llyn's garden, where she sat beneath the shadow of a tree. She had come to hate the sunlight, and didn't care if she ever saw manmade light again, whether it be from candles or hearth. The cool light of the moon was best. It asked so little of her. If only everyone were like that!

For a moment she hid her face in her hands. She could still see the shock of the people—the horror they'd felt just to look at her.

I am a monster, she thought. *A monster who should be hidden away.*

It took a few moments for Llyn to uncover her face again, even here in the privacy of her own garden.

Another wound that will not heal, she thought. *Haven't I enough?*

She heard the lock rattle on the balcony, and then the doors opened with a terrible creak. Llyn pulled her feet into the shadow and stayed very still.

"Llyn . . . ?"

It was Lady Beatrice, Toren's mother. She breathed a sigh. At least it wasn't that rogue Alaan, if that was really his name. But he would never dare show his face here after the humiliation he had caused her.

"Llyn . . . ?"

She did not answer even though she felt a sense of warmth pass through her. A slight softening of her anger. It was like Lady Beatrice to visit at a time like this. She was so kind and had such compassion.

"Llyn, your servants tell me you are in the garden. We must speak."

Llyn released a long sigh. "Lady Beatrice."

"Ah, there you are, child."

Llyn shifted a little so she could see her visitor through the leaves.

"I want to tell you how sorry I am for what happened to you this evening, but first I must tell you . . . I am the bearer of bad news."

Llyn felt herself stiffen. Bad news in the Renné family almost always took only one form. "Who has died?" she asked.

Lady Beatrice took a deep breath and the word came out like a sob. *"Arden."*

Llyn felt the tears begin to flow even before she shut her eyes. She bent forward and pressed her face into the palms of her hands, elbows digging into her knees.

"I am sorry to bring you this news, but there is worse."

Llyn sat up, feeling her heart shuddering within her breast. Worse could mean only one thing. "Toren . . . ?" she said, the name barely making it past her lips.

"No, Toren is unharmed." Again Lady Beatrice drew a breath to calm herself. "Arden was killed by his own cousins—likely Beldor. In the dark they mistook him for Toren."

"I knew something was amiss!" Llyn said, coming to her feet. "I've thought it for months but neither Arden nor Dease nor Toren himself would listen to me."

"It is a terrible thing to be right, sometimes," Lady Beatrice said.

"Poor Arden!" Llyn said.

"Perhaps," came a whisper from above.

"What do you mean, 'Perhaps'?"

"Arden had come to see Toren after the ball to warn him, and to confess his part in the conspiracy to take Toren's life."

"Arden?"

"Yes," Lady Beatrice said with infinite sadness. "Arden . . . of all people." And then she wept. Llyn could see her leaning against the railing, one hand over her eyes, sobbing as though it were her own child who had died.

It was a long moment before either could speak again.

"I still cannot grasp it," Llyn said at last. "Arden? He would seem to be the last person to have been involved in such . . . treachery. Were there others? Arden and Beldor seem an unlikely pair. They didn't much like each other."

"Samul," Lady Beatrice said.

This, at least, was not such a surprise. Samul had never been afraid to take action and had great confidence in his own judgment. "No others?"

"None that we know. Arden was struck down by an arrow as he listed his confederates."

"And what has been done with Beldor and Samul?"

"Toren and Dease have gone after them. Had they not fallen upon Dease at Toren's garden wall, he might have stopped them, but they took him by surprise as he went to speak with Toren after the ball."

"Dease is injured?"

"A little. He'll recover."

"But Toren was unharmed?"

"In body, yes."

"What anguish this will cause him," Llyn said, more relieved than she could say to hear Toren had escaped harm. "His own cousins . . ."

"Llyn? We are not admitting that the assassins were Renné."

"Of course," she said. When had they ever?

Neither spoke for a moment.

"I'm sorry about what happened, Llyn."

"Yes, poor Arden, his sense of honor must have surfaced—"

"I did not mean that," Lady Beatrice interrupted.

"Oh . . ." Llyn drew a long breath. "Worse things have happened this night. I will forget about it in time," she said. "No. No I won't. I'll never forget what happened, but worse things have happened this night, and it's good to remember."

"You are known for your wisdom for a reason."

"Oh, it is easy to be detached when you never leave your own walls. . . ."

This brought a second's awkward silence.

"I have a request. . . ."

Llyn stiffened. "Yes?"

"Lord Carral Wills will be lodging with us for a few days. I have been trying to locate a Fáellute that will do him justice. Do you still have yours, and may I borrow it if so?"

"I do and you may—but do I understand you right . . . Lord Carral Wills, the minstrel?"

"Yes, but I have neglected to tell the other sad news. His daughter, Elise, threw herself from the bridge into the Westbrook. Her body has not been found."

Llyn sat down, shaking her head. It was a night of sorrow.

Alaan—and she—had failed to rescue Elise, and look what she had done. Had Alaan accomplished anything at all this night?

"And her father has come to us," Llyn said, "to exact revenge upon his brother, who gave her hand away against his wishes—and hers."

"No. It is more complex than that. We will recognize Lord Carral as the legitimate head of the Wills family. The Isle of Battle will be ceded to him, and he will become our ally. Menwyn's alliance might totter a little when his supporters hear this. He is a usurper and everyone knows it. It was one thing when Lord Carral lived in the same house and said nothing, as though he sanctioned Menwyn's actions. Then it seemed legitimate, but now . . ."

"Do you think this will have any real effect?"

"Menwyn Wills is not loved by all of the Wills allies. Some might think they now have a justification to refuse Menwyn their aid.

Lord Carral might find he is recognized as the family head by more than one noble house. And now Menwyn and the Prince of Innes will have little justification for war, which is bound to make some of their allies nervous. They will not have the resources of the Isle to add to their war effort. Instead, Lord Carral will raise his own army from the Isle. War will still come. Menwyn wants it, and Prince Neit wants it as well, but we are in a stronger position now than we were a few hours ago. Lord Carral is not without his supporters within the Wills alliance. If the initial battles go our way, they might be convinced that their allegiance is misplaced."

"Do you trust him?"

"Yes. And so will you when you meet him."

"I am hardly likely to do that."

"Oh, I think you will. He will want to come and play for you after you've so generously offered him the use of your Fáellute. Don't forget, Llyn, he is blind."

She had forgotten. Perhaps they would be friends after all.

Ten

An early morning mist lay in tatters over the Wynnd, blotting out pieces of the shore and parts of the river. Where the sun broke through, the river appeared to steam.

Elise ran her hand through the water as they went, leaning her head on her arm on the gunnel. She stared down into the depths of the river, silently watching her hand perform a gentle dance in the green water. And then she sat up and looked back south, the way they had come, her face drawn and anxious. Tam had seen her do this two dozen times that morning—her obvious fear of Hafydd unsettling him.

Tam had said nothing yet to the others about Elise and what she had done—what she had become—and he wasn't sure why. Did they realize? Certainly Baore knew. How could he not?

Perhaps Sianon commands such loyalty of people, Tam thought. *None will betray her.*

He sat up and surveyed the river. It was broad and idle and dotted here and there with boats and barges half obscured by the low mist. Along the shores the tops of trees emerged from cloud hanging over the river, and the occasional small farmstead was lit by the sun falling through a thinning of the fog. Tam ran his eye slowly

along the bank. They were too far from either shore to be the victims of archers, and this gave him a slight feeling of security—
though the river had always been a place of danger for them.

Elise sat up again and sighed, clearly restive. "Baore, certainly a
lady can learn to manage a pair of oars," she said. "Let me take
them awhile. You've done enough."

Baore gave up the oars reluctantly, unable to refuse Elise, Tam
noted. She was soon propelling them along at good speed. Tam
glanced over at Baore, both of them thinking the same thing: she
would soon tire at this pace.

Tam thought that Baore looked both better and worse then he
had in the last few weeks. Certainly his health seemed improved.
He had color in his face, and his substantial frame was filling out
again. But at the same time he seemed even more cheerless, as
though his one great love had run off with another.

Tam glanced over at Elise. Even in the garb of a man and with
her face turning golden from the sun, he thought she looked utterly
beautiful—irresistibly so, in truth. And this was passingly strange,
for Elise was not beautiful in any conventional way. Her face and
nose were long and thin, but her eyes were large and soft, her
mouth as finely drawn as any artist could manage. If the stories
about Sianon were true, then a broken heart was certainly in
Baore's future. Perhaps it had been broken already, who could say?

But was Elise Sianon or not quite, as she'd claimed? Perhaps
even she didn't know the truth.

Elise's efforts propelled them into a dense, cool bank of fog that
settled around them like a sodden cloak. Tam shivered. For a moment they were suspended in that timeless, shadowless place of
dense fog where direction, even motion, lost meaning. Tam half expected great trees of stone to appear, but instead the fog thinned
and he found himself on the river still.

Baore abruptly stood. "Now there is a boat I've never seen!" He
pointed off into the mist. "Do you see?"

"Fáel-scena," Cynddl said, standing up on a thwart.

The boat, stone gray, lay near the eastern shore, its sea-blue sails barely drawing in the still morning. The boat was double-ended and high in both bow and stern, the stem drawing up in a graceful curve like the neck of a swan. It was not an overly large craft—like a small coasting trader in size—but graceful, with a sheer like a curving bow.

"You don't often see them this far from the sea," the story finder said.

"They hardly look like Fáel," Tam said, gazing at the half-obscured figures standing on the deck. "I see none of the colors I associate with your people."

"No, our seagoing cousins have their own ways—their own language, almost, for it is all but unintelligible to my people. On the prow of their ships you'll find carved the head of the whist, for it was the whist that led us to the land between the mountains and warned us of the dangers. On the stern you will find a clan symbol; each ship is sailed by members of an extended family, twelve or fifteen people to each boat. Most often they travel in small fleets, like the land-bound Fáel travel with their caravans of wagons. There are likely other boats hidden in the fog." He turned to survey the river but saw no signs of other Fáel-scena.

"You must be highly regarded among them, Cynddl," Tam said, "descended as you are from the great navigator."

"I am a Fáel of the land, Tam. They look down upon us all no matter what our lineage."

The gray ship sailed into the fog. Tam watched it slowly fade, as though it turned down some other branch of the Wynnd and disappeared from his world.

Though they traveled against the current, it was two hours before Elise gave up the oars, and she had barely slacked her pace in that time—a feat Tam knew he could not equal. This brought them to the southern tip of a small island that lay tight against the western shore, and then, in a short distance, into the mouth of a narrow waterway. The stream itself was smaller than the Westbrook and overhung with ancient walnuts and cottonwoods.

By noon they had come to the foot of a small falls, and beyond that Tam could see white water stretching back to the next bend. They unloaded their belongings then hauled the boat up onto the shore. They dragged it into the bush and turned it over, hiding the oars separately. Anything they didn't want to carry was bundled up and left high in a tree. Pwyll made sure everyone knew where both the oars and their belongings were hidden. No one had to ask why.

With Hafydd after us, who knows which of us will return? Tam thought.

They took the narrow track that ran along the southern bank of the stream.

Pwyll led the way and Tam fell in beside him. He thought the knight seemed . . . if not apprehensive, then alert. He kept his hand near his sword. But the day was quiet and warm and still. Insects buzzed over the narrow little river, and birds flitted furtively among the branches.

"How did you come to know Alaan?" Tam asked when he found himself walking alone with Pwyll.

"Oh, I've known Alaan for many years now. He once saw me practicing the sword with my father. My father had trained to be a man-at-arms but had lost one leg from the knee down. He was given a small holding far to the west, where we managed for many years. Alaan was passing by on one of his travels and saw our practice. He spoke to my father and then, a few months later, an older man appeared. He had once been famous in the tournaments. I remember my father treated him with a respect that verged on reverence. He moved into an old shed that we made comfortable for him—not that he seemed to care much where he slept—and he took over my training. I never really understood why.

"It wasn't till Alaan returned a year later and was obviously familiar with my teacher that I realized he was the source of my patronage. My teacher was strict but not unkind, and under his tutelage I learned more than my father could ever have taught me. Alaan appeared again when I was fifteen and brought me a wonderful horse. We trained it, my teacher and I, and I entered my first tournament that year. I didn't win, but I acquitted myself well against more experienced knights, and thereafter I applied myself to my training with renewed passion.

"I was seventeen when Alaan came and took me with him on one of his journeys. I didn't understand until then why he'd spent those years seeing to my training and my well-being. I thought, because of his noble name, that he was the lord of some demesne somewhere and wanted me to join his household. I only hoped that I could acquit myself well at tournaments and bring some fame and honor to his household to repay him for all that he'd done. I can't tell you how surprised I was to find that he was a landless wanderer.

"But he told me such amazing stories about the past. Stories that I'd never heard, not even from the traveling minstrels. And he told me, too, a little of his purpose. All that really mattered to me was that my teacher treated Alaan with complete respect. That was all that was necessary to gain my loyalty. And so I have traveled with Alaan many times on difficult journeys. And I've been sent on errands of my own, all to Alaan's secret purpose."

"And what is that secret purpose?" Tam asked.

"Only Alaan can tell you that," Pwyll said.

They came finally to an inn that stood near a small bridge and a mill.

"The Inn of the Green Door," Pwyll announced, but stopped the party there and waved them all into the wood.

Not far beyond the inn Tam could see the roofs of a small village. The little trickle of water that later formed the stream had been damned here to make a millpond, and the waterwheel squeaked relentlessly in the spillway. The inn looked out over the pond and the fields beyond. The building was of the sort common to the south, local stone below and half timbered and plastered on its gables. The door, which was large and propped open, was indeed green, but there was no other sign to mark the inn. Ta-

bles were set out beneath the shade of the largest beech tree Tam
had ever seen, and the round tables themselves had once been
millstones, now set on stone columns planted firmly in the
ground.

A few men sat talking quietly over their mugs of ale and mead,
the buzzing of bees and creaking of the waterwheel providing a
sleepy music behind.

"It is kind of you to bring us to an inn, Pwyll," Fynnol said, "for
I am powerfully thirsty, but is this the way into the hidden lands?"

"Indirectly it is," Pwyll said. "You see, I haven't the ability to
travel the hidden paths as Alaan does, but there is a man whom
Alaan once told me of, and he often comes here. I have never laid
eyes on the man myself, but he has the ability to draw maps that
will take one beyond the land between the mountains."

Fynnol did not laugh, as Tam expected him to, and then Tam
had a sudden memory. "Did not Eber son of Eiresit ask us if we
had met the mapmaker?"

Cynddl nodded. He had thrown himself down in the shade. "I
think you're right, Tam. He said something like that, I'm sure."

"How will you know him?" Elise asked.

"His name is Kai, and he is unmistakable, I'm told."

"Well, let's go see if he's there," Fynnol offered, "and if not we
might just have to sample their wares while we wait for him to show
his unmistakable face."

Elise had parted the branches to look out at the inn. "Remember that Hafydd is seeking me, Fynnol. I think it would be better if
only Pwyll and perhaps one other went to the inn. Hafydd will be
asking after me. Better he not have any word of my whereabouts or
how large my party."

Pwyll nodded agreement. "Come with me, Tam," he said.

"But why not take me?" Fynnol said, jumping up. "I'm a much
more pleasant drinking companion than Tam."

"And that is why you must stay," Pwyll shot back as he made his
way through the trees. "I mustn't be distracted from my purpose."

"He means you talk too much," Baore muttered, receiving a wilting look from his cousin.

Pwyll and Tam set off across the open common, stepping carefully among the sheep droppings. "The innkeeper's name is Barnsley," Pwyll said as they walked, "and Alaan says that he knows everyone's business for many leagues around. Be careful what you say to him."

They took a table, nodding to the locals. The innkeeper bustled out with a round wooden tray balanced on one hand, and proceeded to plunk down mugs before several of his customers, dropping comments into each conversation as he went. He was an enormously corpulent man, with wiry hair that was a mixture of black, white, and silver. Beneath bushy eyebrows of the same hue bulged large eyes that made him look constantly surprised. He was quick to smile and almost as quick to laugh. Tam could see why the man knew everyone's business: he looked so pleasant and harmless, even a little comical, that anyone would trust him right away.

"Your pleasure, good sirs," he said as he noticed the strangers.

"A full measure of your darkest ale," Pwyll said.

"I've a black ale that's said to be the finest west of the Wynnd," he said. "It's disappointed very few. The local people call it 'Night.'"

Tam laughed. "I'll have a half measure of the darkness, then," he said. "But does it contain the stars and moon?"

"Never ask for the moon, sir," the man said, and waddled off.

"You needn't keep looking behind you, Tam," Pwyll said, "I've not fallen asleep. Be at your ease. The locals will start thinking we're thieves or highwaymen."

They waited only a moment before the innkeeper returned, two battered mugs on his tray.

"It be a fine day, if a bit too hot," Pwyll said as he found some copper coins to pay.

"Hot, yes," the man said. "But at least you are not traveling as some do this day. We had a visit this morning from men-at-arms all dressed in black. Now, there's hot: riding around in mail and black surcoats!" The innkeeper nodded as he said this as though agreeing with himself. His expression of eternal surprise changed not at all. He shifted from one foot to the other.

Tam tried to hide his alarm as he met Pwyll's gaze.

"We didn't see them on the road, though we came from the river."

"No, these came from the south, toward Westbrook, I'd imagine."

"Many a man-at-arms is returning from the fair," Pwyll offered, leaning back in his chair as if he hadn't a worry in the world.

"And a good number pass through here, but not many as forbidding as these. Frightened all my trade away. I wasn't sorry to see them go. They were hoping to catch up with another party—a lady and her attendants—but none such had passed by the Door." He shook his head. "I hope they don't come back. Only one of them drank anything but water—though my stableman had some business from them." He wiped a bead of sweat from his forehead.

"And where did they hail from, do you think?"

"Not from our little corner of the world." He shook his head. "From east of the river, I would venture . . ." This last sentence turned into a mouthful of air as the innkeeper realized he didn't know where Pwyll and Tam hailed from.

"Well, at least your livery had some profit from them. A large party, were they?"

"Thirty men, I should think. Not many fewer."

Pwyll smiled. "I'm sure you'll see more profitable travelers in the next few days, now that the fair is over."

"Did you see the jousting?" the innkeeper asked. "I've heard that Toren Renné and a stranger made a spectacle not likely to be seen again in a generation."

"We did see it," Tam said brightly. "The stranger would have won the laurels that day had his horse not come up lame."

"It seems opinion is divided on that," the man said and turned to go, but Pwyll stopped him.

"I have an old friend who told me he sups here often. Do you know a man named Kai?"

The innkeeper didn't seem much surprised by this, as though strangers came seeking Kai all the time. "Oh, aye. He's not been here this day but you might see him coming along the Ashdown road by and by. He's generally here for supper, if he comes at all."

"And which is the Ashdown road?" Pwyll asked.

The man hooked a thumb toward the west.

"And these men-at-arms you say visited you, did they go that way?"

The man hesitated. "They took the north road, and in a hurry, too."

"Well, I'm glad we don't go that way," Pwyll said with obvious relief.

The innkeeper regarded them a moment. "Returning from Westbrook, are you?" he ventured, his voice softening a little. Before they could answer, he went on. "Many a man has come back from the fair with neither horse nor armor. 'Tis nothing to be ashamed of. The best knights in the land between the mountains travel there to try their strength, and their lances have shattered many a dream." He shook his head. "And where is it you go now, if you don't mind a man asking?"

"South," Pwyll said. "Far south, where the knights who attend the tournaments are said to be less skilled." He smiled suddenly. "But Kai told me it was worth the journey to Uphill to sample the ales at the Green Door, and I will say our short divergence has been well worth it. Wouldn't you agree?" he said to Tam.

"Oh, aye! I should come thrice as far for half as much." He held up his mug.

The innkeeper was called away before he could respond to this flattery, and Tam and Pwyll gave their attentions to their ale, which was better than common, though not as good as they'd claimed.

"Hafydd's guards have been here before us," Tam said

"Or Hafydd himself. Did you see how frightened the man looked?" Pwyll glanced over at the northbound road. "He has a way of following Alaan, I know—sensing him, really. Perhaps he can do the same of Elise and knew she went north on the river. From Westbrook it would be quicker to ride here than to pull against the current. Drink up," he said. "We should tell Elise. Hafydd will soon know he's overshot and come back."

Tam looked quickly around the common, half expecting black-clad men to come charging out of the trees. He'd met these guards often enough to know how relentless they were in pursuit of their quarry.

A sudden memory of the dying man-at-arms they had buried on the island—the curling thread of crimson—the man's life draining into the river. That poor swordsman had become a man there, somehow—not just an enemy. Certainly he followed the orders of his lord, but he was a man with a conscience for all that. These black-robed knights who made up Hafydd's guard did not leave that same impression. Death's outriders could be no more ruthless, and Tam felt himself shiver. The servants of Death felt no remorse when they came for you. No pity. They had torn through the Fáel encampment with no more compassion than a hurricane, leaving women and children dead. And poor Elffen. Her lovely voice would break no more hearts. Gone. Gone on the wind.

Pwyll put his head back and drained his mug, and Tam followed suit, unwilling to leave a drop behind, not knowing when they might find such refreshment again.

They bid good-bye to the innkeeper and set out over the common again. Tam could feel the locals watching them go. They went back down the road toward the river until they were out of sight, then stepped into the shadowed wood.

"Hafydd was here before us," Pwyll said as they found their companions. "He was looking for a lady."

Fynnol cursed and leapt to his feet.

Elise reached out a hand to Tam as though she would steady herself.

"Are you certain it was Hafydd?" she said, almost whispering.

Pwyll repeated the conversation they'd had with the innkeeper.

Elise sat down on a stone. "It won't take him long to realize we aren't still traveling up the Wynnd. We'd better find your map-maker, Pwyll. If we can locate a track into the hidden lands before Hafydd gets near, the path will close behind us and he will have no way to follow." She looked up at Pwyll. "Unless Hafydd too has heard of your mapmaker."

Pwyll shook his head. "Alaan said this man was secretive. No one knows where he dwells but can only find him here, and not all the time. Only a handful know of his abilities."

"Like Theason Hollyoak," Cynddl said.

"Who?" Pwyll asked, turning to the story finder.

"Theason Hollyoak. He was a man we met on the hidden river, far to the north. He came seeking us with a message from Eber. I have often wondered how he found his way into the hidden lands. Eber knew of your mapmaker, it seems. Perhaps his messenger did as well."

"It is a mystery we have no time to solve or even think about," Pwyll said, taking up his pack. "Hafydd might ride up at any moment, and his party is much larger than ours." The traveler glanced up, trying to find the sun among the branches. "The afternoon is wearing on. Let us go a short way down the Ashdown road and hide ourselves. If Hafydd comes looking, at least we'll have the wood to give us shelter."

Elise nodded. "If we don't find this man Kai by sunset then I should take the boat out onto the river and try to lead Hafydd away while you find Kai. What we do here is too dangerous. Hafydd seeks to kill me at any cost."

He appeared at the crest of a hill on the Ashdown road seated in a wheelbarrow. The old wooden wheel clattered in its forks as the barrow jounced down the rutted hill steered by a man the size of Baore though twice his age.

Tam and the others had been hidden here several long tense

hours, expecting Hafydd to appear at any moment at the head of a column of armed men. It was a wonder he hadn't.

While they'd waited, the twilight collected in the hill's shadow like an eddy behind a rock. Beyond the crest the sky brightened with sunset, and overhead the azure seemed to take on depth and intensity.

"Here is our mapmaker," Pwyll said quietly.

"How do you know?" Elise asked, shifting to have a better view through the leaves.

"Alaan told me he had no legs."

Elise stood, taking up Tam's sword. "But I know this man." She raised a hand to the others. "No, stay where you are. He has not seen us yet, here in the shadows."

The barrow continued its jarring descent, and as it neared, Tam began to make out the features of the seated man, who lolled against an improvised backrest. He was soft-featured and bald, his skin pink as a pig's.

"Take up your bow, Tam, and come with me." She glanced at Pwyll. "Let me speak with him quietly. And do not ignore the road behind. Hafydd will not rest for dark."

As the barrow came near, Elise and Tam stepped out of the shadow of the trees into the middle of the narrow road. Tam followed as she advanced a few paces and then paused; just out of everyone else's hearing, Tam noted. It was a moment before the giant looked up and noticed her, and then he came to a surprised and wobbly stop, jarring the occupant to awareness.

"Kilydd . . . ?" Elise said, turning her head and looking at him out of the corner of her eye as though her vision must be failing.

The man eyed Elise apprehensively. "My name is Kai," he said, "and I have nothing that anyone would want to steal."

Elise shook her head; sadly, Tam thought. In the failing light her eyes appeared to glisten.

"I did not expect you to recognize me for my form is not the same, but even so—that spring in Yarrow . . . was it so easily forgotten?"

The man leaned forward in the dark, his face contorting in pain. "Who are you?" he asked, suddenly breathless.

"It is me, Kilydd. Sianon."

"It is not possible."

"So one would think, but I did not pass through Death's gate, and I have dwelt for many lives of men in the deep river, emerging only now."

The man slumped back in his makeshift seat. "I have heard rumors that there was a sorcerer in the lands again; Sir Eremon some call him."

"Caibre," she said.

The man's hands came up to his mouth; unbidden, Tam was sure.

"But you have seen Sainth," Elise said.

The man shook his head. "No. No I have not."

"He knows of you, Kilydd. He told his companion of you."

The man shook his head in confusion.

"You would not know him, Kilydd, for he appears as another now; as I do."

"Why are you here, seeking me?" the legless man asked. "I am of no use to any now."

"I'm told that you can draw maps that will take one into the hidden lands, Kilydd. I seek Sainth, who is there, wounded we think by the minions of Caibre. Will you put the past aside and help me for the sake of Sainth, who loved you like a son?"

The man hesitated. Tam thought he had never seen a man so overwhelmed. He looked as though he might topple from his barrow—as though the world were no longer steady beneath him.

"Caibre is seeking me even now," Elise said. "Do you want him to find us here? His memory is long for wrongs done him, Kilydd. You of all people should know that none of the children of Wyrr are to be trifled with."

The man nodded. "But where is Sainth? Where should this map lead?"

"Come talk to the man who accompanies him, now, as you once did so long ago." Elise turned to lead the way but stopped, turning back. "But Kilydd, say nothing of who I am to these others. They think me Lady Elise Wills and I would not have them know different." She glanced at Tam. "Not yet."

At the edge of the wood the man Elise called Kilydd produced a quill and paper. Elise told him what she had learned from Prince Michael, and Pwyll added what he knew of Alaan's plans.

"There is such a marsh in the hidden lands," the legless man said. "Those few who have seen it say it is vast and perilous. I would not send any there without cautioning them: very few return from this place."

"It does not matter, Kai," Elise said. "I must find Alaan." She had begun to look pale and unwell again, as she had periodically all day. Tam had seen her squeezing her eyes closed and pressing fingers to her temple.

The man took up his quill in a pudgy hand. "It would be to your advantage to have a boat when you arrive there."

"We have a boat," Pwyll said, "by the falls below Uphill."

The man's hand hovered over the paper in the failing light. "Then I will send you by a small winding stream, but you must carry your boat over a high pass. Can you manage that?"

"If the path is not too rugged," Tam said. "Our boat is not so large. Two strong men can lift it, though they could not bear it far."

"You are six," Kai said. "I think you will manage."

He began to sketch out a map in dark sure lines. Tam had seen enough on this journey to believe that this man could do as Pwyll claimed, but he thought there should be something more to this act of magic. The page should glow, or the lines appear without the aid of a pen. But the truth was, this map-creation would have looked no different if Tam had done it himself.

It took only a few moments. Kai pointed out a few details to Elise, and then rolled the paper and placed it in her hands.

"Such maps usually have a price," he said, "but I do this for Sainth." Tam thought he heard some resentment in Kai's tone.

"I will pay you what you ask," Elise said softly.

Kai took a small bag from his barrow and from this removed a bundle of dried flowers tied with a string. "This is called blood lily," he said. "It is useful for a number of ailments, but I take it for the ghostly pain I still feel in my missing legs. It grows only in the hidden lands, and even there it is not common."

"Then you must know Theason Hollyoak," Fynnol said.

The man's head snapped around toward Fynnol.

"We met him far up the river. He was gathering herbs for healers, he said, and had made a study of the hidden lands, though he would not say how he found his way there."

"Theason should be more careful with what he tells others. And I would ask you to be the same. Most men would not believe it if you told them what I do, but there are some who know more and yet are more foolish."

"We will say nothing," Elise said.

The man nodded, gazing at the lines that etched his palm as though he looked into a faraway land. "If you find Sainth, tell him . . . tell him I do not blame him."

They returned to their boat, stumbling through the dark, but then clouds obscured the moon and they were forced to camp for the night. A fire was debated and finally lit, as Elise was sure that Hafydd could find her fire or no.

They sat by the dying flames, silent, Elise meeting no one's eye. *The others must realize now,* Tam thought. She knew this man—this mapmaker—and how could Elise Wills claim that?

"Who was that man?" Fynnol asked, the faint glow of the fire turning his face golden red.

Elise took a long breath. "With Cynddl's permission I will be the storyteller this night." She didn't wait to hear from the Fáel. "Kilydd was the name of a man born long ago, after Wyrr had taken all his knowledge into the river, but before his children shattered the One Kingdom and began the age of perpetual war. He was an accomplished young man and came to the attention of Wyrr's second son—Sainth. Sainth had the gift of his father, and so traveled across all the world, for no place was home to him, no woman as fair as the one he might yet meet." Elise hesitated a second, a small flame flickering to life but then dying away. "Kilydd served Sainth for many years, his trusted servant and companion of his travels. But as he grew older—and it was one of the gifts of serving Sainth that Kilydd kept his youth for an unnatural span—Kilydd lost his love of travel and perhaps lost his heart, too. But it was Sainth's sister, Sianon, to whom he gave his love, and though she took many to her bed, she took none to her heart.

"He served in her house for many years, as he did for her brother, trusted but never valued, never understood. The wars began with Wyrr's oldest son, Caibre—long, terrible wars—and into these battles Sianon threw all who loved her, and with no more thought than she would have fed wood to a fire to warm her hands.

"Kilydd went to Sainth and asked him for his aid in stopping the wars, for the people of the ancient kingdom suffered terribly in that time. Kilydd and Sainth went to Caibre, but he would not even speak of peace and instead set a trap for Sainth and his onetime companion. What happened then is not clear. Some stories say Caibre had Kilydd's legs cut off for all the years he had traveled with Sainth, and then he was cast into a cell—Caibre must have thought he might have some use for him yet. He should have died in that place, but he found a path out, as though Sainth had reached out from beyond the grave and rescued him. He should have been dead—dead for an age of men—but his long years with Sainth and Sianon had left a taint of magic upon him, and he lived on somehow, forgotten by Death. And then his story was lost."

Elise fell silent.

"And what happened to Sianon?" Tam asked softly.

Elise did not look up at him but continued on in the same grim tone.

"Sianon regretted nothing and no one, sending even her children into battle, and losing them all to Caibre and his armies. The two—Caibre and his sister—met finally upon an island in the center of the River Wyrr. Having killed his brother, Caibre laid siege to his sister's stronghold, breaking army after army upon it until he bent a storm to his will and shattered the gates with the force of it. Caibre was strong then, stronger than his sister, who could not stand against him without her brother. But she was cunning and deep in the arts and laid a trap for Caibre, so that if he managed to kill her, it would cost his life. And so they went into the river, Caibre and Sianon. Into the river, but it did not carry them to Death's gate as it should."

She looked up at Tam, her face dark and drawn. "And now they are among you—the children of Wyrr. And they care for no one but themselves. Themselves and a hatred that has survived beyond the grave."

Eleven

It seemed that Hafydd's ability to trace Sianon's movements was less than perfect. The farther they were from Elise, the less precise the art. His singing blade made barely a low hum now.

They had been riding north, paralleling the river, but inland. Mid-afternoon, Hafydd had stopped his company, strode off into a clearing with orders for the company to be silent, and to leave him alone. Michael had watched as the grim knight held his sword in two hands, the blade angled up toward the sky, and turned in the slowest possible circle, eyes closed. This took nearly an hour, and when he was done he came striding back, mounted his horse and ordered them to turn around and proceed back south from where they'd come.

Sianon, it seemed, had doubled back on them.

They had not gone an hour when they came upon Hafydd's outriders grouped around two men they had sitting on the ground. One of the guards stepped forward.

"We came upon these two on the road, Sir Eremon, and when they saw us they dashed into the wood. As we thought we might question them as to who they'd seen upon their travels, we gave chase, and a good fight they gave us. If the one had not been wounded on his sword arm, we might not all be standing now. We thought them to be highwaymen, sir, but they are fair spoken, and claim to have been victims of thieves themselves."

"But I know these men from tournaments," Prince Michael said. "Lord Samul and Lord Beldor Renné."

Hafydd actually smiled. "And here you are, my lords, horseless, without retinue, and hiding in the forest. What could have reduced two men of such standing to these circumstances? Shall we escort you back to Westbrook and your illustrious family? Or are they seeking you already?"

Neither Renné answered. The Prince had seldom seen noblemen look more wretched.

"I should deliver you back to your cousin, Lord Toren," Hafydd said, "for no doubt some are blaming the Wills or the Prince of Innes for what you have clearly done—murdered Lord Arden Renné."

Lord Samul gazed up at the mounted men—squinting from the sun in his eyes. "We might be able to suggest a more profitable course of action."

"Might you indeed?" Hafydd said.

"Well, the river leads to strange places," Samul whispered to Beld.

They had laid their bedding out away from the others but within the protective ring of Hafydd's guards. Samul thought he had never seen such a grim and formidable-looking company in all his life—except for the son of Prince Neit, who looked like a blossom among thorns in this group.

"I think we are more like prisoners than allies," Samul said. "You realize they could kill us while we sleep."

Beld laughed softly. "They could have killed us while we were awake, Cousin, but there is no reason to do so. They will wait to see if we can be of any real use to them—which I'm sure we can be."

"This is madness, Beld. These are the people we risked every-thing to save our family from . . . and now you will join them?"

"It is not madness, Samul. With such allies we will accomplish what we set out to do in the beginning: we will topple Toren from his stolen throne. We will meet him on the battlefield, Cousin, and ride him into the earth, as he deserves."

Samul felt himself about to explode with frustration. Toren sat a stolen throne now! Then he realized Beldor's gaze was fixed on him, his eyes two cold stars in the shadowed night. Samul's retort died in his throat and he swallowed it whole. He was in danger, and not from the quarter he had anticipated.

He will murder me if I stand in his way, Samul thought.

He had known all along that Beld's involvement in the plot had everything to do with his hatred of Toren and little to do with his disapproval of Toren's policies of conciliation, but now that hatred had grown to sweep everything else aside. Beld would join the Wills to bring down Toren. He would kill members of his own family—for he felt not the slightest remorse over Arden's death. Beld would kill him too, might even be planning it as they lay there.

"You're right, Beld," Samul said quickly. "What choice have we now? Our own family hunt us. Toren will demand our lives if ever he finds us. Better to meet him on a field of battle where we have a chance of survival."

"I thought your reason would triumph in the end," Beld said. "Honor . . . ? It is a hollow doctrine used to keep men-at-arms from making decisions for themselves. But it shall not hamper us. We will do what we must—as the Renné always have. Who knows what alliance we might make with the Wills? There might be a daughter to marry, a dynasty to found."

Samul felt himself nod stiffly in the dark, and then they both fell silent. Now he was talking of dynasties. Samul closed his eyes and consciously slowed his breathing, trying to sound as though he slept. Better not speak of such things with Beld. He might give his true feelings away. He would have to be watchful enough as it was, here among his enemies.

With Eremon's forbidding guard walking the edge of the camp,

Samul did not think he could slip away—and if he did, perhaps they would hunt him down. He should have left Beld behind. Without him to guide Beld, his cousin would have been tracked down by Toren in a matter of days. And look where this had led him! Beld had brought everything to ruin—murdering Arden when Dease had been certain it was not Toren. Leaving Dease behind. Bloody fool! Beld had destroyed all his carefully laid plans . . . and now this.

Samul tried to calm himself. How would he ever sleep now? Either Beld or Sir Eremon might murder him in the night. Eremon . . . Was Toren right, and this was Hafydd somehow come back to haunt them? To have his revenge on the Renné. Now there was an ally for you! An ally only Beld could find.

Despite his seething anger and his growing fear, sleep did find Samul. And for a moment, when he first woke, he wondered if he were in the land of the living or if he had passed through into the lands of the dead. And then a bird cried twice, *whist, whist,* and he knew that he was alive. Alive for a moment but without family or purpose. Living for only one reason—to survive another day—like the most base of animals.

But the whist cried for someone.

Beld, Samul thought. *Let it be Beld.*

Twelve

The two parties of armed, mounted men met at a ford in a small stream where the oaks and hawthorns drew back from the road. In this place, where the earth opened up to the sky, the embankment curved down from either side and the river ran swift and clear over unbroken stone as flat and smooth as a frozen pond. Upon the northern bank double swan banners fluttered against a field of sky blue. The riders to the south carried no banners, nor did they display any coats of arms or other devices to identify them.

Swords were drawn on the northern shore and lances lowered, which caused a reciprocal movement upon the opposite bank.

"I am seeking Lord Toren Renné," a man called over the water. "Is he among you?"

"Who are you who asks?"

"I shall give my name to Lord Toren, if he travels with you. If he does not, I will seek further."

There was a shuffling of horses as other riders appeared on the northern side, and then a hushed conversation.

A rider pushed himself through to the fore. "I am Toren Renné. And who are you?"

A man in a gray surcoat rode his horse down the bank and splashed into the stream. "Gilbert A'brgail," the man called out.

"Gilbert!" Toren pressed his horse forward, splashing down into the stream himself, much to the concern of his own men-at-arms. "I did not recognize you dressed so. You don't look much like a dealer in rare arms."

A'brgail smiled at him, the scar on his mouth almost white in the sunlight. "And you don't look like the young man I often visited, if you don't mind me saying so." He stopped his mount and looked oddly at Toren, as though attempting to find what had changed. "You look rather grim," he said.

Toren shrugged. "I am not upon a happy errand, Gilbert."

"So it would appear," A'brgail said. He pointed up toward his company. "Do you know this animal?"

A man led forward a horse on a tether.

"That is Beld's charger! Where did you find it?"

"It was in the possession of a certain highwayman who has been frequenting these parts of late. We have been after him for some weeks now and finally snared him in a trap yesterday. But take a walk with me, Lord Toren. I have a story to tell you."

The two men rode to the shore and left their horses in the hands of one of Toren's men. They walked down the bank and out onto a small gravel bar where they could see both up and down the stream for a hundred yards.

"It is a perfect day," A'brgail said, gazing down the waterway. "How deceptive that can be."

Toren stopped to look as well. He hadn't thought much about the kind of day it was—his thoughts had been elsewhere—but A'brgail was right. The early morning sun shimmered on the waters, and the shadows of leaves shivered in the soft breeze. High summer in the land between the mountains. One hardly needed to say more.

"I cannot help but think that your knights have taken up their responsibilities rather prematurely, Gilbert," Toren said, tearing his gaze away from the view. "You asked for my family's recognition of the legitimacy of your brotherhood, but I don't remember giving it."

A'brgail did not look away, but met Toren's gaze. "No you had not, but I am confident that you will, for the roads become more dangerous every day. It is difficult to keep up the morale of a company of men who have no purpose. I thought a little taste of the duties we hope one day to perform again might help . . . and this highwayman was getting rather bold."

"Apparently so, if he stole Beld's horse! Where might my cousin be now?"

"That I cannot answer with any certainty, but I had quite a long talk with this highwayman, who had once been a man-at-arms of one of your allies, by the way. Oh, he had a silver tongue, that one! And he had much of interest to tell me. Most interesting though was his story of thieving the horse of your cousin, for you see, he managed to overhear quite a bit of conversation between Beld and another before he grew bold enough to do his deed."

Toren turned his gaze on Gilbert, whose hair, in the sunlight, seemed as white as a cresting sea.

"And was my name mentioned in this?"

"It was, and in a most interesting context, but let me tell my story from the beginning." Gilbert kicked a small stone so that it rolled into the water, sending rings running, then fading away. Toren could not quite get used to seeing the man dressed as a warrior, with the long surcoat over his mail. But Toren thought Gilbert A'brgail looked the part—a stern and noble knight of the ancient days.

"It seems two men who would fit the description of your cousins Beldor and Samul Renné were found roasting a hare and discussing what they might do with their future." A'brgail crouched down, picking up small stones and turning them over in the sunlight. "My highwayman wasn't much interested until one of them mentioned that the other had killed a man named Arden." The knight dropped the stone and picked up another, turning it over as well. "Now this highwayman, like others of his kind, keeps his ear to the ground, so he'd heard about the murder of Lord Arden Renné. The murderers were still being sought, or so he'd heard. It occurred to this man that there might be a substantial reward for capturing the culprits, but as he listened it soon became clear that these two were Renné themselves. There would be no reward for their capture, unless it was his own death to keep him from revealing the truth." A'brgail picked up yet another stone; a perfectly white one.

"Better to keep silent, he realized. But he also realized that these knights would not dare go to the local lord were they to be robbed. The inevitable followed. It seems, however, that your cousins were planning to buy a boat and cross the river. They reasoned that you would guess they traveled south, down the river, not east. And that if you did realize where they went, you would not follow."

Toren reached down and picked up a small stone, as if to see what A'brgail searched for. "Where and when did this robbery take place?"

"Yesterday, not far from here—two hours ride east of Flint."

"I wonder if I can find them before they reach the river?"

"I think you might. I've had riders out looking for them, and they were said to be in the village of Uphill yester-evening. Making for Weir perhaps. A good place to buy a boat, though what they would use for money after the highwaymen took their purses I can't imagine."

Toren looked over at A'brgail. "Did he take everything they wore?"

"I don't think so."

"Then not to worry. Samul leaves nothing to chance. He will have gold or gems hidden away in his clothing. Gems most likely. It is an old Renné dodge." Toren picked up a fist-sized stone and hefted it. "I can be in Uphill in an hour." Toren threw the stone and watched it plunge into the river.

A'brgail nodded. "You could, but I have a proposal for you. We could travel with you and assist you in your endeavor."

"Beware, Gilbert: remember what happened when your order allied themselves with the Renné before."

"But you are seeking criminals on the roads. What task could be more natural for a Knight of the Vow? And we will be allies in the days to come. There is no other way Hafydd can be defeated."

"You seem rather sure there will be a war."

A'brgail paused. "Hafydd lives for nothing else. He is only alive on a field of battle. The times between are painful to him. The inaction drives him to fury. If we cannot destroy Hafydd, there will be a war, your grace. A terrible one."

"Now that I know who you are and a little history of your family, you might drop this servants' address and call me Lord Toren."

"I would be honored."

Toren crouched and looked down the river, seeing how the water bent itself over the shallows and around rocks. "If you are to accompany me you must understand—the fate of my cousins is mine to decide. No other."

"So it should be."

Toren turned and looked back to the two parties of riders gathered warily on either bank.

"Tell me, Gilbert," he said as he rose to his feet. "Did Beld or Samul mention other members of their conspiracy?"

"Then it is true," A'brgail said softly. "I can't tell you how sorry I am to hear it. Your own cousins . . . But no, there was no mention of others. Though you should beware of something, Lord Toren."

Toren turned toward his friend.

"They were debating two things; offering their swords and knowledge to the Prince of Innes . . . and attempting again to assassinate you."

Toren closed his eyes for a second. He turned in one violent motion and flung a stone out over the waters. It skipped several times and then for a moment swam spinning upon the surface before it finally drowned.

Thirteen

Alaan hobbled about his island, chilled now, though he had been bathed in sweat an hour earlier, and had shed his jacket and opened his shirt. He'd also doused his fire. After once awaking to find himself in the hands of Hafydd's guards, he thought it best not to alert anyone nearby of his encampment. Not now when movement was so difficult—if not impossible.

The day was dense with fog, as it seemed always to be in this place. No doubt the sun shone above the clinging mist, but it would not find its way down into the swamp that day. A heron fished stiff-legged along the shore of his island, stalking its prey with exaggerated care. Perhaps this was the way Hafydd sought him now—deliberate and controlled—unlike the Caibre of old.

"But I am different, too," Alaan whispered. "I am capable of sacrifice now."

A crow hopped from branch to branch, observing him as he hobbled. Alaan glared up at the bird. Where was Jac? He hadn't seen his whist in a day or two—not unusual, really, but he would have liked to have seen a familiar face. Even that of his inconstant avian companion. And Jac, when he was in Alaan's company, had the good graces to warn him when danger was near.

Alaan gazed out at the slowly swirling fog, the still water. The place was in tune with his own low mood. He had failed to lure Hafydd to a place where he might finally be stopped. And now what would he do?

"If it comes to war," Alaan said aloud, "Hafydd will win. I cannot stand against him alone."

He could barely stand at all, his leg pained him so. He limped back through the fog to his camp, gazing at the few meager belongings and bits of food, all laid out so he could reach them without rising.

"Fire," he said. "I must have fire."

Just then a bird lit in a tree overhead and the crows took to wing, protesting loudly.

"Jac!" Alaan said. "You have frightened off my guests. Well, so much for them and their manners. Come, I will make us a meal." He found some nuts and spread them on the ground, Jac pouncing on them hungrily.

Crows were larger and stronger than the whist, but Jac was not quite a natural beast. He had traveled with Alaan too long, and other animals sensed it.

Alaan built a fire and boiled some water to make his waterwillow bark tea. If there were any of Hafydd's guards still alive, they would likely not find him, and if they did—well, he would have to deal with that. He unwound the dressing he'd made from his pant leg and examined the wound.

"Ah, look at this, Jac," he said. "It festers and grows more foul. What a place this must be that it could make ill a son of Wyrr." He washed the wound as best he could given how much it pained him, and dressed it again. His clothing would soon be gone at this rate— torn up for dressings.

His tea gave some small relief and cleared his head of fever for a while. He slept, and when he awoke it was dark.

He lay for a moment feeling a light rain, barely more than a cooling mist upon his face. His fire burned still, making him wonder how long he'd slept, but when he turned his head, he saw a figure seated in the curling smoke. At first he thought it was the old man again—the old man he had dreamed—but this was someone else.

"Your wound is deep," the man said.

The smoke turned his way, clawing at his eyes. Alaan lay back and threw an arm over his face. "Why did you kill Hafydd's guards?" he asked.

"The name Hafydd means nothing to me," the man said.

"The men who captured me. You killed them."

"Yes."

"Why?"

"They hunted you, yet you set one of them free, even leading him out of the maze of the Stillwater." The man's voice had an odd quality—the tone of a young man, but the weariness of someone very old.

Alaan turned to look at this stranger, but he was hard to see beyond the flames and smoke. Dark bearded, he was, his face partly obscured by the brim of a large hat. He sat on a bit of log, hunched over with elbows on his knees. The firelight flickered over large hands. He appeared to be weaving a strap of leather, or of firelight, it was hard to tell which.

"They treat you as an enemy," the man said, "yet you treat them with compassion. Why?"

Alaan propped himself up. "It is a weakness of mine. I have this terrible ability to understand the forces that make others act as they do. And I can always sympathize. That man I set free, he was only a man-at-arms. He had no more choice in what he did or where he went than a saddle horse." Alaan found his pot and drank some cold waterwillow tea. It tasted like mud and iron. "And who are you?" he asked.

"Rabal Crowheart, I'm called. Or so I was called long ago when there were others to judge I had need of a name."

"And how have you come to this place, Rabal Crowheart? It is not easily found, and once found not easily survived."

"I came here by accident. But I have remained for other reasons. I think it best you come with me. You will be safer and I will help you heal, for I have some skill in this."

"I think I shall stay here, thank you all the same."

This gave the stranger pause, Alaan could see.

"These men who follow you, they are not all dead and might find you yet."

"But it seems they have orders to kill me only if they must, and keep me alive if they can. No doubt they wish to take me back to their master. They don't yet know that there is no way back from this wretched swamp."

"I have come and gone as I've pleased these many years," the man said, then looked up at Alaan. "And you—you led the man-at-arms out. You found a way."

Alaan squinted at the man through the caustic smoke. "What is it you want of me, Rabal Crowheart?" he asked. The question, the whole conversation, echoed his dream of the old man.

The stranger stopped weaving his strands of firelight, gazing at Alaan intently. "I want you to come see what I've found in the center of the Stillwater."

"And why would I want to see this?"

"Because you are a descendant of a son of Wyrr, and you have an insatiable curiosity."

Rabal Crowheart traveled the swamp in a hollowed-out log, so narrow and tippy that Alaan was sure they would be swimming before they'd gone a furlong. Alaan perched on the bow, where the boat was not wide enough to accept his hips. His wounded leg he stretched out painfully before him, his few belongings in a jumble at his feet.

Jac had disappeared again, and the crows returned to watch their progress through the fogbound swamp. It was clear to Alaan that these overly curious crows followed the man who called himself Crowheart. And this made him a person of very great interest to Alaan.

Rabal Crowheart, however, had managed to sweep aside any questions that Alaan asked, saying only that he should wait until they reached their destination.

A moss-hung tree appeared out of the fog. And then another. Ferns fountained up from the water, green branches splayed like spray. Alaan thought they made their way through a flooded wood and would find the land at any moment.

"Where are we now?" he asked.

"In the Stillwater yet, but another part of it. The swamp changes to this drowned forest. In other places it is different again."

"Then this is not a wood in momentary flood?"

"No, it is like this always. The trees, all the things that grow here, will grow nowhere else. The water here is not so foul. It can be drunk without danger, and the snakes do not venture here, for the wood is too open."

Alaan was doubly relieved to hear this. The few pots of water he had hidden on the island were almost emptied. He thought he saw a light bobbing far off in the mist. He pointed.

"What is that light?" he asked.

"Ghosts," Crowheart said. "The night is haunted with them. I usually don't stray far from my fire at night, but have made an exception to fetch you."

"But ghosts will not hurt the living."

"Will they not?" he said, digging his pole into the bottom and sending them smoothly on. "Does it not hurt to be frightened so that one's heart stops? But perhaps you are braver than I. Braver than the many who have been lost in the Stillwater at night."

"I am not so brave," Alaan said, shifting to relieve the pain in his leg, and failing. "But I've met ghosts before."

Sitting as he was, Alaan's leg began to throb with intense pain, as though someone took a glowing forge hammer and struck his wound again and again. Conversation became impossible. He could only brace himself in the bow of this tiny boat and try to bear the pain without crying out. He opened his eyes, to find pale men draped in mist. They appeared to stop and watch the boat's passing. Sad, they seemed. Sad and despairing. Lost in this place forever.

Ghosts, Alaan knew.

He shut his eyes again. Existing in his own gray netherworld of agony and near-delirium. Time ceased to pass in this place, the only measurement a throbbing metronome of pain, each beat predicting only the next shock of suffering. There was no beginning to this torture. No end.

When the boat finally ran softly ashore, Alaan had to be lifted out. He lay on the damp ground, unable to rise—barely able to breathe—for what length of time he did not know. An hour. A minute.

Finally Crowheart helped him up. He was beyond hobbling with his staff now. Without the help of another he would not have gone a yard, not even on his belly.

They passed through an opening in a stone wall worn away by the mist and the ages. The stubs of other walls grew up out of the brown grasses and broken stones. Between two of these short walls, barely taller than Alaan himself, a wooden roof had been built. The misting rain did not reach here, and in the back of it an ancient hearth had been resurrected, the crudely rebuilt chimney reaching up into the mist above the level of the roof. Here Crowheart soon had a fire roaring. He boiled various mysterious herbs in separate pots, their scents spreading beneath the roof and driving out the damp.

"What is this you do?" the traveler managed through the pain.

"The seeds of blood lily will take away much of the pain. Water-willow bark you have already taken for the fever, but let me make you a poultice of lantern bitter, for it will cleanse the wound of poisons and help it to bind."

Alaan realized he did not much care what he was given if it took any of the pain away. He lay propped up against the wall on some surprisingly clean bedding. Crows fluttered in beneath the roof but sat only on one beam, and if they ventured farther, a word or gesture from Crowheart sent them flapping back to their perch.

Crowheart plied him with the blood lily first, a paste made from the seeds. "A drink made by boiling the plant or fewer seeds will take away minor pains, but the hurt you have I think is greater than that."

In the firelight Alaan could see the stranger now. His round face appeared to be drowning beneath a froth of black beard and hair. It seemed that in a moment Crowheart would be gone. This made Alaan smile, and it was then that he realized the pain, though not gone entirely, was greatly relieved. It was a strange sensation. The pain was still there somewhere but it was as though it had been moved to some other part of the mind: a voice so distant he no longer needed to heed its call.

"Well, that is a noble bloom," Alaan said, feeling the muscles in his body begin to unknot a little.

"Yes, but we must do more for you or you will simply die without pain. This wound is very foul," the man said, staring at Alaan's leg. He had waited for the blood lily to make itself known before he unwound the dressing.

He made a poultice and pressed it to the wound. A clean dressing was applied and his old one placed in a pot to boil clean. An hour later Alaan felt well enough to eat, though his head was not perfectly clear—as though some of the fog from this perpetually mistified place had found its way inside his head, obscuring his thoughts.

Crowheart made them both a meal that appeared to contain no meat, but was made up of vegetables he did not recognize. This had a wholesome, though pasty, flavor. When they had finished their meal, Crowheart went and stood outside the shelter a moment, peering up at the sky.

He came striding quickly back. "I think we might see a little moonlight here in a moment. Can you walk a short way if I help you?"

"I suppose I can," Alaan said reluctantly, "if I absolutely must. I will tell you, though, that where I live moonlight is not so uncommon that I need strain myself to see it."

This made Crowheart smile. "We need moonlight to view the object I wish to show you."

"Can you not just tell me what it is?"

"I could if I knew myself."

Crowheart helped him up, his hands large and heavily callused. With his staff in one hand and Crowheart supporting him on the other, Alaan limped out into the night, surprised at how cool the air seemed after his bed next to the fire.

They passed through a maze of low walls, worn away by mist, apparently. It was a dank lonely place, and Alaan felt nothing but pity for anyone who dwelt there.

"What was this you said about me being a descendent of a child of Wyrr?"

"Of a son of Wyrr," the stranger said. "A descendent of Sainth, to be more precise. Only Sainth had the ability to travel into the hidden lands. After the great sorcerer was murdered by his brother, the only men who could do this were the men who had been Sainth's traveling companions for many years—and their abilities to find the hidden paths were not nearly so highly developed as their master's. Beyond these chosen few, all of whom must be dead by now, only the smallest number of the descendants of Sainth could find the hidden paths. I am one of those, or so I believe." He looked down at Alaan, their faces barely a foot apart. "But you . . . you aren't old enough to have traveled with Sainth, so you must be descended from the great traveler—and kin to me, in some remote way."

Alaan said nothing, but only gritted his teeth and hobbled on. The blood lily seed had taken away most of his pain while he laid still, but this forced march brought much of it back again.

They came to a worn stairway, the stone treads sculpted by rain and wind. Here Alaan insisted he sit a moment and let the pain subside a little.

"It isn't much farther," Crowheart said, staring up at the hazy sky. The moon, a day past full, floated vaguely through the mist. Flat luminescent clouds carried by a high wind obscured the moon like ragged sheets of paper.

The pain subsided enough that Alaan nodded to the stranger, who helped him up solicitously. The stairs were difficult, each uneven tread sending a wave of pain through Alaan's leg. It was fortunate that Crowheart was so strong, Alaan realized, for he bore as much of his weight as he could.

The mist thinned as they climbed up, until the stars appeared and of the mist only a halo remained around the moon. When they reached the top, the Stillwater lay below them, fog like drifting, moonlit snow. Crowheart led Alaan through an arched opening in an ancient wall. Beyond, filtered moonlight played down into what had been a round chamber. A stone floor had cracked and settled so that roots of trees broke through here and there. In the center, surrounded by a border of gray, a single smooth slab of dark stone was set into the ruined floor. It was almost square in shape and twice the height of a man in breadth.

Crowheart led him to the edge of this slab and stopped.

"It looks like slate," Alaan offered.

"So it does, though I think it is not. Watch, though. See what effect the moonlight has."

Crowheart led him to a crumbling stone that stood at the foot of the slab, like a bench. Alaan sat himself down, closing his eyes against the pain. He heard himself curse under his breath.

Crowheart stood beside him, glancing up at the moon that had become veiled by thin cloud. "Here," he said, "the moon will drift free in a moment."

The thin light broke through, just as Crowheart said, and a mist formed over the dark square of stone. It seemed to cling to the rock, not drifting beyond its borders. And then it dispelled, as though the cool moonlight had burned it away.

"There, do you see?" Crowheart said, pointing a thick finger.

Alaan saw nothing, but then . . . "Yes. Is it a man?"

And then it most definitely was; a man seated at a bedside where another lay beneath coverlets of white, his face pale as the mist.

"I have seen this same scene before," Crowheart whispered. "Many times. The young man is dead. The elder grieves over him. Watch."

A tear fell from the man's eye, but when it touched the coverings of the bed, it appeared to freeze, turning not to ice but into a glittering gem. Another tear followed, doing the same, and then many more, until a glittering skiff of diamond-clear stones lay upon the cover.

"The 'stones of sorrow,' " Alaan said.

Crowheart turned to him.

"It is an ancient story," Alaan said softly. "When the sorcerer Aillyn sat mourning his only son, his tears turned to precious stones. But these stones were not natural and contained the father's sorrow so that any who possessed them afterward was overcome by grief and melancholy. The stones were coveted for their beauty, but they were cursed. I hope you have not found them here?"

Crowheart shook his head. "No, only this black stone that reveals strange visions."

The moon went behind the cloud, and the mist wafted over the rock again. They did not have long to wait, for the cloud was small, and in a moment the moonlight returned.

When the mist cleared this time, they saw a boat parting the fog as it made its way over still water. A cloud covered the moon again before Alaan could see the occupants of the craft.

"I've seen that before as well," Crowheart said. "A woman rides in the bow of that boat. She is dressed as a man and bears a sword as though she were born with it in her hand. I don't know who they might be or what it might mean."

"Dressed as a man?" Alaan said. "Are you sure?"

"Yes, and grim and beautiful she is."

A long time passed before the moon appeared again, and this time the mist did not clear immediately. When it did, Alaan saw a great giant of a man bearing a massive sword. He trudged through water to his knees. Alaan leaned forward.

"But that looks like Slighthand . . ." he said.

"Who?" the stranger asked.

"He was a famous warrior, though very long ago," Alaan said. "The legends say that he accompanied Sainth on his travels."

Rabal's eyes narrowed as he regarded Alaan, a deep furrow appearing between his brows. "If he lived so long ago how is it you recognize him?"

Alaan shrugged. "He is rather unmistakable—the two-handed sword, a man the size of a barn." He turned back to the surface of stone to avoid the gaze of Crowheart.

The giant was gone, and in the mist Alaan could now see riders in black, passing over the land like a shadow. *Hafydd,* he thought, but then as the riders appeared to draw nearer he realized it was not Hafydd at all.

"These are the servants of Death," he whispered. "Look at them. They are abroad seeking their victims—which we will all be in time."

A great bank of cloud drifted over the moon then, and Alaan sat back. Crowheart lowered himself to the stone next to Alaan, his countenance as dark as a moonless night.

"I saw you once in this, I think," Crowheart said. "Or so I believe, for the figure was far off. But I think it was you all the same: oddly garbed, bearing a bow, and pursued by costumed men." Crowheart glanced up at the sky. "We will likely see little more this night. On only a few nights each month is the moon full enough to spark the visions, and even then the moon is often obscured in this place, so that a few nights a year one might come here and see anything at all. We were fortunate. What do you know of Aillyn?"

"Little. He lived so long ago—"

A stone rattled across stone.

Crowheart rose, but then did not move for a moment.

"They've found us," he whispered. He snatched up Alaan's Fáel bow and quiver. "Wait here a moment."

He set off for the opening in the wall, leaving Alaan by the black stone. Apprehensive, Alaan struggled to his feet, turned to watch Crowheart, and toppled over. He put out his hands to fend off the ground but fell past it, down and down into darkness.

Fourteen

Hafydd had them riding again the moment dawn was even a hint in the sky. At the Inn of the Green Door they stopped only for warm bread and a glass of wine while Hafydd walked out to the dark crossroads. Here he set his sword singing again. The Prince could hear it moaning in the cool morning air. Hafydd was back on his horse in a moment.

"She is not far," he said, and spurred his horse on, his guards scrambling to take their places around him. They rode now toward the river along a narrow track beside a stream. The Prince fell in behind the last guards, Samul and Beldor Renné riding by him. Already they had been lumped together: he and the two traitors.

Under the shadows of the wood they overtook a family riding in a cart full of produce. The man squeezed his little wagon off the rough track and into the trees. Even in the near-dark Michael could see the fear etched in these people's faces as he passed. The children clung to their mother, and neither parent would look at the forbidding company in their black robes.

A shiver ran through the prince. *Everyone* feared Hafydd. And familiarity did not diminish that. Michael had learned to live with his fear, but it was no less strong than upon their first meeting.

A low, muddied stream bank indicated a drinking spot, but Hafydd's blade led on and he splashed through the dusky waters and up the soft embankment, the hooves of his mount spraying dirt over the stream.

"Oh, aye," the innkeeper said, watching the gold eagle Toren tapped on the stone table, "they were here but an hour ago: a sullen man and t'other fair spoken and courteous. They rode with a company of knights dressed in black livery, though what noble family they served I did not learn. They'd been here the day before with a young nobleman, though the two you've described were not present then." He pointed with a stubby finger. "They all rode off together. Toward the river."

"Men all in black . . ." Toren said, realizing he must sound like a fool. "They wore no devices; you're certain?"

"Oh, aye. There was no mistaking that." The man shivered so that his abundant flesh jiggled. "Their captain sat at this same table yesterday and ordered drink of me: as forbidding a man as I've ever met. He wore a black surcoat, plain as plain. He looked like a man who'd cut your liver out for bringing him dark ale when he ordered pale. I hope he has not come to serve the earl, that's all I can say."

Toren flipped the coin up in the air and the innkeeper snatched it as it spun, displaying more speed than Toren would have guessed. With a bow the man retreated through the green door.

"Hafydd," A'brgail said softly.

"So it would seem," Toren said.

"But this couldn't have been Samul and Beld!" Dease said, confused. He put a hand to his aching head.

Toren clasped his hands on the stone table, gazing at the entwined fingers as though he'd discovered something there. "A'brgail warned me that this might come to pass. Why should there be limits to their treachery?"

"Beld, perhaps," Dease said, "but Samul never. He is man of

principle—misguided principle, clearly—but he would never align himself with the Wills and their allies."

"The innkeeper said nothing of him being in fetters," A'brgail said, leaning forward a little so that others would not hear. "I would guess Samul Renné was here of his own choosing."

Dease shook his head, sitting back in his chair so that it creaked loudly.

Toren looked at A'brgail thoughtfully. "Your highwayman heard no mention of them meeting Hafydd?"

"He made no mention of them meeting anyone."

"Curious . . . Can this have been a coincidence?"

"I would rule out coincidence where Hafydd is concerned. He is more devious than you know," the knight continued. "And more persuasive. Hafydd will find your weaknesses, though those same weaknesses might be hidden from you." A'brgail drew himself up a little, stiffening as though anger kindled within him. "But now we have a dilemma: your cousins are in the company of Hafydd, and Hafydd . . . Hafydd is a sorcerer."

Fifteen

The visitor was white-haired and ancient. He wore clothes that had been cut to forgotten patterns and, like a wise man from an old story, had greeted the Fáel in their own language. He sat on a bent-willow chair before Nann and Tuath, anxious and troubled. Nestled at his feet was a small boy, perhaps three, who regarded Tuath with an impenetrable and unsettling gaze. She had seen such eyes in children before. Eyes that had witnessed too much of life's sorrow and not enough of its compassion.

Apparently he had not seen Fáel before, or perhaps never seen a person without pigment: the pale, washed-out eyes, skin like wax, hair white but gleaming with youth.

Tuath averted her eyes and found that Nann stared at the small boy, her face a mask of sadness.

"When did this begin?" Nann asked.

"Not long ago," Eber said. He caressed his son's shoulder. "A nagar appeared on my island. It came out of the river at night and searched through my rooms, terrifying my servants. But my son, Llya, was unafraid. The specter knelt and spoke with him, or so it seemed, and soon after, Llya began to make words with his hands, teaching them to me."

"A nagar," Nann said. "Are you certain?"

He nodded. "Yes. And not one of the lesser nagar. This was Sianon: Wyrr's only daughter, preserved for a thousand years by the river where her father dwells, sleeping, but not quietly. His dreams are disturbed now, and he mutters and calls out." Eber looked down at his son, his face filled with compassion. "And these are the things Llya hears. The nightmares of a dead sorcerer."

"And what was the nagar seeking in your house?" Nann asked.

"It was searching for a group of young men who traveled down the Wyrr from the far north—one of them Fáel."

"Fáel?" Nann said, sitting forward. "But you can only mean Cynddl. He met us in this very place. What could the nagar want with him?"

"It was not Cynddl the nagar sought but one of the northern-ers."

"How do you know this?"

The old man looked down at his son, who fixed the strangers with his fathomless gaze.

"Llya told me." He looked up at the Fáel. "Cynddl came down the River Wynnd with some others, and their boat fetched up on the tip of my island in the dark. I offered them hospitality and we spent an evening in conversation. I also gave Cynddl something to carry south to a friend."

Nann glanced over at Tuath and then away.

"An ancient flute," Nann said.

The old man regarded Nann. "He told you of it?"

"He showed it to us," Nann said. "A smeagh, Rath thought it might be. Did it draw this nagar?"

Eber sat up in his chair. "What has become of my flute?"

Tuath could see the sudden suspicion in the man's face.

"Cynddl claimed it belonged to another," Tuath said. "He gave it to a man named Alaan. Or that is what he planned to do."

Eber sank back into his chair a little, then glanced down at his son, the suspicion in his face softening, a small smile appearing.

"Cynddl and his friends told me Alaan was dead, and I believed them for a while. But Llya believes Alaan is not dead, though in terrible danger."

The old man shook his head, and Tuath thought he looked close to tears. "Wyrr is restless," he said, almost speaking to himself, "and two of his children have returned, rising from the river. Why? Why would the ancient enchanter have need of them now?"

Llya began moving his hands, the motion swift and fluid.

"What does he say?" Nann asked.

Eber nodded toward Tuath. "He says he wants to see the pictures you've made."

Tuath wondered if she looked as unsettled as she felt. "What pictures?" she asked.

The boy had watched her speak, and now he made signals to his father again. " 'The dream pictures,' he says." A look of sympathy came over Eber's face. "Do not look so frightened. You are a vision weaver, I take it?"

Tuath felt her head bob.

"Then what you witness in Llya is not so different." Eber looked down at his son, considering, then drew a long breath. "He understands the secret language of the river, as strange as that may seem. For hours he sits and watches the patterns of its flow, and he comes to some . . . understanding." He looked up at Nann, meeting her gaze. He no longer looked distracted or feeble of mind. "The river has chosen him, I don't know why. It has chosen him, and he has made a language of movement to communicate what he learns to me."

Nann smoothed her skirt, then looked up at Tuath. "Bring what you have seen."

Tuath hurried off to her tent. In a moment she returned, passing an embroidery hoop to Eber. The old man took it in his pale hands and gazed for a moment.

"That is A'Bert," he said softly. "What is wrong with Alaan?"

"He appears to be wounded," Tuath said. "There is blood on his leg."

Eber squinted, raising the hoop in the poor light. The form of a man could be seen there, lying in a ring of fire among the shadows of trees whose branches seemed to reach down to him in a threatening way.

"That is not the land between the mountains," Eber said, gazing at the image of Alaan. His son had crawled up into his lap and sat with his back against his father, regarding Tuath's vision. Eber pointed at the embroidery. "And these are not shadows," he said. "Nor are these tree branches. They are claws, and the shadows are the servants of Death." He closed his eyes for an instant. When he opened them they glistened. "Alaan is not long for this world."

Llya began moving his hands, looking up at his father.

"Alaan still lives," Eber said. "That is what Llya thinks, and I hope he is right."

"But why is he encircled by fire?" Tuath asked.

Eber regarded the image again for a moment. "I am not sure," he said, though to Tuath he did not sound convincing.

Nann nodded to Tuath and she passed a second hoop to the stranger. He held it up as he had the other, the image almost two feet across. It depicted a woman, her face peering out empty-eyed from a cascade of blond hair, but as the head was slightly turned, one could see the cheek and temple of a second face on the back of her head.

"This is a mask," Eber said, pointing to the most obvious face. "The other face is 'real.' " He gazed a moment longer and Llya spoke again.

"What is he saying?"

"Llya says that is the nagar who came out of the river at Speaking Stone." He looked over at Tuath, took a short breath, and said, "Sianon is back among the living."

Tuath saw Nann's reaction to this. The older woman sat back in her chair, taking a grip on the arms, her face growing pale.

The child began to motion again.

"Llya says not to be frightened. We are waiting for three men who can save Alaan—if they but come in time."

"And who are they?" Nann asked hollowly.

"Three travelers; one who hears the smallest sounds, one older than old, and a third who watches himself from outside."

"And they will save Alaan?"

The boy moved his hands. " 'Perhaps,' Llya says. He asks that you warn your sentries so that they do not turn these men away as you tried to do with us."

Nann sat very still for a moment, then glanced over at Tuath. "I will go speak with the guards." She rose from her seat.

Tuath watched a shaken Nann cross the encampment. Then she noticed Llya's ancient gaze on her. "What is it?" she whispered to Eber.

The boy began making words with his hands again, though he did not take his eyes from her.

"He says," Eber almost whispered, "that you are like the nagar, and that you are like snow. But the nagar have been here forever and the snow lasts but a short time. What of you?"

"I am like the snow," she said quickly. "We are all like the snow."

The boy made two quick motions.

" 'Not all,' " Eber whispered.

Sixteen

"**I**t was a simple funeral," Lady Beatrice said, "the sorrow greater for those of us who knew the truth." She took a long breath. "Arden Renné was a traitor to his family." As she said these last words her voice shook. Llyn could see her, standing at the railing on the balcony overlooking the garden. In the moonlight Lady Beatrice appeared ghostly pale, a small figure of glass and sorrow.

"He was not a traitor at the end," Llyn said. "Toren would be dead if not for Arden. Let us give him credit for that. He could not go through with it."

Neither spoke for a moment. Llyn sat in her garden beneath the shade of a tree; if shadows cast by the moon could be called shade.

"All summer I've felt something was wrong," Llyn said, her voice flat. "I warned Toren, but he would not hear ill spoken of his own family—not even of Beld. And then what did I do? I asked Arden, of all people, to look out for Toren . . . and he promised that he would!"

"And perhaps, at the end, it was this promise to you that he could not break," Lady Beatrice said softly.

"I will take no credit for that," Llyn said quickly.

She saw the figurine that was Beatrice Renné shift on the balcony. Even through the canopy of leaves Llyn could sense the sorrow in her every gesture. Llyn's heart went out to her.

You worry too much about others, she remembered Dease saying.

"And how is Dease now?"

"I don't know. He went off with Toren. Insisted on going, in fact, against the protests of the healers."

"He would not let Toren do this alone. That is his nature."

"Yes. Though their absence means that Kel must prepare us for war, if that is what the months ahead hold."

Llyn looked down into the small pool. The oblong of light from the doors behind Lady Beatrice hung in the water, as though one could dive into the waters and find oneself in a room in Castle Renné.

"Kel will not fail us," Llyn said.

"No. He will not." Lady Beatrice took a sudden deep breath. "Llyn? What were you doing that night at the ball?"

"Dancing, Aunt."

A cold silence seemed to flow down from the balcony like a night breeze.

"I was trying to rescue Elise Wills from Prince Neit and his counselor," Llyn said. She could see Lady Beatrice nod.

"This seems an odd occupation for a Renné. Especially considering Elise Wills is betrothed to the Prince's son. Why were you doing that, pray?"

"Because a silver-tongued rogue convinced me it had to be done," Llyn said, wondering if she sounded as humiliated as she felt.

Lady Beatrice did not continue immediately, but when she did, said, "And who might this rogue be?"

"He called himself Alaan. I know little else about him except that he somehow found his way into my garden. I can't imagine how."

"Into your garden!" Lady Beatrice echoed.

"Oh, we did not meet face-to-face. He accorded me that much

courtesy. But even so, he found his way here and asked me to help him. He knew much about me, I'm afraid. Much of Castle Renné and its inhabitants. More than you would like, I'm sure."

"Lord Carral has told me of a man he met. He seemed to have had the ability to appear and disappear from places he should not have."

"Lord Carral is blind."

"Yes, but even so, I'm sure he's right."

"And what was this man's name?"

"He called himself a ghost."

Llyn snorted softly. "Perhaps that would explain it, for Alaan could walk through walls, apparently." But then she remembered him grasping her hand. That had been warm flesh, there was no doubt of that.

"I think this ghost and your visitor the same," Lady Beatrice said, "for he helped Lord Carral whisk his daughter away from Braidon Castle."

"Yes, he said he'd done that and that friends of his had died as a result. Poor Lord Carral. Imagine losing a child."

Lady Beatrice seemed to stiffen at this, but before Llyn could say anything more, she asked, "Why is this man so interested in the Wills and the Renné? And in Elise Wills in particular?"

"He said he wanted to avert a war, or at the very least delay it."

"Well, he has failed, I fear."

"Is the prospect so bleak?"

Lady Beatrice nodded. She looked behind her as though she had heard a noise. "There is someone here who wishes to play for you . . . to convey his gratitude for what you attempted for his daughter."

Llyn was suddenly flustered and found herself rising quickly to her feet.

"Sir?" Lady Beatrice said, taking a step back and turning toward whoever was in the room. Then she looked back to the garden. "He asks me to remind you that he is blind. You need fear nothing."

"It is Lord Carral," Llyn said in a small voice.

"Yes, my dear."

"But he owes me nothing. I failed Elise. Failed her utterly."

"But you tried, my dear. And at great personal cost." Lady Beatrice led the minstrel out onto the balcony, and one of Llyn's servants brought him a chair. Once he was seated, she could barely see him for the railing.

"Good night to you Llyn."

"Good night, Lady Beatrice."

She heard a door close quietly, and then, without a word, Lord Carral Wills began to play. She found herself drawn out from beneath her screen of leaves, though the song was no more clear out in the open. The music was so sure and beautiful—and so sad! She closed her eyes to listen.

She wondered then if she could walk through her garden in utter darkness—she had done it so often by starlight alone. Llyn began forward, hearing the gravel crunch beneath her feet, but then her toe came up against a rock and suddenly she wasn't sure where she was. Panic gripped her and her eyes sprang open . . . to find her garden around her, quiet and still, the beautiful music of Lord Carral Wills drifting down from above, as though it came from the stars themselves. The stars and the darkness.

Seventeen

A man on foot came pounding up the path. Dease watched him skirt an outcropping and then apply himself to the steeper slope. He arrived at the top breathless, and gazed up at Toren with wide eyes.

"They . . ." he managed, "they're . . . at the . . . bottom . . . of the hill." The last word was inhaled. "Stopped."

"And how far is it to this hill's base?"

The man waved a somewhat limp hand. "Three . . . furlongs."

"We are too close to them," A'brgail said.

"Then we will hold up here," Toren said, deferring to this man as he did to few others. "Or do you think we should go back some distance?"

Dease had been watching A'brgail and his men-at-arms ever since they'd appeared at the ford, wearing their drab gray without markings of any kind. They had been pursuing highwaymen, Dease had gathered, but on whose authority, he could not discover. All he knew was that Toren treated the man with uncommon respect, listening carefully to his every pronouncement. Dease found this annoyed him a little, but his confused brain could not understand why. If only the ringing would stop so he might think!

"No, better to wait here, but quietly."

Dease was not sure what they were doing here. Beldor and Samul were somewhere below in the company of Hafydd and Prince Michael of Innes, but why they were following so carefully, he could not understand. Apparently numbers were on their side, yet Toren refused to take any action, and Toren was not known to dither.

Dease looked down the slope, willing Beld and Samul to flee. He wondered if he could somehow alert them to Toren's presence. He glanced over at the man who styled himself a Knight of the Vow. All this talk of Hafydd being a sorcerer had made Toren cautious, and Dease supposed he should be thankful for that.

Toren waved a hand at the trees. "Would you not think hills of this height would be visible from the river? We aren't more than a few furlongs from the Wynnd, after all."

A'brgail looked around, twisting in his saddle. "I don't know the lands here about." He signaled one of his guards, and the man made his way through the others surrounding Toren and A'brgail. "Here's Tynne," the knight said to Toren. "He was raised not far off." And then to the young knight, "Do you know where we are, Tynne?"

"I don't, sir," Tynne replied. "Not far from Uphill, but we should be in lands given over to pasture here, with small woods on the knolls." He waved a hand around him. "These are not knolls. I don't know of any such hills nearby, nor any forest of such size."

Toren snorted, looking at the man oddly.

A'brgail nodded to Tynne, dismissing him.

"I'm not so impressed with your authority on local geography, Gilbert," Toren said when Tynne had ridden out of hearing.

A'brgail gazed around him once again, rising a little in his stirrups. "I'm afraid that he is not in the least mistaken in what he's told us, your grace."

Toren waved a hand at the surrounding hills. "It would appear he was wrong in every way. This is not a wooded knoll, nor have I seen pasture land for some time."

"That is true, but we are no longer somewhere near Uphill. In fact we may well be quite far from those places."

Toren turned toward the knight, his manner impatient and grave. "Gilbert, we are less than a day's ride away."

"So it would appear, but we are following a sorcerer, and things might not be what they seem. Have I ever told you about my half brother? No? Well, he is a traveler, though unlike any you have ever known."

Six of them and their belongings sank Baore's boat down into the water and gave it an odd, tender motion. Fortunately, the stream they followed was barely more than waist deep, so tipping would not be disastrous. It was also not wide enough in most places to employ the oars, so they took turns poling them along with all the speed circumstances would allow.

They traveled in silence, not knowing if Hafydd pursued them still or if passing into the hidden lands would free them of him at last.

Trees leaned over the narrow stream, so that the waters appeared brown and shaded, changing to green where the sun found its way through. The banks were low, crumbling in places, and turtles and dusky herons watched them pass; unafraid, it seemed—or too frightened to move. Warblers and kinglets flitted through the branches and wove in and out among the underwood. A wren appeared, to scold them from the top of a drooping branch.

Pwyll studied the map that Kai had made them, angling it this way and that in the filtered light, as though he would uncover the trick of it.

"How far to the carrying place?" Baore asked quietly.

"It's difficult to know. The map is surprisingly accurate but doesn't show every twist and turn." He pointed up. "There appears to be a cliff through the trees there, and if so, it's likely this one our mapmaker marked on his drawing. If that's true, then we have come about halfway, and I would guess are well into the hidden lands."

The day wore on, becoming hot and muggy, the air still in the small valley of the river. Tam had given his sword over to Elise, who kept her hand near the hilt. Both she and Pwyll were watchful and silent, and this put the others on edge. Even Fynnol became quiet and grim.

They did not stop to eat but made a crude meal in the boat, though someone kept them moving even then. By mid-afternoon they found what Pwyll and Cynddl agreed was the carrying place Kai had spoken of. Pwyll, Cynddl, and Elise hurried up the wooded hillside to examine their route.

"Pwyll and Elise look worried," Fynnol said when the others were out of sight.

"You are likely right," Tam said, quietly beginning to unload their belongings. "Alaan did not return as he said he would, which would cause worry enough, but for all we know, Hafydd pursues us still. He might even be very near." Tam glanced over his shoulder. "We should go as quietly as we can." He stood up, stretched his back, and examined their surroundings, then took out his bow and quiver and set them where they would not get lost in the clutter. He might have need of them yet.

An hour passed before Elise and Cynddl returned.

"Where is our good tourneyer?" Fynnol asked.

"Still reassuring himself that these hills hide no black-robed men-at-arms," Cynddl said. He threw down his bow and quiver and knelt to drink from the river. He splashed water on his face and sat back, water running from his short gray hair and dribbling off his chin. "It is not steep, the way up, but it is more overgrown than we might hope. From the top we could see a great swamp stretching off into the misty distance."

"How long will it take to pass over?" Tam wondered.

Cynddl shook his head, throwing beads of water off in arcs. "We won't be there this day. We didn't walk down the other side, so I can't guess the state of that path."

Baore found his axe amidst their gear and turned to look up the hill. "I'll start clearing our way," he said. "As narrow as we can make it. We'll take the boat up on its side. We've enough strength in numbers to carry it so." He strode a few paces to the trees and began taking down saplings and loping off branches. The trees shook from his assault, the cracks of steel on wood tracing his progress. Tam saw Elise look at Cynddl, clearly worried by the noise. But if they were to take their boat over the pass, they must have a path.

All the gear was carried up the hillside to the summit—two trips for each of them—and piled on the crest. Baore toiled up the slope, clearing their path. His shirt was soon left hanging on a branch, and he glistened with sweat as he worked.

A quarter way up the slope Baore stopped to hone the edge of his axe, and then surrendered it to Pwyll. The big Valeman lumbered down the path, stripped, and threw himself in the cool stream. Elise did not seem to care or even much notice, Tam realized. She was not the young noblewoman he had met on the River Wynnd, that was certain.

They pulled the boat up onto the bank and turned it on its side, sliding it along the soft ground on its gunwale.

"Mind the rocks!" Baore called out, concerned for his paintwork. He was out of the river and dressed in a moment, catching up to them quickly.

"You've done enough, Baore," Elise admonished him. "Take a deserved rest. We have hands enough here."

But Baore would have none of it, though he said nothing to gainsay Elise, but only took hold of the stern and bore the boat up. Every few moments they set their burden down, balancing it on its side so they might rest. They were all soon covered in sweat, their hands slick where they gripped the wood.

In less than an hour they caught up with Pwyll, who had been slowed by a section thickly overgrown.

"I hope this is Kai's carrying place," Fynnol muttered, "after all our work."

It was dusk when they finally reached the top, letting the boat down onto the summit with a thump. Tam stretched his aching back and arms.

"A meal!" Fynnol cried.

"We can't make a fire here," Pwyll said, bending to gather firewood. "It would be a beacon to anyone below." He pointed off down the slope they had just conquered. "We'll build it down there on that level spot, but not till after dark." He looked up into the sky, which was showing signs of clouding. "Rain," he said. "Good for us. Wind will hide the smoke."

Good for us? Tam thought. The hot day turned cool as the sun set, and a wind from the south began to batter the trees of the hillside. Baore kindled a fire after dark, and clouds dangling skeins of rain appeared in the moonlight. Squalls of wind and fierce downpours found the companions, but these passed quickly, leaving them in relative peace beneath a starry sky.

They set two to watch at a time that night, one on the crest of the hill, while the other sat in the dark beyond the fire's light to watch the lower path. No one could make their way through the shadowed wood without being heard. Tam was worried that the sound of their axe had not gone unnoticed, for it had echoed over the quiet valley all that afternoon.

He drew the second watch, and slipped up the wet slope to the crest of the hill. He found Pwyll standing in the shadow of a tree, staring out over the mist-wreathed lowlands. Tam came and stood beside him but stopped as he was about to speak.

In the mist below torches wavered—hundreds of torches.

"What in the world?"

"An army," Pwyll said softly. "But made up of ghosts, or so I've come to believe."

"Ghosts? Those lights look real enough to me."

"They do until you've watched them for a time. They waver and fade and pass through each other. And they cast no light. No faces appear, no signs of ground or tree or vegetation. They are not lit, one torch from another, but simply appear, and they never smoke.

I can smell the rotting swamp below, when the wind comes up the slope, but no smoke. No signs of men at all."

"I don't much like the idea of a ghostly army," Tam said, a shiver passing through him. "Will they march up here, do you think?"

Pwyll shrugged. "They've shown no signs of moving, but that might change."

"Perhaps Elise should see this," Tam said.

Pwyll looked at him in the moonlight. "She is not Elise Wills anymore. You know that, don't you?"

Tam nodded. "Should we fear her—what she's become?"

Pwyll tilted his head to one side, as though considering this. "I don't know. I have traveled far with Alaan so I have grown used to the presence of . . . such people."

"She made a bargain with the nagar, didn't she—the one that has followed us?"

"The nagar are cunning. It waited until she had no choice. Alaan told me it is always so—they sense your moment of weakness."

"But she seems much herself, even so," Tam said hopefully.

"The nagar . . . the nagar have purposes of their own, Tam. Never forget that."

"But you serve Alaan. What of him? Are his motives suspect as well?"

Pwyll stood silently staring out over the army of mist. For a moment he said nothing, and then finally: "Alaan told me how to kill a man who has made a bargain with a nagar. No, not just kill the man, but kill the nagar as well—send it through Death's door."

"In case it is left to you to deal with Hafydd."

"No, in case it becomes necessary to deal with Alaan." Pwyll turned to Tam. "Do not be too distracted by this ghostly army. It is Hafydd's guards we should be wary of, but anyone traveling in these lands could be a danger. Anyone real." He nodded once and disappeared down the path toward their camp, his footfall so light that Tam soon lost it in the sounds of the night.

He stared out over the great lake of mist that lay below. Moonlight illuminated it here and there as the shadows of clouds passed over. When a shadow fell upon the milling army, the torches disappeared, proving that Pwyll had been right.

Elise appeared beside him so silently that he jumped.

"Pwyll says there are ghosts in the swamp below."

Tam pointed. She still carried with her the heat from the fire, and he could feel it close beside him in the cool night.

"What can your new 'memories' tell us about that?" he asked.

"Very little, I'm afraid. This land is strange to me, its history unknown. But Pwyll is right. That is an army of ghosts, and a great army it once was. Look at the numbers!"

"Are they a danger to us?"

"No, I don't think so. Not unless they await our coming, and that seems very unlikely." She touched his arm as though reassuring him. "They will disappear with the coming of morning, that is what I think." Her hand lingered a moment on his arm, and then, Tam felt, pulled away reluctantly.

He turned to look at her in the moonlight and found himself eye-to-eye with her, for she was nearly as tall as he. Her eyes seemed to explore his face, as though it were a landscape with a secret. They leaned toward each other, and as they kissed, a gust of rain struck them. In a moment they were drenched; Tam could feel her pulling at his clothes, the cold rain running inside his shirt and down his chest. He tore a button loose, fumbling with her clothes. Water ran down his face and into his eyes. Her skin was like ice, cold and smooth.

And then she was pulling her clothes together, pushing his hand away from her soft, wet breast. "Someone is coming up the path," she said, and suppressed an almost girlish laugh.

"Tam . . . ?" It was Fynnol. "Cynddl thinks there is a fire; down below us and to the south. He caught the scent of their smoke— burning cedar he said, which we are not."

Fynnol's face appeared to float, a small mass of gray in the teeming rain. Below them moonlight still illuminated the lowlands, and torches still flickered in the fog.

They stumbled down the dark face of the hill, pulling their sodden clothing together as they went. Cynddl was awake, but no others stirred. The fire had burned down, and the story finder was separating the charred logs, letting it die completely. He motioned for Tam and Elise to follow, and as they passed through the small clearing in which they camped, Elise found Tam's hand and squeezed it once.

When they were out of earshot of the sleepers, Cynddl spoke low. "I went a short way down the path toward the stream, just listening, when a gust must have eddied up the valley and I smelled smoke, very clearly—smoke from burning cedar. It is most distinctive. We have burned no cedar this night. Is it Hafydd, do you think? Could others dwell in this place?"

Elise drew a deep breath through her nostrils. "I don't know."

"Perhaps it is Alaan," Tam offered.

"Perhaps." Elise sniffed the air again. Tam imagined she shut her eyes in the dark, trying to sense the smoke on the wind. "Someone should go back up to the crest lest we are surprised from that direction."

"I'll go there," Cynddl said.

"Don't be alarmed by the lights in the swamp below. They are ghosts, I am certain, but can do us no harm."

Cynddl hesitated only a second at this, then patted Tam on the shoulder and was gone.

"And you, Fynnol, when is your watch?" she asked, assuming command of the situation with alarming ease.

"Next watch is mine."

"Then you should sleep. I will sit up with Tam awhile to see if I can smell this smoke. But even if it is true, there is little we can do about it until morning. Get some rest. With the wind blowing as it is I think it's very unlikely the smoke from our fire would drift to them."

Fynnol didn't take much convincing, and was headed back to his damp bed immediately.

For a brief second Tam hoped Elise had sent the others away so they might resume what they'd begun, but as they stood in the teeming rain she made no move to come closer.

"I can smell nothing, Tam. Can you?"

"Our own fire, now and then, or so I imagine."

"Let's go down to the streambed for a moment."

They stumbled down the path, hand in hand, Elise leading the way, for her night vision seemed better than his. The moon lit a little patch of running water, otherwise they were in the dark shadows of the wood. They stood for a moment, listening, a precaution Tam felt they had inherited from the animals. Elise crouched down, still as stone. A little rain began to fall, pattering on the leaves and stream, but the small moonlight did not waver.

"Perhaps I do smell smoke," she said.

"Hafydd, do you think?"

"Better to know than wonder all night."

Elise stood and began rustling about in the dark. It took a moment for Tam to realize she was pulling off her clothing. He took a step toward her, but heard a plunge into the river. In the faint ribbon of moonlit water she appeared, but was it Elise? She was pale as the moon. Her hair seemed longer and strangely matted. She looked back at him once, and then dove into the darkness, her legs drawn into shadow after her.

Tam found her pile of sodden clothes in the dark and gathered them up, intent on keeping them warm while she swam. He twisted as much water as he could from them, bundled them together, and pulled them inside his light coat, the scent of Elise rising unexpectedly to fill his nostrils. He thought of her, rain drenched, her wet lips meeting his.

Men loved Sianon, but she loved none in return.

They were camped some distance off, Elise found, guards standing sentry, a small fire burning back from the river. She could see no sign of Hafydd.

He must sleep, she thought.

Just knowing that he was this close almost paralyzed her with fear. But then she realized these men did not wear the black robes. Two came down to the bank, barely discernable in the small light of the fire.

Dease gazed at his cousin in the poor light, the noble face, carved in sadness. Fair-haired and blue-eyed, Toren was handsome in the common way. In the moonlight he looked younger—like their cousin Arden, Dease realized. And this caused Dease to close his eyes for a moment.

Toren's intentions always eluded him, and even more so now, with his brain addled from Beldor's attack. What were they doing here? Certainly this man A'brgail was not of sound mind. All this talk of sorcerers and hidden lands and . . . Well, he could not remember all that had been said but he didn't believe a word of it.

The ringing in his ears mingled with the sounds of the stream and the evening wind to produce a cacophony inside his head. His thoughts seemed to flee like frightened spirits.

"I think he's a dangerous lunatic," Dease said.

"Keep your voice down, please, Dease." Toren was looking at him with that measuring look of concern. "I have known Gilbert A'brgail for many years. He is more sane than you or I—and I know something of madness."

Dease nodded. A vision of Toren's father flickered in the confusion. "I know you do, but what this man has said makes no sense. A brother who travels through lands others cannot reach. Yet somehow we have managed to find them—or so he says."

"You know this country well enough, Dease. There are no hills or such a forest by Uphill. We are in a wilderness, it seems, where there should only be pastures and small woods. You heard A'brgail's man, who grew up nearby."

"I heard him, but as you say, he was A'brgail's man—one of his Knights of the Vow. Excuse me if I find it a bit hard to believe that we are pursuing a sorcerer. A blackguard I can accept. I will even accept that he is Hafydd not Eremon, as difficult as that is to believe, but a sorcerer? If such men ever existed, it was an age ago, Toren. No, the man you call your friend, this man who thinks he is a Knight of the Vow—a Knight of the Vow!—he is either lying or mad."

Toren reached out and put a hand on Dease's shoulder. "And how fares your poor head, Cousin?"

"It is not just my state, Toren, that makes me say these things! It is common sense!"

"It is common sense to believe, when you travel among mountains that should not be there, that something extraordinary has occurred."

Dease opened his mouth to protest but Toren held up his hand. "Believe what you will, there is no denying that our cousins are in the company of Hafydd, and that is deeply strange and more than a little disturbing." He glanced up the steep slope that ran behind their camp. "I hope Hafydd or his guards do not smell our smoke this night."

"They are far enough away and there is wind and rain. I should not be so worried. And what if he does find us? Let him try his guards against the Renné. We have not been champions at every tournament this summer without reason."

Toren ignored this. "Dease, Dease, you are not listening. This man is not natural. . . ." But he gave this up, changing his tack as something else occurred to him. "Do you think Samul and Beld conspired with Hafydd to murder me?"

Dease was trying to concoct an answer in his addled brain, but Toren went on.

"Beldor was the one who insisted we go after Hafydd for what his guards did to the Fáel. His hatred of the man seemed genuine."

"Perhaps that's what he wanted us to think, Cousin."

Toren gazed at him reflectively. "You think he knew I would not allow the Renné to break the Peace of the Fair?"

"I could have predicted it myself," Dease said.

Toren nodded. "Yes, but your intellect is a good deal more subtle than Beld's." He frowned and a deep crease appeared between his eyebrows. "Perhaps I underestimated Beld's hatred of me all along. But that doesn't explain Samul . . . He might have been involved in the plot against me, but it would have been out of 'principle.' It's almost impossible to believe that he would betray the Renné to an ally of the Wills."

"The innkeeper's description left little doubt, I fear."

"That is true, but there is something very odd at work here, Dease. Something we cannot see—not yet."

Dease could hardly have agreed more. What in the world were Beld and Samul up to?

Toren put a hand on his shoulder and met his eye in the poor light. "I say we continue as we are for a while and see what it is our cousins are involved in. It would be foolish to do otherwise. Don't you agree?"

Dease hesitated, then nodded. He could think of no argument against that—no argument that wouldn't cast some suspicion on him, especially now with his mind in turmoil. But then he immediately wondered if that was merely his own guilt speaking. Likely he could argue that they go back and Toren would suspect nothing. Why should he?

"We might go on for a while," Dease said, "but if anything A'brgail says is true, I'm not sure we should stray too far into these unknown lands."

Toren broke into a grin. "A moment ago you called Gilbert a lunatic. Do I hear you now giving some credence to his words?"

Dease did not answer.

Toren clapped him gently on the shoulder. "Try to sleep, Dease. Rest will do more to help you than anything a healer might offer."

Dease nodded. "I'm not quite ready to sleep yet." He looked up at the sky visible through the trees overhanging the river. On the hilltop it would still be light, but here in the valley they were in shadow. It occurred to Dease that this was somehow like his own mind—lost in shadow while almost within sight it was light and clear.

"I want to have a word with A'brgail," Toren said, and rose with the particular grace that he always displayed.

Dease grasped his cousin's hand as he went, feeling the strength of Toren as his cousin returned his own pressure. He listened as Toren made his way back to the fireless encampment and the cold comfort of these Knights in gray.

Alone, he drew a long breath and gently rubbed his temples. Conversations with Toren seemed to make the pain in his head worse. "I owe you for this, Beldor," he muttered.

"Is that why you follow him? Because you've a debt to discharge?" came a strange hissing voice.

Dease shot up from the rock upon which he sat, fumbling his sword free of its scabbard. There, in the shadow of an overhanging tree, he could see a woman—in the water!

"Who in the world are you?" he asked.

She moved a little farther out in the stream, eyeing his sword. "You wouldn't believe me if I told you," she said.

Dease could see her a little better now. Her hair, wet and shining, and . . . strange—like seaweed—fell about her pale shoulders. Her face remained in shadow. He put a hand to his head. Leaping up had sent a hot knife of pain slashing through his addled brain.

"You are not well," the woman said with surprising compassion.

"No, and I am having . . . visions, as well." He sat slowly back down on his rock and lowered his sword.

"I have not often been called a vision."

Dease closed his eyes hard, then opened them again, but she was still there.

"Your cousin is right," she said softly. "Hafydd is a sorcerer, just as this man A'brgail has said. You should beware of him."

"I cannot convince Toren to go back."

"So it seems. What is it he wants? Revenge on Hafydd and your two cousins?"

"Revenge? No. It is not Toren's way. Justice for Beldor and Samul, that's his intent. Hafydd? I'm not sure what will be done with Hafydd. He is our enemy, certainly, and A'brgail's even more so; but A'brgail is afraid of him. That's what I think."

"A'brgail and his Knights of the Vow. Isn't that what you called them?"

"Yes. Toren claims A'brgail is a descendent of a knight who survived the fall of Cooling Keep—or was not present or something. He is trying to revive the ancient order, and, incredibly, my cousin is allowing it. Why am I telling you all this?"

"Because I am a vision. Who better to talk to?"

Dease snorted and shook his head, causing the pain to tear through his thoughts again.

"Where is Hafydd now?"

Dease motioned with his hand. "Up on the other side of this hill, camped. They've tried to keep to their horses, which has slowed them considerably in such rugged country." He gazed out at the spirit floating in the river. "If you were not a vision," he said, "what would you be?"

The specter paused a moment. "I would be the past of your race returning to haunt you."

"Then you are a ghost?"

"Better that I were, Dease Renné, for then I could do little harm." She gazed at him thoughtfully. "I might take away the pain in your head—at least for a few hours."

"How would you do that? Magic?"

"Something like that." She swam toward him. "Bend closer."

He pulled back involuntarily and she smiled.

"Come now! You are a trained man-at-arms bearing a sword, and I am a woman . . . wearing not even a stitch of clothing. Which of us should be afraid?"

Dease leaned out over the water, keeping his sword ready.

Cold hands took hold of his wrist and the back of his neck. Soft, cool lips pressed to his forehead. And then she sank back into the water. For a moment he wavered there, his head spinning. He sat back clumsily. The searing pain in his head was gone!

"It wouldn't be wise to go telling the others what you saw," the water spirit said.

"Toren already thinks my brain is addled." Dease leaned forward, trying to see her better in the dark. "Th-The pain is gone."

"Try to convince yourself now that I am a vision." And she swam off into the gathering gloom.

Eighteen

Toren found A'brgail in a small grove of trees. Candles on long stakes cast an inconstant light on the tall man. Two of his gray-clad followers stood by with their long swords bared. A'brgail was standing unnaturally still, the end of a short loop of cord held out in his hand. From the cord a knife was suspended at its balance point so it hung like a compass needle.

At a word from one of his guards A'brgail looked up. "Ah, Lord Toren."

"Are you performing arcane rituals here in this mysterious land?"

The knight looked very serious in the dull candlelight, his eyes dark, almost melancholy. "No, but I am contemplating them."

Toren started to laugh but stopped when he realized the knight was not joking. "What have you there?" he asked, nodding toward the knife.

"A dagger, as you can see."

"But of very old design! What a beautiful piece, Gilbert. Where did you find it?"

"It is one of the artifacts that was hidden when the Knights of the Vow were destroyed."

"Ah. May I?" Toren said, reaching out.

"No!"

Toren pulled his hand back, surprised.

"I have sworn a vow to let no others handle it," A'brgail said apologetically. "You should not have even seen it, really, but I have instructed my Knights that you are to have a certain latitude where some of our . . . *rules* are concerned."

"And I am honored that you have allowed this. Unfortunately, you have now awakened a certain curiosity in me. We are allies, after all. . . ."

A'brgail took a long breath. "More so than you realize. I don't think we can accomplish what must be done without each other. The dagger, you see, once belonged to a sorcerer named Caibre. This was a long age ago. Caibre was the son of the great enchanter, Wyrr. In fact, the dagger might have been a gift to Caibre from his father."

"Wyrr? Is that not the ancient name of the Wynnd?"

"It is. The stories of Wyrr and his children are bound up in the story of the river—bound up in its course, you might say."

"And why do the Knights have this dagger that once belonged to a sorcerer?"

"Many Knights of the Vow have asked the same question, myself among them. The answer is not really simple, but without giving you a long lecture on our history—much of it history never told to others—this dagger gave the Knights power. Caibre, you see, was a warrior, perhaps the greatest warrior who ever bore a blade. He made a realm for himself that would make the old Kingdom of Ayr look like a duchy. He was a sorcerer of astonishing power. And when he died . . . well, he did not quite die. He went into the river where his father had gone, and never passed through Death's gate. Instead he became a nagar—not quite a ghost, nor a river spirit. Something altogether more dangerous and frightening."

"I have heard old songs of the nagar."

"There are a few, though they were written by men who knew

almost nothing of their subject. The nagar were powerful in ways the minstrels would never have believed, and more frightening than they could imagine. But using this dagger . . . and other objects, the Knights of the Vow found ways to make use of the nagar—to turn such powers as they still possessed to our purpose. But this was a dangerous endeavor, for the nagar were wily and as patient as stones. A grand master was ensnared by one, and his own order burnt him upon a pyre for his failure."

"Then why do you keep such a perilous object?"

"Because we might have need of it one day. That is one answer. The other is that Caibre has found a way to return—or at least partly so. He has made a bargain with a man, and that man is now very dangerous."

"*Hafydd!*"

A'brgail nodded. "But I have this object still. Hafydd has another that also belonged to Caibre, but he does not know that I possess this one."

Toren waited. A'brgail was telling him far more than he should, the nobleman sensed, and he did not want to say anything that might interrupt the flow of this confession.

"Caibre is connected to these things in ways difficult to understand," A'brgail went on. "The objects themselves are merely objects—they have no power. This dagger is not even particularly sharp. But the connection cannot be broken. When Caibre was a nagar, the Knights of the Vow had ways of controlling him, of bending him to their will. But now he has become something we don't quite understand, and the knowledge for dealing with the nagar possessed has been lost. There has been much . . . speculation, actions we might take to curb Caibre's powers or even to break the bond with Hafydd, but it is just speculation, and almost certainly very dangerous to attempt." A'brgail pulled up on the cord and took the dagger in both hands so that it laid across his open palms.

"Then what were you doing with this just now?" Toren nodded to the blade.

"I was 'dousing.' Assuring myself that I can use this to locate Hafydd—or Caibre, more accurately. The dagger tells me that he is on the otherside of this hill—which we know to be true. But what is strange is that there is another . . . presence, perhaps even two."

"And what would these be?"

"My brother; or half brother, to be more precise. You see, he stole another of these forbidden objects—a 'smeagh,' as they're called. He did things that I cannot condone. For which I might even be forced to call him to account. But more importantly, it would seem that Hafydd is seeking my half brother—Alaan. And if that is so, he plans to murder him, and I will tell you that is no easy task. But if anyone can do it, Hafydd will."

"What will you do?"

"I don't know. It is most likely that Alaan is leading Hafydd somewhere with purposes of his own, but Alaan does not possess an army or even a small company." He paused, looking suddenly terribly sad and anxious. "Despite all my reservations about Alaan, and putting aside issues the Knights of the Vow have with him, I will support Alaan against Hafydd, if it comes to that."

"You're talking now like an older brother," Toren said.

A'brgail smiled. "And so I am."

"Different fathers, Gilbert?"

"Yes."

"Your father was descended from the knight?"

"No, his."

Toren looked at the man's face in surprise. "And yet *you* have brought the knightly order back into being."

"I am the son our . . ." He paused. "Alaan's father wanted."

"Then whose son is Alaan?"

"He is the son of Wyrr, in some ways, and even Wyrr disowned him."

Toren shook his head. All of this was too strange, as though the conversation was a dream. "Then Alaan has become *Caibre's* brother?"

"In a way, but Caibre hates him with a passion that we will never fathom."

"Oh, my family knows much of hatred, Gilbert."

A'brgail turned his gaze on Toren for a moment but said nothing.

"You say there is a third?" Toren asked. "Another son of Wyrr, as well?"

"He had only two sons. It is a nagar the dagger senses, that's what I think; a sorcerer that did not make the long journey to Death's kingdom. If this dagger really did belong to Wyrr, then I would guess that it will find his children: Caibre, Sainth, and Sianon. Sainth has made a bargain with my brother. Sianon . . . Sianon has been lost since the fall of Cooling Keep, but that might have changed."

"So you will risk much to support your brother, Gilbert."

"Yes, but for a purpose. I would see if I can break the bond between Alaan and Sainth. If we can do that, then I will know how to deal with Hafydd."

"It is a complex family tree, Gilbert. A half brother who has become the sibling of Hafydd. What does that make you?"

"A High Judge, Lord Toren. Perhaps an executioner. We will see. Hafydd must be stopped. And so must Alaan."

Elise emerged from the water in one smooth motion, like a fish sliding up onto the land. She shook herself, spray flying in the dark. Tam could barely make her out.

"It was not Hafydd whose fire Cynddl smelled, but he is not far off."

"Who is it, then?"

"A company of Renné and some of their allies. Now where have my clothes gone?"

"I've been keeping them warm for you," Tam said.

"That is chivalrous of you!"

She came toward him in the dark, and Tam found he was a little apprehensive—he had not forgotten the *thing* that had haunted them down the length of the Wynnd.

Elise stopped. "You have no need to fear me, Tam."

"You travel beneath the waters and have no need of air . . . ?"

She did not answer right away. "May I have my clothes, please? It is a chill night."

"You do not feel the cold either."

"No, but I feel the coldness of others. I am not without feelings."

"That is not what was said of Sianon."

"I am not Sianon, Tam. Take my hand," she said, and he had a vague sense that she reached out to him in the dark.

"It is cold as ice," Tam said.

"But my heart is warm," she said, and put his hand on her breast, soft and wet and slick as a fish.

"I feel no warmth," Tam said.

"You can feel it if you try," she said, stepping close to him. She seemed to flow against him, like a current, and he felt himself pressed forward. Her breath was scented with the river, her hair wet and matted, like kelp. She pulled him down and they spread their clothes over the wet grasses that grew beside the stream. Beneath his touch she grew warm, though the night air was chill as autumn. She was knowing beyond Tam's experience, and yet she was as innocent as a girl. Beside the whispering river they rolled in a bed of pillowing grasses, and left a tiny crimson blossom upon the summer green.

Nineteen

They had performed rites for Arden Renné the previous day, and the smoke from his pyre still seemed to linger about the castle cornices like a ghost reluctant to leave. The sorrow was greater among those few who knew the truth—that Arden Renné had been a traitor and had plotted his cousin's murder. Truth, Llyn thought, could be a cruel comfort.

Today the rites for Lady Elise Wills were being performed in the courtyard beyond her garden. Her servant leaned a ladder against the garden wall and she climbed up, peering through the wisteria, hidden, hearing every word, every sigh. There was no body to set on a pyre, no remains to inter, no ashes to pour into the river, if the Wills family embraced that superstition. There was only a small knot of mourners, most of whom had never met Elise Wills: Lady Beatrice Renné, a few of her nieces and nephews, a number of minstrels who seemed to know Lord Carral, and Carral himself, ash pale and looking as though he had lost his sense of balance and could not regain it.

They stood in a circle around an artful arrangement of flowers, smooth stones, and fire. Traditionally there would also have been objects dear to the person who'd died, but any such objects were far away, so members of the Renné family had offered things they deemed appropriate: a hoop bearing an unfinished embroidery, a book of poems, a small harp, a girl's doll.

A flaming vessel of pitch belched a dark line of smoke into the sky, where it scrawled in a strange hand across the high, flat gray.

Out of respect for their guest, Lady Beatrice spoke the rites, and Llyn thought her voice somber and filled with compassion and dignity. The darkly dressed mourners stood silently when she had finished, the white linen of the men's shirts stark beneath the overcast.

Silence stretched on. In the distance a crow called twice.

"Lord Carral?" Lady Beatrice said. "Whenever you wish . . ."

Llyn realized he was unaware that the others bowed their heads, for his blank stare remained directly ahead, unwavering. He took a long ragged breath and began. "Though I am a minstrel of undeserved reputation," he began softly, "I have no song for my daughter. I haven't the skill to dignify such a life. A song for Elise would have to contain every moment of her days and would take twenty years to perform. It would encompass her sleep, her breathing, her laughter, her first steps. Her first kiss . . . her last. It would lay bare her love for me . . . and mine for her." He paused a moment, his mouth working soundlessly, and Llyn thought he would not be able to continue—but he did. "Her song would contain all of the things I could not see: her beautiful smile, the gold of her hair beneath the evening sun, the grace of her movement as she crossed a room, her hands laid upon the strings of a harp. All of her childhood would be found in this song; her first words, the hours of play, the ten thousand 'whys' she asked when she was two. Her first dance. Her first ball." He closed his sightless eyes, and a tear streaked his cheek, though he made no sound.

"The young woman Elise became," he said quietly, "would be a verse. Her beautiful voice, her child's sense of justice, her indomitable spirit, the refutation of the feud which led to her doing . . ." he almost whispered, "what in the end she did." He struggled with the last words. "If I could write such a song I would leave out only her death . . . for I could not bear to write that. No, Elise's song would end with her defiance of my brother, for Elise did not commit herself to the river out of despair. I knew my daughter. She was defiant and willful and proud and would not allow herself to be subsumed into the plans of my brother and his allies." He paused, tears flowing freely now. "Or perhaps I would end it with her last good-bye to me, her last dance, that is, if I could bear to end it at all, for I will play my daughter's song over and over until the day I follow her into the river. Over and over in all of its thousands of precious moments, all of my dreams for her future." He paused, still staring off into the distance. "Good-bye, my darling," he said with heartbreaking tenderness, and tossed the rose he held toward the flame, only barely missing. He began to sob without care for others or what they might think of him. He cried with the abandon of a child, and Llyn cried with him. She placed her head against the stone of the wall and felt the tears flow. Shakily, she climbed down the rungs and lowered herself to the nearest bit of low stone wall. She trembled with grief, for someone she didn't know.

"The poor man," she whispered. "The poor dear man. He has lived a life of loss. Far greater than mine. Far greater."

The minstrels who had worked up their nerve to play before this man on this, of all occasions, began a slow sad air. The sun plunged into a bank of cloud on the western horizon, drawing the day after it, and the mourners retreated from the courtyard, but the minstrels stayed to stand vigil, playing in turns throughout the night, as though by their mere endurance they would make this man feel their love and respect—as if that would mend even the smallest part of his broken heart.

The smoke from the burning pitch still sent forth its smoke, etching a few last lines across the paper-gray sky.

Twenty

"They are Renné," Elise said softly. "They want revenge."

"For what?" Pwyll asked.

She shrugged.

Tam and Elise had returned to the camp to find the others stirring, readying themselves to leave at first light. Elise had told them what she'd learned. Tam could make out the silhouettes of his companions, slumped about the camp, still as stumps. A vague unsettled mood had crept over them, like the wisp of smoke that washed up from their dying fire.

Pwyll shifted where he sat. "If it is Toren Renné, as you say, then I don't think his motives are so simple. I jousted against him. He is a man of great integrity—more like a king out of story than one of his squabbling kinsmen. If he is following Hafydd, there must be another reason." He seemed to turn his gaze on Elise in the darkness. "I'm not sure if you were brave or foolish, sneaking through the bush in the dark to spy on them. It is a wonder they did not hear you."

"Oh, let us give up this pretense!" Fynnol said. Tam could just see his raised arm, a hand pointed at Elise. "You are no more Elise Wills than I am Toren Renné. Everyone must realize that. Look at you! You are as strong as Baore, as comfortable with a sword as Pwyll, and as shy as . . . me. Why not tell us the truth? We have met nagar before."

Tam sensed Elise become very still. "Fynnol is right," she said, her voice cold and controlled. "I went into the river, for the river is my home, in many ways. The Renné are camped downstream from us. I overheard Toren Renné and his cousin Dease talking. They were trying to imagine why their cousins, Samul and Beld, were traveling in the company of Hafydd, who they are following."

No one spoke. The clear notes of a sorcerer thrush fell into the awkward silence.

"Who are you?" Fynnol asked, his tone filled with dread.

"I am Elise Wills, Fynnol, and you should have no doubt of it. But the nagar with whom I made my bargain was called Sianon and she was a sorceress, great and terrible."

"And what do you . . . does she want with us mere mortals?"

"A terrible war is about to wash over your lands like a storm. You may choose not to help me avert it, Fynnol, but it might find you all the same. It is my purpose to stop Hafydd, to kill him if I can and burn him upon a pyre. You may help me or not. The choice is yours."

"To stand and fight a sorcerer or run and be taken from behind." Fynnol threw up his hands. "It is not much of choice you offer—if I am to believe you."

"I believe her," Tam said, surprised to hear himself blurt this out. "Hafydd has been our enemy since the night we met Alaan at Telanon Bridge, and he will remain our enemy until either we or he are dead. I don't know why we have been chosen for this but it's clear we have."

"The river chose you, Tam," Elise said. "You can let that fill you with fear or you can take comfort from it. The river chose you, and it chose well."

"Could it not have chosen some others?" Fynnol said softly. "Some men-at-arms who have spent their lives in combat? Perhaps such men would have been equal to the task."

"If any will prove equal to it, Fynnol Loell, it will be you and your companions. Did you not fight Hafydd's guards down the length of the Wynnd? And many of Hafydd's black guards died while you have all lived. The river does not make mistakes, Fynnol. It does not."

Tam did not take much comfort from this. No one spoke for a long moment.

"Well, the arrival of the Renné seems fortuitous to me," Cynddl said at last. He put one end of his bow on his boot and flexed the yaka wood, dropping the string over the end and into its notch. "If we have to fight Hafydd we will have allies."

"Little good it would do us," Elise responded. "Hafydd would sweep us all aside without effort. He is more fearsome than an army, while I . . . I don't understand this change that is taking place inside me." She sat down on a rock, her hands clasped between her knees. "I must find Alaan. Only he might be able to help me see my way through this." She looked up at the others, all her anger gone. She seemed suddenly alone and frightened. "Sianon was powerful beyond our understanding—I know that— but I am unable to make order of all these memories that are flooding in." She shook her head, almost a tremor. "They are all a jumble, fragments. . . ."

"Like the stories I find," Cynddl said. "Perhaps like finding stories, you must wait patiently. In time it all makes sense."

Elise nodded, clearly not believing. "I do know what Sianon would do about the Renné. She would set them against Hafydd to give herself a chance to escape . . . and she would be right."

Tam felt all the companions look away from Elise, unsettled to a man by this show of ruthlessness. She was less Elise than she claimed, Tam realized, this woman he had made love with that night. A memory of her emerging from the river—not quite nagar but not quite human, either. This strangeness had enticed him then—the coldness of her body had soon warmed with passion and pleasure. Apparently her heart had remained untouched.

"I will not be party to the murder of innocent men," Fynnol said evenly.

Elise's head snapped up. "What a great luxury to be able to make such decisions," she said. "Tens of thousands of innocent men will die before year's end if Hafydd is not stopped. Tens of thousands—perhaps all of these men who travel with Toren Renné, and Lord Toren himself. And you will not be party to the murder of innocent men. Let Hafydd continue as he is and you will have more blood on your hands than the river can ever wash away."

Elise was on her feet, her bearing proud. "Hafydd will kill us all if we are still here at dawn. He knows he must murder me now before I become strong. We have no choice but to bear the boat down to the swamp tonight and be gone by daylight." She paused crossing their encampment. "Gather up your belongings. I'll go look at the way down. My vision in the dark is better than any of yours."

She strode past Fynnol and the others and went deliberately up the slope. Baore rose as if to follow, and Tam spoke before he thought.

"Let her go, Baore. She needs a moment to think."

Baore hesitated, and Tam could feel him looking at him oddly in the dark.

"You should not speak to her so, Fynnol," Baore said mildly.

"She is a nagar, Baore," Fynnol answered. "Were you not listening? She made a bargain with that thing you refused."

"Perhaps, but we will perish without her, that is certain. And you should not speak to her so."

Tam looked around at the shadowed faces of his companions, feeling the silence that descended between them like darkness.

"Rath once told me a story," Cynddl said, and lowered himself down onto a flat rock. He kept his gaze fixed on some distant point, and in the near-darkness Tam thought his ancient voice seemed to emanate from the rocks themselves. "It was of a blade that bore a curse. No one knew where it came from—Naral Tynne brought it back from the Winter Wars, it was said, though he told different stories of how he came to possess it. The blade was said never to nick nor need sharpening, and that no rust ever touched it. Within a year of his return Naral Tynne died of a strange fever, raving at the last and cursing the sword as though it were a demon. His son took it up, and his son after him, but after that it became a possession of A'borel Keep, and was only wielded in times of desperation. Each time, the man who took it up died within a year, falling ill with the same strange fever that killed Naral Tynne. And each man who died raved at the end and cursed the sword that had brought them victory. After a time the sword acquired a name: 'Death's Dagger,' they called it.

"For many many years it lay locked in a room in A'borel Keep, no one daring to touch it. No battle had ever been lost in which that sword was wielded, and its reputation spread across the lands. Armies came to wrest Death's Dagger from A'borel Keep, for some thought the stories of the fever deaths were contrived to scare others away, to keep the sword for themselves.

"There came a time when an army made camp in the vale beyond, bringing up their siege engines. The old lord of the keep looked out from his battlements over that great army and knew that the keep would fall. From the locked room in the armory he had servants bring a sealed case. He opened it before his gathered knights and family, laying bare the shining blade. 'Who will take up Death's Dagger,' he asked, 'and protect our wives and children from what lies outside our walls?' But all of his knights hung their heads and said nothing.

"The lord looked down sadly at the blade. 'Then it is my burden to bear,' he said, reaching out, his hands trembling with age. 'Not yours, Father,' said his eldest daughter, Lenta. 'Your days of making war are long past. Death's Dagger needs stronger hands than yours.'

"Before the lord could protest, Lenta stepped forward and swept up the sword. 'Who would dare take it from me now?' she challenged the knights. But they all stepped back and averted their eyes from the gleaming blade.

˙ "Lenta led out the host of A'borel Keep and drove the army from the field, cutting down their champions. She returned to the keep with her army, but no cheering met them, no trumpets or drums—only tears and muffled sobbing.

"Her father carried the case for Death's Dagger forward and had his daughter return the sword, then he retired to his chambers with the blade. With only his old equerry standing by, he offered the sword his life in place of his daughter's, and before dawn threw himself on the point.

"The lord of A'borel Keep was mourned by his people, and by Lenta most of all. Within a month she fell ill with a fever that no healer could break. But as she raved in the throes of the delirium, a calm came over her and she said to her sister, 'Here is my part of the bargain: my death for all the lives I took. For all the lives I saved.' And she passed away. Death's Dagger was locked in a room in the armory, where it waited like a plague."

The distant songs of frogs and insects added their voices to the wind in the trees.

"Are you saying that Elise will die because of this bargain she's made?" Baore asked.

The story finder shook his head. "Not necessarily. I've only told this story because it seemed appropriate somehow: there will be a price for what Elise has done—and she will pay it." Cynddl turned to Baore in the poor light. "No one can pay it for her, Baore. No one."

Twenty-one

They were wet, bruised, bloody, and foul-tempered when they slid the boat into the murky waters. The whole slope down had been slick and treacherous, and they fell and several times all but lost control of the boat. It would have been difficult enough to manage in the daylight, but by night it was perilous.

Dawn was just a hint in the mists and cloud. Before them lay a swamp beneath a rolling cloud of mist, reeds, and swamp grasses clumped in spreading stands. No trees could Tam see, but open waterways wandered into the fog and reeds. Mist blotted out the sky, like water on paper, and the position of the rising sun could not be discerned.

"Damn that bloody boat," Fynnol said, and threw himself down in the wet grass. Most of the others did the same.

"Alaan told me this swamp was filled with serpents." Pwyll stood looking about him.

Cynddl got slowly up. "If Alaan says it is so," the story finder said, "then we should be wary. There can be few travelers more seasoned than he."

Fynnol still sprawled, red-faced, on the grass. "Let the snakes have me," he said. "If I don't rest a moment I will die anyway."

Baore eyed his cousin then bent to drink from the waters, but Elise reached out and stopped him with a hand on his shoulder. "No, we best fill our water skins from the stream. This water is not healthful." She took up Tam's sword. "We've no time to rest. The sooner we are out on the water the safer we'll be."

Baore stood, nodding. "Yes, we've all our gear to lug down. Best be about it."

The others heaved themselves up, reluctantly. Only Fynnol lingered.

"Give me a moment," he said, trying to smile. "Even a snake deserves an even chance."

They toiled back up the slope in the damp morning. Tam wiped sweat out of his eyes with a sodden sleeve. The thought of plunging into the stream drew him, but there was much work yet to do and they'd wasted too much of the day already. Hafydd and his men were no doubt making their way through the wood even now. He only hoped the boat would let them travel more quickly.

They climbed to the summit of the carrying place, and Baore and Pwyll immediately shouldered bags and took up an oar each. Cynddl looked over at Tam and sighed, dragging a bag up reluctantly and throwing it over his shoulder. He staggered one step from the weight, steadied himself, and set off down the slope.

Elise busied herself collecting their scattered belongings, and Tam did the same. But when he looked over at her, she was sitting on the ground as though in pain.

"Elise? Are you hurt?"

She shook her head, not opening her eyes or turning toward him. "Hurt? No, it is worse than that. I have offered myself as refuge to a monster, Tam. Her memories come back to me. . . . They are horrifying." She shook her head hard, and then a tear slipped down her cheek. "She lived for war, Tam, and I can feel it, feel her excitement and pleasure at the prospect of battle. At all other times she felt as though half dead. Only in war was she alive, but ruthless and heartless.

"She had children she could not bother to raise. Some grew up to be warriors, to win her approval, and she spent them in battle as readily as any other—and mourned them not at all when they died. It is as though this is who I once was—like a drunk who's come late to sobriety and sees all the harm that he has done, yet still thirsts for the bottle. That is who I am now. A woman who was drunk on war, but has reformed—as much as any drunk ever does. I see war stretching out before me, and I am in despair, Tam, and yet I welcome it like a lover. Let it begin today, a secret voice says; a war that cannot be avoided. A just war! Give me command of an army and I shall be like a reformed drunk locked in a wine cellar without water to slack my thirst."

She turned her tear-streaked face up to look at him. "Give me command of an army and I shall throw men into battle like wood into an inferno, and care not at all. No, the blaze will warm me—warm my cold heart. Oh, Tam, what a fool I was to make this bargain."

He knelt down beside her and she cried in his embrace, sobbing like her heart had broken. And then they heard Fynnol singing below and she pushed herself up, disappearing down the path toward the stream without a word or a glance behind her. Tam stood and watched her go. She slipped into the trees, and he felt his heart go after her. How pitiful she was.

And then Fynnol appeared, smiling.

"Slacking off, are we?" Fynnol said. "Come on, Cousin, keep up! You're forever falling behind. I can't always be doing your work for you."

Half an hour later they were all down by the swamp, Baore and Pwyll carefully loading the boat. Elise stood looking anxiously up the bank.

Fynnol called out quietly from where he stood a few yards away. He was staring down into the reeds at the water's edge.

The others gathered quickly to see what he'd found. In the shallow water at the swamp's edge lay a man, facedown, his bright costume stained and torn.

Elise bent down and turned him over.

"He was stabbed in the throat," she said, and stepped over him to reach down into the water. "But I will have this." She drew out a dripping sword. Before the blade was clear of the water, however, she recoiled as though she had been struck. For an instant she stared at the blade in shock, then reached down and lifted it again, standing with the blade in the water.

"Hafydd is here," she said, pointing down the shore. "Not distant. We must be gone." Saying this, she hurriedly unbuckled the dead man's scabbard. Then they made a run for the boat and in a moment were afloat.

"But where now?" Fynnol asked. "How do we find Alaan in this great fogbound swamp?"

Elise settled herself into the bow, the blade of her new sword cutting a thin wound in the water's skin. She pointed. "We go this way. With all haste and as quietly as we can. Hafydd is all but upon us."

The boat silently parted the mists, slipping through the water, though heavily laden. The odd, smoky blade she had found, Elise kept in the water. After a time she seemed to relax.

"He is not so near now," she said, not whispering as before, though there had been little speech among them.

Tam noticed that Cynddl was bent over, his face pale and contorted. "What is wrong?" he asked.

The story finder seemed to straighten with difficulty. "Wrong . . . ?" He shook his head. "It is this place, Tam. There are stories here in profusion, as though all the stories of men in this world have flowed here, where they lie in layers, like mud, deep, deep beneath us. And under those there is a greater story yet. The story of an enchanter, I think, but I hear only echoes of that. The greater story eludes me."

"It is the story of Aillyn, Cynddl," Elise said, not taking her eyes from the way ahead. "He was the brother of Wyrr, for whom the Wynnd was once named. The father of Aillyn and Wyrr was Tusival, their mother a swan. Tusival cast an enchantment upon her so that by moonlight she became a maiden: the 'even swan,' she was called. A clutch of three eggs she laid. If they hatched by night they would be even swans, like their mother; by day they would be the children of man. Two eggs hatched before the sun set, but one was too late—a girl child. The sons were Aillyn and Wyrr. The daughter was Sianon, who did not live to see her third year. Wyrr named his own daughter for her: Sianon—even swan."

Elise reached out a hand to the rail and cleared her throat before going on. "But long before the children of Wyrr came into the world, the brothers' love had worn away. Aillyn's mind fell under a shadow, and though he had long been domineering and unbending, he grew suspicious and filled with dread. The saying was that no one breathed in Aillyn's kingdom save the king. His son, his only child, self-murdered to escape him." Elise paused. "But Aillyn was a great sorcerer and followed the paths of knowledge to places his wiser brother would not go. A great spell Aillyn cast, greater than any spell cast before or since. The lands were sundered so that none could travel between the brothers' kingdoms, or so it was intended. But the spell was imperfect and paths would open up from time to time, as you found traveling down the river. And now he lies here, in a long sleep, dark with dreams. All the stories of men have collected in these waters, for Aillyn would control even that. And now we are here, looking for a son of Wyrr, with yet another son following, bent upon murder."

Twenty-two

Hafydd looked out over the cloud-drowned swamp.

"Is this not the place my father's man-at-arms described?" the Prince said softly.

Hafydd did not answer for a moment, then nodded once.

"Did you not say that Alaan tried to lure you here so you would not become aware of Sianon's return? But here we are all the same."

Hafydd's guards began to silently move away from their master. Even Samul Renné sensed the anger emanating from the man. Michael knew that he should stop. Baiting Hafydd was both frightening and dangerous.

"Perhaps this is too perilous," he said, his mouth dry. "Two sorcerers, after all."

Hafydd turned and glared at him until the Prince could bare it no more and averted his eyes. When he looked up again, Hafydd had turned away.

"We go into the swamp," he ordered his men.

Michael let out a sigh of relief. Hafydd had not struck him down, as he feared one of these times he would.

"You're gambling with poor cards," Samul Renné said. He stood near to Michael, hardly looking at him—as though he did not want to be seen associating with him.

The Prince shrugged. "I cannot help it," he said truthfully. "Everyone is so afraid of him. Someone has to take a stand."

"It is a risk—perhaps even a foolish one."

It didn't surprise Michael that Samul Renné would say so. Samul was the most easily overlooked man he had ever met. He was almost a shadow, he was so unobtrusive. And yet the Prince had a sense that Samul was no fool.

Perhaps only I am the fool, Michael thought. He took up his bag and slung it over his shoulder.

Prince Michael pulled one foot up from the sucking ooze and lost his balance, stumbled and plunged his foot down hard into the bottom again. The man next to him, one of Hafydd's guards, looked at him in annoyance. For most of that morning the floor of the marsh had been soft but did not try to steal one's boots at each step. This mud they had found now, though, seemed intent on dragging them down into the depths—or at least slowing their pace to a crawl.

He glanced down the ragged line of men-at-arms disappearing into the mist. They moved forward with a dreamlike slowness, struggling to maintain their balance—and occasionally falling. They tried to stay to the open channels now. Not an hour after they'd entered the swamp, one of Hafydd's men had been bitten by a snake. Hafydd had sent him back with another to aid him. But two hours later they'd encountered the men wandering lost in the featureless fog. Not long after, the snake-bitten man had died, and they went on, a quieter company—and more wary.

Hafydd was "dousing" periodically with his sword: holding the blade in the waters while remaining very still, his eyes closed. Then he'd point off in a direction and they would begin looking for open channels that would lead them that way. Gusts of insects swept over them, biting whenever they could alight. A particular reddish-brown horsefly took chunks of flesh that would have put a vulture to shame.

They straggled on, a few of Hafydd's men in the fore, followed by their master, who was flanked by guards behind and to either side. The Renné lords trailed them, the rest of Hafydd's minions, then the Prince, followed by a rear guard of four black-robed men-at-arms. Their world was small, enclosed by walls of dense fog. It would be easy to slow for a moment and be separated from your companions. The Prince was certain that one would then wander in circles until either the sun came or one collapsed from exhaustion. Where would you rest in such a place? He shuddered at the thought of sitting down in the murky swamp and trying to sleep while keeping his mouth above water. It would be a terrible and ignominious death. Or perhaps a snake would get you, and then death would be quick, but agonizing.

The Prince was considering dumping his mail into the swamp and trusting to fortune to protect him, but he assumed Hafydd knew more about these things than he did, and the knight still wore his mail. The Renné had not cast aside theirs either, though they might be doing as the Prince was and following the example of Hafydd, for they were no more versed in war than he despite their prowess on the tournament field.

With some effort, he dragged one leg, slowed by sodden clothing, through the waters. Then the other. Ahead of him Hafydd cursed loudly—and then again. The knight stood still, his blade submerged in the murky waters, his eyes suddenly wide, and then he shook his head and cursed once more.

The Prince was willing to bet that the knight had sensed both Sianon and Alaan.

An hour later they stopped for a moment's rest and Hafydd called for him. Prince Michael slogged forward to where Hafydd and his guards stood sinking into the ooze.

"The man-at-arms who we questioned in your father's pavil-ion . . . you knew him?"

Michael was surprised at how mild, even thoughtful, Hafydd's tone was. As though he'd forgotten about the earlier incident. As though Michael taunting him was not a matter of great concern.

"I wouldn't go so far as to say that I knew him. He has served my father for a number of years, as did his father."

"Did you trust him?"

"Certainly, yes. I would trust any of my father's men-at-arms."

Some hint of a smile crossed Hafydd's serious face. "That would be a mistake, I think, but we are concerned with this one man. You can think of nothing that would make you doubt him in the least? Not the smallest incident?"

Prince Michael considered a moment, though in fact he was wondering why Hafydd was so interested in this. "Nothing, but then I did not know him well."

Hafydd contemplated this, his gray beard, hair, and pale skin seeming almost to fade into the mist on this dull day. He glanced over at the Renné lords. "Stay clear of them," he said softly. "If this is a trap we have fallen into, my guards will dispatch the Renné without waiting to find out whose side they are really on."

Prince Michael nodded and Hafydd went back to his guards. The Prince wondered if the man-at-arms who had lain dying in his father's tent could really have been allied with Alaan. But why not? the Prince wondered. Hadn't Alaan enlisted his own aid?

The water grew shallower, barely to mid-calf, and the ooze disappeared. They marched on now through a kind of coarse grass, though it was sparsely spread. They stopped once because Samul and one of Hafydd's guards thought they'd heard a call, but it didn't sound again and they went on.

The day had worn on to afternoon, Michael guessed, though there was no sun to tell him the truth of that. The daylight had not wavered since it first appeared. No shadows grew or shortened. He felt as though time had paused to take breath and left them to wander through an endless gray with no place to sit or lie to rest from their long march.

He ran into the backs of the others then, and there before them in the mist, on the mossy stump of a long dead tree, stood an old man in armor, an ancient broadsword in his hand. He raised the thick blade and pointed it at Hafydd.

"You are beyond the lands of your father, son of Wyrr. What is it you seek in my master's realm?" The old man's voice rolled out like distant thunder.

"My purpose is my own," Hafydd said, his manner proud and frightening.

"This is not the One Kingdom," the old knight said, apparently not at all intimidated by this man who intimidated everyone. "You do not have leave to journey here, nor will you find your way out again without my aid. What is it you want?"

The Prince looked at Hafydd, trying to read that iron-jawed countenance. The knight took a moment to answer, and when he did his voice was mild and even of tone.

"I have come here hoping to make peace between my brother and sister, who have fought and cannot conquer their passion. I mean no harm to you or any other."

The old man still held the point of his sword toward Hafydd's heart, though he stood a dozen paces off. "Turn back now and you will find your way out. Continue on and your stories shall end as have all the others. Turn back. This warning has not been given to any before you."

"I cannot go back and leave my siblings to murder each other. I owe our father more than that. Will you not let us pass? We shan't be in these lands for more than a day or two."

The Prince could see the old man pause to think, skeins of mist twisting around him. "Pray your brother will lead you out, son of Wyrr."

Mist broke over the old man like a wave, and when it cleared he had been washed away.

"Who in the world was that?" Samul Renné asked.

"That?" Hafydd said. "That was 'Duty' draped with the form of a man. A thousand years he has been here, waiting, watching these borders."

"Guarding them against what?"

The knight shook his head, staring into the mist as though he might catch another glimpse of the old man. "Guarding what? That is the question. Why would his master leave someone to stand such a long thankless vigil? What does he hide here, and what does my whist know of it?"

Hafydd shook his head, as though surfacing from a daydream. He plunged his blade into the waters, then pointed off to their left. "This way. Make haste."

Michael's legs had begun to ache from dragging them through the water, pressing to keep up with Hafydd and his relentless guards. Looking forward at their black robes passing into the featureless fog, he felt like a prisoner being marched to the final gate by Death's silent servants.

The guard who led the way suddenly disappeared into the water with a great flailing splash, and others rushed forward to drag him up, but the first of these disappeared as well. He did not fall forward into the waters but went straight down.

"A sinkhole!" Hafydd shouted, holding out his arms to stop others from following the first. Hafydd and his lieutenant cautiously sounded out the edge of the hole with their feet, then, with others grasping them from behind, leaned down, straining forward and casting about with their hands. Hafydd ordered his guards to pull, and he came back dragging a choking man-at-arms. It was a few moments before the second was found, and he came out limp, like a sodden leaf, and could not be revived.

The first man coughed and gasped until at last he could stand on his own.

"Who among you can swim?" Hafydd asked.

Several men claimed this skill, Prince Michael among them.

Hafydd pointed at him. "Then you shall go first. Doff your

mail." He turned to Samul Renné. "And you shall accompany him." He turned to the others. "Follow directly behind. Do not wander. These sinkholes are made by some kind of fish to lay their eggs and could be common in places. I've no time to rescue every damn fool who cannot watch where he places his feet."

The Prince shed his fine armor, sloughing it off like a skin, watching it sink into the dirty water. The padded doublet that went beneath this he left on, but even so, he immediately felt both lighter and cooler. He noticed that neither Hafydd nor anyone else followed suit.

"Well, I see we're more expendable than his own guards," Samul murmured to him as they set off. Prince Michael shrugged.

He and Samul led on, feeling the presence of Hafydd behind them, driving them forward like an invisible current. Though they sounded with the tips of their swords, they twice stumbled into sinkholes, flailing into the water and down-soft silt. They swam free, guiding the others around.

This duty jangled the Prince's nerves, even though the worst that happened was that he found himself swimming with a heavy sword in hand, something he would not have been able to do for more than a few yards at most. A vision of the two guards swallowed by the dark waters kept appearing to him, as though they had been pulled down by something more than their own weight.

Samul Renné kept glancing over at him, raising his eyebrows a little or shaking his head. The Prince did not react, but tried to keep his attention on the swamp bottom before him.

After a couple of hours they encountered no more sinkholes and the Prince began to breathe more easily. The fog persisted and the company carried on in grim silence, broken only by Hafydd quietly ordering them to go this way or that. Prince Michael managed a few bites of food as they slogged, and sipped from his water skin now and then, though he was both ravenously hungry and thirsty.

The swamp seemed unnaturally quiet, as though their passing

disturbed the inhabitants, though Prince Michael realized only Hafydd could have such an effect. After all, it was Hafydd the old knight had singled out, no one else. What did he mean, *Your stories shall end as have all the others?* The Prince did not like the sound of that, nor the feel of this place. He regretted coming now, wondering what in the world he had been thinking when he volunteered. He had promised Elise that he would spy on Hafydd, but even so . . .

Elise.

Sianon was the name Hafydd used. He remembered Elise aswim in the Westbrook—she was not herself, that was certain.

A distant clamor interrupted his thoughts. He almost stopped so that his progress through the water would be silenced.

"Do you hear that?" Samul said quietly.

"What is it?"

Samul shook his head.

Then the Prince smiled. "Crows!" he said, and laughed for the first time that day. But as the sound drew nearer the smile disappeared. There seemed to be a thousand of them—like carrion crows descending on a battlefield.

They came out of the low fog in a black squall, falling on the men, their bloodthirsty bills snapping at eyes and throats. Prince Michael flailed about him with his sword and arms, but still they bit him, tearing at his scalp, his ears, ripping into his neck and arms. He heard men howling and stumbling into the waters, and still the birds came, a black horde falling out of the sky, tearing at them like a vicious wind. A sword knocked his own blade from his hand, and he was going mad trying to keep the birds from his eyes and throat. He felt their claws dig into him as they sought purchase on his body, and as he swatted each crow away, three took its place.

He stumbled and fell to one knee in the water, and still they came after him. A hand dragged him up and he ran, tripping and plunging into the waters, rising again, to fall a few paces later, for he could not see for the crows diving at his eyes.

A deep, resonant ringing broke over the crying of the crows. Prince Michael knew that sound: Hafydd's haunted blade.

The crows took flight in a desperate flutter of wings, and then there was only one bird, clawing at his face. He drove it down into the water, pushing it into the soft mud with his foot. It struggled beneath his boot and then was still.

"Michael?"

"Lord Samul? I'm here." He wiped blood away from his eyes, finding his brow flensed. His hands, too, were bloody and torn.

The Renné lord appeared out of the fog, and Michael was shocked at the man's appearance—as though he'd been flayed from head to foot. Even his eyelids bled!

"Have you your eyes, yet?" Samul Renné asked.

"I have, though it is a wonder."

The ringing of Hafydd's sword faded away, and they heard men calling out, their voices filled with dismay.

Samul Renné bent over, his gasps nearly turning to sobs. "To what place of horror has this man led us, Prince Michael? Should we not go back? The others would never find us were we to set out now."

"Set out in what direction? I fear we'd have no more luck than the man who was snake bitten. No, this place is a maze without a sun for direction. I fear only Hafydd might get us out, though as you say, we are the expendable ones."

"He is your father's man, yet he makes no effort to protect you."

The Prince shrugged. "I have opposed him, and spoken against him to my father. I don't think he would kill me outright, but if I were to perish on this journey, he wouldn't grieve."

Samul forced himself to stand erect. A small noise made him jump. "Am I as much of a ruin as you?"

Prince Michael was still surveying the extent of his wounds. No single bite was terribly serious, but there must have been nearly a hundred that he could see, and the back of his neck felt as though it had been gored by the tines of a rake, over and over.

"A thousand crow bites are preferable to a single snake bite." He looked about him. "I've lost my sword."

Voices called out, and with a shrug Prince Michael led the way. It was not too difficult to follow his path for he had disturbed the fine silt on the bottom, leaving a track. They found Hafydd and a few of his guards still in the channel, and with a little effort the Prince managed to dredge up his sword. As he retrieved it, dripping from the bottom, he saw Hafydd staring at him as though he were a stupid child.

Yes, he thought, I dropped my damned sword in the water as no man-at-arms should.

In the end their numbers were reduced by one—a man who ran off into the swamp to rid himself of the crows but never returned. Beldor Renné they found enmeshed in tangle vine and bellowing like a bull. A second man was gashed badly by another's sword as they'd tried to beat off the crow's attack, and they were all slashed as though by a hundred tiny knife wounds.

"We go on," Hafydd said. "My Prince, Lord Samul, resume your places . . ."

And they did, sounding the bottom with their swords, listening intently for the sound of crows, or any sound that might turn out to be a threat; and what couldn't after a flock of crows attacked like wolves?

For a moment Michael and Samul were a few paces ahead of the others, who were organizing themselves behind.

"One by one we are dying," Samul whispered. "One by one. I will guard your back and stand watch turn-about if we ever find a place to sleep. Will you do the same for me?"

Prince Michael nodded. And they continued into the perilous fog, listening for the sounds of birds.

Twenty-three

The island seemed to rise up out of the waters before them, murky dark trees tangled in mist. They circled it once and then Pwyll and Elise went ashore, the others ready with their bows. In a moment they waved to the others, and Baore nudged the boat up to a fallen tree.

It was a rocky island, sparsely treed, and grown over with low bush and moss. Cynddl stopped, reaching up to pluck the leaves of trees and the needles of evergreens. He gazed at them with a profoundly puzzled look on his face.

Elise called out and the others converged at an abandoned campsite. She pointed to a bloody dressing.

"Stay back from this a little," Pwyll said to the others, "and let me look."

He stepped with care into the campsite, crouching to examine the ground. A sodden gob of dark material drew his attention. "Waterwillow bark," he said, glancing at Elise. "He was wounded or injured in some way. There was another here, as well. Look at these footprints—too large to have been Alaan."

"Had he a confederate awaiting him?" Cynddl asked.

Pwyll shook his head, not lifting his gaze from the ground. "Not that he ever spoke of, but that means little. Alaan was close about all his doings—even with me." He pointed down at the ground. "There is something odd here. Look at this small round depression. It is everywhere."

"It is the butt end of a staff," Elise said.

"Then he was wounded on a leg," Cynddl said. The story finder reached into a low bush. Entwined in his fingers was a long, black hair. He glanced over at Elise, who shook her head.

Fynnol bent and retrieved a dark feather from the ground. "There are more than a few of these. Would his whist be molting?"

"Those feathers look too long to be Jac's," Pwyll said.

The Fáel reached down and retrieved another of the dark feathers. "They're crow feathers, I'm almost certain."

From the shore of the island Baore called out. They left the encampment and scrambled down to where he was.

"Look here," he said. "Someone nudged a boat up to the shore. You can see the mark."

Elise glanced over at Pwyll. "When he arranged my escape from Braidon Castle he had Elffen and Gartnn awaiting us with a boat. He must have done the same here."

"That is not impossible," Cynddl said. He stood rocking gently from one foot to the other, bending a small willow wand in his fingers. "There is something strange about this place that I didn't understand at first." He fell silent then and Tam thought he looked terribly grave. "Every story I've found since we came into this swamp ends here."

Silence.

"Be less cryptic," Fynnol said. "What does that mean?"

Cynddl looked up at the Valeman. "No one has ever found their way out, Fynnol. No one whose story I've discovered, at least. They wander here, sometimes for years, but no one escapes—except perhaps Alaan."

"And Alaan hoped to lure Hafydd here," Elise said.

They were silent and still absorbing this until Elise plunged her blade into the stagnant waters.

"Hafydd is near," she said, and pointed off into the mist. "Alaan is that way, and traveling quickly."

Hafydd stirred at the coals and ashes with a stick, but no wisp of smoke twisted up, pungent and telling. The fire had been cold for some time. Hafydd moved silently about the encampment, lost in thought. To Prince Michael the knight suddenly looked unsure of himself, if that were possible.

Michael wondered if it had been the appearance of that ancient man-at-arms, claiming to be someone's herald, who then disappeared into the fog. The Prince shuddered at the memory. Had the old man been responsible for the attack of crows?

Hafydd poked his stick at a mass of bloody cotton strips—a dressing, cast aside. A dark sodden mass caught his attention.

"What is that?" Prince Michael asked, the knight's quiet mood making him forget how little Hafydd liked to be questioned.

"Waterwillow bark," the knight said softly. "Used to bring down fevers." He turned toward the west and stared off into the still, thick mist.

"Whose camp was this?" the Prince asked. "Certainly we are not so far behind Sianon that her party would have camped here last night?"

"No. My whist camped here."

Michael considered this. "Will we rest here this night?"

Hafydd shook his head. "No, we must not let these two find each other."

"Who is Sianon?" the Prince asked, realizing he could push this too far.

Hafydd did not answer for a moment, and just when the Prince was sure he would not, the knight said, "A sorceress, my Prince. A very powerful one. Long she slumbered, but the men I sent to be sure no one disturbed her failed—and she is among us again." He rubbed the hard plane of his cheek absentmindedly. "And now she is seeking my whist."

"Why?"

"They are brother and sister, my Prince. Brother and sister, and together they could become very strong. We must catch Sianon before she finds Sainth or our war will be long and bloody. So long that it is unlikely any alive today will see its end."

Hafydd walked off, looking again at the ground, stopping here and there to turn something over with his stick.

Michael stood dumbfounded. But who were they chasing? He had thought it was Elise Wills, who had somehow gained arcane knowledge, but she had no brother. And this man Hafydd called his whist was a man Elise called Alaan—and she claimed only to have met him this summer.

"What did His Grayness have to say?" It was Samul Renné at his elbow.

"There are two sorcerers in this swamp—a brother and sister— and this has unsettled him like nothing else I have ever seen."

Samul considered this. He was very still, this Renné lord. Michael had noticed it before. When he was not addressing you directly, you tended to forget he existed at all. The Prince found this both fascinating and disquieting. Who was Samul Renné? He doubted that anyone knew.

Samul smiled. "Do you know why we are here, Prince Michael?"

"We are seeking one of these sorcerers—a sorceress, named Sianon, to be more accurate—but what she means to Hafydd, I do not understand."

"Well, whoever she is, I hope we find her soon. None of us will last much longer at this. If the snakes or birds don't find us, we'll all collapse and drown from exhaustion." Samul met his eye. "Will you follow him unto death, my Prince?"

"Will you, Lord Samul?" Michael replied.

Samul smiled, then chuckled under his breath. But before he could answer, Hafydd called out to his lieutenant, who hovered near at hand. "Gather my guard."

The man nodded and rushed off, rousing the men who sprawled on the solid ground: Hafydd's guard actually showing signs of being human. If Prince Michael had not been so utterly exhausted, he would have taken some pleasure from it.

Reluctantly, the men rose, shouldering their burdens to travel, but Hafydd marshaled them together near the burned-out fire. The Prince stood there with the others, as confused as any. Samul Renné caught his eye, raising his eyebrows in question, but the Prince could only shake his head.

Hafydd took a rope one man-at-arms carried and laid it down in a careful circle around the gathered men. Over this he spread ashes from the fire. Prince Michael could hear the sorcerer muttering as he did this. He then stepped inside the circle himself and took a log from the fire. He spoke a word to this and a section began to glow orange. He touched it to the rope and loudly chanted a string of unknown words.

The rope burst into flames of blue and green, which wavered around them like breaking seas. Michael felt all the men around him press together, away from the flames. Beldor Renné cursed under his breath. Again Samul caught the Prince's eye. He looked both frightened and astonished. And then the flames were gone. A line of dark cinders lay where the rope had been, not a scent of smoke in the air.

"Stay where you are," Hafydd ordered.

He collected up a handful of this black dust and beckoned his lieutenant. With the ashes, he put a mark on the man's forehead, and then another on each cheek.

"You may step outside the circle," Hafydd told the man. "But all of you others wait."

Each man in turn he marked as he had the first. Prince Michael fought the urge to flinch as the man's large hand came toward his face. But the marks had no feel of magic to them. He was hardly aware of them at all.

Last, Hafydd put the marks on himself, and then stepped beyond the circle of cinders. "Let Sianon wonder where I have gone," he said to no one in particular.

He set off immediately for the swamp, and his lieutenant ordered the men into their places to follow. Prince Michael slung a bag over his shoulder and fell into line.

One by one they disappeared back into the fog, back into the timeless, featureless void where a cold numbness filled the heart and Prince Michael felt that he was neither alive nor dead.

Twenty-four

She wondered if it were merely curiosity, this strong desire to see his face: to see it close up. Llyn had not felt this drawn toward many men. If that were not strange enough, this man's last name was Wills. Although this particular Wills was an ally of her family, or claimed to be so. Llyn had begun to believe him.

"When will you sign the writ?" Llyn asked.

"In a week. There are still details we've not agreed upon. I will sign the treaty between our families at the same time." He stood up on the balcony, staring blankly out over the starlit garden.

"Lord Menwyn has condemned your actions," Llyn said. "He has said publicly that you are a traitor to your own family and nothing more than a lackey to the Renné."

"Such moderation of phrase is unlike Menwyn. I would imagine that he is furious, as is that fatuous prince he calls an ally. Without Hafydd, neither of them would have the skills to fight a battle, let alone a war. What a straw man my brother is. I wonder if, in his heart of hearts, he knows it? Perhaps that is why he is the way he is."

She leaned out from beneath the parasol of leaves that protected her anonymity.

He cannot see you, she reminded herself, but still she ventured no farther.

"You have not brought your Fáellute today," she said.

"It is your Fáellute," Lord Carral answered.

Llyn made a small shrugging motion, forgetting for a moment that such gestures did not register. Before she could speak, he went on.

"I've not felt much like playing, to be honest."

"That seems out of character: not that I can claim to know you." She took the smallest step out from her hiding spot, like a timid animal overcome by curiosity.

"It is more out of character than you can imagine. I would have told you that my heart would stop beating first." He placed both his fine-boned hands on the balustrade, leaning forward a little, as though he looked down into the garden bed below.

She stepped quickly back into the protection of her tree, and then smiled at her action. "Then why have you stopped playing, if I do not pry?"

She thought he began turning the gold band he wore on the ring finger of his left hand—his wedding ring, though this wife had been dead these many years.

"My love . . . my *fixation* with music led me to avoid the responsibilities of my birth, Lady Llyn. It led to my younger brother Menwyn taking my rightful place in the Wills family." He stopped turning the band but still held it tenderly between his fingers. "It led to Menwyn trying to marry my only daughter to someone she would not choose, so that Menwyn might form an alliance—an alliance of ambition." Even at a distance she could see his face change, the mouth draw thin, the planes of his face harden. "And all of this led to my daughter's death and to breaking faith with my wife, who charged me to protect Elise." He paused, and closed his eyes a moment. "Music does not seem such a wonder to me now. No longer the bright woman of purity, but the temptress who draws a man away from his true wife and his children. That is how

I think of my former calling. But for my weakness, Elise would be alive this day."

Llyn was shocked, not so much by what he said, but by the bitterness of his voice. She heard the beginnings of self-loathing there, in this man of wondrous talent. "You blame yourself," Llyn said, "but your brother stole your place from you. He took advantage of your affliction and turned your own family against you, convincing them you were not competent. What could you do?"

"There was much I could have done. I could have fought him, made alliances within the family, as he did himself. There were some who did not support Menwyn—at first—but I let them down as well."

She stepped out onto the path now, as though afraid the leaves would soften the urgency of her words. "But even had you resisted, would Menwyn not have won in the end? He is devious and a liar and men must hold your blindness against you."

"They do that, and yes, perhaps Menwyn would have won, but had I fought back, fought with all my strength, then at least my conscience would be clear."

"You would not feel such terrible guilt?"

"Yes."

"Guilt is a wasted emotion, Lord Carral." She felt herself take a step closer—almost out into the moonlight.

"It would not be wasted in my family, Lady Llyn. More guilt would perhaps have controlled some of the Wills excesses. Perhaps if the Wills had a greater capacity for guilt there would not have been a feud with the Renné which has claimed so many thousands of lives."

"I would not count on that. My family might have drawn the Wills into it. I have studied the history of the Renné, Lord Carral. Many of their actions would have driven the most moderate of people to desire revenge." The toe of her slipper drew a short arc in the fine gravel.

"There have been too many wrongs committed by both families," Lord Carral said. "There must be an end to it, and Toren Renné is the key to that."

"As are you, Lord Carral."

"Perhaps. My daughter was a determined young woman, Lady Llyn. I will do everything I can to thwart Menwyn and make a peace between our families. I cannot bring Elise back or undo the things I have done, or not done, but I can try to do this one thing. Perhaps then I too will find peace. Peace that will let me sleep at night."

She was standing almost directly beneath the balcony now, gazing up, when a drop of rain touched her cheek. Rain from a star-filled sky? Or was it a tear? A tear from the darkness?

Twenty-five

A'brgail crouched near to the ground, a dagger in his hand. With his gray robe, white hair, and waxy complexion, he looked like he had been spawned in this place, had grown out of it, one of the ghosts come back to life.

Using the point of his dagger, he prodded at the coil of ash that encircled the fire. He had warned them all back, but without explanation.

Toren stood looking over A'brgail's shoulder, as respectful as always, which led the Renné men-at-arms to treat him in the same way.

"What have you found, Gilbert?" Toren asked.

A'brgail continued to gaze at the ground a moment, his lower lip thrust out. "It is a sorcerer's circle, or so I believe."

"And what exactly is that?"

A'brgail combed fingers into his white hair. "It is a kind of enchantment—a way for a sorcerer to concentrate his power. Little is known of them now. They were difficult to make and sapped much of the maker's strength away."

Toren went down on one knee to see more closely. "And why was this one made, do you think?"

A'brgail shook his head. "I don't know, but whoever made it must have felt they had strong need. This kind of enchantment was not made often."

"Could it have something to do with us?" Toren said, speaking so low Dease could hardly hear. "Does Hafydd know we follow him?"

"I don't imagine he would go to such lengths to deal with us, but tell your men to stay clear of it all the same." A'brgail rose to his feet and walked slowly around the outside of the circle, examining the ground. He bent to look at a small pile of sodden bark, and again to look at a flag of bloodied cotton. This seemed to give him pause, and he rose to stare off into the fog a moment. The daylight was all but gone and the mist darkened like smoke.

"Someone with a wound was here," he said. "That is waterwillow bark that has been boiled, and there is a bloody dressing."

"Your brother, do you think?"

A'brgail shrugged. "It is difficult to be sure. Many men have been here. Do you see the way the footprints have all been walked over and then over again? I can't claim to solve this puzzle. Someone made a camp here by this fire. Whether it was that person who was wounded, I cannot say." He turned and looked out into the gathering dusk. "I don't know if we should wander through this swamp by night, Lord Toren. It is a dangerous place." He pointed to one end of the island. "Let's make our camp far from this."

After the others had gone, Dease stood a moment staring at the dim line of ash, both fascinated and horrified. Enchantments. They were finding evidence of enchantments now. Dease shook his head, which caused it to throb. Dusk darkened the world around him, and the frogs and insects filled the air with such a clamor he wanted to plug his ears. It was good that they would rest. He could hardly have gone another step. With a little luck, Samul and Beld would escape during the night and never be caught.

Toren saw A'brgail slip away with two of his guards, leaving the warm light of the fire to go into the damp night and clinging mist.

It took Toren a moment to decide, and then he went after the knight, thinking A'brgail might be going back to the sorcerer's circle. A'brgail was so secretive, and Toren was consumed by curiosity about him and the things he did. Imagine reviving the Knights of the Vow without anyone knowing!

Fifty feet beyond the fire the darkness was so complete that he could not see where to put his feet. He stumbled forward waving his arms before him. But then the moon broke through the cloud, its frail light filtering through the mist. There, before him, ghostlike, stood A'brgail and his Knights. They looked up as he appeared.

A'brgail held his ancient dagger on a cord. His pale face showed his utter surprise.

"He's gone!" he whispered.

"Your brother?"

"No, Hafydd. It must be Hafydd."

"He's left this place? I hardly blame him."

A'brgail stood perfectly still, like a man listening. "No. He's used the circle to hide himself. That is what I think. He's hidden himself from Alaan and from Sianon. What danger they are in now!"

Twenty-six

Alaan stumbled and fell, but instead of striking flat stone, he landed on a steep stair and went rolling and skidding down. He came to a stop and lay writhing from the pain in his injured leg, which had been battered by every step.

When he finally propped himself up on an elbow and looked around he was no longer in the ring of fallen walls, but lying on a smooth stone floor. Nearby, two great columns soared up into murky darkness. Torches flickered on the walls, their smoke pluming up. He could see only one wall, the others lost in smoky shadows.

"Well, Alaan, you have found many a hidden path, but never so accidentally as this," he said aloud.

Using his staff, he hauled himself up painfully and stood a moment, his head spinning. The sound of his breathing seemed an intrusion in this place of silence. After a moment he recovered sufficiently to move. The shuffle of his feet as he limped along and the hollow thud of his staff sounded dully among the columns, and the dim light cast his twisted shadow down upon the stone.

He knew he was not well, and not healing as he should. Not as he was used to, that was certain. He stopped and leaned against one of the columns, waiting for the pain to lessen enough for him to go on.

He had no idea if he was in danger in this place, and had little means to defend himself: a sword, a dagger. Any enchantments that he might fashion took both time and stamina, of which he had only the former in any measure.

It was unfortunate, he reflected, that the arts were nothing like the "magic" found in songs and stories. There, a sorcerer had but to wave a hand to cause anything to happen that he might wish—clouds to rain fire, enemies turned to stone. In truth, the arts were both more laborious and more narrow in application. Oh, great enchantments had been wrought—even Sainth had managed a few—but these took months, even years, to fashion, and stole away so much of one's life force that they were seldom attempted. Besides, they sometimes went wrong or failed to do precisely what you hoped. And for all that, enchantments had never held the fascination for Sainth that they had for his siblings—or their father. No, Sainth was a traveler, a man who wanted to see what was beyond the next hill and the hill beyond that. And look where this had led him!

In the shadows between the columns, Alaan could make out two enormous doors that stood closed. They appeared to be made of the same stone as the walls, but he suspected they were actually wood contrived to look so. He stared at them, wondering.

They were not locked or barred in any way, but swung heavily open when he pulled upon the ring with all his weight. He stared into the near-dark for a moment, then made out a stair descending before him. Torches burned here as well, if dimly, their wavering light illuminating the treads as streaks of stone.

Not knowing what else to do, Alaan put his staff on the first tread and awkwardly stepped down. It was an ordeal, descending the steps, and after a few he sat down and continued on his bottom like a child who'd not yet learned to walk. It was slow, and if he had not been in such pain, embarrassing, but he made progress.

The stair was not long and he was soon at the bottom. There, he found himself in a gallery overlooking a large, round chamber. In the dim torchlight he saw a pool at the center, filled with what appeared to be a silver liquid, like mercury, though not so thick and congealed.

Upon the smooth stone floor—the color of aged ivory, like all the room—lines were drawn and characters etched, and these lines also appeared to be silver. Torchlight reflected in them, so they sometimes appeared crimson or the deepest orange. Up the walls they ran, where words were written in scripts so ancient that even with Sainth's memories Alaan could not read them.

"It is an enchantment," he breathed. But what an enchantment! An entire chamber had been devoted to creating it. A lifetime of effort.

"It is more than that," a voice said behind him. "It is the most elaborate enchantment ever created."

The old knight who called himself the Herald of Aillyn stood a few paces off, staring over the balcony and down into the chamber.

"My master wrought this spell over a great span of years. It sundered his lands from those of his brother. It was the greatest work of sorcery ever seen, and none has equaled or even approached it since."

"And now it is failing," Alaan said. He raised a hand and pointed at the wall. He had at first thought what he looked at was another one of the hundreds of lines, but it was a crack running down the wall.

The old man nodded. "It is failing. And Death waits not far off, hoping always to take those who have avoided him longest."

"Death is breaking down the enchantment?"

"No. It is his ally, Time."

"What will happen when the spell fails?"

The old man shrugged. "The lands will join again, with a great wrenching of the earth. Mountains might fall, plains be cast up." He put both his hands on the railing and closed his eyes. "No one can really predict, but it will shake the earth that you know, that is certain."

"It should never have been made—this spell," Alaan said.

"And when you died you should have passed through Death's gate," the old man said, looking over at Alaan. "But here you are, in the Stillwater. And where do you find your way? To this chamber that no man has found before. It is not an accident, son of Wyrr. You were meant to discover this place and come to my master's aid."

Alaan snorted. "I owe nothing to Aillyn. And my knowledge of enchantments is far less than you think. I couldn't even begin to understand this spell. It must have taken him a lifetime to create."

"Longer than a lifetime," the man said. He turned and came a little closer, still difficult for Alaan to see in the shadowy chamber. "You don't need to understand. Aillyn will guide you."

Alaan took a painful step back. "Aillyn passed through, Herald. Have you forgotten?"

"I have an object—"

Alaan drew his sword awkwardly. "Stand back from me," he warned. "I will not offer myself to bring your master back. He was a monster, Herald, the greatest who ever lived. Why Death would want him, I don't know. He bargained uncounted thousands of lives to preserve his own."

The old man took another step, but stopped, looking around. And then Alaan heard it. A sound echoed beyond the doors, then rolled down the stairs.

"What is that?" he asked, attempting to keep his voice even.

"You opened the moonstone gate but you failed to close it after you," the old knight said. "It would seem that others have followed."

"It has ever been my problem. I open paths and others pursue me down them. Who are these 'others'?"

"The men who have been hunting you. Some number of them, by the sounds."

"And will you not stop them yourself? Are you not the guardian here?"

"It is not my place to interfere in your wars. You, son of Wyrr, owe nothing to Aillyn, which means I owe nothing to you."

Alaan did not wait to speak further, but turned and began making his awkward way along the gallery. He could hide in the shadows on the other side and hope they did not come looking for him there. Without even a bow he wouldn't stand a chance against armed men. Even two or three might be enough to master him.

When he looked back, the ancient man-at-arms was gone. Alaan limped on and hid himself in the shadows on the chamber's far side, pain stabbing through his leg like a hot blade. He stripped off the cloak he wore against the rain and all but fell to the floor. Lights danced around the edge of his vision and darkness seemed to flow in from the sides like thickened ink.

He lay his cloak out on the floor and, taking his dagger, began to speak softly over it. He made marks upon the cloth with the point of his blade, mumbling quickly. How much time he had he did not know. A few moments, perhaps, not more. Probably not time enough.

The first men poked their heads warily into view, retreated, then appeared again. They were quick to hide themselves behind the balustrade. Alaan could see them through the intricate scroll work. If he only had a bow, oh, how he would make them pay!

When these two thought themselves safe, two more appeared, and then two more. They were dressed in costumes from the Renné Ball, the colors soiled and fabrics torn. They would have looked comical had they not been so dangerous. Alaan hoped that he was right and Hafydd had ordered them to take him alive if at all possible. But he feared that killing him would not be unacceptable.

Six trained men-at-arms to one. Alaan was not hopeful. Still . . .

The men didn't speak but only nodded to each other and split into two parties of three. They went in opposite directions, circling the chamber, probing the shadows left by torchlight. He could see the three coming toward him, swords in hand, wary and ready to pounce. They walked like the best trained men-at-arms; knees bent, swords held ready. They positioned themselves to guard each other's backs as best they could, not all looking in one direction.

As the first group came near, Alaan spoke a string of words, and his cloak swept up from the floor. It flew at the costumed men out of the shadows, and they all turned upon it.

Alaan had three steps to make before he could strike, and even in that distance the man saw him and turned. It was almost pure luck that Alaan managed to land his stroke before the man's blade could find him.

The second lunged at him. Alaan spoke, and the cloak threw itself over the man's head, allowing him to cut that man down too. Then he stumbled and almost fell, only barely recovering by leaning on his staff.

The third man leapt back, brushing aside the cloak and saving himself. His three companions came running, and now it was four to one. Two down. Not enough. He knew he needed to have cut down three to have a chance. Now it was just a question of whether they would kill him or try to take him alive. And that depended on how enraged they would be by the murder of their companions.

They spread themselves out as best they could in the confines of the gallery, swords ready, crouching low, watching for the cloak that Alaan had sent back into the shadows. The arts did not seem to frighten them. Many a man would have run just seeing the cloak flying about like a great bat.

"I shall stop all of your hearts," Alaan said, "and send you through Death's gate. I have stood before it and watched the darkness spill out. I will warn you this once: stay among the living while you can."

But the men did not waver. Hafydd had trained them well; or perhaps merely frightened them more.

He was about to send his cloak at the nearest one and attempt to bring him down, but the darkness dripping about the edge of his vision washed out suddenly, and the world tilted beneath him. He felt himself hit the unyielding floor, but he did not feel the pain.

The last thought he had before the blackness drowned him was, *You were meant to come to my master's aid.*

Crowheart could see the men coming up the path—eight of them, grim and unsettled, but determined all the same. They were armed with swords, and likely with daggers too, but he could not see a bow among them. He nocked an arrow, took careful aim, and let fly. He took one man in the arm. Not good enough, but he didn't know Alaan's bow, even though it was of the finest craftsmanship.

The men scattered into shadow then. He knew they would come up from either side, clambering over the walls easily enough. He let arrows fly at two more shadows, then retreated as silently as he could.

But Alaan was gone! He was not to be seen in the circle that enclosed the moonstone.

"I thought he was more crippled than that," Crowheart growled, and sprinted for the wall. He scaled it, landing heavily on the other side. Alaan apparently had been exaggerating the effects of his wound and had not trusted him, running off at first chance. "Men who walk the hidden paths can be hard to follow," he whispered. He wanted desperately to go back and look at the ground to see which way Alaan had gone, but in the faint moonlight he would likely find nothing—and going back now was impossible. He would lead these men into the swamp. There, either he would pick them off one by one or the Stillwater would see to them. It was a wonder they had stayed alive even this long.

As for Alaan . . . Well, who knew where a descendant of Sainth might go? But Crowheart wondered if Alaan realized that the servants of Death they had seen were seeking him.

Twenty-seven

"**I** have never been put off so graciously in my life," Lord Carral said.

"I don't doubt that is true, your grace. A little to your right, sir."

Carral Wills was walking down a corridor with Josper Twill, his servant of twenty years. Though he would occasionally take someone's arm, even Josper's, Carral and his servant had worked out a series of signals, both of word and light touch, that allowed Carral to walk independently most of the time.

"Have I made a terrible error, Josper? Is that what I've done? Has Menwyn been right all along?"

"I don't know, sir." The tone of Josper's voice told his master that this was something of an understatement. "Toren Renné does seem to be away. None of the servants know his whereabouts."

"Yes, but his signature isn't strictly necessary. Lady Beatrice told me this herself. *She* can sign the documents ceding the Isle to me. Toren has already agreed."

"But perhaps she is being honest when she says she prefers Toren be present and that he sign as well. It is reasonable that the politics of her own family make this necessary."

"Of course her explanation would be reasonable, Josper. She has a subtle intelligence informed by a lifetime of intrigues and family politics. That doesn't mean she isn't merely obstructing matters for other reasons, or that the Renné haven't reconsidered and that I am about to be abandoned. Where will we go then? Not back to Menwyn, that is certain. We will be in danger, Josper. I have claimed Menwyn's place, after all, claimed it with the promised support of the Renné. And what is becoming of that support?"

"It is not Menwyn's place, sir," Josper said softly. "It is your place." He touched his master's forearm lightly, restraining him a little. They had reached the door of Lord Carral's rooms.

Carral waited while Josper opened the door, letting his master pass through first. Josper's footsteps followed. Carral heard a distinct punching sound and an almost simultaneous grunt as though from pain. Someone collapsed to the floor. The door closed.

"Josper . . . ?" Lord Carral spun around.

The footfall of another person sounded in the quiet room. Lord Carral began backing up without thinking.

"Josper!"

"*He has a knife,*" Josper grunted, and the footsteps stopped. The distinct punching sounded again, a gurgling breath, and then silence.

Carral stumbled over a small table, almost falling, and something hot singed his hand. He lifted his walking stick, to use the nob as a cudgel. The footsteps advanced again, but haltingly now.

Whoever stalked him stumbled over the fallen table

I've put out the candle! Carral realized.

He leaned forward and quickly pulled off one boot, then the other, balancing himself on his stick. He slipped back now, toward the other rooms. Rooms he knew were unlit.

The footsteps were suddenly muffled.

He's on the carpet, Lord Carral thought.

And then a strange, disturbing thought came to him. *Find me,* he thought. *Send me to join my beloved Elise.*

But the thought was as brief as the fall of a star. The instinct of self-preservation was stronger. Lord Carral had a mental map of the room that he suspected was better than any sighted person's. He knew how many paces between the window and the most comfortable chair, how many paces between the divan and the table. Where everything was in relation to everything else, in fact.

His assassin—he could assume the man had no other intentions—was feeling his way along the wall now. He was about to reach the small writing desk where Josper did their correspondence. There was a loud thunk of bone hitting wood, a muttered curse.

A floor plank creaked. If the assassin stepped onto the small rug, Carral knew he was coming toward him; if he continued on bare wood, he was going toward the sideboard.

The footsteps were muffled again. Two chairs sat side by side behind Lord Carral, a small table between. Carral reached back and pushed over the table so it clattered on the floor, then he stepped quietly behind one of the chairs. He raised his walking stick again, the heavy weight of the nob hovering uncertainly in the air.

He felt a wave of panic surge through him. He didn't even know how tall the man was. Where would he strike? What if he missed, as he almost certainly would?

But it was too late for any of that now. He could hear the man moving forward. The scuff of his soles on the floor. Ragged breathing. Another plank squeaked, not a yard away. Then something patted the leather of the chair. The assassin would almost certainly proceed between the two chairs. A hand brushed along the chair arm.

He must have bent down to do that.

Carral held his breath and brought the cudgel down with all the force he could muster. It glanced off something hard and he heard the man stumble to the floor. Carral bent forward and felt the man kneeling. He ran his hand up his spine to his neck and hit him again right on the back of the skull, and again. The man collapsed, and Carral dropped to his knees. He hit the man twice more, then gingerly reached forward. The man's skull was a mass of hair, oozing fluid, and shattered bone. He felt him twitch once and then lay perfectly still.

Carral dropped his walking stick on the floor and sat back. He was overwhelmed by nausea and dizziness. He turned to one side and went down on his hands and knees. Twice he retched violently, but then he crawled back toward the door, the floor beneath him slanting this way and that.

"Josper . . . ? *Josper!*"

He sat, brandy glass in limp fingers, huddled over his grief, stricken by silence. Lady Beatrice thought his face as blank as the unwritten page, yet eloquent with the language of sorrow.

He had lost his precious daughter, and now the man who for twenty years had been his loyal servant—his very eyes.

And he no longer trusts us, Lady Beatrice thought.

"I shall send you the best manservant in Castle Renné," she said, knowing how inadequate this would be.

"Will you?" Lord Carral said.

She wondered if he had even heard her. "It was not my family, Lord Carral," Lady Beatrice said, and not for the first time.

The minstrel stirred himself, shaking his head. "Oh, it was not you, Lady Beatrice, I have no doubt of that."

"It was not any Renné," she said, tone firm but voice soft.

"I don't know how you can be so sure. You told me yourself the cause of Lord Arden's death."

She was not so sure. That was the truth. But her intuition said that the assassin had been sent by Prince Neit of Innes or his cursed counselor. He might even have been sent by Lord Carral's own brother, Menwyn. That man was capable of anything. But Renné . . . ? It seemed more than unlikely. What faction of her many-factioned family would benefit from the death of Lord Carral Wills?

Those who wanted war with the Wills—and there were more than a few of those. But there would be war anyway, whether or not Lord Carral took control of the Isle of Battle and became their ally. If Prince Neit could not find a legitimate excuse for war, then he would simply invent one. It would be all the same to him. So why would any Renné try to murder Carral Wills?

Kel, Toren's cousin, came in then. Lady Beatrice thought he looked careworn and harried. He kissed her hand and then bowed to Lord Carral, who stood when he heard Lady Beatrice rise from her chair.

"May I offer my most profound condolences, Lord Carral," Kel said. "That such a thing could happen within Castle Renné . . ." He didn't finish. The safety of the castle's inhabitants was Kel's duty—and not an enviable one, Lady Beatrice thought.

Kel sank into a chair and nodded to a servant, who brought him brandy. He still wore his Renné blue surcoat and shirt of mail, having come directly from his search of the castle.

"Two servants of Lord Maban have gone missing," he began. "It is the problem with fair time—too many guests and not all of them entirely welcome. The dead assassin was recognized by at least two of our staff, and they remembered seeing him in the company of one of Maban's missing servants. It is not hard to imagine how this man gained entry to the castle. Who he was, though, we still don't know." He sipped his brandy. Lady Beatrice thought he looked tired and grim.

"His purse was surprisingly heavy for a supposed servant." Kel's eyes came to rest on Lord Carral Wills. "I think it is safe to assume, Lord Carral, that the assassin gained admittance to the castle by posing as one of Lord Maban's servants. Very likely Maban's servants were bribed and didn't even know his true purpose, but thought him a thief. He may even have offered to share in the profits of his larcenous efforts. I spoke at length with Lord Maban and am quite certain he had no part in this. The marshals of the fair have taken it upon themselves to run down these missing servants, but even if they're found, I think they will add little more than confirmation of my suspicions, though they will certainly find a harsh justice for their part in this matter." He took a deep breath and applied himself to his brandy again.

"It seems you have been most thorough, Lord Kel. I thank you." Lord Carral fell silent again, his sightless eyes staring off into a lifelong darkness. "It has been a most trying evening," he said, abuptly, rising.

Lord Kel and Lady Beatrice did the same, and a servant hurried to take the blind minstrel's glass.

"Andris will see you to your rooms," Lady Beatrice said.

Carral thanked her distractedly.

"And fear nothing, Lord Carral," Kel added. "Your rooms will be guarded. You have only to call out and my most trusted men-at-arms will be at your side."

Carral muttered his thanks again. A servant came forward and took his arm somewhat awkwardly.

"Let me express my regrets again," Lady Beatrice said. "In a short time you have become a good and valued friend, Lord Carral, and it pains me to see you suffer such losses. It pains me terribly."

"Kind of you," the blind man said softly, and then the servant led him out.

Lady Beatrice stood for a moment, staring after their guest, then returned to her seat, the skirts of her black mourning dress settling about her.

"Was it one of our own, Kel, do you think?" she said after the door had been closed for a moment.

He nodded to the serving man to leave the brandy bottle on the table and then dismissed all the servants. When the room was empty and the silence had lingered just a moment too long, he said, "I don't know, my lady." He shook his head. "I think it unlikely but I would not bet anything I truly valued on it. There are many who think that Lord Carral will betray us. That he will take possession of the Isle of Battle and raise an army which he will then put at the disposal of his brother Menwyn and Prince Neit of Innes."

"He hates his brother."

"I hate several members of my own family, but I would not take up arms against the Renné because of it."

"No, you wouldn't, but if Menwyn Wills was your brother, I'm not so sure you'd be saying that—especially if he did to you what he has done to Lord Carral. Carral Wills will not betray us. I am sure of that."

"And I am sure you're right. I believe him myself."

"It is hard not to, isn't it? Have you ever met anyone who exhibited less guile?"

Kel shook his head. "It is no wonder his brother was able to steal his place," he said, lifting his brandy glass.

"He worries that the assassin was hired by someone in our family," she said.

"As do I."

"Waiting to receive the Isle of Battle is undermining his confidence in us, as well. If only Toren would return!"

"I thought he would have returned by now," Kel said, reaching for the bottle again.

"I expected him two days ago at the latest. I don't understand what has happened or why we have no word of him!"

"I'm sure nothing has befallen him, my lady. Toren's judgment is very good and he is seldom rash. But I do wish he were here, now."

She looked up at her nephew, his face lined and serious. "What a terrible burden you've been left, Kel. How go your preparations?" She could not bring herself to say "preparations for war."

"Well enough. That is not true, they do not go well at all, but they progress as well as we can expect. Our allies are wary. They don't like the idea of us turning over the Isle to a Wills—any Wills. They want to meet with Toren, to hear his reassurances. I do what I can, but they know I do not speak for him. They wait, as do we all, for Toren to return."

"Pray he does so this very night."

★   ★   ★

A throat was cleared.

"Lord Carral?" It was a woman's voice.

"Yes."

"Lady Llyn sends her compliments, sir, and asks if you might join her for a moment?"

"But the hour is late."

"If it is inconvenient, Lord Carral . . ."

"No, no, not at all. I—I will visit your mistress, gladly."

"If you would follow me."

The three sets of footsteps proceeded down the empty hall, echoing ever so slightly, overstepping each other so they sounded here and there like clapping. For a few steps they walked in dance time.

They passed through a door, the manservant releasing his unwanted hold on Lord Carral's arm. The blind minstrel felt ahead with his cane. He was in the room with the balcony that overlooked Llyn's garden. He could smell the lavender. The maid's light touch replaced the manservant's and Carral was guided gently to a chair.

"Shall I not go out on the balcony?"

"Not this night, sir."

He heard the maid's footsteps retreat across the room, which was cool with a scented breeze wafting up from the garden. A door opened. Someone whispered, and then the rustle of skirts; footsteps he had heard only at a distance.

"Lady Llyn?"

"Good evening, Lord Carral. I'm sorry to ask you here at this hour. I have presumed a great deal. I thought that you would not likely sleep this night and that my company, for a time, would be preferable to being alone."

"That is not presumption, that is wisdom. And I am honored by your presence." No one was allowed into the presence of Lady Llyn but her servants. Not even Lady Beatrice.

He heard her settle into a chair quite nearby. The night's silence seemed to flow into the room—acrid, scented with burning charcoal. Unsure of what to do, Lord Carral sat down.

"Your manservant was dear to you," Llyn said suddenly.

"As dear as one's eyes can be."

"Yes," she said softly. "I'm so sorry. And with your other loss so recent."

"I feel truly blind for the first time in many years. Oh, you needn't worry. I am more capable than you realize. But Josper did much for me, and not all of it utterly practical. Sometimes he would describe things for me; people, a sunset, the view from a window. He had a way of making these things, which I had never seen, take some sort of substance and form. But now I sit in a darkened room, with only the scent of your garden and your perfume, mixed with burning charcoal."

She did not answer and they fell silent again.

"My garden is roughly rectangular," Llyn began in a halting voice, "bounded on two sides by the castle, and on the others by a high stone wall with no gate. Except for the doors and the windows in my rooms, all the windows that look into my garden have been mortared up. A small spring feeds a tiny pond with water lilies. From this a stream winds across my garden and disappears beneath the castle, where I'm told it emerges again in the kitchens. It is the true voice of my garden."

"My wife made a garden with a voice," Carral said. "I would sit there and listen by the hour."

"And what did you hear?"

"I heard promises. Promises made but never kept."

"In my garden I hear a voice that is trying desperately to tell me some truth—some monumentally important truth—but I cannot understand it." She took a quick breath. "Do you think the assassin was Renné?"

He tried to say something suitably polite, but somehow he felt the moment called for utter honesty.

"How could you not wonder?" Llyn asked. "We are a treacherous family."

"You include yourself among them, which certainly is not true."

"How do I know what I might do, Lord Carral? I have never been tested. Not here in my quiet garden. Lady Beatrice does not believe the assassin was sent by anyone in our family or from among our allies."

"Lady Beatrice wants to believe the best of everyone."

"That is the truth." She paused. "A gravel path winds among the flower beds and trees; doveplum, cherry, chestnut, and willow. This time of year the gardens are bright with flowers. Each color . . . is like a chord, it comes in many shadings and is composed of more than one note. Some colors are warm and calming, others are bright and jarring.

"Wisteria grows along the top of the wall. In springtime its purple pendants dangle overhead and drop small flowers on the gravel walkways—"

"You tell me much of the flowers, but what of the beautiful lady who dwells in this garden?"

"She is hideous!" Llyn hissed. "With the face of a nightmare."

"No," Carral said firmly. "I know her. She has a heart like no other, a compassion that is incomparable, a voice that is warm and wise and musical. I have dreams of her."

"You cannot see her."

"I look beyond the things other men see." Carral felt a strange movement inside him, like a flower opening, and suddenly he did not care if he looked foolish, or even if he were foolish. It only mattered that he find words for these feelings.

He heard Llyn move, and then fine-boned fingers took his hand. For an instant he thought she would raise it to her lips, and his breath caught, but she did not. She laid his fingers along her cheek, the skin rough and bubbled and stiff as leather. He felt a tear roll down his cheek and swallowed. She drew his fingers slowly over the ravaged skin. Her nose had almost been burned away entirely. He tried to hide a gasp by clearing his throat.

"My left eye has only half a lid," she whispered hoarsely. She moved his fingers down to her mouth, which to his relief was full and soft and unharmed. Llyn let his hand fall away.

"Now you know," she said tonelessly, her voice almost disappearing into the acrid breeze.

"I say you are beautiful still."

"You are kindness itself," she said, her voice emotionless and frightening.

"But you don't for a moment believe what I'm saying?"

Her answer was so quiet he did not hear. Then she said, "There must be a thousand beautiful young singers who would be honored by your attentions. Five hundred noblewomen who would do anything to bear the Wills name."

"Yes, but who among them would be interested in a blind man if his name were not Wills, or if he had not such undeserved fame among the minstrels? You see, we are not so different, Lady Llyn. You don't believe anyone will ever have feelings for you because of your disfigurement, and I distrust any woman who expresses love for me because of the attraction of my name and my reputation. Do we really distrust others so completely?"

He heard the rustle of her skirts as she rose to her feet. Before he could follow suit, she was moving across the room, faster than a blind man could follow.

"Lady Llyn?"

She paused at the door.

"I—I'm sorry," he said. "I did not mean to offend."

She was very still for a moment. "I am not offended," she said softly. "I am . . . perhaps I am merely bewildered. Confused, and more than a little unsettled. I must go." The handle rattled and the door creaked open. "Good night to you, Carral Wills."

"Good night, my lady."

Twenty-eight

It was a long, musical flight of stairs, each tread creaking a different note. Lord Carral ran his hand up the worn banister, which released the smell of honeycomb polish. Lady Beatrice went before him, her step light and slow. A servant held his arm, unnecessarily.

"Not much farther," Lady Beatrice called back.

Not much farther to where?

Lady Beatrice had requested he accompany her, and as he was her guest, he had readily agreed. If he had not been so polite he might have asked where they went, but he was still trying to convey the impression that he trusted her utterly—though it was becoming less true with each day.

"Your grace," came a man's voice from above. Carral had the impression that more than one man bowed: armed men. How did he know that? Did steel have a smell?

"He awaits you, your grace," the man said, and a key rattled in a lock.

"Still calm?" Lady Beatrice asked softly.

"Yes, ma'am."

"Lord Carral? We have arrived. Would you mind waiting a moment?"

He said he would not, and the door creaked open, her soft footfall retreating inside. Voices reached him, the words unclear.

Footsteps came from the room a moment later: not Lady Beatrice's.

"We may go up, your grace," the servant who held his arm said.

They passed between the guards and into the mysterious room beyond.

"Lord Carral?" came Lady Beatrice's voice. "My husband, Lord Culan Renné."

Carral tried not to seem surprised, but Lord Culan was said to be mad. No one had met him in years. It was this madness that had brought Toren Renné into his power early.

"Lord Carral," a deep, hoarse voice said—a voice that seemed to echo from a large chest. Lord Culan was standing, and very tall. Carral could tell by the source of the voice.

"Lord Culan. It is an honor."

"An honor to meet a madman? Hardly. But I am almost sane at the moment, and might stay so until nightfall, if fortune smiles upon me."

It was said that darkness brought Lord Culan to madness. He could not bear it.

"Please, Lord Carral, be at your ease," Lady Beatrice urged. "Show Lord Carral his chair." She was near to her husband, he could tell. How often was the man sane? Was she giving up these few precious moments to him? And if so, why?

"I would for all my life like to spend a few hours getting to know you, Lord Carral," Lord Culan said, "but I haven't the luxury of such time. Lady Beatrice tells me that you have become an ally of the Renné, and I never doubt her. The Isle of Battle will be yours. That is the decision that has been made, by Toren, who stands in my place, and by my wife, who was always my most valued advisor." He stopped and the silence dragged out far too long. Lord Carral could hear the people in the room begin to shift about. He could feel the embarrassment, the growing trepidation. "Do you doubt us, Lord Carral?" Culan asked quietly, the hoarseness of his voice noticeably worse, as though he dined on shattered glass.

"I would like to see the documents signed, and I am sure they will be," Carral added hurriedly.

"Your doubt is reasonable—it is not well founded, I will tell you—but it is reasonable. My family have not been known for honoring their promises. But Toren and Lady Beatrice . . . they would die before they would betray you. And I do not mean that figuratively. They would die. You have taken a terrible risk coming to the Renné, Lord Carral, but if there is ever to be an end to this feud, more of us will have to take such risks. I honor you for having the courage to do it first." He was silent a moment. "The feud, Lord Carral, is the true madness, I . . ."

Lord Carral could feel the man's focus slip away, like a wandering eye.

"Lord Carral?" It was Lady Beatrice. "If you would not mind . . ."

"Certainly." He rose and a servant took his arm. "It has been an honor, Lord Culan," he said, but there was no answer.

Just as he reached the door Lord Culan spoke. "Lord Carral? You have lived all your life in darkness?"

Carral stopped. "Yes, all my life." He could hear the hesitation.

"How . . . how do you bear it?"

"Lord Carral? If you would, sir . . ." the servant said, and tugged gently on his arm.

The door closed behind him, but only a few stairs had been descended when a frightful scream followed, a scream that would tear out a man's throat.

The servant beside him began to talk, to cover the ghastly noise, but it chased them all the way down to the foot of the stairs. Lord Carral feared one would never escape that terrible wailing once it had been heard.

She had asked to be left alone—alone with her sorrow—but her maid disturbed her all the same.

"It is Lord Kel, your grace. He says it is most urgent."

"Then I'm sure it is," Lady Beatrice said with little conviction. "Show him in."

A moment later Kel appeared in his usual mail and surcoat, as though he were a captain of the guards. He bowed quickly.

"We have an unexpected visitor; the Duke of Vast—"

"Not so unexpected, I should say."

"It is who accompanies him, Lady Beatrice. Lord Carl, A'denné's son."

"That *is* interesting," she said, sitting up. She felt the lethargy that had overwhelmed her since visiting her husband wash away. "But where is his father?"

"Attending upon Prince Neit of Innes."

"Ah."

"The Duke and Lord Carl await your pleasure, Lady Beatrice, though it was Toren they hoped to meet."

"I will have to do," she said, almost jumping to her feet.

As they made their way beyond the rooms of her closest family she said, "It is an odd assortment of noblemen we have calling at our gate. First Lord Carral, and now the son of Lord A'denné, a man who is an ally of the Prince of Innes."

"A reluctant ally," Kel said. "Everyone knows that."

"That is the rumor, but he has rejected even our most delicate overtures in the past."

"War was not then iminent, Lady Beatrice. Now he must declare himself."

"If he declares himself an ally of the Renné, the Prince of Innes will overrun him in a week. And how can we defend him, there across the river, and unprepared as we are?"

"Let us see what this young man has to say. Perhaps he has simply run off, unable to bear allying himself with Innes and Menwyn Wills."

"Yes, and lightning will rain down upon our enemies, and plague lay waste all their domains."

Lord Carl A'denné looked like his mother. That was the first thing Lady Beatrice noticed when they were introduced. He had the blond hair and cautious manner, the same disarming smile. Oh, how she would like to possess such a smile!

He was introduced by another name, and the servants sent scurrying for food and drink, for both Carl and the Duke bore the mud and dust of travel upon their cloaks. They declined to refresh themselves, however.

"Then you have come on a matter of some urgency," Lady Beatrice said. "Shall we dispense with pleasantries this night, and look forward to them another time?" They were seated around a cold hearth. "Lord Carl, it is a pleasure to finally make your acquaintance. I have known your father long, though not well, I regret to say."

"Something he regrets as well, Lady Beatrice."

"Then perhaps you and I shall make up for it by becoming friends. What brings you to Castle Renné, Lord Carl? I will admit your visit is something of a surprise."

"It did not seem wise to give warning," the young man said.

Lady Beatrice nodded, encouraging him to speak. He looked very wary, yet she also sensed great resolve in his manner.

"No doubt you know the Prince of Innes and Menwyn Wills are readying a war against you," he began. "My father is with the Prince as we speak. Because of the position of our holdings, we are perforce allies of the House of Innes, though we have tried to retain neutrality whenever it could realistically be maintained. At the moment this is not possible: the present prince has not the respect for others that his father displayed. We must prepare what forces we have to join him in the field."

"How soon?" Kel asked.

The young nobleman hesitated an instant before he said, "Sooner than you hope."

"I sympathize with your position, Lord Carl," Lady Beatrice said. "My family would do anything we could to help you, if only we knew what could be done."

Lord Carl took a sip from his wine cup. His hand shook just perceptibly. "My father would be willing to enter into an agreement with the Renné, Lady Beatrice. We would take the great risk of becoming your secret ally—your eyes and ears within the council of the Prince of Innes and Lord Menwyn Wills."

"And in return for this invaluable service you would want . . . ?"

"To be treated as your ally once the Renné have triumphed. To be given a suitable portion of the lands of the Prince of Innes, so that the House of Innes will threaten us no more."

Lady Beatrice glanced over at Kel. "It seems to me, Lord Carl, that if we were to agree to this, the A'denné would be on the winning side no matter who finally triumphed."

He did not look away. "This is so, Lady Beatrice, but how likely is it that my family will survive to the end of this war—this war of the swans? The Prince of Innes has spies within your house, as you must know. If they find out I visited this night, my family will be dead within three days. It is very unlikely we can maintain this secret for more than a few months—perhaps not even a few weeks. Great risk deserves great reward."

Lady Beatrice nodded. There was truth here that she could not deny. "If the risk is so great, why have you made us this offer?"

"Because we despise the Prince of Innes and are tired of shaping all of our policies to please him. There is only one answer to this—eliminate the House of Innes, and take over a significant portion of their estates."

"You think that by becoming one of the great noble families your problems will be solved?"

Lord Carl bit his lip as he considered this. "Perhaps not, Lady Beatrice, but we will solve this one problem, at least. If we survive the coming war we will worry then about dealing with the problems the great families face."

She glanced over at Kel. "How do we know you have not been sent by the Prince of Innes to spy on us, to divine our own intentions?"

"Tell me nothing," Carl said quickly. "In truth, I wish to know nothing. In that way, if we are caught, I cannot betray you. I believe, Lord Kel, it is the A'denné who take all the risks here. We are willing to do so because my father believes that Toren Renné and Lady Beatrice will honor their commitments to us."

The Duke of Vast cleared his throat. "I believe this young man, Lady Beatrice. I believe he speaks for his father, who is a man worthy of great respect, no matter the size of his holdings."

"Then I will make this decision in the absence of my son. The Renné will give you half the estates of the Prince of Innes if you will act as spies within the Prince's house. But you must keep your side of the bargain, Lord Carl. We will not gift you half the estates of Innes for a few paltry scraps of information. You must do better than that. And you must find a way to send this information to us."

"We will not disappoint you, my lady," he said warmly, his beautiful smile appearing. "Let me begin to do our part this minute. The Prince of Innes and Menwyn Wills are planning to overrun the Isle of Battle within the week, putting to rest all these problems caused by the defection of Lord Carral Wills. They have made this decision in the absence of Sir Eremon, the Prince's counselor and their chief general and strategist. If Sir Eremon does not return before then, this could be a great opportunity for the Renné, for neither the Prince nor Menwyn Wills have ever fought a battle before."

"Do you know the details of their battle plan?"

"I do not. And to be honest, I don't know if I can provide such details before their planned action. But you now know that they will attack and when. The lay of the land and the Isle's known defenses will dictate much else. To my mind, that knowledge is of great value in and of itself."

Kel nodded, his mind racing. "Certainly, yes. We can put men in the field to discover the movements of their armies, and as you say, the existing defenses and the land itself dictates much strategy."

The tower bell chimed the hour of eleven, and both the Duke of Vast and Lord Carl rose to their feet.

"You will spend the night in Castle Renné, I hope," Lady Beatrice said.

"Forgive me, Lady Beatrice, but I fear my presence will become known here, and if it does, my family will be in danger. It would be better for all concerned if I spent this night under a tree in the wood. The squirrels are not in the pay of the Prince of Innes."

Lady Beatrice offered her hand and he kissed it shyly, becoming a boy suddenly. Before leaving he pulled up a traveler's hood that did much to hide his face. At the door he stopped.

"Pardon me, Lady Beatrice. Is it true that Elise Wills drowned in the river?"

"Alas, yes, Lord Carl. Did you know her?"

He put a hand up to his face, which she could not see within its hood. "I met her but once, and briefly, but it is a terrible loss for all. She was against the feud and refused to marry the Prince's son for that reason."

"She was courageous," Lady Beatrice said. "Her father lodges with us awhile and so I feel I have come to know her through him. A terrible loss, yes. And not the last, I fear."

"No," he said sadly, "not the last."

Twenty-nine

Hafydd was gone. Elise held the blade in the water, her eyes closed—"listening" with every fibre of her being. *Hafydd was gone.*

"He's left the swamp?" Pwyll said.

Elise shook her head. "Not if Cynddl is right about this place. No, he has devised some way to hide himself from me. Hurry us on, Baore, I cannot judge where Hafydd might be now. Make as little noise as you can. Whisper only if you must. And string your bows. The fog does not matter to Hafydd—he can sense me."

Darkness came and they went on, plunging into patches of fog and then out into starlight, the sky clear and black as the pupil of an eye. Elise sat in the bow, her sword in the water to guide them—guide them toward Alaan. The others took turns at the poles; pushing them into obscurity, Tam thought. Voices were heard—distorted and strange—and there was movement in the fog patches. Here and there they saw lights, dim and distant, moving jerkily through the swamp. After a time they realized these were apparitions, not Hafydd, though it was of little comfort.

A gray horse stormed out of the darkness, tossing its mane and casting its head about desperately, and then it bolted into the mist as though chased by lions. Everyone stared, disbelieving.

"Was that real?" Fynnol whispered, but no one answered him.

Lights appeared again, and the ghost army passed by like a silent tide, the men bearing torches, their faces forlorn and defeated. Among them Tam saw a woman carrying a small child, darting this way and that, barely there at all in the fog.

In the frail light of stars and the waning moon, Tam could see the others trying to peel back the folds of fog and darkness. Ghosts were bad enough. The thought that Hafydd might be about to overtake them had unnerved everyone. Even Pwyll shifted about in his seat as though an arrow might find him at any moment. Tam could hear his companions breathing—quick and shallow. Dawn was a century away.

They ran aground often: it couldn't be helped in the poor light. As they backed their boat into deeper water, Tam found his fears would rise, as though they were suddenly vulnerable. He felt safer when the boat moved, though he didn't really know why.

As the night wore on, Tam began to nod off, despite the danger. *Hafydd is nearby,* he told himself, but it did not matter—exhaustion feared nothing. It overwhelmed him like an invading army. He awoke some time later, to the sound of birds.

Their varied songs preceded the dawn, as though the birds could sense light that the mists hid from mere men. Swallows greeted the morning with their thin calls, then thrushes and golden-crowns. A gang of marauding crows added their grating cries.

Daylight angled off the mist like light off a mirror. *And we are moving through the glass,* Tam thought. Crows pounced on swaying branches, crying and lamenting. Tam was reminded of Alaan's whist, Jac, and their first meeting at Telanon Bridge. How long ago that seemed! If they had known what troubles would come of it, they would not have been so hospitable that night. That one act of kindness had led to them being hunted down the River Wynnd, and then to the Renné Ball, and now here—to this place where all stories ended; or so Cynddl believed.

Tam looked around. He didn't want his story to end here. The crows hopped along from branch to branch, scolding and rattling their bills.

"Have we invaded some sacred domain of the crows?" Fynnol asked, stretching his arms and yawning. They had grown less afraid of ambush with the passing of hours, and Tam hoped this complacency was not a mistake.

Pwyll hissed at the dark birds and waved his arms, but this only increased their agitation. "Is this some sorcery of Hafydd's to find us?" the man-at-arms wondered.

Elise shook her head. "Hafydd knows where we are." She looked up, squinting at the clamorous birds, who bent down, stretching their necks to scold the companions. Faint sunlight gleamed on their dark bills as they bounced from branch to bobbing branch, following the boat's progress.

And then the whole raucous flock was off, swallowed into the fog, their cries muffled and quickly distant—then gone. The companions all looked at each other. Tam didn't think that anyone believed for a moment that what they had just seen was some natural flocking of birds.

"This place is too strange," Fynnol said. "The sooner we find Alaan and get out, the happier I'll be."

"Yes," Baore echoed. "Assuming Alaan can lead us out."

Thirty

They all stood. That was the first thing that struck Lady Beatrice. Stood as though they were all about to rush out and ride off to fight a battle. Kel leaned with his fists on the table and stared down at the map. He was Renné blond but green-eyed, and more squarely formed than was common in the family, as though he'd been more roughly carved than Toren or Arden. She closed her eyes at the thought of Arden, and an ache began somewhere at her center.

Fondor stood to Kel's left, the largest of the Renné, tall and strong and forty-four. He was of an in-between generation, being a very late son of one of Lord Culan's uncles—twenty years younger than his next eldest brother. Fondor was her husband's youngest cousin. In his day he had been a successful tourneyer and a great favorite of the ladies, but now he was settled, growing stout, and commanded a significant army of children ranging greatly in age.

The third man was Tuwar Estenford, who had been her husband's chief military advisor and general. He was gray, but he was far from frail, and though one leg was wood from the knee down, he did not ask for a chair. His weathered hands rested only gently on the table, and his face was remarkably untroubled, as though he had done this so many times it no longer unsettled him.

They were planning for battle. More precisely, they were considering the defense of the Isle of Battle.

Fondor tapped a large finger on the map. "If they cannot take one of the bridges, they will need to have some barges ready. It's been done before. Place them side by side at a narrow point of the channel. Four barges will span the gap. A few planks nailed in place and they can ride horses across.

"I've sent riders ahead to warn the marshal of the Isle of the pending attack. Of course, there are any number of barges loading and discharging cargo in the channel, but if the Prince does not realize we are aware of his treachery, we can fire most of them or capture them and send them out into the river. The bridges can be defended or torn down, whichever the flow of events dictates."

"You won't stop them from landing on the Isle for long," Tuwar Estenford said quietly. "A day or three at most. The channel is too long, and there is the river to think of. They can land a force large enough to catch us from behind and hold a piece of the channel bank while their army crosses. It is part of the reason that Toren wanted to return the Isle to Wills control: the cost of defense was too great."

The Isle of Battle, Lady Beatrice knew, was not really an island in the true sense of the word, but a large piece of low-lying land that sat inside a bend of the river on the eastern shore. To its east an ancient and dry channel of the river had been laboriously dredged into a narrow canal that barges and larger river craft could transit in the seasons of high water. At low water only a skiff might make its way through, but even so, the narrow channel aided in its defense, for it was soft-bottomed and could not easily be ridden through. Water levels had passed their high point this year but the channel would remain navigable now until the autumn.

"Then what do you suggest?" Kel asked.

"We should meet the Prince's army before he gets to the Isle. Meet him in the field and force battle where he least expects it."

Kel looked up at the old man. "But then it will be said that we started the war."

"Perhaps it will, but would you rather wait for them to arrive at the Isle and lose? Will it matter what is said then? No, I think we should preserve the Isle if we can, or make them pay a great price for it. How large an army can we muster? That is what I should like to know."

"That is what I should like to know as well," Kel said, "but some of our 'allies' are being very coy."

"Perhaps if the documents were signed and the Isle transferred to me, we would do away with one source of doubt." It was Lord Carral, who had come in without anyone realizing.

Lady Beatrice swept to her feet and crossed to him, taking his hand.

"Lord Carral, how pleasantly you surprise us."

Carral did not turn in her direction, but stared blankly ahead. "It should be no surprise that I am interested in the defense of the lands I am to hold. I fully intend to accompany any army you will send to aid in the defense."

Lady Beatrice looked over at Kel, taking advantage of the minstrel's blindness to mouth her horror at this suggestion.

"It is unnecessary, Lord Carral," Kel said on cue. "We shall secure your lands for you, as we would any ally. Better you stay here in both safety and comfort."

"I have wasted my life in safety and comfort, Lord Kel, and the consequences have been too great. No, I will accompany you. I can ride as fast as any company of armed men, and live as roughly as need be; you will see."

"But Lord Carral," Lady Beatrice began, not sure what she would say, "the defense of the Isle is in the most capable hands, and if you will permit me an observation, you are neither trained nor formed to be a man-at-arms. What do you hope to accomplish?"

"What do I hope to accomplish? To show the men who will risk their lives for the defense of my small realm that I am willing to stand among them, and die with them, if I must. That I do not value my life above theirs. I hope to accomplish no more than that."

The emotion in the blind minstrel's voice caught them all off guard and silenced them for a moment. Kel opened his mouth to speak but Tuwar Estenford interrupted him.

"That is reason enough," the old man said. "Let him come."

His heel ground down on gravel, and the maid let go of Lord Carral's hand. He scribed a small arc with his walking stick, measuring the width of the gravel path.

"Lord Carral."

It was Lady Llyn; her voice was unmistakable. The warmth of it touched him as though he were the string of a Fáellute.

"My lady," he said, making a small bow. She put her hand in his and he brought it to his lips. How soft the skin of her hand. Immediately he remembered touching the burns on her face. How dreadful that this accident had befallen her!

"Come sit. I have a small table and refreshments. Would you take my arm?"

He would, whether he needed to or not. She fell into step close beside him, the scent of her perfume mixing with the lavender of the garden. She led him to a chair, where he settled himself, the music of flowing water sounding nearby.

"Tea?" she asked him.

"Please." Carral could feel the awkwardness. Was anyone welcomed here but her own servants? He wondered where the balcony was from which most of her visits took place. To his left, he guessed.

"Is this true what they tell me that you will accompany Kel to the Isle of Battle?"

"It is true."

She said nothing. He heard her cup rattle as she placed it back in its saucer, as though her hand shook just perceptibly. He waited for her to speak, to contend his decision, but she did not.

"I feel I must go, Lady Llyn," he blurted out. "If I am to govern, I must gain the respect of both my subjects and the men-at-arms who will fight for me. I cannot do that by remaining safely here."

"You would not be the first to govern who left the fighting to others."

"That is true, but were such men respected?"

"Some were, in fact, for they governed wisely."

"But I have not governed at all, so I cannot claim respect for something I've not done."

He heard her lift her cup again. A breeze moved through the garden, disturbing the branches above.

"I shall not argue this with you. It is a noble but misguided choice you have made. Such choices have made men heroes in the past—gained them the admiration of even their enemies. Though some were dead and could not appreciate the moment appropriately."

He thought he could feel her looking at him.

"You will stay in the rear, won't you, Carral?" she said, addressing him as though he were an intimate. "Take no unnecessary chances."

"I shall stay at the rear . . . Llyn. I don't want any men-at-arms to have the distraction of having to rescue me." They were silent again. "Kel is having a suit of mail altered to fit me."

"Well, that is something."

"I shall feel a fool in it. I have refused a sword. What would I do with a sword?"

"I'm sure it is for appearances only."

"The blind aren't much impressed by appearances," he said.

She laughed, which broke the tension of the moment. "It is a good thing," she said, but did not elaborate.

"Now that I am in your garden, Llyn, I feel I know something of it . . . from the description you gave me." He moved his hand toward the sound of water. "Here is the small pool with water lilies. The water has a voice, as you said, though the trees each have their own particular tongues as well. Did I tell you I can recognize many types of tree by the sound of the wind in their leaves?"

"Now I believe you are teasing me, Carral," she said, only the slightest pause before she used his name.

"No, no. This is a doveplum we sit beneath. Is it not?"

"It is indeed! How did you know that?"

"Close your eyes."

"I have."

"Now listen. The doveplum branches are very stiff, so the leaves must take all the force of the wind. This gives the sound a different timber, as though the leaves vibrate more quickly, like the high strings on a Fáellute. If you go stand beneath a chestnut you will hear the leaves there move more slowly. They are larger, their sound more defined. A weeping willow is unmistakable. It whispers. The sway and shush of the branches can almost be understood. Of course, in a stronger breeze the sounds change, and larger trees have voices both louder and richer, but if you listen you will soon come to recognize the voices of the trees you have here." He reached out and found his tea cup, though the tea had grown cold as he spoke.

"You are the only person I know who can name a tree by its sound. How those aunts and cousins who are so proud of their garden lore would be put to shame by that! How did you learn this?"

"By listening. It is amazing what you can learn by listening. It is always a wonder to me that people who must talk all the time know anything at all. I once wrote a song that attempted to represent the sounds of the different trees."

"Oh, I would love to hear it," she said immediately. "Shall I send for my Fáellute?"

"But I have not played in days. My fingers are not limber."

He felt her beautiful, warm hand cover his. "You mustn't give up music. It is a gift you were given. A gift to hear and to create beauty. You cannot give it up. It is like bearing a child: you must put all your heart into its rearing. Anything less is unacceptable."

"Would that I had done more in the rearing of my child, Llyn. Perhaps she would still be alive. But I forsook everything in favor of music. And now I shall try to make amends. Let some other take up the Fáellute. I have done my part there."

She did not argue with him, which was a relief. He felt as though all his joy in music had died with his daughter.

"Lady Llyn, when we last spoke . . . I said certain things—"

"You have reconsidered?" she said quickly. "Will you take your words back now?"

He was surprised by this outburst. "I—I do not wish to take them back. I want you to know I meant them with all my heart." He could hear her shift in her chair, her soft breathing. "Will you say nothing? Is it true, then, that your heart belongs to Toren Renné?"

"Where did you hear that?"

"It is what everyone says . . . within the castle."

She laughed, but her mirth sounded false. "Lord Toren and I are not made to be together."

"That does not mean you don't love him."

She took a long shaky breath. "I am confused," she said softly. "Never have I been so confused. I have hidden myself away from others all my life, and then you . . . you have stepped over my garden wall as though it were not there. And here we are, face-to-face, as I have been with only my most trusted servants. And now I am tossed about like a tree in the wind. I want to hide myself and never speak to you again, and I want to throw myself into your arms and weep with gladness. At times my anger is so great that I could strike you for what you have done."

"And what have I done?"

"You have wakened feelings in me that I thought were long dead. It is as though you have recalled me to life. As though I dwelt here only half alive, and you reached out your hand and drew me out of my beautiful grave. How I hate you for that," she said with feeling, and then in a very small voice: "And how I love you."

Carral rose to reach out for her and discovered she had risen, too. He found her lips in the darkness, and then as they embraced, she pressed the unburned side of her face near to his. A tear touched his cheek. He was not sure whose it was.

Thirty-one

The creak of leather and fetor of horses had become oppressive, like a single note plucked over and over again. Lord Carral rolled with the constant motion of his mount, surprised by the silence of the Renné men-at-arms.

Kel had been gathering an army since the night of the Renné Ball, and this task had been aided by the time of year. Many of their allies had attended the fair, and most of these had brought with them their best knights, archers, and swordsmen. For this reason, Kel had explained, they were traveling with a gratifyingly elite company.

Not wanting to alert the Prince of Innes to their plans, Kel had split his force into many smaller companies, and these were instructed to tell any who asked that they were merely returning home from the fair. The Renné had arranged transportation across the river from various points, none of them from the usual towns where ferries landed.

It was a simple plan, and likely to be more effective for it. The total number of men was not large, but added to the forces stationed on the Isle of Battle and coupled with an element of surprise, Kel hoped they would carry the day. There was little other choice but to hope, for more men were not available on such short notice, and as Fondor had pointed out, a larger force would likely be noticed by the Prince's spies.

Fondor had been left the unenviable task of continuing to ready the Renné for war, a task that Kel was only too happy to abandon for the more simple and direct act of battle.

The scent of the river carried on the wind, and Carral thought immediately of Elise. Her body had never been found. There was a place in some corner of his heart that took this knowledge and held out hope that she had survived, even though his mind knew that this was not so. She could not swim, and had not meant to survive. And if somehow she had, certainly Elise would have sent word to him by now. She was gone. Utterly gone, as though she had sailed across the ocean to some distant and unknown land from which she would never return. There were times when he imagined her living out her life in such a place, still vibrant and somehow at peace. He fought back a tear. The human heart was so frail, the thought of a loved one's death was almost beyond its ability to endure.

He had this thought, suddenly, that they would find her body as they crossed the river. A man-at-arms would call out and they would gather her up and lift her onto the deck, where she would lay, cool, her flesh soft from the waters. She would smell of the river, no trace of Elise left.

"Lord Carral?"

It was Kel, who rode at his side.

"Yes?"

"Is this proving too much for you?"

"Not at all. I love to ride, and often ride for pleasure much greater distances than this."

"Ah," Kel said awkwardly. "I wondered . . ."

Carral took a long breath. "I was thinking of Elise. If I looked to be in pain, that was the reason."

"You have every right to suffer for such a loss, Lord Carral. Forgive me for interrupting your reverie."

"No need to apologize. My mind goes there too often when not occupied by something real and immediate."

The leather of their saddles creaked, hooves pounded down upon the hollow ground.

"Lady Beatrice is concerned that you blame yourself too much for your daughter's death," Kel said tentatively.

"Too much? No, I don't blame myself too much."

"But you blame yourself."

"It is undeniable that shrugging aside my inherited duties played a part in what eventually happened."

A bridle rattled as a horse shook its head. Somewhere to his right a wren scolded.

"May I tell you something about going into battle?"

"Please do. As you know, I know, nothing of it."

He heard Kel shift in his saddle. "I have known men who went into battle before, consumed by feelings of guilt." The wren fell silent. "None of them survived."

"Let me put any fears you might have at rest, Lord Kel. I have no desire to self-murder."

"Neither did they, Lord Carral. Not the slightest intention, yet none of them lived to battle's end."

The sound of a horse trotting toward them was heard ahead.

"Your grace," a man said. "We've arrived."

"If you'll excuse me, Lord Carral. We've reached the river."

Carral heard the two horses trot away as the line of riders came to a halt.

"Where are we?" Carral asked his servant.

"We've come to the river, sir. There is a small stream here with a bridge over it, if my memory hasn't failed entirely."

A quiet order was given and riders began to dismount, some speaking softly to their horses and then leading them away, probably to the river to drink. The footsteps of men were all around him—footsteps he did not know. The metallic ripple of mail and men sighing told him that some had cast themselves down on the ground.

His servant dismounted as well. He could feel the interest of his horse increase, then she tossed her head once, quickly, and was still.

"I have her head, your grace," the man said.

Carral swung down from the saddle unaided. A walking stick was thrust awkwardly into his hands. Oh, how he missed Josper Twill!

"Look! There!" someone cried out. "In the river."

There was a sudden confused splashing.

"It's a girl!" a man called. "Where is the healer? Call the healer."

"What is it?" Carral said. "What have they found?"

"I can't see, sir," his servant said uncertainly. "But it seems to be a girl floating in the waters."

Men jostled past him, heading toward the bank.

"Take me there," Carral ordered.

"But the horses—"

"Damn the horses! Take me there."

The man grasped his arm and they clambered up a short incline from the road. In a few steps they were at the riverbank and sliding down the slope, colliding with horses and men.

"Can you see?" Carral asked.

"It's a girl, your grace. She's not moving."

"Is it Elise? Is it my daughter?" He shook off the servant's restraining hand and stumbled down, slipping in the mud, colliding with someone. "Where?" he said. "Where is she?"

Abruptly, the men on the bank were silent.

"Here's the healer," a man said quietly, and Carral heard men move aside.

"Is it my daughter?" Carral asked again. "Is she costumed?"

"It is a small girl, your grace," a voice said. "Perhaps ten years. Dressed like a commoner. She's dead."

Carral sat down where he was. He felt the tears streaming down his cheeks. No one spoke.

"The poor child," Carral managed. "The parents must be found. They can't be left to wonder; wonder and never know."

Thirty-two

Currents gripped the barge, pulling it this way and that without warning. Oars thudded between thole pins, and the rudder creaked like an ancient door opening. Carral half expected someone to step through, and he was afraid of who it might be.

"Tuwar Estenford, Lord Carral," the servant said.

He heard the thump of the wooden leg on the floorboards and then the old man took his place alongside Carral at the rail. In the cooling air of evening the minstrel could feel the heat of the man, could smell the oil he used to keep his sword from rust. And Carral could hear the wheeze of his lungs, for Estenford's every breath was a labor, as though he must wrestle the air just to stay alive.

"There will be few stars tonight, I think," the old man said.

"It will be all the same to me. Will it rain?"

He heard Estenford shift about. "The breeze has fallen away and it feels muggy and still. Perhaps."

Tuwar Estenford never looked at him when he spoke. Carral knew this by the tone of the man's voice.

"Why did you support my coming on this endeavor?" Carral asked.

The old man took a deep, difficult breath, more labored than most. "Because it was a noble gesture, to come here and face the dangers the men-at-arms will face. If you survive, it will endear you to the people of the Isle and the fighting men, and that will carry you far."

The tiller creaked loudly, and the helmsman called out to the men at the oars. Luckily, Carral had a good hold on the rail or he would have been thrown to the deck. Josper would have warned him and then given an explanation of what went on without being asked, but no one around him spoke, as though he were not in the dark.

"We will reach the shore soon."

Carral said nothing.

The man cleared his throat but it did not relieve his labored breathing. "Do you know that I lost my leg in battle?"

"I am told very little these days but for some reason that information was given me."

"This will sound strange, but I can feel it still, feel the pain. Sometimes it itches terribly, but cannot be scratched. It is as though one part of me passed through into the netherworld and became ghostly, while the rest of me is still here. Sometimes I dream that this ghostliness begins to spread, and bit by bit I disappear, passing through into that other world until I am insubstantial, all of my feelings strange and distant." He stopped and fought for a few breaths of air. "I have wondered what you see in your mind, Lord Carral. Do you have pictures of what things look like, created, perhaps, by having handled them?"

"It is darkness inside and out, Tuwar. I can hear voices in my head, and music. I remember the scent of my wife's hair after washing, the touch of her lips upon my own. All my memories are made up of the senses that I have, but no light, no 'pictures,' as you say." Carral rubbed his hand over the rail which had been worn smooth by ten thousand hands doing the same. "But I do have dreams not unlike yours. I dream that I begin to lose my senses; first touch, then my sense of smell. My hearing fades to whispers and echoes that might or might not be real. Food turns tasteless in my mouth until I am left stumbling around calling out but unable to hear my own cries, feeling nothing, smelling nothing, tasting nothing. It is a dream of death, I think."

"Yes," Estenford said. "Men-at-arms have many such dreams, often about Death's gate and the overwhelming darkness. I'm sure my dream is the same: a dream of death. It is my experience, however, that such dreams are almost never prophetic."

"Everyone dies."

"Yes, but not commonly the day after their dream."

Carral heard the bargemen pass quiet orders down the line of oarsmen. The clatter and thumping of wood on wood followed. Suddenly the craft was still, bumping gently against something hard—a stone quay, Carral assumed.

"Welcome to the Isle of Battle, Lord Carral," Estenford said.

Urgent whispers and quiet curses passed down the line of men aboard.

"Sir Tuwar?"

Carral did not know this voice, but the man who spoke was somber and sure.

"Sir, the Hilltower and Canalkeep are under siege by the Prince of Innes."

Thirty-three

Alaan woke to find himself being dragged across the antechamber on his formerly animated cloak. The pain in his leg was unbearable, and he would have cried out had he not been gagged.

"He's come back to life," one of the guards said.

His progress over the floor stopped and a head appeared in his small circle of vision, the face shadowed and blurry.

"If we see you doing anything that looks like sorcery we'll cut your throat so fast you won't see the blade coming. Do you hear?"

Alaan nodded.

"Good. We will take you back alive if we can, but none of us will mind killing you either." The man grabbed Alaan's hair and pulled his head roughly to one side so he could check the knot on his gag. "Good. Let's get on."

They hauled him roughly up the stairs by his arms and legs, the pain in his leg so great that for a moment he lost consciousness. He felt himself lowered to the ground. Voices mumbled words too jumbled to understand. Someone shook him by the shoulder, rolling him onto his back. They untied the gag and pulled it free.

"Watch him. That might be a trick to get you to take off his gag."

"It was no trick. He was no more sensible than a rock."

Filtered moonlight fell around him now, and Alaan took a few deep breaths of the damp air. Morning, he decided, could not be far off. What had become of Crowheart?

"Let's get him down to the shore," their captain said. "We'll use that boat. If it's still there."

Two of the guards lifted Alaan and bore him down the path. Crowheart's boat remained, drawn up on the shore. They all but tossed him into it, causing him to double up with pain again. Before he had even begun to recover they pushed him out into the waters.

A couple of the guards went up to the encampment and gathered up Alaan's belongings and anything else they could find. To Alaan's relief, they stuffed some blankets under his back, giving him a little support and easing the discomfort a little. Then two of the guards pushed his boat forward through the waters, the waning moon hanging in the branches of the strange aquatic oaks.

Dawn transformed the sky to mother of pearl, and Alaan could see his captors now—a nobleman, a seer, a blacksmith, a squire. Two certainly belonged to Hafydd's guards. The other pair were no doubt men-at-arms to the Prince of Innes. All of them looked spooked and wary from their short time in the swamp, which did not surprise Alaan.

"Take us out of this forsaken swamp," the captain of the guards ordered.

Alaan raised his hand and pointed randomly. He wondered how he would escape these men in the condition he was in. One thing was certain: he would not lead them out so that they could return him to Hafydd. He would let them kill him before he would fall into Caibre's hands again.

And then, from a branch overhead, a crow spoke.

Thirty-four

Lord Carral sat in a camp chair beneath a rippling sailcloth spread between trees. A light rain stammered over the canvas while Lord Kel Renné and Tuwar Estenford questioned a man-at-arms who'd met them at the quay. He was one of the garrison on the Isle of Battle, a local but obviously of good family, by his manner of speech.

"They landed a mounted force on the northern tip of the Isle," the man said. "They came down the river by night, and before we knew, they'd used barges to build a floating bridge not far off. They had most of an army across the canal by early morning, and by the time we'd learned of it, we could not muster a large enough force to drive them back." The man paused. "They caught us looking the wrong way, sir, despite your warning. We expected them to try to take one of the bridges."

"They moved more quickly than we'd expected," Kel said. Carral could hear the anger in the man's voice. Lord Carl's intelligence had not saved them, and Kel was not happy. Things weren't going as planned. It was the Prince of Innes who was supposed to be caught off guard.

"Do they know we're here, I wonder?" Carral asked, thinking aloud.

He heard the man shift about on the rain-soaked ground. "Certainly they have excellent knowledge of the Isle or they should not have landed so easily and without resistance."

"But do they know we've landed in force?" Kel asked.

"I wouldn't think so, but we should curtail the movement of any residents nearby so word doesn't spread."

"Or better yet," Estenford said, sucking in a difficult breath, "spread rumors that Renné forces have landed at any number of different points. Let the Prince wonder if we've landed a vast army and then spend much effort in worry and in trying to discover our whereabouts."

Lord Carral made a slight bow toward the source of Estenford's voice. He wouldn't have thought of that. The reason for Kel's deference to this man was becoming apparent.

He could hear men moving about the camp, smell the smoke of their fires. Every so often a barge would arrive and there would be some subdued commotion while the newcomers were settled. A cool breeze blew from every point of the compass, as raw as a wind off the sea. The leaves of poplars shook nearby, as if complaining.

"Are you sure of the numbers?" Kel asked, and not for the first time. He paced back and forth beneath the covering, his boots squelching on the damp ground.

"I am, sir."

Kel stopped. "But these are not large enough forces to take the keeps."

"They have siege engines, sir."

"Even so . . . Is this just inexperience on the part of the Prince and Menwyn Wills?"

"Their landing here did not look like the result of inexperience," Estenford said. "They must have some old soldiers in their camp, though I would not have thought the Prince wise enough to listen to them." Unlike Kel Renné, Estenford did not move about, but stayed solidly in one place—a blessing to a blind man.

"Do not underestimate Menwyn," Carral said. "He is sly and

patient. He knows his own abilities well and finds others who have mastered the skills he cannot. I don't know that the Prince is listening to him, but I've seen Menwyn convince a man that an idea was his own when it definitely originated with Menwyn."

"Has he made a study of war?" Estenford asked.

"Not that I know of, but he is secretive. One can never be certain with Menwyn." Carral felt chilled and somewhat miserable, and this talk of his brother made him feel worse. Menwyn had always bested him before—always gotten his own way.

"Well, it is apparent that we can't count on them making mistakes," Estenford said. "We must assume they're formidable."

"Then why have they sent so few men to siege the keeps?" Kel began to pace again. He was slapping something against the palm of one hand.

"Because they hope only to keep the forces in the towers occupied, I would guess," Estenford said.

"Then they are still landing men," Kel said.

"That is what I would think." Estenford gulped down air. "They expect the Renné to respond by bringing our own army across the river. If they defeat that army, then they will have delivered a great blow to the Renné."

"Then we have some advantage yet. But it will not last. I think we should march this night and attack the army they are landing. If we can drive them back into the canal before the forces sieging the keeps are alerted, we will have time to turn our attention to them."

"It is a risk," Estenford said. "If we don't defeat the landing army quickly, then the sieging forces will come to their aid. We'll be fighting armies before and behind us, which is as much like a death wish as I can imagine."

"Some risks are worth taking. Once the Prince knows we are here, everything will change. Our small army will be outnumbered, and I for one don't believe that a Renné is worth half a dozen Wills. I say we attack now, before their army has formed and is effective."

"But we have not even landed all our train," Estenford said. "What will men eat?"

"Whatever can be scavenged until our train arrives. Are you with me, Tuwar?"

Carral listened to the old man wheezing like a leaky forge bellows. "Aye, I'm with you, but let us hope we can drive this army back into the canal. If we can't . . . the Prince of Innes will have the great victory he is looking for."

They rode by torchlight along the winding lanes of the Isle. Kel could just make out the dark shapes of the riders between the seemingly solid hedgerows. A light rain splattered the leaves of overhanging oaks, and a fitful wind came from one point of the compass and then another, rattling the leaves forlornly. Drops of water ran cold down Kel's neck.

Carral Wills appeared just ahead of him now, as Kel wound his way up the line of mounted men. It surprised him what a good rider this minstrel was. Certainly blindness seemed to be no handicap here, for he was as graceful in the saddle as Toren Renné, and that was saying a great deal.

"Lord Carral?" Kel said as he brought his mount alongside.

"Ah, Lord Kel. We make good progress, do you think?"

"As good as can be expected in the dark. We've most of our archers on horse now and the rest on hay wagons and drays we have been finding along the way. We'll move faster now."

"You have no infantry, no foot soldiers."

"We've been gathering some from outlying garrisons, but I don't know if they'll arrive in time. It might be horsemen and archers and nothing else."

"May I offer a piece of advice, Lord Kel?"

"By all means." Kel wondered what a minstrel might hope to add in this situation, but Carral Wills was to rule the Isle—he could hardly be ignored.

"Give my brother Menwyn no quarter, nor even warning. He

will eke an advantage out of anything. You must give him no opportunity to recover. None whatsoever."

"But certainly it is customary to give your enemy time to draw
themselves up to fight. We would never ride down men who were
not even armed."

"The way Hafydd rode down the Fáel women and children? I
know it is not in the code of a man-at-arms, but I beseech you to
give them no warning whatsoever. Attack them as soon as you can
arrange your forces. Give them no warning but arrows. You cannot
afford to be chivalrous now, and let me assure you, Menwyn would
not be so if it suited him. He would murder you in your sleep if it
gave him advantage. He would murder me, and not lie awake suffering remorse. No, this is all-out war, Lord Kel, we do what we
must to win."

Kel gathered his companies beneath the boughs of a small wood
that sat astride a hillock overlooking the canal. A subdued dawn,
misty gray, revealed the labors of the men below, even through light
rain.

"We are outnumbered, that's certain," Estenford wheezed, "but
their position is not good. Their backs are against the canal. They
have no line of retreat and there is no natural defense. They should
have spent time throwing up some earthworks, but they have not.
We might drive them into the water if we do as Lord Carral has
suggested—attack without warning—though I know you are loath
to do so." Estenford sat upon his horse, covered in a thick wool
cape that glistened with rain. The hood was up, so that he seemed
to be speaking from the depths of a tunnel.

Kel gazed out through a screen of trees, wondering what he
should do. Certainly Toren would never attack without fair warning. He would rather lose a battle than sully his reputation. But
Toren was not here, and the Isle would almost certainly be lost if
they failed to carry the day.

"No sign of the Duke of Vast?" Kel asked.

"None, your grace. We have riders out looking for him."

Kel snorted. "You know, Tuwar, it was the Duke of Vast and Carl A'denné who warned us of this attack. And here we are, ready to repel the Prince of Innes, but the Prince seems to have arrived several days early. . . . Early enough to catch us off guard had we been but a few hours later. And now where is the Duke, do you think?"

"Lost, I hope, sir."

"Lost is what I hope, too. Not waiting to attack us from behind."

"The men below do not look forewarned, at least."

Kel considered this. His horse shifted beneath him and tossed its head—it sensed battle coming. "That is true. Can we slip the archers down that hedgerow without alerting the Prince?" Kel pointed, his hand shaking rain down from the sodden branches.

"They have outriders who might see them."

"Send our best archers and woodsmen ahead to deal with the outriders. How long until the archers could be within striking distance?"

Tuwar thought a moment. "An hour if we do it properly."

"Then do it, there is no time to be lost. More men cross the bridge by the minute."

"No fair warning then, your grace?'

"No, Tuwar. Lord Carral is right—the time for such niceties has passed. The Prince of Innes lost his right to fair treatment when his counselor attacked the Fáel." Kel reached out and moved a small branch aside. "Do you think that Carl A'denné and his father are down there?"

"Shall I give the order that they are to be spared?"

Kel had been contemplating this very question. He shook his head. "No. They will be of no use if their allegiance to us is revealed. Better hope they're not there or that they manage to swim back over the canal. Lord A'denné understands the dangers of his choice, though I have some pity for his son, who I think came to us in all sincerity."

★   ★   ★

They had ridden all the previous day, crossed the River Wynnd, and then ridden through the night. Carral Wills had to admit, at least to himself, that he was exhausted. How these men-at-arms would fight a battle now he did not know, but that is what Kel proposed to do.

His legs had begun to ache and his saddle had turned to stone. Around him he could hear hushed voices and men moving, both mounted and on foot. Tuwar Estenford wheezed out orders, and men jogged off, without question, to carry them out. His horse threw its head and pranced a little sideways, sensing the disquiet in the air. Battle was about to be joined, and what was he doing here? Here where he could offer nothing, but only get in the way. And if they were to lose? He did not fear for his life, at least not overly, but his claim to the Isle would be at an end. Menwyn might even have him killed, accidentally in the heat of battle, of course, but his brother would not stand another challenge to his authority.

"Archers are in place, Lord Kel," Estenford reported.

Kel sat upon his horse at Carral's side. There were a number of others on horseback as well—Carral's small honor guard—the men who were to whisk him away if the battle went wrong. They would take him back across the river if at all possible. So much for his desire to face the same dangers as the men-at-arms.

"Are the riders mounted?"

"Mounted and awaiting your order."

"Then let us go without trumpets or battle cries. We might cover half the distance before they're aware of us."

This order was passed down the long line of knights who waited, hidden in the shadows of the wood.

"Forward, then," Kel said softly, and Carral heard the horses set out down the grassy slope toward the canal. His own horse began to strain at its lead to follow the others, but his servant and his own hands on the reins soon had her under control.

"Can you see?" Carral asked.

"They go proudly, your grace, though quietly, yet. There is no sign at the canal that they have been seen. It is a great sight, sir, all the mounted men in their Renné blue, the double swan flying overhead. Still they have not been seen, but as soon as they are . . . There! The Wills have sight of them now, sir! The signal has gone up for the archers. There they go, sir, the first wave of arrows. And how they have hit their mark! Men are falling, sir, falling and running. There is confusion now, your grace. Even on their damnable bridge men are falling and pushing each other into the waters to escape.

"The riders have passed by our own bowmen, sir, and are on level ground. How they fly forward now! Can you hear their cries?"

Carral could, and hooves thumping relentlessly over the earth. Had he advised this? Attack without warning, he had insisted; it was the only way to ensure victory.

"What happens now?" Carral asked, afraid of the answer.

"They're all but there, sir. Our archers have ceased to fire."

There was a loud report like a great door slamming in the distance.

"They're upon them, sir."

Only a few had managed to scramble into their saddles, though foot soldiers had quickly formed a ragged line. Not enough of them, though. Kel had driven his charger into the hastily formed line. It appeared to happen very slowly, his mind taking in every detail. The pale grim face of the young man, helmless, who fell beneath Kel's first stroke. The sound of iron-shod hooves on mail, on bone.

Most men broke and ran. The rest were trampled or cut down. It was a slaughter, though the greater numbers of the Prince of Innes preserved them for a time. Men flailed into the river, where they sank beneath the weight of their mail, and others fought to cross back over the bridge, where knights had drawn swords and began killing their own to stay the rout.

"The horror of victory," it had been called, and Kel understood it now. He spun his horse and looked around. Everywhere, he saw men in purple and black and in the Wills evening blue running from the Renné and their allies. Small pockets of men, surrounded by sky blue, were sullenly laying down arms. A sword in one hand, a torch in the other, and controlling his mount with his knees, Tuwar Estenford led a battle for the bridge, driving the Wills and their allies back.

Kel turned again and spurred his horse forward to go to the aid of a group of knights hard pressed on all sides, but horns called out in the early morning, horns and the cries of men. He looked up to see mounted men swarming down the slope under the dark, double swan banners of the Wills.

A shout went up from the Wills and the men of Innes. They were delivered! Suddenly they turned from flight and renewed the battle, engaging the Renné as equals rather than conquerors.

And now it was Kel who was being driven back, back from the bank of the canal. He saw Tuwar, almost on the bridge, throw his torch into a barge and begin to fall back.

Above the din Kel heard the whistle of arrows, and flinched before he realized it was the Renné archers sending their arrows into the arriving Wills. Where had they come from? he wondered.

The battle hung in the balance, he knew. Either the resurgence of the men of Innes would spend itself, or they would push the Renné from the canal bank. It might take only a few minutes for that to be known. If the archers couldn't drive the Wills reinforcements back, then they would fall upon Kel and his men from the rear and they would be encircled. It would be a miracle, then, if they could extricate themselves and escape.

Kel was isolated and surrounded so quickly he didn't know how it had happened, but suddenly he was beset on every side, he and one other who would not hold this position long.

Horns sounded again, and a cheer went up from the men of Innes and the Wills. More reinforcements had arrived, Kel thought, but could not look up. A sword shattered on his shield with such force that he lost his grip on it and felt it fall from his hand.

They were driven south, into a stand of trees and bush, and stayed alive by maneuvering themselves in among the trunks so that not all the men-at-arms could attack at once.

Kel's companion was thrown down from his horse, and the men surrounding the Renné lord screamed for his blood. He could see the enraged faces beneath their helms. He tried to keep the fallen man's charger between him and those on his right, but this ploy would not last long. His own charger kicked out and bit on command as he hewed about him with his sword. But he could not hold and he knew it. He was already exhausted and knew his end was near. A sword caught him across the back, but it was a weak blow and his armor turned it, though the breath was knocked from him and he almost fell.

Then one of the men who assailed him turned and cut down the man to his left, then cut down another.

"See! See!" someone shouted. "A'denné! A'denné betrays us!"

Kel had no time to determine if it was Carl or his father. Suddenly there was hope! A new strength grew in his arms, and he threw a giant from his saddle, then cut down another. Riders in sky blue came to his aid then, and he had to protect the man in A'denné crimson.

Kel looked up at the slope above to see a mounted host riding down on them beneath the banner of the Wills. To the north a second mounted company appeared from beneath the trees of a wood and spurred their horses to gallop.

"The Duke!" someone called. "The Duke of Vast!"

Thirty-five

Above the sound of slaughter Carral could hear the banners fluttering in the breeze: the double swan standards of both his house and the Renné. How many such massacres had these swans presided over? he wondered.

"I hear horns to the south of us," Carral said. "Who?"

"I don't know, your grace."

Over the distant cries of men and the grim sounds of battle, Carral heard a horse go forward. In a moment it came trotting back.

"They're Wills, from the siege of one of the towers," the rider said, "and I fear we've been seen. They're sending a company our way."

Carral's guard swore. "Out of this! We'll go west and hope they give up on us for the larger battle. Hold tight, Lord Carral, we must go at speed."

And so they did. Carral found himself in the inglorious position of clinging to his saddle pommel, and hunching low while branches raked over his surcoat and the mail protecting his arms. He lowered his head so that his helm took most of the blows, though now and then a branch would scape across his face or strike him in the chest and try to hurl him from the saddle.

The pounding of hooves and the shouts of the men were all that he heard. No one could tell him what happened, and he expected a sword to bite into his back at any moment.

And then they were sprinting forward, no branches battering him.

We're in an open meadow, he thought. Carral heard the man leading his horse curse, and then something flicked over his shoulder.

"Ride on!" his guard called, and Carral found himself on his own. The lead from his horse had been thrown over his shoulder, and he grabbed at it desperately, knowing what would happen to him if his horse were to tangle a foot in that.

His guard had gone back to help his companions, and Carral raced on into the darkness, not knowing if he pointed his horse toward a barn or a stone wall or a sturdy oak. Disaster, he was sure, would meet him at any moment, for this was nothing short of madness, to keep on so—but what choice had he? The men pursuing him would certainly take him back to Menwyn if he were caught. He didn't think they would kill him in his evening blue surcoat, but he might be wrong at that. He was seen as a traitor to the Wills, after all.

His horse began to shake its head, fighting the bit. Carral gave the horse its head, hoping it had the sense to keep him from harm. It swerved suddenly, and he all but lost his saddle, thrown far over so that a tenuous grip on the pommel with one sweating hand was all that preserved him.

The horse slowed to a trot. Carral pulled himself back up into his saddle, gasping and frightened. He listened as he'd never done before, but no sounds of battle came to him. No sounds of horses in pursuit. What had happened? Had his guards all fallen?

"You wanted to face the same dangers as the men-at-arms, you damn fool!" he cursed himself.

He steered his horse to the right now, certain from the sun on his face that she was going in circles. He drove her forward, trying to let her find her way while still keeping her going, west, away from the men who pursued him. If his guards drove their pursuers off, then they would find him. For all he knew he was visible for furlongs. If the Wills won, then it would be better if he pressed on. They might give up after a time, knowing that there was a battle going on and their fellows perhaps falling.

His mare began to fight him again, throwing her head and shaking her bridle. He eased his hold on the reins and she veered to the left, this time throwing him to the ground. He landed on one shoulder and the pain cut into him like a sword. He felt the mare's lead ripped from his fingers and he was horseless.

Staggering up, he called her name quietly. "Lady Gray," he whispered. "Lady . . ." But she ignored his entreaties. Nothing he tried would coax her back, and though he could hear her not far off, she stayed out of his reach. Twice he stumbled and fell. And then he sat down and cursed her under his breath. Now, when he was most in need, the treacherous animal would act so—like a coy woman!

In a moment he was up. He stood feeling the sun on his face, oriented himself by the time of day he imagined, and set out. But he lost the sun quickly and wondered if cloud would hamper him. A gust of wind blew and he stopped. He was beneath a massive hornbeam—he could tell by its voice. He strained to hear. Yes, there was a wood before him. There would be no sun there, but it would make finding him more difficult.

He went gingerly forward, waving his hands before him. In a moment he stopped and pulled off his helmet. Feeling about, he tossed it into a thorny bush and hoped it was not too visible. Deciding not to do things by half, he stripped off his surcoat and then, with great difficulty, his shirt of mail. The padded doublet he wore beneath this he threw off as well, and felt the breeze immediately begin to cool him.

Now, at least, if he were to encounter hostile forces they might think him only a blind man who lived thereabouts. Unless of course they were men-at-arms who recognized him, which was not impossible.

He tripped over a stick, which did more to benefit him than harm. Breaking it to the right length, he had a walking stick again, which let him go forward more surely, though here and there the underwood was dense and he could not push through but was forced to find his way around.

The wind was his compass now, and he just prayed that it would remain constant and from the same quarter as it had all morning. He imagined he was a sailor on a starless night, navigating by the feel of the wind, the sounds around him.

How long he stumbled through the wood he did not know, but the day wore on, warm and cloying. Carral Wills was scraped and bruised, and limped from forcing his way through the wood. He wondered what had become of the Renné, Kel and his allies. Had the arriving companies turned the tide of the battle? Perhaps the Isle was lost to Prince Neit and Menwyn and he was of no use now to the Renné. A blind man without home or family. It occurred to him that he could become a traveling minstrel. Though once war spread, even minstrels would not be safe on the roads.

The ground abruptly gave way, and he toppled down a slope of dirt and grass, landing at the bottom in an awkward heap. He lay for a moment, catching his breath and steeling his nerve to go on again. Beneath him he felt the rut of a cart track, though whether it was a road or some farmer's lane he did not know. The breeze hissed in the trees around him and a warbler sang its soft song. Cattle lowed far off and bees in number swarmed some innocent bush to his right. Honeysuckle, he realized, breathing in the scent.

And then, from a distance, came a repetitive squeaking, like a cartwheel that had never been greased. Carral lay where he was, listening, and when he was sure the sound approached, he sat up. His first impulse was to hide, but then he decided such a noise was not made by men-at-arms. Perhaps it was a farmer, though he could hear no sound of draft horse or donkey.

The squeaking continued, growing louder, until it was a squeal that rose and fell in pitch. Even the warbler paused to listen. The noise appeared to reach a crescendo, and then suddenly it ceased.

Kel looked up. He could see the two mounted companies thundering down the slope, lances in hand, hear the cries of the men. Beside him Carl A'denné huffed like Tuwar Estenford. For a moment the fighting seemed to have moved away from them.

"Do you have faith in the loyalties of the Duke of Vast?" Kel shouted over the din.

"Utter faith."

"Let it not be misplaced."

Beneath the banners of the Wills, men began to tumble off their horses as they came within range of the Renné archers. Horses fell, causing others to topple over them, but still they came.

"They will meet just before they reach us," Lord Carl said.

Kel turned toward the young man, who looked like a boy dressed up in his father's armor.

"Let me cut you out of that crimson," Kel said, "before someone murders you."

"No. I must go back. I have my side of an agreement to keep."

"But men saw you here defending me."

"They're all dead, and we are hidden by the trees."

"You take a great risk."

But the young man only saluted him with a sword and set off at a gallop, back into the fray.

"And I would not give the order to preserve him or his father," Kel said, wondering at the strange turns life took.

He waited only a moment before following. The battle swayed in the balance, neither side holding the advantage. He heard the crash of the two armed companies driving one into the other and knew that much would be decided there. He threw himself into the fighting around the bridge, which was afire now. Men with buckets threw the river onto the flames to preserve their link to the other shore.

Kel found Tuwar, and the two of them tried to force a path to the bridge.

"Vast!" someone shouted. "Vast will carry them!" Others took up the Duke's name and it became a battle cry. "*Vast! Vast!*"

But the battle for the bridge still raged, swaying back and forth like a cornered serpent.

"Good day to you, good sir," a voice called out.

"And to you," Carral said in return.

"Are you hurt, or have you lost your way?"

"I am blind, good sir, and lost, and there is fighting all about."

"Where is it you go?"

"West, to the river. I hope to cross and escape the war that has erupted here."

"As do many. Where are your family, your belongings?"

"I have neither. Not on this side of the river, at least."

The man spoke quietly to some other and then the terrible squeaking began again. The cart, or whatever it was, ranged near.

"We must go quickly," the man said, "and our way is not easy, for soon all the tracks and lanes will be clogged with people in flight. Already the main roads are filling with wagons."

"I will come as quickly as I can, if you will guide me."

"Come along, then, and we'll see what happens. I have pity for any who have an affliction of the body, for I have lost my legs and go about now in a barrow."

Carral followed obediently along, walking on the grassy strip between the wheel ruts. He could almost have managed just by following the screech of the barrow's axle, but with his walking stick he could sweep ahead of him and feel the ruts to either side. Whoever pushed the barrel was strong, for he went uphill and down at the same relentless pace. The man who rode spoke occasionally—when the ground was most even, Carral noted—but Carral required all his breath to just keep his legs moving. The third man did not speak at all.

After perhaps an hour they turned off this track and onto a narrow footpath, which went up and down over the small hills of the gentle landscape. It was not an even path, and much overgrown in places, but the man in the barrow followed it unerringly.

After a march of some hours they stopped beside a creek where waterwillow whispered. Carral knelt down beside the stream and drank from his cupped hands. He could hear the man in the barrow laboring to breathe, though he had not walked a step.

"Hurry," he said to his companion, the word pressed flat.

Pain, Carral thought. *He is in great pain.*

The man who wheeled the barrow quickly built a fire, likely having carried hot coals with him. Water was boiled, and then a sweet peppery odor Carral had not smelled before reached his nostrils.

"What is that you make?"

"A kind of herb," the man said, his voice still pressed and hard. "I take it for an infirmity."

The sound of liquid being poured, then of someone desperately drinking. A sigh that was almost a sob. Carral said nothing for a while, but only listened to the sounds of the creek and the forest.

"There," the man said after a time. "There. I'm human again. How are you bearing up?"

"Well enough. Is it much farther to the river, do you know?" Carral asked as he sprawled back on the soft ground.

"Some distance yet. We shall not be there this day." The man took a deep breath and let it out slowly. Carral could hear relief in his voice.

"I am ill prepared to spend a night in the wood, though I suppose I shall survive."

The man laughed. "My name is Kai, and my silent companion is Ufrra."

"Carrel, I'm called. I'm surprised we've met no families fleeing the battle. Nor have we encountered men-at-arms."

"We shall see some of each when we strike the road, I'm sure. How is it that you are traveling with no belongings? You are a man of good family, clearly."

"A family much reduced in both numbers and circumstances, I fear. I possess little, and what I did have was taken by marauding soldiers. I was lucky to be left alive, and was likely only left so because I could not identify them. I hope to cross the river, for I have a daughter there."

"Such crimes and worse follow behind war like carrion crows," Kai said. "But we should go on. This herb has only whet my appetite. Perhaps we will find a meal along the way."

Carral heard Ufrra approach, his footsteps now quite familiar. The fire went out in a hiss of steam, and then the terrible screeching began again.

The path continued to twist and curve, worming into fragrant woodlands and over poppy-scented meadows. They would stop in the shade of trees and rest every so often, for though the walking was not hard, it was difficult for Ufrra wheeling his charge.

"What tree are we beneath?" Carral asked as they rested in the grass. He breathed in the unfamiliar scent.

A slight pause answered him, and then Kai said, "I don't know. A kind of elm, I think."

"It does not sound like any elm I've ever heard."

"You recognize the trees by their sounds?"

"Yes, many of them, and the elms are familiar to me. They all sound much the same, though I'm told there are several varieties. But this is a tree I've never heard."

"Well, I can't explain that. It appears to be an elm but perhaps I'm wrong."

They were soon up and moving again, though Carral was having trouble keeping up in the more rugged terrain. Kai soon realized as much.

"The path curves to the right and goes down somewhat steeply here," he called. "Mind the roots."

And the pathway did go down, much farther down than Carral would have thought possible. Had they really gained so much elevation? He would not have thought there were hills so big on the

Isle, but the only other explanation was that they were descending into a valley that lay below the level of the river.

They walked beneath trees with voices Carral did not know, and he found this passing strange. The day began to cool and he could feel the shadows wash over them. He guessed the sun had gone far into the west, though he'd long since lost any sense of what direction they traveled, for the path twisted all over the compass.

He smelled wood smoke, and as they went a little farther, animals and perhaps a garden.

"Orlem?" Kai called out as they came to a halt. "Orlem?"

There was silence and then a muffled reply. A creaking sound and then wood bumping wood.

"Who is— Kai! I've not seen you in . . . well, it seems like a century!"

The sound of boots thumping down stairs followed, and then footsteps on softer ground. The man had emerged from whatever dwelling place they stood before.

"Kai, Kai!" and then all the enthusiasm and joy vanished into silence. "I know you've not lost your way," the man said slowly. "So what is it you've come to old Orlem for?"

"Can a man not visit an old friend? This is Ufrra, who carries me about the world, and good Carral. He was wandering blind upon the road when we came upon him, fleeing a war that was erupting on the Isle of Battle."

"There always be war in the land between the mountains."

"So it seems, good Orlem, so it seems."

"It be late," the man named Orlem said. "I'll make us some supper and you can tell me your story after. Carral? Would you care to sit?"

"With all my heart, thank you."

He heard the man walking toward him and then some heavy object placed close by. Carral reached out and found a large, rough-hewn chair, into which he collapsed, on a blessed pillow of horsehair. It was not his legs that ached, but his right arm and shoulder and his back—from feeling his way with his cane all day. Josper would have made such efforts unnecessary.

Orlem cooked outside over what Carral guessed was an open hearth, perhaps only cooking indoors when the weather grew cooler. He had an odd manner of speaking, using older forms of words which he put together in an archaic manner. His voice sounded like the wind through an ancient hawthorn; hollow and complex.

Carral nodded off after a few moments, unable to keep his eyes open.

When he awoke the nightjars called, and the frogs were in full choral harmony. He lay still, listening.

"I think we tired the poor man near to death," Kai said.

"Why have you taken him on?"

"I don't plan to take him beyond the river. He was lost and certain to run afoul of the war as it was breaking out. I took pity on him. We made a fine trio—me without legs, Ufrra without voice, and the third man blind."

"Huh," was all Orlem answered to that. "So what's brought you here then, Kilydd? You were never much one for sentiment." He began making a scraping sound as he talked—sharpening something, Carral realized. And why did he call him Kilydd and not Kai?

"Oh, I've not forgotten the old days, Orlem, don't worry. In some ways I think they're more with me these past years than ever before. I often wonder why." He paused to clear his throat. "They've returned, Orlem."

"Who've returned . . . ?" The scraping sound stopped. Carral could not hear the man breathing. "How is it so?"

"They had smeagh hidden that we did not find."

"River take them," the man cursed softly. "Do they know we worked against them?"

"No . . . No, I don't think they do. Not yet."

"Are you sure they've returned?" Orlem said, a bit desperately.

"Sianon I've had speech with. She was looking to find Sainth, and said that Caibre was close behind her, seeking her death."

Carral heard Orlem rise and pace across soft ground to the fire. Liquid ran into a small container—tea into a cup. The sweet peppery scent came to him again.

Something creaked, and from the source of the voice, Carral thought that Orlem returned to his seat. " 'Tis not pleasant to face one's failures, Kilydd. Not this one, at least."

"They were more clever than we, Orlem, hiding their smeagh, leaving things behind. We know they laid spells that lasted for centuries, though how these were wrought, I do not know."

"But why has this come about now, I wonder?"

"I've only pieces of the story. We've long known that our Knights betrayed us, hiding smeagh away until they found ways of using the nagar. Bloody arrogant fools, they were."

"Yes, the Knights of the Vow were a mistake, but the task was too great for us to manage alone. In the end, though, we should have contrived their downfall sooner, Kilydd. It was a mistake to let them go on so long, hoping they would come to their senses."

"Yes, it was a mistake—and not the last. I thought the Renné had destroyed the Knights to a man, but it wasn't so. Some few escaped, Orlem, and a handful slipped out of Cooling Keep with their treasure. No, we were not diligent enough. Sainth would have been disappointed in us."

"But he is back as well?" Carral heard Orlem's voice rise, almost in elation.

"Back, yes, but with Sianon leading Caibre toward him. She had only just wakened, I'm sure, and hadn't yet come into her full understanding."

The rasp of metal on stone began again. "Caibre will never catch Sainth."

Kai began to answer but Orlem interrupted.

"I don't know what we can do now, but hide, perhaps, and hope that Sianon and Caibre never learn that we conspired against them for so long."

This was answered by a brief silence. Carral could sense a tension here.

"Sainth is in the Stillwater," Kai said. "I sent Sianon after him, with Caibre in pursuit."

Carral heard a creak and rustle of clothing, as though someone sat forward in his chair. "Into Aillyn's lair?"

"Aye."

The man called Orlem laughed. "Well, you be a canny old fox!"

"I wish it were so. Sianon came to me demanding a map to take her there."

"Sainth has lured them there, Kai. That can be the only answer."

"Perhaps, yes. But there is more to it. Sianon claimed that Sainth was wounded, and very gravely, too. He might not be able to escape."

"Do you think she told the truth?"

"I believed her, yes."

They were both quiet then, listening to the forlorn cries of nightjars and the whispering of strange trees.

"What does she look like now, Kilydd? Like she did . . . then?"

"No, not a bit. She has hair the color of fall wheat now, thick and curly and long, though she goes about in the clothes of a man as she did of old. She is not so forbiddingly beautiful, but more womanly and kind—though she did threaten me!" he said, and they both laughed. "I don't know what will become of her, or the young woman she made her bargain with."

"It should never have been done, Kilydd, but some will weaken and fail."

"Neither you nor I have stood before Death's gate, Orlem. Who knows what we would do?"

"I know what I would do, Death's door or no. But others know less of Wyrr's children than I." Carral heard the man shift about in his chair, as though he couldn't get comfortable.

"Let us hope that Sainth has lured his brother and sister to the Stillwater with a purpose, and that they wander there for many lives of men. Aillyn lets few escape his grasp."

"True, though Crowheart seemed to have immunity to this," Orlem said. "He came and went into the Stillwater as he pleased, though I never knew why."

"He went there seeking a vision, or so he claimed." Kai sipped at something.

"I've not heard of him in a hundred years or more. I can't think that he lives yet. There are none left but you and me, now that Gwyar has passed over—"

"And Lansa, don't forget. She lives still, on the very edge of the hidden lands. She can walk out her front gate into the land between the mountains and out her back into the hidden lands. She hides herself from people now, as do you, Orlem. Do you not grow lonely?"

"I have my garden and my wood, Kilydd, and my peace. I had my peace of mind, too, until you came to disturb it."

"I thought only to warn you, Orlem, nothing more."

"And I thank you for it, Kilydd. I thank you. But what shall I do with that warning? I've not strayed into the land between the mountains now for many years. Oh, if I must have something that I can't make myself or do without, but that has hardly been frequent. Without a map from you, no one will find me but Sainth— and Sainth I would welcome."

Carral could almost feel the two men's minds slipping back to some distant past. What had he fallen into? Who were these men who talked of figures out of the oldest songs and enmities that endured the centuries? Where was he? Why were all the trees so strange?

"Well, they are all best left in the Stillwater. Only Sainth was worth anything at all. Caibre and Sianon were loyal to nothing."

"That is true," Kai said softly. "Do you remember when Sainth came back for us at Braeleath Castle?"

Orlem seemed to think a moment. "Oh, aye. I do. I never thought to see the light of day again, and then in he strode with the ring of keys in his hand as easy as you like."

"They thought they were laying a trap for him—and they had— but Sainth was more cunning than they. Even so, he risked his life."

"And more than once, too. I've not forgotten."

Silence, as the two men considered these ancient events or others like them.

"And now he lies wounded in the Stillwater, his foul brother not far off," Kai said.

This statement produced a long, difficult silence.

"My service to Sainth was done centuries ago, Kilydd. There is no reason to come to me now."

"No? I would go, Orlem, had I legs. I would not see him die in that place—he who risked his life for mine."

"If Sainth dies, his brother and sister will perish with him. None escape the Stillwater. None but Crowheart."

"I wonder, Orlem," Kai said slowly, "if the children of Wyrr will not escape. Will the dreamer in the water hurt them? They are his own blood, after all."

"They've made bargains with men and women who will die."

"Yes, but look how long we've lived, Orlem. Longer than Sainth and his sister would have thought possible. Even if they do die, they will become nagar again, and wait. They are more patient than the river, Orlem, wearing away stones if it takes a thousand years. I fear they will escape in time. And if they do, and Caibre has killed Sainth and burnt him upon a pyre, who will be left to stop the two who remain?"

Carral could hear Orlem breathing now. As though he labored at some task. "The nagar were sustained by the River Wyrr. Outside the river, outside the land between the mountains, I think they will fade away in time."

"Perhaps they will, but how long will it take?"

"An age of men."

"Will they not find their way out in all that time? You know how cunning they are, how resourceful. Caibre and Sianon were only ever held in check by Sainth, by the knowledge that if he allied himself with one, the other could not stand against two. He held the balance . . . until Caibre saw his chance and murdered him, betraying all that was honorable."

"But we are old men, Kilydd. Older than old," Orlem said, his voice sounding frail and ancient. "What can we do now but run afoul of the children of Wyrr? They have already taken your legs. What offering will you make next? No, it were one thing to work against them when they'd gone into the river, but now that they're returned . . . Best to hide yourself away, Kilydd. Make yourself a map to some far place that none can find. And hope that if the nagar find their way out of the Stillwater, we'll be in the grave. Let it be sooner rather than later, for my life has gone on too long. I've seen sorrows enough to break a hundred hearts. I've outlived all my children and their children's children, too. Our time is done, Kilydd. It should have been done long ago."

"But Caibre and Sianon think differently. They come into their power again, and the people of this time know nothing of them but their names in ancient songs. If Caibre kills Sainth—"

"But certainly Sianon will save him. And if she can't, what can two old men do?"

"The Stillwater is treacherous and difficult to navigate. Only Crowheart can claim to know it. He might reach Sainth before either Sianon or Caibre do."

"But where is Crowheart? Can you answer me that?"

"I think I can. Some years ago I sent a man into the hidden lands to find my blood lily—Theason he was by name. On the edge of the Stillwater he chanced upon Crowheart, and the two struck up an acquaintance of mutual benefit. Crowheart brought Theason healing plants that grew in the Stillwater, and Theason would bring him necessities from the land between the mountains. They arranged a signal that Theason told me of."

"And what do you think I could accomplish? You know what I would be facing. The power of Wyrr's children is beyond our understanding. You saw it, Kilydd. You saw them shatter the doors of great fortresses, call down lightning on their enemies, cast spells that changed the face of the land. No one but Wyrr could ever hope to stand against them. We failed to keep them from returning, and when they have leisure, they will come seeking us for this crime against them. They never forget ill done to them, Kilydd. You know that. Caibre and Sianon both were vengeful as no mortal could ever be. More than once Caibre exercised his wrath upon the children of the man who'd wronged him, when he found the man already dead. No, they are monsters and will make us pay for our offenses."

"Well then, you best find someplace more distant than this, Orlem Slighthand, for they will find a path to this valley, near as it is. Good night to you, Orlem. My blankets, Ufrra."

Carral woke to the singing of birds and realized that morning was not far off. The first songs come before light, he'd been told, and men rose with the dawn. He could hear soft snoring nearby—more than one man. It seemed that some had slept outside. It had been a fair night, warm and quiet. Carral found he had been covered in a coarsely woven blanket that prickled through his shirt.

He'd been so tired he'd fallen asleep where he sat, and now the arm of the chair—once the branch of a tree, for he could feel the bark—pressed into his ribs. The night felt like a dream to him. The strange conversation about the children of Wyrr. He knew songs about Wyrr and his children. Wyrr was connected with the River Wynnd, somehow.

When he closed his eyes the forest shivered
Though he did not die as mortals do
But slipped into a dreaming river.
While overhead the dark swans flew.

He searched among the thousands of tunes in his memory. A song about the gifts Wyrr gave his children, each gift with a price, though Carral could not recall the lyric now. Kai—or Kilydd—and Orlem talked like they had lived in that time, that time of ancient songs.

Though the chair bit into him, Carral lay still, hoping the others would wake and continue their conversation. The mystery had a hold on him. These men did not sound mad. No, they sounded terribly sane—sane and frightened and sorrowful.

How could children of a long-dead sorcerer come back to life? Nagar, they had spoken of, and Carral knew many songs of nagar. They were of the river, that was certain. He couldn't think of a lyric where they did not dwell in the Wynnd or some tributary, though they sometimes emerged onto the banks, ghostly and frightening. The nagar were never named, and it was unclear whether the songs spoke of few or many. One thing was always the same: the nagar made bargains with men, and the mortals always paid the greater price.

Orlem stirred first, Carral could tell by the man's heavy footfall. He must be larger than Ufrra, at least in girth if not height. He disappeared for a time and then returned to kindle the fire. His footsteps sounded inside the dwelling and then emerged, scuffing over stone before stepping down onto dirt. He began to hum softly, every now and then singing a word, a phrase. After a time Carral recognized the air, though much changed. It was the tale of a man's love for the daughter of a great king—but as Orlem sang it, it was a man's love for the daughter of Wyrr, which made much more sense, for, in the version Carral knew, the "king" performed magic.

Orlem began to sing the song in its entirety then. He had only a passable voice, but he sang the lyric with conviction, as though he told the story from his own experience. The poor lover was spurned and driven off by Wyrr, chased far away, where he took up service with her brother—which was not in the song that Carral knew.

Ufrra woke next, lumbering off to perform his toilet. And then the crackle of the fire and the smell of cooking roused Kai.

"Poor Carral," Kai said. "I all but did him in yesterday, it seems. Hi, Car—"

"Do not rouse him yet," Orlem said. "Where will you go now? What will you do?"

"I don't know. I cannot send Theason to find Crowheart, for I don't know where Theason is. The journey to the Stillwater is not long but it is arduous. I don't think Ufrra can carry me there. I don't know what will become of Sainth, with Sianon and Caibre bearing down on him."

Carral heard Orlem take a long breath. "I will seek him for you, if you will make me a map. A map that will take me both there and bring me back."

"Once you are in Aillyn's lair there is no map that I can make that will guide you out. But you can find Crowheart without going into the Stillwater. Theason would signal him from the shore."

Neither man spoke. Carral could feel something in the air, like the moment before a lightning strike.

"Then I will sharpen my blade. You find a quill and paper."

"You have always known the meaning of loyalty," Kai said warmly.

"Have I always? But I was younger then. I am old now, nothing but a book of memories. What tales we could tell if men would believe us! Tales of sorcerers and nagar . . ." He laughed bitterly. "Do you think it will happen to us?"

"What?"

"Will we fade and become nagar, half alive in the river?"

Kai did not answer right away. "It is possible. I can only say do not drown, Orlem Slighthand. Do not give yourself to the river. The lesser nagar are nothing more than the faintest mist. At least the children of Wyrr were clouds or rain. They could be seen. But you and I . . . we would be nothing more than yearning, Orlem."

"That would be a fate," Orlem said so softly that Carral barely heard. "How strange the world has become. The children of Wyrr awakening again after uncounted years. How could this be so?"

"I do not know for certain but I have suspicions. Do you know of a man named Eber son of Eiresit, Orlem?"

"I do not." Wood settled on coals.

"He served Gwyar of Alwa for a time."

"I heard that Gwyar passed over," Orlem said. He raked ashes, Carral was sure.

"Yes, and he went a bit mad at the end. I'm not sure what he told this man, but Eber learned more than he should, though I don't know to what use he's put it. He keeps himself hidden on Gwyar's island and hasn't ventured off in years. My friend Theason would sometimes visit him there."

"And what did your man tell you?"

"Eber knew much about the nagar, and had sighted them . . . more than once. My friend thought Eber might even have been searching for smeagh, perhaps thinking Gwyar possessed such objects."

"Do you think he found a smeagh? Certainly Gwyar knew the danger of possessing such things."

"Theason did not know. But I will tell you something stranger about Eber: he claimed to listen to the river and would sometimes hear it speak."

"He was mad. Mountain ranges have fallen away in the years that Wyrr has been dead."

"Yes, but Theason did not think this man was mad."

Orlem considered this a moment. "Let us break our fast. I've much to do this day."

"Carral?" Kai called. "Ufrra, give him a shake. I fear he has died on us. I've hardly heard him breathe all night."

Thirty-six

The barges and planks of the floating bridge blazed so that thick caustic smoke drew over the battlefield like a shroud. From the saddle of his poor charger, lame in one foot, Kel surveyed the field. The remains of the army of Innes and Wills had either fled or surrendered.

The dead lay all about, among the fallen horses and banners. A river of Renné blue seemed to flow among the purple and black of Innes and the shadow blue of the Wills. In the field of purple and blue, Kel thought the crimson of the A'denné swirled like blood upon the waters. He was certain he would find Carl A'denné lying there, and perhaps his father, too.

The crackle and hiss of the burning barges reached a crescendo, and suddenly the planks that made up the floating bridge collapsed. One barge rolled on its side, a spectacular cloud of steam boiling up through the flames.

Prisoners sat in circles, back-to-back. He could see one cleaning his sword, for they were allowed to keep their weapons. Noblemen were never deprived of their weapons, their word was enough to keep them.

Yes, Kel thought, but we attacked them without fair warning.

Perhaps all the rules have been suspended for the duration of the conflict.

His attendant rode up with a second horse and Kel dismounted stiffly. He was about to climb into the saddle when he saw Estenford walking toward him.

"What is the news, good Tuwar?"

"I bring bad news, Lord Kel. We have lost Lord Carral," Tuwar said.

Kell stopped. "He's been killed?"

"I hope not, but he's not to be found nor are any of his guard."

"Give Sir Tuwar your horse," Kel ordered his equerry. "Let us go up the hill and see what can be found. We can't lose the Wills— not now."

The two climbed wearily onto the backs of horses and set off.

"I bear much of the responsibility if anything untoward has befallen Lord Carral," Estenford said. "It was I who insisted he be allowed to come: a foolish whim in hindsight."

A guard was quickly mustered to follow them, for there were Wills and their allies about yet. At the crest of the hill they found the place where they'd left Carral Wills with a small company of mounted men. The marks of horses led into the trees, and they followed these through and out the other side. Kel found that each time his horse set a hoof on the ground, pain shot through his back where a sword had struck him. Breathing seemed to have become more difficult, and Kel feared he sounded like Tuwar. He'd have to visit the healer, though they were occupied with men more direly injured than he.

A meadow revealed nothing at first but the trampled pasture where horses had passed. And then they came upon the first rider—lying facedown in the long grasses, his arms twisted strangely.

"Dead when he hit the ground," Tuwar said, gazing down grimly. "Not one of ours, thankfully."

"There are horses, sir," one of their guards said, pointing.

"Leave them for now," Kel said, and they rode on. They found two more men down, one their own, both dead as well. The trail of carnage stretched on until all Carral's guard had been accounted for and a number of their enemies as well.

"They put up a good fight,"Tuwar said, climbing down from his horse to look at the ground. He began to walk then—awkwardly— leading his horse. His pegged leg sank into the soft earth here and there, throwing him off balance, but still he managed to crouch down and part the grasses to examine the earth several times.

"I think one horse went on alone," he said, rising and shading his eyes to look up at Kel.

"But was it Lord Carral?"

"If it had been one of our guards, he would have come back to the battle, which this man did not. If it had been one of theirs— well, there would have been two horses, for Lord Carral is not among the dead we've found."

"Though perhaps we've missed him somehow." Kel looked off across the meadow. "Where would Carral Wills get to on his own?"

Tuwar turned and looked as well. "Who can say? Not far, I should think."

Kel turned to one of his guard. "Find a huntsman and take a party to follow these tracks. If it is Lord Carral, we want to find him before some stray troop of Wills."

Kel and Tuwar rode back toward the field of battle. At the crest of the hill they stopped to gaze out over the canal and the carnage. Men moved slowly among the bodies, bearing them up and lying them in neat rows. The wounded were treated similarly and laid not far off. Many of these would make the short journey to the ranks of the dead before the day was over.

Woodsmen were readying a place for fires; all the men would be stripped of their armor, their devices recorded on the roll of the dead, and the bodies would be burned on two separate pyres. Mounds would be raised over the fire pits, like so many others in the land between the mountains.

"After all Toren did to avoid war," Kel said, "it has begun anyway, and over this scrap of land that he tried to give them to keep the peace."

"Menwyn Wills and the Prince of Innes wanted war, Lord Kel. It could not be avoided by any statecraft of Lord Toren or anyone else, though I honor your cousin for trying."

"So do I. There is a siege which must be lifted," Kel said, thinking out loud.

"Perhaps, but I think that army will appear soon enough. Unless they have already received word of what happened here. In which case they will make for the bridge at Tumley Mills. If they fail to cross there, they'll be seeking boats to ferry them across the canal."

"Then we should find them before they escape. Let us hope they have the good sense to surrender. I've seen enough blood for one day."

"I agree, though this was a minor affair as such things go, with only a small number killed. If this blossoms into a large scale war, it will seem almost a pleasant day compared to many we'll see."

"You do much to cheer me, Tuwar. Let us find all the men fit to travel. We can secure the Isle by nightfall—at least for the time being."

Kel could not take his eyes off the flame, which swayed and jumped and lifted up toward the stars. The awful reek of bodies burning permeated the air and clung to hair and skin. He wondered if he could ever wash it off. Still he stood, watching, feeling the heat of it on his face, watching the tower of smoke climb the heavens, staining the very stars.

He coughed and shut his eyes tight from the pain. Cracked ribs, the healer had pronounced, perhaps broken. Tuwar appeared at his elbow.

"Tuwar?"

"He has not been found."

"We have secured his kingdom and he is not here to enjoy his triumph. Where has he gone?"

"We do not know. The huntsmen had his track, plain as plain, they said. His footprints just grew more faint, though the ground was soft—as though he grew lighter and lighter and then floated up into the sky, like a cloud."

"Keep searching. Someone must have seen him. Unless he has fallen victim to a wild beast and been devoured."

"Unlikely here. The Isle is more civilized than that."

"Why did they not surrender, Tuwar?" Kel asked, still staring at the fire.

"I don't know, sir."

"Their army had been routed. They accomplished nothing by their action. Oh, they killed a few more of our good men-at-arms but not enough to matter in the long run. Was it bravado, do you think?"

He could see Tuwar's shoulders shrug in the light from the flames. He too stared at the pyre. "There are some leaders whom men will follow anywhere—to certain death. Perhaps such a man commanded here—and would not be taken prisoner. Perhaps they simply did not understand the situation. It doesn't matter now. They fought to a man, and one must respect their courage, no matter how foolhardy."

"Well, I will never again allow anyone to say, in my presence, that the Wills are cowards. Fools, perhaps, but not cowards."

"What are your orders now?"

"Keep searching. Every man we can spare, regardless of his rank, should join the effort. I don't know how I will explain this to Lady Beatrice. I won the battle but lost Lord Carral Wills. She will not be pleased. Toren will be livid. Lord Carral must be here somewhere, alive or dead. He cannot have disappeared into the air—as these poor bastards do."

"No," Estenford said, "unless he were somehow among the fallen here."

Thirty-seven

They did not go quite so quickly that morning, though the track was no more difficult. Carral followed behind, as before, and Kai described the way for him, becoming more and more adept as each furlong passed. Very quickly he learned the things of which Carral needed warning. He was no substitute for Josper, however.

They stopped by a small stream, collapsing in the shade. Carral could hear Ufrra lifting Kai from his barrow. It seemed that Kai could shuffle about on the stumps of his legs, though his progress sounded painfully slow. Bouncing in the barrow all day, however, would be excruciating, and Carral suspected that Kai was driving himself to the limits of his endurance, traveling as they were.

Fire was kindled and Kai's tea steeped. After a time he spoke. "So, what did you think of the conversation last night? Have you ever heard such madness?"

Carral was about to deny having listened but then could think of no reason why, other than the appalling bad manners it indicated. "It did not sound mad to me. Fantastic, yes, but not mad."

"And you are a Wills. Is that true? Carral Wills?"

Carral tried not to act surprised. "What makes you think that?"

"There are a small crests of the Wills family embroidered on the points of your shirt collar. And your breeches are evening blue."

Somewhat abashed, Carral reached up and felt the embroidered double swan on his collar.

"You are obviously a man of some standing, by your speech and your manner, and you are blind. I had heard that Lord Carral Wills recently was ceded the Isle of Battle by the Renné. How came you to be wandering alone without guard or horse?"

"I was attacked by a company of men-at-arms serving the Prince of Innes. They had come late to the battle and saw me and my guard upon a hill overlooking the battle. I escaped, but my guard, I fear, did not. I dared not go back, in case my family and their allies had won, but hoped to meet up with some company of Renné, or perhaps find a way to cross the river to safety."

"If you listened last night you will know that there is no place of safety, not in the land between the mountains."

"You said a great deal about the children of Wyrr. They've returned, you said, but how can that be? Even if they once lived, which no one believes, they would have been dead a thousand years."

"Dead? No, Lord Carral, they've not been dead. They've been lurking in the river, sustained by their father. Waiting for the smeagh to fall into the wrong hands, so that they might prey upon the fears of some poor man or woman. But they have returned now, for I have met one of them; Sianon, with her brother Caibre in pursuit. Two more terrifying sorcerers have not walked the earth but for Wyrr and his brother. But you, Lord Carral Wills, have the ear of the most powerful nobles in the old kingdom. You they might listen to, whereas a legless man of no property would never have a chance to speak with them. But how can I convince you that I am speaking the truth?"

"It might be easier than you think. You see, I believe I have met two of your sorcerers. One was a man who called himself Eremon, though I now believe that he was once called Hafydd and we thought him dead after a battle against the Renné. The second was a rogue who would not tell me his name, who disappeared from the top of a tower in Braidon Castle, though he did not avail himself of the stair. Hafydd was seeking him with a passion that one could hardly imagine. Could one of your sorcerers have escaped a tower room without descending the stairs or sliding down a rope from the window?"

"Sainth has done such things before. He once escaped a cell in a dungeon, though the door was still locked and bolted from the outside and there was no window nor even a hole big enough for a mouse to slip through. The jailer swore a cockroach could not have escaped that cell, yet Sainth did."

"But I am not sure what I can do that will help. We are not the best suited men for heroics."

"What? A blind man and a cripple? Who would dare stand against us?" Kai laughed. "We will see. There are strange forces at work in the land between the mountains. Our meeting was not an accident in the usual sense of the word, nor was it fated, as some might say, but we were cast together all the same, me on my way to visit Orlem Slighthand, and you wandering in the darkness."

"Who is Orlem Slighthand, if I might ask?"

Kai considered a moment before answering. "He was once a great warrior and a commander of armies. Songs were sung of him then, and he was honored and feared. He rose to prominence under the tutelage of Caibre, Wyrr's eldest son, but was seduced by Sianon and became the commander of her armies. Sianon, however, was capricious in her love and he left her, one of the few to have done so. For many many years he wandered with Sainth, which is how I came to know him. Both of us had been cast aside by Sianon and we bore our wounds like brothers in arms. I was with Sainth when he went to Caibre, trying to keep the peace between brother and sister. We met on a barge in the River Wyrr. I can see that boat to this day, with its swan banners flying. Sainth tried everything to maintain the peace, but to no avail. In the end he threatened to join Sianon in her war against Caibre, and Caibre broke all the rules of honor by which they lived and slew his own brother, for which he bears a curse to this day. He cut off my legs and threw me in the river to die, but . . . I did not die as I should have.

"Neither Orlem nor I were present when the last children of Wyrr fell. And we lived on—and on. For several lives of men we dedicated ourselves to destroying the smeagh of Wyrr's children, but we failed. We created the order of knights you know as the Knights of the Vow. The songs and stories say they were created by King Thynne, but the order existed long before, and its secret vow was to our purpose: to seek out and destroy the smeagh. The vow was broken and the smeagh hidden, and the Knights, in their pride and ignorance, took to communing with the nagar. After the fall of Cooling Keep we thought their smeagh had been destroyed, but we were wrong, it seems. And now Orlem will take up his sword again and go seeking our friend Crowheart, whose knowledge might now come into play." Carral heard the man shift on the ground where Ufrra had placed him. "Do you believe any word of that?"

"I have listened to so many ancient songs that what you say seems just another story, another lyric passed down through generations of minstrels."

"There is more truth in old songs than you know, and more lies as well. Do you know the Song of the Wanderer?"

"There are many such songs."

"Yes, but this one was the first." In a surprisingly high thin voice Kai sang:

"He traveled roads unseen by men
True Kilydd beside him, bright blade free
Through shadowed wood and hidden fen
He rode through fire to come to me.

"Of course there was more, but that is all I can recall—the only lyric I know of that included my name. It was a song much sung, long ago, but only few remember it now."

"I have heard it. You are Kilydd, the companion of Sainth."

"Well, one of a long succession of such companions, but yes, I was among that proud company of wanderers. I have seen things men would not believe, but I paid a price for it."

Carral could imagine the man reaching out to touch his severed legs.

"You should be warned, Lord Carral Wills, if we fall afoul of Caibre, he will take his revenge on you, cut off your hands so that you can never play again, perhaps worse."

"I am already his enemy, good Kai, or Kilydd, if you prefer. There is nothing I can do to change that now."

"Then call me Kai. Kilydd disappeared into the river long ago and the man who emerged was not the same."

Carral took a deep breath of the forest air. "How much farther have we to go?"

"The river is near. We meet a road just ahead and it is but a short journey along that way to the Ravenwood Ferry."

"Ravenwood! But that is on the south end of the Isle. Certainly we have not walked so far!"

"I know a shorter way," Kai said.

"So it would seem. Then we are traveling somewhere else, as Sainth did?"

"I have not a hundredth the ability of Sainth. We are barely over the border, just around the bend from the land between the mountains. I can draw maps that will take one deeper into the hidden lands, but not too far. There are places only Sainth can find."

It was perhaps half an hour before they reached the road, and there Kai told him families trooped past with wagons piled high with valuables and frightened children. Kai was cautious and wary of men-at-arms, for reasons he did not explain. When the way was clear, they went out into the road and set off.

They had not gone far when they heard from behind the sound of horses.

"Take us off the road, Ufrra," Kai ordered.

Carral was led forward by the gentle Ufrra, who seemed a giant when Carral reached out to put a hand on his shoulder. Behind a fallen tree Carral crouched down, as he was asked to. Horses cantered by—Carral could not be sure how many, but fewer than six, he guessed.

"There," Kai said. "We can go on."

"Who were they?"

"Men-at-arms."

"Serving whom?"

"The Prince of Innes." Carral could hear Kai shift about in his barrow. "Will they recognize you?"

"Some few might. I think it unlikely that we would meet them, though."

"Even so, we should take no chances. Ufrra? Can you do something about Lord Carral's collar?" There was the scratching of straw on wood as Kai shifted about in his barrow. "Among his other skills Ufrra is a master with a needle and thread. If you will permit him?"

"Certainly." Carral removed his shirt, dropping one stud into the long grass. Ufrra found it quickly.

His shirt was placed back in his hands in a moment and he reached up to feel the collar. Its shape was altered but still acceptable. He thanked the silent man.

"Let us go down into the town," Kai said. "Perhaps some honest man can be found who will carry us across the river, for I think it is a danger for us to stay here."

A few people were passed as Carral followed the tortured barrow into town. They learned that the soldiers of the Prince were stopping wagons of grain or other foodstuffs, but people were being allowed to cross the river. There were so many waiting that the ferrymen were said to have increased their price fivefold.

"Perhaps I should wait here," Carral said when they neared the crowds gathered by the quay.

"Better to stay with us, I think," Kai said.

"Do you know no shortcut across the river?"

"I do but it is too difficult to travel in a barrow."

Carral was jostled and reached out to find Ufrra, the screaming barrow close by. "Who is here?" Carral asked, to assure himself somehow that he had not been lost.

"Farmers, tradesmen, maidens, children, the industrious, the feckless, millers, tanners, noblemen, thieves."

"Are there minstrels?" Carral asked casually, afraid that his identity would get out here, where the Prince's soldiers were present.

"I'm sure there are or soon will be, a steady stream of humankind has begun to flow down the narrow road. There is even a small company of Fáel, it seems. Here . . . here is a woman selling boiled potatoes and sausages."

Food was thrust into Carral's hands, Kai paying whatever was asked. The minstrel had forgotten his own hunger, or it had been pushed aside by fear, but now he ate like one who had been long starved.

"Come," said Kai. "Let's try to make our way down to the quayside. We have no belongings like these others, perhaps there is a small boat that can take three so unencumbered."

They pushed through the crowd.

"You!" said a voice. "Wait your turn."

"You've no authority here!" someone in the crowd shouted.

"I've the authority of the Prince of Innes."

"The Renné still rule the Isle," another spat out.

"Then why are you all here, scrambling to the other shore? You in the barrow? Where do you think you're going?"

Carral turned away and tried to hide his face. Men-at-arms of the Prince of Innes were here. They would have him in a moment.

"Leave the man alone!" someone hollered. "Can't you see he has no legs?"

"Lost them fighting the Wills, no doubt," some other called.

"I told you to stay back!"

Carral knew the sound of swords being drawn, and suddenly

he was shoved, violently, and struck by another who knocked him savagely to the ground. He tried to rise but a man landed on top of him, knocking the wind from his lungs and pinning him down so that his mouth was filled with dirt. People were running. Boots kicked into his ribs and landed hard on his back, one on his head.

And then a huge hand dragged him up and carried him under an arm like a child. Carral could feel the crowd seething around him, pushing them right and left. People screamed and cursed.

"They're throwing cobbles!" Kai yelled almost beside him.

And then they were out of the running stream of people who had been tumbling them this way and that. Ufrra set Carral down on his feet, where he collapsed against a stone wall, shaking like a frightened child.

"I'm unhurt, Ufrra. And you? Lord Carral? I though we'd lost you there."

Carral could not speak for a moment, but spat out the bitter dirt that choked his mouth and drifted into his airways.

"I think I have a loose tooth where someone's boot landed on my jaw and I'll have bruises all across my back and the backs of my legs. River save me, how they pounded over me."

"Well, it's less than those men-at-arms received. When the cobbles started landing they made a charge to frighten their assailants off, but those farm boys and villagers stood their ground. The Prince's men retreated instead. We shall not find a boat here. There was a panic to get out of the riot and several boats were overturned; the rest were set out into the river and won't be easily enticed back."

Carral could hear Kai shuffling about on the stumps of his legs.

"It looks safe enough now. If our poor barrow wasn't shattered and our meager belongings scattered to the winds."

Carral heard Ufrra's resolute footsteps set off. There was not the slightest sign of ambivalence in that walk. His soles hit the ground firmly, and his step was measured and constant. No shuffling or scuffing. When Ufrra set off to do something, he went with all his will.

The terrible screeching began and in a moment had reached them.

"Well, it could have been worse," Kai said. "It looks like it will hold me until we can make repairs. Gather me some fresh straw from that stable, Ufrra. I'm sure the ostler won't mind—for a cripple's comfort.

"I see no choice now but to go along the riverbank and hope to find someone with a boat or to wave down some passing craft. I haven't much money to offer, I'm afraid, and the cost of passage will be high this day."

"I will pay our way," Carral said.

Ufrra's certain footsteps returned.

"Ah, hay! We have hay instead of straw this day. We are rising up in the world. Just lay it in, I will soon squash it down. And what is that? A walking stick! Do you hear, Carral? A walking stick for you. I hope no one misses it soon. Let us be off. We can't expect poor Ufrra to take us, one under each arm, and jump the River Wyrr. We need a boat. Even a raft would do."

The awful screeching began again, and Kai called out the hazards of their path. Very soon they were on a narrow track that ran along the riverbank. Carral could hear the sweet voice of the river and the rustling of the familiar poplar leaves overhead.

At a cottage, they bought a chicken for their dinner as well as potatoes and beans. Along the way they found children picking wild strawberries and bought a small basketful.

"We shall eat well this night, Lord Carral," Kai said. "But then I should stop using your title if we are trying to keep your identity secret. Do you mind?"

"No. Call me Carral, or any other name you like."

"Well, I have always liked the name Mellisa, though it does not really suit you. No, we'd better call you Carral."

They made a camp beneath the stars near a little running spring and cooked their meal over a bed of coals. Kai sipped the "tea" made from his herb. It had a slight soporific effect, Carral thought, for the man always became quiet afterward and his vowels became noticeably prolonged.

"Who was this man Crowfoot you spoke of?"

Carral heard Kai stir himself. "Crowheart. Rabal Crowheart." Kai fell silent a moment, and Carral began to wonder if he'd fallen asleep. "Crowheart is a mystery. He is old, though not so old as Orlem and me. I first began to hear rumors of him after Wyrr's children died—for so we thought at first. It was not until later that we realized the river sustained them. He traveled the countryside with his flock of crows, his clothing festooned with the bright gifts they brought him. He is an odd-looking man, at once both striking and comical. Farmers and villagers knew him for his skill with animals—though skill does not begin to describe it. He would heal their flocks and calve their cattle. He was said to mend the bones of horses, which I did not believe until I witnessed it myself." Carral heard Kai shift on the grasses Ufrra had cut to cushion him from the ground. He gave a small moan.

"I did not much care to meet him for some time until I heard two things about him. He was once set upon by highwaymen— rather desperate highwaymen they must have been, for Crowheart had no wealth or possessions—and the crows defended their master, leaving two of his attackers blind. Another time he was chased by a mob of superstitious villagers, and they claim that he led them into some strange wood none had seen before, and when they made their way back out they were many furlongs farther from their homes than they should have been.

"Then I knew something about him. He was one of those who traveled with Sainth. Traveled with him long enough that he began to see the secret paths opening, and recognize them. I sought him out, and he was not easily found for he ranged all over the land between the mountains with no pattern to his wanderings. But I did find him, one day, almost by accident.

"I went to him, telling him my horse had cholic, which it did not. I traveled in a cart then. But he knew me, or quickly recognized me for what I was. When I first saw him he was in a barn, the rafters and haystack punctuated by roosting crows: his constant companions. Of his life he would tell me nothing, though he was amicable enough, if peculiar. He would not eat eggs or the flesh of animals, saying that they were not in this world to sustain him. Milk and cheese he would eat, calling them gifts, but I believe he would have starved before eating animal flesh. I told him of our purpose—to stop the children of Wyrr from returning— and this seemed to interest him a little. He was of some help once or twice, but mostly he seemed content to wander and find his living among grateful villagers and small landholders, for he shunned the nobility.

"He was somewhat interested in my stories of the children of Wyrr, but nothing else seemed to matter to him much. He did not desire wealth or even a roof, nor were women of any particular interest that I could see; though in his youth that might have been different. Friendship meant little to him, even the friendship of those who, like him, lived long.

"I heard stories of him now and then and a few times our paths crossed, apparently by happenstance. But then he disappeared, and after a good number of years had passed I came to believe he might have died. And then I met him again. He was sitting at a crossroads, as though waiting for me. He had found something in his travels. Something he had never heard of, not in song or story. It was a great flooded area he called the Stillwater where ghosts appeared by night. 'It is a place of strong magic,' he whispered. I had never seen him so. Why this place excited him this way I could not fathom, but finally he admitted to me that it was the resting place of the brother of Wyrr.

"Now, the story that Wyrr had a brother named Aillyn was something that many regarded as fable. Many, even among the learned, did not even believe that Wyrr had existed. Sainth, however, had told me that Wyrr was indeed his father and the most powerful sorcerer in an age of sorcerers.

"Why Crowheart was so intrigued by this place, I did not understand. 'It is a maze,' he said, 'where men wander until they die. Before Crowheart, none escaped, but I have learned its secrets, now. The dreams of Aillyn appear at night, ghost warriors fighting terrible battles. Kingdoms won, and kings fallen. Loves and songs and journeys and sorcery. It is a frightening place but I have not been able to tear myself away. There are secrets there, Kilydd, secrets we have never dreamed of.' But I was not tempted and let him return alone. As I said, he was strange, and it was not really surprising that something like this would fascinate him."

Carral heard Kai sip his elixir.

"And everyone now is in this place—the Stillwater?"

"Well, not everyone, but at least two of Wyrr's reborn children, with Caibre likely close behind Sianon. And now Orlem, and likely Rabal Crowheart."

"What do you expect of him?" Carral wondered. "It seems this Crowheart has little interest in the affairs of this world. You said he was of little help before."

"Yes, but no one knows the Stillwater like Crowheart. It was his dark fascination. It was the first and only passion that had taken hold of him, and such single passions get a grip on a man like no other. I would not have sent Orlem off to such a dangerous place had I not thought Crowheart would be there and be of some help. Theason claimed to have met Crowheart on the edge of the Stillwater only a few years ago. Crowheart is like Orlem and me: hidden from Death by the magic that clings to us. It is from serving Wyrr's children for so long. If we are alive, he will be, too. That is what I think."

Thirty-eight

They had passed through a fog so dense the boat's bow could not be seen from the stern, and now found themselves in a drowned forest, as alive and verdant as any wood near the Vale. The smooth gray trunks held aloft a canopy of green, moss-hung and lichen-cloaked. Beneath the reaching branches of the trees a sparse underwood grew up from the water, and sword ferns thrust up here and there. The water was as clear and cool as water from a spring. To their relief, the biting insects had all but disappeared, and they had seen no snakes or other animals that had dwelt in the swamp.

"It is too much like the forest of stone we passed through for my liking," Fynnol said.

"These are different trees," Baore said, "and fully alive, but they're all strange to me." He pointed. "That appears to be some kind of oak, but I know of no oaks that grow in the water." Baore twisted about, trying to take in the whole scene at once.

Elise had gone over the boat's side, and stood with her blade in the water, still as a hunting heron. For a long moment she did not move, a slight wind rustling her blond hair, roughly tied back. Then she raised a hand and pointed.

"Alaan is this way now. He's moving." She remained still as stone, like someone listening. "But Hafydd is still hidden from me." She shook her head, anxiety clear on her pretty face. "I don't know how near he might be."

She clambered back over the boat's side, dripping, and they went on, Elise urging them to hurry.

"But is Alaan going back the way we've come?" Cynddl asked.

"Yes, almost." Elise dried her sword on her vest. "I fear I'm not as sure at this as Hafydd might be."

Cynddl twisted around to look back at Tam, who, along with Pwyll, was taking his turn propelling them along with a pole. "Hurry, Tam! If Alaan leaves the swamp before we find him there'll be no way out for us."

Tam and Pwyll redoubled their efforts. Trees appeared in the fog, and they steered around the boles, though at times the mist was so thick that they were obliged to slow, for the trees would loom out of the mist so close that Elise would have to fend them off with her hands.

Elise cut a long, fine slit in the surface with her blade, her eyes closed and head cocked to one side. The day wore on and dusk settled, no sunset or warm evening light. Instead the dull daylight appeared to be absorbed into the mist and dark water. Nightjars began to cry overhead, and the frogs and insects began their songs, quieter here away from the swamp. Silhouette islands passed, like the tops of hills in a flood.

They were forced to stop and wait for the moon to rise, for the drowned forest was too dark to navigate by night. The moon finally floated up into the watery sky, where it cast a thin light down among the trees and onto the tendril mist.

Elise went into the water again and thrust her blade into its moonlit skin. She nodded. "North," she said, having a clear sense of direction for the first time that day, for the sun had been hidden by the mist.

They set off at once, taking turns at the poles, no unnecessary speech. No one knew where Hafydd might be, which kept them constantly anxious.

"Do you see?" Fynnol hissed, his hand snapping out, a finger thrust into the thin mist. Tam nocked an arrow. He squinted into the mist that swirled and thickened then blew away in strands. There was movement more than there was form. Tam almost wondered if it was nothing but imagination and fear.

"But they appear to be on horseback."

"Make no noise," Elise whispered.

In a moment the movement was lost in the dark and mist.

"Who was that?" Baore whispered after a while. "Hafydd?"

Elise shook her head. Tam could see how she gripped the gunwales, and her face was ghostly pale in the moonlight. "No, not Hafydd."

"Who, then?"

"I don't know. Let us hope we have no reason to meet them." She pointed with her sword, and Tam thought her hand trembled. He also thought that she was not telling them what she knew—and he wondered why.

The fog clung to trees, here and there; shredded skeins of wind-blown wool. Prince Michael slogged on, so impossibly tired he'd begun to see things, things moving in this haunting landscape—a forest drowned. But when he looked more closely, and blinked his eyes several times, they were only trees and mist and shadows.

Two hours earlier Hafydd had suddenly stopped, his blade in the water, and then sent them in a new direction entirely, pushing them to make more haste. As usual, he offered no explanation for his decision.

"On that island . . ." Samul Renné said. "Do you see?" He pointed off into the forest where a bit of solid land arched out of the water, crowned in trees. And there the Prince saw movement.

Men!

But the men on the island spotted them at the same time and

rushed to take up arms. For a moment they stood peering into the mist at Hafydd's company, who stared back.

"Sir Eremon . . . ?" one of the men called.

"They are ours!" Hafydd said almost in triumph. He turned then and smiled at Prince Michael with the most obvious pleasure. "They have captured my whist!"

"But were we not seeking a sorceress?"

"We were, until my whist drew nearer. I thought at first it might be a ruse to lure me away from Sianon, but look . . ." He pointed with his sword, his stern countenance almost gleeful.

The Prince looked away. He could not bear to see Hafydd gloat.

They all went splashing ashore, the Prince so tired he wanted to fall on the ground. But instead he forced himself to walk over to the rough encampment the men had made. There, on a soft bed of moss, lay Alaan, blue-pale, his limbs thrown out limply, like he no longer cared for comfort. He was dead, the Prince was sure. Kneeling down, he put a hand before the slack mouth but could feel no breath.

So you have already escaped, Michael thought. *No making a fool of Hafydd this time. No leading him on a merry chase.*

Hafydd stood over Alaan. "He is not dead!" he said firmly.

"I'm afraid that he is." Prince Michael stood up, looking at the limp figure lying before him.

"No! Not here! Not in this place!" The knight looked around desperately. "There is water. He will escape me again!"

Hafydd crouched down and put his hand on Alaan's chest. "He still breathes," he said with relief. "But this will not do. He cannot die here. There can be no water, either standing or running." He looked about as though he would find a suitable spot for Alaan's death.

"Build a fire," Hafydd said. "Who has something dry to cover him?" The knight glared up at Prince Michael, who stepped back in alarm. "We must keep him alive—I will not have him escape into the waters again!"

Thirty-nine

He felt the rise and fall and the soft lapping of water across his face, his chest. Beside him, his arms moved gently to the rhythmic swell; down and up, down. There was no sun, only a muted gray, like a fog-filled eye.

The gentle rhythm of his movement lulled him so that thoughts would not wholly form. Who was he? Who?

Perhaps I am a leviathan, asleep on the breathing sea, dreaming that I am a man. Perhaps.

Time lost its focus, and he drifted without name or purpose or even a sense of where he left off and the sea began. Perhaps he would have drifted thus until time ran still, like a frozen river, but a change in motion disturbed his peace. He was jolted each time the sea let him down.

He opened his eyes. It seemed to be the cusp between dusk and night—neither dark nor light. A stone quay lay near, and he had floated onto a shelf or step just below it. With some effort he raised himself, falling onto the dry, gritty stone. He lay there panting, the world spinning and tilting.

Alaan? Was that who he was? But no, there were other memories . . . Sainth. He had once been called Sainth.

A terrible grinding sound shattered his thoughts. Part of the stone cliff seemed to be moving, swinging out.

Death's gate!

He knew it now. Some age ago he'd stood here, and the nagar had come to him, slipping in through the tear where his life seeped out. But there would be no nagar this time. He looked up at the gate, grating open, a stain of black cast down on the stone. It crept toward him, a dark tide. He tried to back away, back into the lapping waters, but could not.

"Death awaits you, child of Wyrr," said a wisp of a voice, soft as a leaf falling. "He sits upon his black throne like a shadow among shadows. Like the dark between the stars. Long you have eluded him, but now his servants will cast you down on the cold stone at his feet, like an offering."

Alaan turned his head and found what looked like a thin rag of fog upon which some silver light reflected. Was that a face? A hand outstretched? Troubled eyes, gazing at him hungrily?

"And what are you?" Alaan asked.

"I am Aillyn, the brother of Wyrr. Or so I was." He glanced up at the gate, which continued its movement, shaking the ground.

"And how is it you are here?"

The eyes appeared to blink. Alaan could see the face a little now—gaunt and grim.

"Because I need something of you, nephew. I will give you back your life for . . . But where is my stone? Was it not given to you?"

"I refused your herald's 'gift,' old man," Alaan spat out. "What did you think you could offer me? You were my father's enemy. Why would I do anything to aid you?"

"Because I thought you wished to live, and because what I had to propose should have come to pass a long age ago."

The terrible grinding stopped and Alaan heard whispering within, and anguished muttering.

"I do not trust you, old man. You who smothered everyone and everything so that only you might breathe. No, Sainth will find another. And I will go the way of all men. I shall not bring you back to this life. Come through the gate with me, as you should have done when your true life ended."

"Ah, you are brave, nephew—brave and foolish—but Death cannot see me," the old man said, his words insubstantial, hardly a whisper. "And I cannot pass through his gate, as I am less than alive, though not yet dead. Now you shall see what no living man has seen—the Dark Kingdom. May you not find an age of torment."

A scurrying of feet on stone, whispering like wind through an empty window. The patch of mist drew back, then stopped, the face gazing into the darkness, fascinated and fearful.

They will come and carry me in, Alaan thought, *into the night from which none return.* He closed his eyes, unwilling to look upon Death's servants. He lay still, fighting for each breath. A part of him would tear away, he knew. Sainth would go back into the waters, back into the Wynnd, somehow. He braced himself, expecting to feel something akin to having his heart ripped out.

But there was nothing. The ghost of a cry, far away. Whispering like wind through the trees, water over stone. Alaan opened his eyes to find a sea of flame rising around him, blue-green and cold as the river.

A fire was kindled and Alaan laid near its heat. Some rough bedding was found and he was covered as warmly as they could make him. Hafydd set half a dozen of his men-at-arms to gathering dried grasses that grew on the peaks of the islands, and when they had enough, he twisted a rough coil and laid it in a circle around Alaan and the fire. For the second time he set a circle on fire, and Prince Michael was glad to find himself outside this one. Hafydd stood over the ring of flame, muttering words the Prince could not quite hear, or perhaps not understand. The fire within the circle grew, and suddenly the flame jumped to Alaan. The Prince leapt forward to strip off the flaming bedding but a black guard grabbed his arm and held him back, saying nothing.

Alaan moved and moaned like a man in agony, the flames covering him completely now. Twice he cried out, and then began to convulse.

Prince Michael closed his eyes. He would have saved him if he could, but there was nothing that could be done. Hafydd had won.

The horror of the scene seemed to draw him, and he opened his eyes to see the flame burning low and flickering out. Hafydd had fallen to his knees like a man struck down on the field of battle. For a moment he swayed over Alaan, as though he would fall.

The Prince realized then that Alaan showed no sign of being burned. He lay still, untouched by the flames. The blankets that covered him were not even singed by the heat. And then he opened his eyes, giving his head a little shake. He smiled.

"Ah, Brother . . . you have come!"

Hafydd raised his head with some effort. "Do not think you will escape me again," he said. "I shall take you away from this place of water and see an end to you . . . again."

"That is where you are wrong, Brother, for you shall never leave this place. Only I can find the path out—no other. And I have no intention of leading *you* anywhere. Look around you, Brother." Alaan raised a hand weakly. "See your new kingdom—for you shall never rule another. Kill me, if you will. That will see the end to all your ambitions." Alaan laughed. "I would rather have managed this without being trapped here myself, but no matter. You shall not lay waste the land between the mountains in this lifetime, that is certain."

"You cannot frighten me with lies," Hafydd said, but Michael thought he heard doubt in his tone.

"And I don't need to," Alaan said, fixing his gaze on Hafydd. "You are in Aillyn's lair, Brother. No one has ever found their way out but myself, and a man-at-arms I sent back, hoping to entice you into coming after me. I didn't really think it would work. But here you are. You have ways of discovering if I'm telling the truth. Apply them and you will see."

Alaan looked around. "Prince Michael? How sorry I am to see you! You didn't deserve this!" Alaan tried to prop himself up on one elbow but his strength gave way and he fell back. "Could someone bring me water? I have a terrible thirst."

Hafydd staggered to his feet, pulling his sword free of its scabbard. He swung it up over his head and seemed poised to cut Alaan in half where he lay, but instead he let forth a scream that echoed through the drowned wood, echoed with centuries of anger and malice. He spun to one side then and slashed viciously at the nearest man—one of his own guard—who dove aside.

Hafydd stalked off toward the crest of the island, muttering and cursing under his breath. He hadn't gone ten paces when he stopped and pointed with his sword at the man lying by the fire— the man who called him brother. "You will not stay in this place, Sainth! I know you! You could not bear it. No, you will weaken before me, and then we will come to an arrangement. You'll not last a month, Alaan." He pointed at one of his guards. "Tie his hands and hobble him. Two guards will stand over him at all times. He is never to be out of their sight, not even for the blink of an eye." He turned toward Prince Michael. "Bring him water. You can serve as his nursemaid. At least you'll be useful in this." He strode off over the crest of the island and was lost to view.

Prince Michael found a drinking skin and filled it. When he returned to the fire, he had to rouse Alaan, who had fallen into a stupor. He helped him drink, unsettled by how weak the man was.

Alaan tried to smile at him. "He's no fool, Hafydd," Alaan whispered. "He thinks I will try to escape and leave him here, and that I will convince you to aid me. That is why he has put me in your charge. But I will dwell here the rest of my life before I will unleash Hafydd on the land between the mountains again. I'm sorry, my Prince, but that is the price we are forced to pay."

Forty

Orlem gazed at himself in the pool, a large man dressed in a style of armor not seen in centuries. Good armor, though, made link by link by Womma Fourfingers, a man who knew his business. His blade was even better—it had been forged by Corlynn, and there was not another like it in all the lands, nor had their been for many hundreds of years. For a man of normal size it would have been a two-handed sword, but Orlem could wield it with one.

He took the carefully folded map from the pack that lay at his feet, feeling a slight tingle as he touched it: Kilydd's magic. Orlem didn't think he could find his way to the Stillwater without it. He'd not spent nearly so many years traveling with Sainth as Kilydd had, and he was not so able at finding his way in the hidden lands.

Kilydd. He shook his head. To think that he went around now in a broken-down barrow, sitting upon a pillow of straw, like some pig being wheeled to market. Kilydd, who had once been loved by Sianon and had been great among the great. All his wealth and comforts had been renounced to travel with Sainth. Orlem, of course, had done the same, as had many others, but even so, Ki-lydd's fall had been far. And now there was no place for him among men—which was the fate of those who traveled with

Sainth. Once you had seen the beauties of the world, even a castle appeared a prison.

A leaf fell into the water. Little rings rolled outward, Orlem's reflection reeling like a drunkard's vision.

Were they mad, taking up this fight again? Two old men—older than old. He did not look elderly, he knew. Oh, he did not look young, that was certain—no maiden would lose her heart at the sight of him!—but he could be taken for an unusually hale and strong man in his sixth decade. He had seen more centuries than that.

Orlem spread the map on an almost flat rock and examined the sure, dark lines that Kilydd had laid down. He must go up now. That's what Kilydd had told him. Up over a pass, and then down to the Stillwater, where Crowheart was rumored to still dwell—if he were alive.

He folded the map, returned it to its place, and shouldered his pack again, settling the straps in place. He did not carry much for he was adept at taking his living from the land. A pot, he carried, a small axe, flint, a length of rope, blankets, some food, though not much. A bow of yaka wood. This he had seldom used to slay men, for he was a swordsman of legend, but it was useful when something was needed for his dinner pot.

He began the ascent of the ridge, picking his way among the outcroppings of rock and thicker stands of trees. The underwood became more sparse as he climbed. It was an ascent of some hours, rugged and steep in places, but finally he reached the crest, where he gazed out over the great swamp, half hidden beneath a blanket of mist.

"Well, Crowheart, what kind of forsaken home is this you've chosen?"

He dropped his pack and sat down on a rock, drinking from the skin he carried. An uneasiness grew inside him and his gaze kept turning back the way he'd come to the green sunlit lands. He could walk back to his valley in little more than a day. But then so could

Caibre. He'd cut off Kilydd's legs for being an ally of Sainth. What would Caibre do to a man who had served him once and then became the ally of his enemy? He shivered at the thought.

Forcing himself up, he lifted his pack and set off down the slope to the swamp below. A breeze brought the odor of the place to him—a stench he thought too much like death. The scramble down went quickly, the shore of the Stillwater appearing through the trees, the mist swelling out over the solid land.

"Well, Rabal Crowheart, now to let you know I am here." Orlem set his pack down, doffed his armor, and took up his axe. There were a number of dead trees standing along the margin of the swamp, and these he addressed with a will. He soon had such a blaze going that he couldn't stand within ten feet of it. He couldn't help but think that it looked like a pyre. Scrambling back up the slope, he cut down a large section of flowering vine that was strangling a substantial fir. This he threw on the blaze, and a stink like a rotting beast filled the air. He walked a good distance upwind of the smoke and sat down, drawing on his water skin.

"Kai's friend claims this will draw you. Let's see if it is true."

Orlem waited late into the afternoon, feeding his blaze now and then but wondering if Kilydd was mistaken and Crowheart was gone. Sleep called to him but he fought it; he had the habit now of a short sleep in the afternoon, and knew such self-indulgence would no longer be possible. To keep himself occupied, he took out his whetstone and honed the edge of his blade, not used now in many lifetimes of men. It had not dulled, though, nor had he ever let rust touch it. His ancient armor and this blade were all he had left to remind him of the past. A past so remote that he hardly felt he had lived it at all.

Had he really cut his way through a pride of lions sent by Caibre to kill him? What beasts they had been! Bigger than natural lions and far more fierce. He had been first through the shattered gates of Geahmor Wal, and faced the rage of Andor Shotte and his sons. How many men had fallen that day! And he had been the lover of

Sianon—for a time. He did not forget that either, though he no longer dwelt on it as he once had.

What was she like now? Different, Kilydd had said, kinder, more womanly.

Something croaked and he looked up to see a crow gazing at him from the low limb of a tree.

"Have you turned into a crow, then, Rabal?" Orlem asked, and laughed.

The crow took to wing, flying to pass directly over him, but it turned suddenly and something bounced off a rock at Orlem's feet. He had to search around a moment to find it, but there it was: a ring set with a fine stone.

He stood up and searched around for the crow, which had returned to its perch. "Well, it is a kind offer, my good crow, but I am too old for marriage, while you are young and a beauty still."

The crow bounced from its branch and into the air, where it circled overhead and then set off into the mist-laden marsh. He could hear it crying as it went. In a moment it was back, alighting on its slender perch and cawing at him as though scolding a bothersome child.

Orlem found his pack, sheathed his sword, and walked to the edge of the Stillwater. He was reluctant to go farther. Kilydd had said there was no map that could lead him out. Only Sainth or Crowheart might do that, and Sainth might already be gone—or dead.

The crow hopped into the air again and flew, crying overhead.

"All right. All right!" Orlem said. "I will come." And he plunged into the foul waters of the marsh.

It was slow, difficult going. The crow circled overhead, disappeared into the mist, then returned. It was already late in the day when Orlem began, and he wondered how he would go on by dark. Would the crow fly after sunset? It seemed unlikely, but then it was not a natural bird. It was one of Crowheart's and capable of any surprise.

The day grew more and more gloomy, and finally Orlem realized the sun had set and darkness would soon be upon him. What would he do then? Follow the crow by the sound of its voice? He thought this swamp might be a dangerous place by night. The bugs swarmed about him but did not alight, though this small benefit of having once traveled with Sainth would not extend to the greater beasts. They would not fear him. Twice he had seen snakes that day, and he was sure there were many more lurking in the reeds. He had tried to stay clear of those, keeping to open pools and channels.

Something large and dark appeared in the mist and fading light. A tree, he realized, and in a moment he waded ashore upon an island and walked up its spine. Here he found the remains of a camp—one that looked like it had been abandoned quickly and recently. The crow settled on a tree, croaked at him once, and began to preen its feathers.

In the failing light Orlem looked around: there was a small supply of firewood, enough for one night; a pile of waterwillow bark; some bloodied cotton—a shirt torn into a dressing. He bent down to look at a long root growing across the ground, but a touch caused it to crumble into dust. He followed it a few feet and then realized it made a circle.

Orlem stepped quickly outside it and cursed. A sorcerer's circle! Had Sianon found the wounded Sainth and performed some enchantment to save him? But Kilydd had said Sianon had not come into her full understanding. Could she perform such a difficult enchantment already?

In the last of the light he searched the ground once more. There had been many men here, their tracks walked over by others. It was impossible to read anything from this. Only the bloodied dressing and the waterwillow bark told him anything at all.

Orlem built a fire some distance from the sorcerer's circle and took out a bit of the food he carried. He knew there would be fish and turtles aplenty in the swamp, but he wasn't inclined to go seeking them by night. He wondered if lighting the fire was wise, but reasoned that Crowheart's emissary had led him here and it was unlikely that the crow was leading him into danger.

The first torch appeared in the mist, bobbing up and down as it went. Orlem was on his feet and out of the fire light in a instant, his sword in hand. Other flames appeared, moving in procession through the mist. There was no sound of men, though the numbers were great. Then they began to pass by the island, an army of men going east, pale and silent.

"Ghosts," he muttered. "An army of ghosts!"

He'd never imagined an army of such size: knights on proud chargers, company after company of archers, and foot soldiers by the tens of thousands. It was a long time before he realized that they were not going to battle but were in retreat. How could an army of such size be defeated? But it was so. They went bearing their wounds, silent and sorrowful.

"And they went to their deaths," Orlem whispered to no one. "All of them."

Even in the battles of Sianon and Caibre he had not seen armies of such scale. These ghosts could only have served Wyrr or his brother, Aillyn. Who else could have commanded so vast a force?

For a long time Orlem stood watching the solemn procession, but finally he could bear it no longer and turned back to his fire. An old man sat there staring into the flame, a sword across his knees.

"The last army that rose against Aillyn," the old man said, "marching to its doom."

Orlem had raised his sword to guard without thinking. "Who are you?" he asked.

"I am the Herald of Aillyn, Orlem Slighthand, and I have come to warn you. Death is abroad in this land. I have seen him riding with his servants, their terrible hounds hunting before them. Like a shadow, he is, his steed like the darkest storm on a moonless night. He is looking for those who have long escaped him, for Death does not care to be thwarted."

"And what of you, Herald of Aillyn? How long have you escaped Death's embrace?"

"Longer than you, Slighthand. Longer than any but my master and his brother. But I am hardly more than a ghost myself, dwelling here, in this netherworld. What is it you seek in Aillyn's dream?"

"I look for a man named Rabal Crowheart."

The gray old man looked up at him. "Crowheart," he said bitterly. "Long he slept within the bole of a tree, guarded by spells none could break. He stirs again now, and he gathers his feathered army. Be sure you are his friend, Orlem Slighthand, for if he looses his crows upon you, they will take out your eyes and feed your heart to their young."

"I will take the risk. I have no choice."

"And what is it you want of Crowheart?"

"What is it you want of me?"

"Your life, if the answers to my questions displease me. What is it you want of Crowheart?"

"I seek a child of Wyrr."

"There is more than one child of Wyrr in the Stillwater. What do they seek here?"

"I wish I knew, Herald of Aillyn. They have returned from their long age of sleep and will spread ruin wherever they pass. It is in their nature. I hope to stop them."

"Then you must be mightier than you appear, for the children of Wyrr are powerful and ruthless. How will you stop sorcerers with your small magic?"

"I will tell you honestly that I don't know. That is why I've come seeking Crowheart, or Sainth himself. Perhaps Sainth will know a way to send his brother and sister through Death's gate."

"Perhaps, but he is almost before the gate himself."

"Sainth . . . ?"

"He is wounded, and the wound has grown foul from these dark waters. Death rides toward him, drawing nearer with each word we utter."

"Then I must go!"

"Go where? Into the dream by night? No, better to wait until morning. There are ghosts afoot that you should not want to meet, and the beasts that stalk the swamp by night are fearsome. Your guide will not stir, I can tell you." The old man stood, sheathing his sword. "I will give you leave to travel the Stillwater and seek Crowheart. But tell Crowheart this: his time here is drawing to an end. Aillyn will tolerate him no more. And you, Orlem Slighthand, do not tarry in this place. Do what you must and get out or you will die here and join the wandering army. As to the children of Wyrr . . ." He paused for a long moment, as if choosing his words with particular care. "Tell them . . . tell them there are matters greater even than their hatreds and their craving for endless revenge."

The old man stepped back into the mist, and in two paces disappeared from sight.

Orlem stood, staring into the fog that seemed to cling to the trees on the edge of the firelight. He did not think he would sleep that night.

Forty-one

Lord Carl saw the keep in the distance, down the long line of sullen soldiers who followed the twisting road. Did retreats always look so, he wondered, men defeated in spirit as well as on the field?

Was it this same army that had landed triumphantly on the Isle of Battle and built its bridge, easily driving off the small resistance that had been offered? One thing was certain: the information he had given the Renné had preserved the Isle of Battle for them. They would certainly never have had an army in place in time. His family would be owed something for that—if they lived long enough to collect.

Lord Carl A'denné had not slept peacefully since he had spoken that night with Lady Beatrice Renné. He felt as though all the joy had been drained from his life that night. He went around now performing a poor imitation of himself, hoping none would notice, living in constant fear that he would be discovered and the A'denné name erased from the land between the mountains. And what he'd done this day had increased the chances of being discovered a thousandfold. Would Kel Renné have rescued him? he wondered.

The Prince of Innes had commandeered a small keep not far removed from the canal where his forces had been defeated that day. Lord Carl and his father had rooms there, as had most of Prince Neit's principle allies, many of them traditional allies of the Wills.

He dreaded his arrival there. Certainly the waiting would be over quickly. If his act of reckless nobility had been witnessed by any of the Prince's men-at-arms, he would no doubt be called to account this very night. If the Prince did not send for him by midnight, and likely his father as well, then he would have dodged an arrow.

As he rode through the gate of the small keep, his mouth was dry and he was almost shaking.

"Are you injured, your grace?"

"What?" Carl looked down to find his equerry staring up at him. He had not seen the man since he had crossed over the makeshift bridge on his way to fight. "No. No, I'm not injured."

"Where is your armor, sir? And this is not your horse."

"Everything was left behind so I could swim the river. Only my blade I preserved by floating it on a fallen branch."

A dozen times he had crossed the river, bringing men with him who could not swim. Each time he crossed he could see the anxious faces of the men who awaited him. How many could he take before the Renné found them? And the Renné had found them, sooner than he'd hoped. So many men had been lost there on the bank, though a few managed to surrender, casting down their arms and falling to their knees, hands up in supplication. The sight had torn his heart, and he had fled wiping tears from his eyes. All the good, noble fighting men who had died that day!

He dismounted, the cobbles jarring him all the way up his spine to his neck. Had he lost his balance dismounting? His attendant kept a hand on his arm all the way inside, and Carl did not try to shake it off. He sank down onto his bed when he reached his room.

"Can I be of service to you, your grace?" A pause. "Sir? Shall I tell your father you are safe?"

"Yes. Do that."

"I can bring you food, sir. Hot water is in scarce supply but I might find you some—enough to wash if not to bathe."

Carl hoped that he nodded.

The servant placed a goblet in his hand, and he took a long drink of the dark wine. It tasted bitter in his parched mouth.

"Shall I bring you a supper here, sir?"

"Yes, please do."

The servant was bustling around, laying out clean clothes. "I'll see what I can find."

Carl was not certain how long he sat there, his mind as blank as the sky. A maid came in with candles, alerting him for the first time to the arrival of darkness—or almost. He rose and went to the window. Dusk was far advanced, and he could still see stragglers coming down the road and the wagons and drays that bore the wounded. He thought he had never seen so melancholy a sight in all his days. Like a funeral, though it was men's hopes that had died.

A soft knock brought his attendant back, followed by a small troupe of servants bearing a tray of food and buckets of steaming water. A tiny metal bath was set by the window and the water sloshed in.

"It will cool just enough while you eat," his man said, placing a jug of wine on the table beside the plates and bowls.

Carl had no want of food but ate to please his equerry, who had gone to such efforts on his master's behalf. It did him some good, though, as did the wine.

Alone, he undressed and slipped into the small bath, folding himself to the size of a child. He poured water over his head with a dipper, letting it run through his hair and over his face. So that had been his first battle. Some thousand men must lay dead upon the field, and many more would die of their wounds in the days to come—all because of him. All because he had given the Prince's plans away to the enemy.

The Prince was *his enemy,* he reminded himself. The Renné might not have been the A'denné's natural allies, but they were better than the House of Innes and the Wills. At least this current generation of Renné were better.

At a strong knock on the door, he started.

"Yes?"

"Carl? Are you well?"

"I am well. I am also in the bath. Give me a moment."

He crawled out and dried himself quickly, throwing on clothes. He was dragging a comb through his hair as he opened the door, to find his father's worried visage staring at him.

"Tomas said you were not yourself."

"Tomas exaggerates. I'm perfectly hale, given the results of the day."

His father came in, putting a hand on his shoulder. The older man stared at him as though he'd not seen his child in many years.

"I thought you might be lost this day. So many were."

"I was almost among those but swam the river to escape."

"So I've heard. I've also heard it was not so simple. You carried a dozen men across before the Renné found you, the last with arrows falling all around you."

"Thank the river you taught me to swim. I should have been captured this day, or worse." Should he tell him about saving Kel Renné? Was it safe to even whisper such a thing here?

His father nodded. "You've made yourself a hero to the men-at-arms, Carl, and this will serve you well in the weeks to come. Risk your life for them and they will do the same for you. I must go now. The Prince has called for all his generals. It only remains to be seen who will take the blame for today's debacle. Rest. You need rest. Do not be ashamed of that. All who fought feel as you do."

But he did not rest. He lay awake through the night's early darkness. The smell of smoke from the many fires of the fighting men drifted in his window, but there were no songs this night, no laughter. He could almost hear the whispers passing from fire to fire: so-and-so had fallen, and this man too, and that. Another was not expected to see the sunrise. He could imagine the litany of names, like an endless poem of loss and sorrow.

A pounding at his door startled him, and he realized he had dozed at last. Before he could rise, three men-at-arms in the purple of Innes burst into his room, and he knew then that the life of Kel Renné had been bought at great cost.

The Prince of Innes and Menwyn Wills stood by the cold hearth, each appearing to have drawn himself up to his greatest height so they might look down upon Carl A'denné. Menwyn Wills betrayed nothing in his face but a studied calm. The Prince, however, was pale, his jaw taut and eyes narrowed.

"He said it was you. He had no doubt."

"And where is this man who accuses me of such treachery?" Lord Carl said, drawing himself up as well, clipping off his words like a man wronged.

"He is wounded and under the care of a healer. Do you deny it?"

"Of course I deny it. But if your man is not a liar then there is a traitor among our men-at-arms."

"I'm sure he is not a liar, and he is certain it was you. He recognized you, and your bay horse with the white face."

"I have such a horse but this day rode a dark bay into battle, for my other had gone lame. You may ask my equerry and any number of others."

"But they are all your people, Lord Carl," the Prince of Innes said.

"Am I to be convicted because my own witnesses serve the A'denné? These were the men I fought among this day. And they are all honorable men. If I were a traitor they would be the first to tell it."

Carl almost breathed a sigh of relief. He had changed his horse as the battle began. Whoever had seen him rescue the Renné was mistaken about the horse: easily done in the heat of battle.

"Perhaps they would," Menwyn Wills said, "but you know, Lord Carl, that such things must be looked into with care. It seems almost impossible that the Renné should land an army with such timing. There is a traitor among us."

"There could certainly be a spy, just as we have our own people among the Renné. But perhaps that does not even explain it. Perhaps they merely landed an army here as a precaution. I have heard that there was a Wills banner flying on the hilltop and a rider dressed in evening blue. Lord Carral might have come with a force to secure his domain. It would have been a wise thing to do. We might simply have underestimated them."

Carl immediately regretted this, for he could see that Menwyn Wills and the Prince would rather believe there was a traitor who had warned the Renné than admit their precious plan had been in error. But then, perhaps, when they repaired to their rooms alone that night, doubts might begin to wear away at their confidence, as doubts tended to do in the hours of darkness.

"Carl," said his father, "look at me. Swear to me that you had no part in this."

"I swear it, Father. Do you doubt me as well?"

"Never, but our position has been difficult. Some might think we were inclined to support the Renné rather than our natural allies." He turned to the Prince of Innes. "But who would be foolish enough to trust the Renné? They have betrayed their closest allies in the past. They have murdered their own. Indeed, there is no end to their treachery. So I say my son is innocent of these accusations and your man is mistaken. It was a battle. Many men wore the crimson of our family, and several rode bay horses. I will bring these men to you, and your informant might look at each one and see if he can find the guilty party."

The Prince of Innes looked down at the floor. "Well, yes," he said, "but this man passed over not an hour ago." He looked up suddenly. "But when Sir Eremon returns he will want to speak with you. He has ways of hearing lies, Lord Carl. I have watched him do it before. Good night."

★   ★   ★

Carl sat staring out the window at the fires that had burned low. Around some fires men still gathered, dark, silent forms standing their vigil. He breathed in a deep draught of the night air. He felt that he should thank some benevolent spirits for saving him that day. The man who accused him had died. Couple that with his mistake about the mount and it was enough to cast doubt on the man's claims. But not enough to erase all doubts about him, Carl knew. They would be watching him now. Finding ways to pass news to the Renné would be much more difficult and dangerous.

The handle to his door rattled, and he turned to find his father letting himself in.

"Have you no candles?" his father asked.

"I wished to sit in the dark."

His father came and stood behind him, where he sat with his arms upon the windowsill.

"You must get away before this Eremon returns," his father whispered. "He is a sorcerer."

"Do you believe that? I think it worth the risk of staying."

"No, it is not. The man is a sorcerer. I know much about him. His name was once Hafydd and he served the Renné, only to be betrayed by them. His hatred is turned toward them now, but I fear he will turn on his allies if the Renné are defeated. You must escape before he returns."

"Then we must both escape."

"No, I will stay. The Prince does not dare to subject me to the sorceries of Hafydd. His other allies would rebel. But you must escape so that the A'denné name does not disappear from the land between the mountains."

This sentence took the wind from Carl's lungs. "You will be found out, Father," he whispered. "You will accomplish nothing dead."

"Perhaps, but we cannot go on as we do. If we merely escape and go to the Renné, they will give us nothing, for we have nothing to offer them. We will be lucky to have our estates returned if the Renné triumph. Once you have escaped I will denounce your treachery and disown you. I will call you a coward and traitor to my name. But with this scorn I want you to know I am saying that I am proud of you, my son, that I admire the man you have become, and that I love you more than my honor, estates, or even my own life. You will know that."

Carl felt his father's large hand on his shoulder, and he reached up and took it in his own. Before him the fires blurred as though a sudden rain fell, though the sky was bright with stars.

Forty-two

Dawn was but a diminishment of darkness. Orlem rousted out his crow as soon as he could see a dozen feet and the bird scolded him angrily before setting off again into the watery air.

Orlem sloshed through the fetid waters, lost in fog. After all his years with Sainth he had an uncanny sense of direction, yet here all points of the compass seemed the same to him. The sun was never bright enough to give away its position, as though it had burned low, like a guttering candle.

The day brightened only a small amount, but the fog thickened, as though in response. The first tree was a surprise, but the forest was utterly unexpected. Orlem stood for a moment looking around at the mist-hung branches, the moss covered trunks. A breeze clattered through the leaves, casting a rain of droplets down upon him and across the opaque surface of the water. He skirted a stand of sword ferns, green blades waving at him in the breeze.

"Well, this is not the Stillwater I was expecting. It is a forest in flood."

Yet the ground never dried, as he expected; instead the waters became clear and cool.

The crow would wait for him, alighting upon a branch and calling out like a foul-tempered guide. After some hours Orlem waded ashore on what he guessed was an island, and the bird went on before him, up the slope among the rocks. At the crest he found a dark-haired man sitting by a small fire, a pot of thin broth bubbling on the blaze. Crowheart.

"I'm glad to be shut of that guide at last," Orlem said. "Poor manners he has." He realized that a host of silent crows perched in the trees, gazing at him with glittering eyes. It was a little unnerving.

"My crows have little patience for men."

Orlem smiled, though to Crowheart perhaps that was not a jest. He looked much as he had been described; dark of hair and beard. He wore the skins of dead animals, which Orlem knew he always claimed not to have killed. The bright trinkets brought to him by his crows were strung all about his jacket. Nearby a wide-brimmed hat lay on the ground. He was a solid man of good height, his face cut into sharp creases by years in the sun. He was brown-eyed, like his servants, and seldom looked at you when he spoke.

"I've been waiting for you," Crowheart said, "though I wonder what brought you here?"

"Kilydd found me, saying that the children of Wyrr were abroad again and that Caibre pursued Sianon to this place, where she came seeking Sainth."

Crowheart did look at him then, twisting around where he sat.

"Abroad again?" he said. "The children of Wyrr have been dead for centuries."

"Not dead, Crowheart, for they went into the River Wyrr, where their father sustained them. They became nagar and lived on. Now they have made bargains with men and a woman and are abroad again, though what they want none of us know."

Orlem could see Crowheart absorbing this, like a man who'd received a sharp blow. "Then that man I met was Sainth?"

"You've met him? Do you know where Sainth is now?"

Crowheart turned back to the fire, then shook his head. "He was pursued to this place by men-at-arms. Six of them, crafty and skilled in arms, found us and took him from me. I could not best them alone, not in a short time, at least. And then my crows told me you had come."

Orlem cursed aloud. "We can only hope that Caibre will not let him be killed here, where water lies everywhere."

Orlem stood looking down at the strange man, who didn't look back, but stirred his broth and added some small sticks to the fire. He wrapped his sleeve about his hand and lifted the pot by its bail. Dipping a crude wooden spoon into the broth, he brought it to his lips. "Almost," he pronounced, and returned the pot to the flame.

Orlem crouched down, bringing himself nearer Crowheart's height. "What are you doing in this place, Rabal Crowheart?"

It was not a question the man had an immediate answer to, it seemed, for he thought long. "I came here seeking a vision, and to study the dreams of Aillyn, which become manifest by moonlight. In my vision I saw what I thought were descendants of Wyrr, wandering lost among events they did not understand." He turned his head a little and looked at Orlem from the corner of one eye. "And I saw you, Orlem Slighthand, though I did not know your name then. You came to the Stillwater, and we had a task to accomplish. Would you die to see Sainth set free?"

Orlem hesitated. He felt a cold flush like a precursor of fever. He nodded. "I would."

"Then let me tell you something more of my vision. The children of Wyrr have not returned at this moment without reason. Aillyn and Wyrr are both restive. They stir from their long sleep, disturbed by dreams. Why they need the children of Wyrr, I do not know, but Sainth . . . Sainth must be preserved." Crowheart took up a stick and prodded his fire. "Sainth has some larger part to play in all of these matters, Orlem Slighthand. Aillyn dreams of him. But Death seeks him." Crowheart looked at Orlem from the corner of his eye. "Few dare stand before Death and his servants, and not waver."

Orlem could find no words for a moment, and then said, "An old warrior, calling himself the Herald of Aillyn, came to me last night and said that Death and his servants were abroad in this place."

"He is a half-crazy old man, as lost as many who wander here, his master drowning in a dream. But about this one thing he was not mistaken. I have heard the horns of Death and the baying of his hounds."

"The old man said to tell you to leave this place and not return."

Crowfoot gave a small laugh, rubbing a large hand over his slick, black beard. "If we die in this place, Orlem, we will never leave." He bent forward and tasted his soup again. "Join me. They say the hunger of ghosts is a torture."

Forty-three

Samul Renné appeared, wet to the knees, with a pair of glistening trout suspended by the gills.

"How fares your charge?"

"He rests," Prince Michael said. "He has need of it."

"He has need of sustenance, as well." The nobleman held up the fish and smiled. "And you could use a little yourself, I think."

The Renné laid the fish down on the grass and carefully raked out the coals of the fire, fanning them until they glowed red. He disappeared and returned with two forked sticks that he drove into the ground and supported with other bits of wood and stone so that they leaned over the fire. Taking out a dagger, he split the fish and shoveled out their guts. With a nod to Michael and the two guards standing by, he went down to the water, scraped away the scales, and washed the fish clean. Michael came down and filled a drinking skin some feet away.

The Renné looked around casually. "Hafydd is weak from making his enchantments," he said low. "There could be no better time."

Better time for what? Michael wondered. Hafydd's guard was reduced but still numerous. "Three men are not enough," the Prince said, keeping his attention on filling his skin.

"And we are but two."

"Hafydd could deal with us without his guard, even weakened. Trust that I know what I'm saying."

Returning to the fire, Michael put water on to boil and made tea from waterwillow that had been gathered. Samul Renné spread the dead fish out and, with a small lattice of twigs, suspended them within the crotch of his sticks.

"They do not cook quickly thus, but they cook beautifully."

"It seems an odd skill for a nobleman and man-at-arms."

"Oh, many the night my cousins and I spent out beside some remote stream or lake, fishing and sleeping under the stars—or with the bugs, as we used to say."

Oil from the fish began to drip on the coals and flame quickly erupted, sending up a small cloud of acrid smoke. Hafydd's two guards began to cough and repositioned themselves on the other side of the fire.

"Might I have some water?" Alaan said, his voice hoarse and faint.

Michael brought him a skin and helped him drink from it. Alaan looked terribly ill, his cheeks sunken, face glistening and deathly pale. He twisted his head a bit to find Hafydd's guards.

"I might have made a mistake," he whispered, leaning nearer to Michael. "I thought I'd found this place by accident in my wanderings, but now I've had time to think, a moment of lucidity. There are things in this place Hafydd should not learn. Better he make his war in the land between the mountains . . . What am I saying?" He blinked his eyes several times as though something were in them. "I hadn't time to think. No time. I meant to lure Hafydd here. To trap him, but I didn't understand the dangers." He coughed, and Michael gave him more to drink. He helped Alaan lay back down and arranged his coverings. The face that stared up at him was definitely fevered, the eyes intensely bright in the fading light. Was he raving?

"Beware . . . " Alaan closed his eyes and a tremor ran through him. "Beware an old man who calls himself the Herald of Aillyn. If he should appear, you must put an arrow in his heart—then let no one touch him, not even Hafydd. And take nothing that he offers you. Do you hear? No matter how sweet his words, how reasonable his explanation. But we must slip away. Hafydd will follow. That is his hope, that we will lead him out. But he must never reach the land between the mountains. Never."

And then Alaan closed his eyes. Michael sat back on his heels, near to tears. What could one make of that? Was there any part of it that was not raving? How was he to decide what course to take when Alaan raved like a madman? Who was to guide him? He looked around at the darkening wood, the fog drifting through it like a shroud, and thought for the first time that he would die here. That he would never escape.

They left their boat tied to a tree and waded through the clear waters of the drowned forest. How strange a place, Tam thought. How utterly strange.

"Certainly Hafydd is here before us," Pwyll said.

Elise did not answer but only shrugged, keeping her attention ahead, where her blade told her Alaan waited.

"Does he know you're here?" Cynddl asked quietly.

"Hafydd need only hold some iron in the waters, but let us hope we have outdistanced him in our boat."

"There—do you see?" Fynnol pointed into the fog.

An island rose up, looking much like all the others they had seen—a rocky knoll lifting out of the waters to a height of four or five fathoms. It was treed with birch and black willow, with an underwood of stoneberry and sword fern.

"Men-at-arms, several of them," Cynddl said.

"And wearing black surcoats," Fynnol whispered, "or so it appears in this dull light."

They hid themselves behind the bole of a massive tree, staring out. Cynddl clambered up into the branches but could see little more. The mist would waft in, obscuring the island for minutes at a time, then it would thin, but never enough to reveal the whole island at once.

"I fear it is Hafydd," he whispered. "There are two or three not wearing black, and what might be a man lying by a fire. If that is Alaan, he has two guards standing close by and he does not move."

"Cynddl should stay in the tree and watch," Elise said, "but the rest of us should go back so we can't be seen. Hafydd knows I will come here, eventually."

Leaving Cynddl hidden in his bower and armed with bow and sword, they waded back to their boat.

"But what will we do now?" Fynnol asked. His hands moved jerkily as he spoke and he kept glancing back toward the island.

"Into the boat," Elise said.

But once aboard, she asked them all to turn away, and in a moment she slipped into the water, her clothes tossed over a thwart. She surfaced to look back at Tam.

"I will see what is to be seen: if Alaan still lives, and how Hafydd has placed his guards. He will expect us to try to rescue Alaan, so we must be wary and cunning as crows."

She swam off, as unlike a crow as Tam could imagine, but as lithe and swift as an otter.

"I never dreamed that the water spirit who haunted us down the length of the Wynnd would become our traveling companion," Fynnol said.

"She is more than a water spirit," Baore said, glancing at his cousin and then at Tam. "You do not begin to know her."

"Let us keep silent and watch in all directions," Pwyll said. "Hafydd might have guards posted or moving among the trees. Keep your bows ready, Tam and Fynnol. And Baore, take up a pole. We are near Hafydd now, and there is no one more dangerous in the land between the mountains."

"If we only were in the land between the mountains," Fynnol

sighed, but he took up his bow with only a slight tremor to his hands.

Elise slipped through the water, surprised again by how natural it felt, as though she had spent centuries as a creature of the depths. It was her intention to circle the island and see what could be seen. Caibre might sense her but, unlike Sianon, his centuries in the River Wynnd left him with a hatred of water, and he would not take to it willingly.

The wood grew dim as she swam, dusk spreading its dark wing over the Stillwater. Caibre had placed his few guards carefully in the shadows of trees, so they were difficult to even sight, let alone shoot with a bow. It was unlike him to travel with so small a company—he who valued his life above all else. She began to look up into the surrounding trees, thinking that he might have placed men there, but she could see none.

She ventured a little nearer the island as the dull daylight of the Stillwater drained away. Where was Caibre? Perhaps he hid himself out of fear—but fear of what? The Renné might still be seeking him with their cursed ally—the man who called himself a Knight of the Vow—but why would Hafydd fear them? What if Hafydd had not used his sorcerer's circle to hide himself from her but from the Knights? Could that be?

One of the guards walked down to the shore and waded out into the clean waters to fill a water skin. *Prince Michael!*

She slipped beneath the water, surfacing so that he stood between her and the island. When her head broke the surface, he started back but then composed himself and continued filling his skin.

"I feared it was you Hafydd was following," he whispered. "Can none escape this place? Is that true?"

"None but Alaan," she said quietly.

"Elise, Elise! Alaan is terribly ill. Hafydd brought him back from the brink of death but he does not heal. His fever has returned and he raves and trembles like he will shake himself to death." The

Prince looked like the young who had gone to war—aged in some mysterious ways that one could not explain.

"Does Hafydd realize where we are? He will die here if Alaan is not saved."

"Who knows what that madman thinks?" Michael hissed. "Why doesn't he save Alaan if we will be stranded here otherwise?"

"Because Caibre was ever a servant of Death, not a healer. I might be able to save Alaan, but we must somehow get him away. Where is Hafydd?"

"He sleeps, with his black guards hovering over him. It seemed that the making of his sorcerer's circles exhausted him. I could try to kill him now but it would certainly cost my life."

"It is unlikely you would manage it. He is more careful than you realize and would almost certainly kill you. How many are his guards?"

"Twenty-one, plus Beldor Renné. Samul is with me, I think. The rest succumbed to the swamp . . ." He reached up and touched a wound over his eye. ". . . or its inhabitants."

"You are covered in small wounds!" She was surprised by her distress.

"Yes, a flock of wrathful crows fell upon us and tried to take out our eyes. Not everyone survived."

"We saw crows. They followed after us calling and calling."

"You were lucky they did nothing more. These crows were ferocious."

"And unnatural," she said, "for natural animals will not attack a child of Wyrr. They sense their power."

"I don't know what to do, Elise. Alaan is raving and I . . . I am lost in this place."

"I can't stand against Hafydd, Michael; not yet. He is too strong for me. I need time to prepare—time, and an army."

"Alaan will not live that long."

"But perhaps I can draw Hafydd's attention for a moment. Could you get Alaan away—we have a boat."

"Perhaps. There is also a small boat on the island. We might get him into that, but Hafydd can track him with his blade." He glanced up toward the island to see if any watched. Elise thought he looked haunted, and felt her heart go out to him. He seemed too young and beautiful for this task.

"Yes, but we will worry about that after. If there is a sudden attack on your island, get Alaan to the boat if you can, and go into the Stillwater. If nothing happens between now and morning, meet me here again at dawn. Can you do that? I will wait behind that tree."

"I will try. Luck to you."

Elise reached out and took his hand, pressing it briefly to her lips. She watched him wade clumsily through the thigh-deep waters. She wondered at this ache she felt. It was different than the desire she had known before—more certain, more knowing.

Did Sianon feel so about every comely young man she happened across? Perhaps so. Look what had happened with Tamlyn Loell: a youth from a place so small and unheard of that it was on no map she had ever seen. A young man from the Wildlands.

But Tam was something far more than that. She sensed it. He could lead armies if he so desired. She had seen that kind of presence before. A quiet certainty that made others listen and take note. What he would do with his gifts, she did not know. She suspected he wanted nothing more than to go back to his home in the north and fade into obscurity. At least that was what he had wanted before their encounter on the grasses. She wondered if she had the power of Sianon. Would Tam love her now? Pity him if he did.

She had not swum far when movement in the growing darkness caught her eye. It was not one of Hafydd's guards, as she feared, but a man-at-arms robed in gray. *A Knight of the Vow*. Elise fought an urge to murder him where he stood. Sianon's hatred of these Knights was boundless and frightening.

He was alone, watching the island, hidden in the underwood. She struck out silently, searching away from him, and in a quarter of an hour had found an island peopled with silent, gray-robed men and a company of Renné in their sky blue.

How like Hafydd's silent guards these Knights seemed to her, their colorless robes only a shade away from black—dusk rather than night. It had been the Knights that had found and kept the smeagh safe, guarding them with their lives, which meant the children of Wyrr had the Knights to thank for their resurrection, though Elise was inclined to curse them.

She realized how much Sianon feared the Knights who had ensnared her for so long. And now they had allied themselves with the Renné. For all that Elise Wills believed there should be peace between the families, she distrusted and feared the Renné still.

You are not being wise, she told herself. These men were the natural enemies of Hafydd. Perhaps the self-proclaimed Knights of the Vow even had the means to defeat Hafydd, for they had once known much of the nagar and their weaknesses.

Hafydd was nagar no more, she reminded herself. *He is at once more dangerous and more vulnerable.*

She continued to swim, trying to count the men gathered in the quickly falling darkness. They would light no fire that night. But what did they plan? Would they attack Hafydd? It seemed the Renné were more concerned with their cousins—unable to see beyond their own concerns, as she would expect.

Of course, Toren Renné was with them, and his interests were greater, his vision wider. Certainly the Knights would have told him who and what Hafydd was.

She circled the island, quite close to the shore now that darkness was falling. If any did see her, they would think she was an otter, nothing more. She would be gone beneath the surface before any had time to draw a bow.

"I claim no knowledge of sorcerers, Gilbert, as you know, but have we traveled all this way only to turn back? What of justice? Samul and Beldor are murderers and traitors. I vowed I would bring them back."

"And you would have, Lord Toren, if they had not allied themselves with Hafydd."

This was the man who claimed to be a Knight of the Vow! And the
other was Toren Renné. She could just make them out, standing on
the shore.

"We would only be asking to die in this place," the man went on.
"I am capable of sacrifice, and so are my Knights, none more so,
but not without purpose. If we are to give up our lives, at least let
us sell them dearly."

Elise could feel the tension between the two men. It reached her
like a ripple on the water.

"What of this artifact you carry? Does it have no powers? No
use but to find the children of Wyrr?"

Elise felt herself rise up a bit in the water.

"None that I know of, and I don't want to find out more.
Smeagh are not objects one toys with. The Knights of the Vow
never learned that. They thought to enslave the nagar, but the
smeagh brought about their downfall. This dagger should be
destroyed."

"Then why have you not done it?"

A'brgail took a long breath and let it out in a heavy sigh. "I don't
know, Lord Toren, that is the truth. Because the children of Wyrr are
abroad again and it might yet have some purpose. I don't know."

Elise could hear in this man's voice the conflict he felt. Did he
really have a smeagh? Who could it have belonged to?

"You tell me that Hafydd will murder Alaan. Will you do nothing to stop it?"

"I will do everything in my power, but you do not understand,
Lord Toren. Hafydd will not kill Alaan here where there is water.
The sorcerer with whom Alaan made his bargain would only slip
back into the water and become a nagar again. No, he will not kill
him here. So we will follow and wait our chance. We can do nothing more. Hafydd would destroy us if we attacked him now. Trust
that I know what I'm saying in this matter."

"I do trust you, Gilbert. I am only impatient. Impatient to have done with this and get back to the land between the mountains, where who knows what has transpired in our absence."

"But you may return to your home anytime you wish. Alaan's welfare is not your concern. I fear there will be no chance to bring your cousins to justice now. Not while Hafydd has them under his protection."

"I'm sure you're right, as much as it galls me to leave them. But I will not go back without you, Gilbert. If we are to be allies, then we will not abandon each other at the first sign of adversity. That is how we will keep the trust between us. Renné and Knights of the Vow have a history that we must overcome."

"All right, but I am concerned about your men. The Knights of the Vow bear much blame in this matter. We will not risk others to pay our debts."

The two men fell silent and then retreated up the slope. Elise swam on, wondering who else she might encounter in this strange wood. But there were no others, only her own companions, waiting in the darkness.

"Let us get Cynddl down from his perch," she said. "There is another island not far off. We might make a cold camp there."

Elise stayed in the water, clinging to the painter and taking them forward with a little help from Baore with a pole. In a moment they had Cynddl down from his tree and they set off through the dark wood. A watery and waning moon and a few dull stars showed through the mist, making haunting silhouettes of the overhanging trees, which seemed to reach down at them with branches like bones.

They beached their boat on rocks and went quietly ashore in the dim light. Tam thought a fire would have been welcome. He was hungry and tired, and sick of worrying that Hafydd would step out of the fog at any moment. He did not know what Hafydd could do, but Elise and Pwyll were both afraid of him, and two people more formidable would be hard to find.

Elise, who had dried herself and dressed, came up the slope from the water. No one seemed much concerned now by what she was—not that they really understood, Tam thought.

Baore still hovered near her, like a guard. The big Valeman had not spoken to him all day, though he had not spoken much at all. Still, Tam wondered if he suspected what had happened between Elise and him? He had wondered what had happened, as well. He suspected some aspects of Sianon's personality were asserting themselves, and she was known for her propensity for taking and then casting aside lovers—or so Cynddl had said. It caused difficulties in the past and would no doubt do so again. He felt guilty when he looked at Baore—not that the big Valeman had any claim to Elise's affections.

She sat down and told them what she had found and overheard, and a whispered debate began.

"We should go to the Renné and these Knights," Pwyll said. "We cannot ignore possible allies here, no matter what their last name or history. We must rescue Alaan. And as soon as possible. It is a wonder Hafydd has not killed him already." Pwyll sounded tired, his voice rising, revealing his concern for Alaan.

"The Knights of the Vow enslaved Sianon when she was a nagar and would do it again," Elise said. "I would never trust them—"

"But what shall we do?" Fynnol interrupted, clearly uninterested in hearing Elise rage against the Knights.

"Hafydd intends that I take Alaan off the island. I could see it by the way he has stationed his guards, and he is supposedly exhausted and asleep. Alaan is the only one who can lead us out of the Stillwater, and Hafydd hopes I can heal Alaan. Hafydd will let me do so and then follow us out when we leave, planning to kill us once free of this place. That is his plan." Tam could see Elise shake her head in the pale moonlight.

"But this is a dilemma!" Cynddl said. "We can hardly leave Alaan in Hafydd's hands—especially if he is gravely ill."

"No," Elise said. "We must save Alaan. Without him I cannot

hope to stand against Hafydd. It is now all a matter of when he will strike. Hafydd must kill me before I come into my powers, but if he attacks too soon, I will not have healed Alaan and Hafydd will be stranded here."

"But can you heal Alaan now? Have memories returned that will let you do that?"

Elise took a long breath. "I don't know, Tam. I really don't know."

They sat in silence for some time, the frail moonlight illuminating ghosts of mist that hovered around them as though listening, drawn to the living and all their turmoil.

Cynddl cleared his throat.

"There are so many tales gathered here that a story finder can hardly begin to pry them apart," he began. "But I've been piecing together a story—the story that seems to lie beneath all the others, coloring them like paint bleeding across a canvas. This place was once called 'Aillingbrae'—'Bay of the Golden Sun'—and was the end of a long finger of the ocean that pointed inland. It was a place of surpassing beauty then, and people dwelt along the shores, fisher folk for the most part. But Aillyn made his spell that sundered the lands, and the Aillingbrae was inundated, its people swept away. The Stillwater was what remained—the great marsh we have found." Cynddl shifted, his dim form hardly a silhouette in the shadow of a tree. His voice seemed to echo out of this shadow as though the land were speaking to them.

"Elise told us that Aillyn's son self-murdered to escape his father, but she did not say that Aillyn blamed his own people for this, claiming his son had been murdered. He had long been suspicious of others, and now he unleashed his armies upon his own people, driving them into the mountains or killing those who were not swift enough. The nobles of his kingdom raised an army against him, the largest army ever seen, but Aillyn was strong in sorcery and defeated them in a battle that raged for three days and nights. Now they march across this swamp every night, in endless retreat.

"Wyrr heard many disturbing tales of Aillyn from his son Sainth, with whom he was not yet estranged. Sainth led people out of Aillyn's kingdom into the land between the mountains, and they told tales of their ruler's madness. Wyrr despaired of his brother, but was powerless to stop him without bringing about a war so great that even more people would die. Instead, he spread a rumor that he'd discovered a stone that had belonged to his father—he found it around the neck of a swan swimming on the river. It was an object of immense power, and in it were locked the memories of their father, who had been a great sorcerer.

"Wyrr well knew his brother's jealousy and knew that Aillyn would want this stone for his own. What Aillyn did not know was that the jewel contained a spell, so subtle that it was all but undetectable. Wyrr called the large emerald the 'Jewel of Remorse.' Toward the end of the lives of the two great sorcerers Aillyn stole the jewel, but when he hung it around his neck he slowly became aware of all the horrors he had caused, and felt the pain of those he had murdered and wronged. He lies here in misery to this day." Cynddl stretched out his legs. "And that is what you feel in this place. The horrifying remorse that followed Aillyn beyond this life."

Elise would not try to steal Alaan away until the depths of night. She was not willing to take the chance that Hafydd had other plans. They set one person to watch the island and Elise told all the others to try to rest. They might have need of all their strength.

Tam was not sure if the others slept. They lay in the various places where the ground was not too rocky, rolled in their bedding. Tam for one could not sleep, though he was deeply tired. He lay looking up at the blurred stars and moon, wondering if they would ever get out of this place alive.

"Tam," came a whisper.

It was Elise. She appeared out of the shadows, bending over him. Without saying a word more, she pulled his blanket aside and lay down beside him, shifting until she was pressed close, her head on his chest. For a moment they lay like that, very still, listening to the breeze in the branches.

"Tam? Why did you journey down the river? What led you from your home in the north?"

It was not a question Tam could answer without thought, for it seemed now that he had set out on the river for one reason, but larger currents had taken hold of him, sweeping him off and offering no choice in where he traveled.

"It is odd," he whispered. "I left the Vale to find out what had happened to my father, in some strange way. Oh, I knew what had happened to him. I think I had to meet the kind of men who would kill a stranger for no reason. I had to see them for myself. I know this must sound strange, and I can't explain why."

"You wanted to meet such men and have revenge."

"No, I wanted to meet them and find out what had happened to their humanity. Where had it gone? What had worn it away? Or perhaps I merely wanted the nightmares of brutal, faceless men to go away. It is like being afraid of a serpent, yet fascinated by it at the same time. What makes it act as it does? Can it kill me or can I learn to master it, to master my fear?" He stopped to puzzle out his own emotions. "I did not leave my home for one reason only. I knew my place in the Vale, knew what I might do there, what I might accomplish. Who I might marry, even. But could I find a place in the larger world? Do you know what I mean? Was there something more that I might accomplish?"

She patted his chest. "Was there a greater man in here. Someone who might make his mark in the world."

"Something like that."

She shifted herself, running her fingers over his chest. "In the world I was born to, Tam, they have a term: a drawing room ornament. It is used to describe the most foolish and worthless of the nobility—though the truth is the term might be very widely applied with some accuracy. It has been my fear that I would never be anything more."

"And look where it's led you," Tam said, and felt her smile.

"Yes, to intimacy with a rogue from the Wildlands."

"I'm not a rogue."

"No, Tam, you're not. But let me answer one of your questions for you. In this world, you might do what you want. Oh, it might not be easy, and little will be gifted to you, but you might find a place among the great if that is your wish. You can accomplish much."

"Can I escape this place and go back to the Vale?"

She didn't answer immediately. "If we live through these next few days—then, yes."

He felt her hand take hold of his shirt and ball it into her fist, and then a tear soaked through to his chest, and then another.

Forty-four

Hafydd loomed out of the mist, a dark and silent presence, and Samul Renné started back, his hand going to his sword before he could stop it.

Hafydd raised his own sword hand, palm out. "Be at peace, Samul Renné," he said.

Samul had been gathering firewood in the faint moonlight, but had dropped it all with a clatter when Hafydd appeared.

"I have been watching you, Lord Samul. You and your cousin. One could do better than rely upon him. . . . His passions lead and his mind merely stumbles along behind, like a lame mule."

Hafydd had positioned himself so his face was in shadow, a tall, unmoving silhouette, like a standing stone.

"You, however, have your passions on a tight rein. You speak seldom, yet you have much to say, you are still when others act without purpose. You disappear into the crowd and let others come to the fore. You are wary and careful as a fox, caring nothing for personal recognition. Men think they know you but they do not."

A ghost of mist wafted between them so that it seemed Hafydd faded. The mist blew off slowly and Hafydd reappeared.

"Men might never even think to ask what Samul Renné could want. However, I have considered this question with some care. Samul Renné would be the hand behind the throne, unseen, unheard, largely unknown, yet the power all the same. Let some other know the adulation and the jealousies of the courtiers. Let him also risk the daggers of assassins. Samul wants only the power to rule and make difficult decisions. And you deserve to do that, for you have the wisdom of the watcher, the knowledge of the listener. Your cousin Beldor should be relegated to cleaning your boots and keeping your stables." Hafydd paused but still he did not move. "Let us be candid with each other, Lord Samul. I will rule. The Wills family will be swept aside, as will the house of Innes. But my kingdom will be too large for me to rule alone. I need someone I can trust, someone raised in a noble house who understands the workings of the nobles and the necessities of rule. That could be you. Yea or nay?"

Samul stood as still as the specter before him, his hand on the pommel of his sword. He felt that he was hearing a man speaking the utter, simple truth for the first time in his life. Hafydd would rule. None could stand against him. The Wills and even the Renné would be swept away. Only Hafydd would remain—Hafydd and those who served him.

"Yes," he said, "I—" But Hafydd raised his hand and cut him off.

"Prince Michael plans to whisk Alaan away. You will go with him. Out in the wood a woman awaits him. She is a sorceress and will try to cast a spell over you. Beware; she loves no one. She is loyal to no one. Her name is Sianon and she will heal Alaan, who will then lead Sianon and her companions out of this place. When he is ready to do that, open this." He held out his hand, revealing a hard leather case smaller than his palm. "You will find a small blue egg. Crack it open and I will come. You will kill your cousin for me then, to seal our bar-

Sean Russell

gain." He held up his hand again. "If you cannot do this thing then I cannot trust you. If I cannot trust you then I will kill you. Do you understand?"

Samul nodded.

Hafydd turned and went back into the mist, leaving Samul standing with one hand on his sword. A hand trembling and slippery with sweat.

Forty-five

The squealing of Kai's barrow wheel had become so aggravating, like something sharp jabbed into a rotting tooth, that Lord Carral had taken to walking farther and farther behind. Without Kai to warn him of changes in the path, he stumbled and would force himself to catch up. Then the irritating screech would dig its way into his brain again and he would find himself dropping back, going more slowly. As someone who loved music, this dissonant squeal was more than he could bear.

About midday they stopped by the edge of the river, so Ufrra could kindle a fire to brew Kai's elixir.

"I met a man-at-arms once who had lost his lower leg," Carral said when he sensed Kai's brew had taken effect. "He told me that he could feel it still, as though part of him had disappeared but still remained. 'Ghostly,' he called it, even saying that part of him dwelt in the netherworld of ghosts. He wondered if it would begin to creep over him and the rest of him would slip slowly into the ghostly world."

"Well, that is a comforting story," Kai said. "The thought has occurred to me. But what a world of pain this netherworld must be! Without my blood lily I should die of the agony. I have only a small supply of it, Carral, and if I can't soon get more. . . . Well, then you will hear my moans and my curses."

"But do you not trust Theason to bring you more?" a voice asked.

"*Theason?*" Kai said loudly, and Carral heard him turn quickly around.

"Yes, 'tis Theason. And just in time," said the soft voice. "But you are far from the Green Door, good Kai. It is the greatest luck that Theason should find you."

"Luck?" Carral heard Kai say softly. "We are on the banks of the River Wyrr, my friend, and it will take you places you don't expect."

Carral heard something soft plop to the ground and then the sound of cord being drawn.

"Ah, Theason, I should make you a hundred maps for this! What brings you, now, to the Isle of Battle? Don't you know war has come here?"

"Theason has seen people on the roads and many boats crossing the river—even rather unriverworthy rafts. Is that what it is? A war?"

"The Renné and Wills, or the Prince of Innes to be more precise. They have gone to war over the Isle."

"Well, it is all very strange to me. Are their estates not large enough? Have they not the finest horses and castles? What do they want, Kai? Theason does not understand."

"Kai does not understand either," the legless man said. "Though once I thought I did."

Theason cleared his throat. Carral was certain he shuffled his feet. "Well, Theason should find his tick weed, then, and go before someone makes off with his boat."

"You have a boat?"

"That is how Theason travels, good Kai, as you well know."

Kai laughed. "Of course. But can you carry us across the river? Is it large enough?"

"The river is very large, Kai."

"No, is your boat large enough?"

"Yes, yes. Certainly, but who is your companion?"

"Good Ufrra you know. This is Carral, who cannot see. What a company we make; blind, dumb, and legless. You shall be the only one whole among us, Theason."

Theason apparently did not know how to answer this. The sound of the river running and the high, liquid peeling of a skylark were heard. A gusting breeze shivered through the leaves of a copper beech.

"Is it far to your boat, Theason?" Kai asked gently.

"Not far, no, but farther by barrow, for the way is not smooth. We should be there before sunset. Perhaps we might cross before the stars return. Come, I will lead you."

Carral went on all that afternoon, walking with Theason, who warned him of dangers and steadied him when he stumbled. He did not seem to be a large man, but he was surprisingly strong and walked on without need of respite. Carral could not help but smile at Theason's habit of referring to himself by name or in the third person. What did it say of the man's inner life that he almost never used the personal "I"?

"You have known Kai for some time?" Carral asked.

"Many years. But the blink of an eye to him, for he has lived long."

"So I gather. He is a sorcerer of some kind?"

"Theason does not know all of Kai's story, for it is painful for him to tell—his past has been cut away, like his poor legs. It seems that good Kai once served a sorcerer and from him learned this ability to make maps that lead . . . elsewhere. From association he gained his longevity, for sorcerers lived many lives of men and sustained those loyal to them."

"It is almost too remarkable to believe."

"Yes. It is a remarkable world, good Carral. Theason has seen a white hart drinking from the river at dawn, trees that grow flowers like yellow trumpets, a vine that tangles the unwary and then devours the flesh with blossoms the color of blood; black swans, Theason has seen, and a lion and her cubs, though too close. He has traveled over lakes where no man has ever dwelt or perhaps has ever been, the waters so clear that you could see the fish swimming far beneath. It is a world so inspiring of awe that one can lose one-self in it, for one man seems so insignificant."

They went on a little farther and then Theason said very quietly, "It is agony for Kai to travel like this. What has brought him so far from his usual haunts?"

"I don't know him well enough to answer," Carral said, trying not to tell an outright lie. "Perhaps you should ask him."

It was dusk when they found Theason's boat, pulled up in a stand of long grass and bushes. She had not been disturbed that day.

Kai was in need of his blood lily, so a fire was quickly kindled, which Carral found caused unwarranted frustration. He had begun to wonder what happened in the larger world—or perhaps it was the smaller world. Had the Renné triumphed or been defeated? Had war broken out elsewhere? Had the forces of the Prince of Innes crossed the river? It seemed unlikely, but being without news had suddenly made anything possible.

Theason and Ufrra slipped the boat into the water and put Kai and his barrow aboard. Carral was helped in and sat down on some soft bag, holding onto the gunwales to either side. He did not much like water and could not swim a stroke. He was sure that such a small craft as this seemed to be could upset at the slightest provo-cation.

"Where will you go?" Theason asked as he stepped aboard, the boat bobbing and rocking alarmingly, though Theason did not seem concerned.

"I don't know," Kai said. "Carral? Where must we go now?"

"To Westbrook," Carral said without hesitation. "All of my for-tunes wait there."

"I can take you there, but we must cross the Wynnd first and work our way up the bank where the current is less. Ufrra can use an oar, for it will be difficult for Theason to manage alone."

Carral felt, as they went out onto the dark, cool river, that he was leaving behind a terrible failure. He had gone to brave the same perils as the men-at-arms and had been driven from the scene of the battle, his guard likely killed, and he had wandered lost, fleeing the fighting in which he could do nothing.

What had Hafydd said? He could neither bear a child nor use a lance so he was of no use to any in this world. Or words similar to that. Carral hoped his vanity of riding with the knights would be quickly forgotten.

He listened to the night river; the calls of hunting owls, a loon, the frogs along the shore. A breeze sang down the valley, luffing his clothes like sails. A scent like new cut hay drifted with it. And then he heard a song from some riverman on his barge, deep and melancholy.

The night wore on and he slept as Ufrra and Theason bore them on. Several times he awoke to feel them still struggling against the current.

He awoke again at dawn, stiff in neck and shoulder and hip, from lying propped up in the boat. He worked his arm and shoulder.

"Is it morning?" he asked.

"Yes," Theason whispered. "The sun is about to rise, and spreads a glory of colors across the eastern heavens."

"You did not stop to rest?"

"No, the night was too beautiful for sleep, and Ufrra never tires. We are almost at the small isle that divides the Westbrook at its mouth."

"Almost at the Westbrook?" It was Kai. Carral could hear the man rustling about, probably stretching.

"Yes, there are still Fáel camped there," Theason said.

"Can you land us there?" Carral asked. "The Fáel are friends to me."

"The Fáel are friends to few," Kai said.

"Nevertheless, they know me. You will see."

Smoke drifted down to them on the morning breeze, and the

sounds of livestock. Carral had heard the tents of the Fáel described many times but still they were difficult to imagine. Sighted
people tended to describe objects in terms of other objects—all well
and good when you could see, but if you could not . . . Elise had
differed in this, he remembered, and felt a wave of anguish wash
through him. Reaching over the side, he trailed his hand in the
water. If only her hand would come into his.

"Perhaps the wanderers are gone," Kai said. "That boy is not
Fáel."

"Theason!" said a man who did not speak like a Fáel.

"Eber. What do you here, so far from Speaking Stone?"

"Llya has led me here. He has been waiting by the river with
hardly a rest, telling me that you would come."

"But your son has no voice," Theason said.

"That is true, good Theason. That is true. But he told me you
would come all the same."

Forty-six

Lady Beatrice drifted out onto the balcony like a ghost, Llyn thought. Pale as ice by moonlight, her gaze fixed on another world. When she did not speak right away, Llyn felt her eyes close and her throat tighten, like a loop being drawn closed.

"News," she managed. "I was told you had news."

"Yes, Llyn," Lady Beatrice say.

"It is Toren, isn't it? Something has befallen him?"

"No: at least not that we know." Lady Beatrice took a long breath. "It is Lord Carral. He was lost at the battle on the Isle—"

"I knew he should not have gone! It was a foolish—"

"You have not let me finish, my Lady Llyn. When I say lost, we do not know his whereabouts. He has been found neither among the living nor the dead."

"How can that be? Kel said he would guard him."

"And most certainly he did, but the guards were killed and Carral chased—perhaps taken, perhaps escaped."

"Then his family has him back."

"Perhaps, but it seems he was thrown from his horse after escaping the men who killed his guards. A huntsman was sent after him but his footprints faded away. Kel thinks he might still be wandering somewhere on the Isle of Battle or has gone to ground."

"The man is blind," Llyn heard herself say. "He can't cross a room that he does not know."

"He is more formidable than others think. He killed an assassin, don't forget, and I dare say the assassin knew his business. Kel thinks he is still on the Isle, though, which is worrisome as there are still parties of armed Wills and men of Innes at large."

"How in the world did Kel let such a thing happen?"

"It was merely bad luck, Llyn. I'm sure Kel was most exacting regarding Lord Carral's safety. A party of Wills came upon him and attacked. His guard fought to a man, and Kel thinks Carral's last guard fell after he had dispatched the final attacker. By then Carral had been driven away from the place where he was to wait and wandered off, lost."

"How long has he been gone?"

"More than a day, unless they have found him, which we can hope. My news is a little out of date."

"Some nefarious men have come upon him, I fear. They will rob him or ransom him back to the Wills." She felt tears welling up. The poor man, wandering through the daily darkness with no friends or servants. Certainly he could not survive. Even the Isle of Battle saw wild animals now and then.

"Llyn? They will find him. Kel has companies of men looking in every corner of the Isle. He does not think the Wills could have got him back across the canal, even if he did fall into their hands. I did not want to worry you with this but thought that you, of all people, should know. . . ."

Llyn felt herself taken aback by this. *She of all people?*

She felt a sudden urge to deny . . . what? She glanced up at Lady Beatrice, whose steady gaze looked down into the garden. Quickly, Llyn stepped farther back beneath the branches of her tree, as though she had been seen.

Forty-seven

He slipped out through the gate wheeling a slaughtered hog in a barrow. Torches made a shadow of his face beneath a disreputable-looking hat, and the guards missed him among the throng.

The encamped army smelled of cooking food, unwashed bodies, bitter smoke, and defeat. Lord Carl made his way to the cooking fires and spent an hour toiling for the master baker before slipping away. He crossed the camp to the banners of his family, which hung limp that windless night. The man he was looking for was not an officer or mounted man-at-arms, but a mere equerry, and an aging one at that. He had, however, served Lord Carl's family loyally all his life.

"There is no horse for you, your grace," the man said softly. "That is to say, we can't get one past the Prince's sentries."

"Then how am I to make off?" Carl hissed. "They will be after me by mid-morning. How long will it take to ride down a man traveling on shank's mare?" Carl wondered for a second if the man might have been corrupted after all.

"Many days, if you've cunning. There be a waning moon to light your road this night, and you should be halfway to the Isle by morning. Hide yourself by day. Cross the canal by night. But first we must slip you past the Prince's sentries, and that'll be no easy task."

They went first to a tent where the man found a sword and scabbard, and a small cloth bag which he carried as they made their way through the tents and across the encampment. The problem with the sentries, Carl knew, was that their function was not just to guard the camp from outside attack or intrusion, but to keep potential deserters in. To this end there were three rings of sentries. The *inner men* stood at their posts and watched the camp. Between these, fires burned to light the darkness. Beyond them a ring of riders rode a constant circle, watching for deserters or for any trying to infiltrate. Outside of this ring a second circle of sentries watched, and a second circle of fires burned. These *outer men* gazed out into the darkness.

The equerry led the way to the northern edge of the camp, and standing back from the guards he pointed out into the night.

"Do you see that small dark spot on the grass?"

"It looks like an ink stain . . . there?"

"Yes. That be a small scoop in the ground where a man lying flat can't be seen. Get you there and wait for the rider to pass."

"And how will I 'get me there'?"

"This sentry has a terrible thirst and can be too easily distracted from his duties by the sound of a sloshing bottle. I'll see to him. The outer sentries stare into the dark. Get you to the hole in the ground and wait for the change of guard, which will occur in less than an hour. When the guard changes, stand up and walk out as though you are going to your post. I'll cause a bit of a fuss here and no one will be looking too closely at you."

"It might work," Carl said.

The old man could not hide a smile. "Oh, it'll work, your grace. It's worked often enough in the past." He passed Carl the sword and pressed his hand as though he were a grandson, which made Carl smile.

Do I look so anxious? he wondered.

The old man took up station not far from the sentry and began to drink from his jug as conspicuously as possible. He had the sentry's attention immediately.

"What you got there?" the sentry demanded, sauntering over toward the old man.

"Bit of bee's nectar, if it be any of your business."

"You've a lip that'll get you in trouble, granddad, that's for certain."

The sentry took in the old man's clothes and stopped. "Oh, aye. Your master could be hearing from the sergeant-at-arms about you, drinking when none's allowed," he said, though without much conviction.

The old man laughed. "And what do you think the sergeant-at-arms and my master be doing this moment? Have a sip of this and forget your damned rules for a moment."

The man looked around quickly, not spotting Carl where he waited in the shadows. The old equerry moved so the sentry's back was to Carl, who did not wait a moment but shot out into the night, his eye out for riders. He was lying flat in the low depression in the ground in an instant, his heart beating like a war drum, hoping the old man was right and that he was not lying on the ground in plain view.

With his ear to the earth he heard the horse before he saw it. Carl had the sense to bury his face under his arm and even pull his hands into his sleeves. If the horseman spotted him, Carl knew he would have barely a second to leap up and cut the man from his saddle. Hard to manage before the man sounded the alarm but he would try. Otherwise he would be going back into the keep and into a locked cell from which he would only emerge to be judged by a sorcerer.

The rider went slowly past, the pace of his horse never changing. Three more horsemen rode by, the last horse lowering its head to sniff him, so close had it come, but the rider only pulled on his reins and cursed.

The hour sounded in the keep and the change of watch was called from man to man. Carl watched the nearest sentry pass, and there was a sudden shouting and cursing. Carl jumped to his feet and walked slowly out as though taking up his post. He looked back only once, when his station had been reached, and then kept going out into the night. One sentry and an old equerry would be in some trouble in the morning. Drinking while on watch was an offense punishable by flogging—and giving liquor to a sentry was punished the same. He cringed at the thought of the old man taking a flogging for him and hoped his age and the position of his master would spare him.

Finding himself beneath the branches of some trees, Carl stopped to let his eyes become used to the dark. He could hear singing within the camp and the mournful lowing of cattle destined for the bellies of the gathered soldiers. In the high walls of the keep he could see lighted windows, and wondered again at his father's decision. His rank would only protect him so long. Yes, he would denounce his son as a traitor and coward once his absence had been discovered, but this was thin paint and would disguise the true wood only a short time. Carl feared that his father's sacrifice would gain his family nothing, and his life would be surrendered to no purpose.

He felt tears gather on his lids as he crouched in the darkness. How alone he felt. How utterly alone in a world of cruelty and betrayal.

It was his duty to survive, even if he would have nothing more in this world than a place in the Renné army. At least he might live and reestablish the name of A'denné.

Orienting himself by moonlight, he skirted the camp until he found the western road. He kept to the shadows along the road's edge and set himself a brutal pace. The farther he was from the army by daylight, the more country they would have to search, and the better his chances of going undiscovered. He stumbled in ruts and potholes often, but recovered and pushed himself on, not slacking his pace. From within the wood an owl hooted, answered by another not far off. Thankfully, he stepped into a patch of moonlight and increased his pace while he could see.

Men tumbled noisily out of the wood, surrounding him in the cool light. Four of them. His sword came to hand and he turned this way and that, keeping them at bay. Two men brandished long cudgels, another a short sword, the last no weapon at all, but he was twice the size of Carl.

"Now, now," the man with the sword said soothingly. "No need of bloodshed, lad. We'll take your purse either way, you decide what it's worth to you."

In Carl's case it was worth quite a bit more than any of these men had seen in a lifetime. He was not going to hand it over peacefully.

"You can decide what price you'll pay for it," Carl said, "for I'm a trained man-at-arms and will leave the four of you here for the crows unless you fade back into the wood, and quickly."

The men laughed.

"Aye, look at this boy, will you?" the giant said. "He's run off with his master's blade. I'll be having that for me own."

"You'll be having it in your bowels," Carl said. "I've warned you once."

The man to his left stepped forward with his raised cudgel, but Carl knew it was a feint. None of these men were going to risk their skins over the few coins a servant would carry.

He sidestepped the feint and put the man between himself and the swordsman. Spinning, he cut toward the giant who was reaching for him, but he leapt back, more nimble than Carl would have expected—or more timid.

He faced the four of them now, the wood to his back. He hoped they'd left no reinforcements lurking there.

"Did you see that, Jamm? He spins like a dancer," the tall one said. "Maybe he is a dancer. That's where he learned his sword-play—on the stage."

"Did he put his blade in your bowels, Big Toll?" the man with the sword asked.

"Not so's you could tell, Jamm, but I'm an ignorant man and might be mistaken."

Carl lost his patience. He feinted at the nearest man with a cudgel, driving him back, nicked the arm of the man next to him, and took the blade from Jamm's hand, all in one smooth motion. He'd turned back toward Big Toll before the man had taken a step.

The highwaymen were gone into the wood in a trice, and Carl had to put on a burst of speed to trip up the leader, Jamm. He held the man by his collar, the point of his sword against Jamm's stomach. The robber did not beg, but only gazed at him in surprise. Carl could hear his stalwart companions crashing through the underwood. They likely thought it was a trap and other men-at-arms would be upon them in a moment.

"Have you a blade in your bowel, Sir Jamm?" Carl asked.

"Sir . . ." the man grunted, but no more.

Carl hauled the man to his feet and let him go. "How badly are you cut?"

The man looked down at his wrist in the poor light.

"I've had worse," he said.

"Haven't we all. You know that robbery upon the Prince's roads will bring you a short trial and a quick death?"

The man said nothing.

"Well, the stars of luck shine upon you this night for I'll not give you over to the Prince's yeomen. How well do you know the paths between here and the canal?"

"You're a deserter, then," Jamm said.

Carl lifted the blade of his sword just perceptibly.

"I know the paths as well as anyone, sir."

"Can you keep us both from the Prince's huntsmen?"

"I've managed it now these three years."

"That is a good recommendation, Jamm. See me safely to the

canal and I shall give you a reward, besides your life. A greater reward than you shall get to turn me in. Do you agree?"

The man nodded. What choice had he?

"Bind up that wound, then, we've far to go."

Carl took up Jamm's sword and made him lead the way. He was wary of this robber, not because he was a formidable man, but because he could never be trusted and would possess a certain cunning, as thieves often did. There would be no sleep with this man for a guide. Courage was not likely one of Jamm's traits but he was brave enough to slit a sleeping man's throat, Carl guessed.

They had walked for some hours, Carl thought, when Jamm stopped at a crossroads.

"We should leave the road now," he said. "If the Prince sends huntsmen after you, they'll follow the road to the canal. Little will they find, for the summer road is dry and hard as stone. They'll watch for places where a man might leave the way and slip into the wood, and they'll ask after you from all the country people and in the villages. If we're seen, they'll be on us in a moment. But Jamm knows places to hide that have never been found."

"Lead on."

They took the south road, but didn't go far before climbing over a crumbling stone wall. Here they found some untended fields where a few sheep had been left to graze.

"This shepherd has dogs," Jamm whispered. "Make no sound."

They traversed the field along its margin, climbed over a pile of stone that had once been a wall, and were in another field even less well tended. Saplings grew out of the long grass here and there, and thistles and brambles encroached on the pasture. They passed over three more such fields before Jamm crawled into a thick stand of thorny bush just as the sky turned gray. To Carl's surprise they found a little, low shelter, roughly built of old boards. It might accommodate four men if they all sat up but how they would rest he didn't know.

"It leaks a bit in hard rain," Jamm said, "but it keeps off the sun of a hot day." The robber uncovered an earthenware jar. "Spring-water," he said, and Carl drank.

As the sky brightened, the face of his guide became clearer. He was pockmarked and sunken-cheeked, like someone who had been hungry most of his days. His frame was slight, but Carl guessed stronger than it appeared. The man's face had been badly shaven a day or two past and he smelled like sour cabbage and old sweat.

"You sleep," Carl said, his stomach growling for food. "I'll keep watch."

"You've no need to fear me," Jamm said. "The Prince's yeomen have been after me these three years. Were I to turn you in, they would draw and quarter me before they dealt with you. That would be my reward."

"That might be so, but I'll stand watch anyway."

The robber shrugged. "It might profit you to conserve your strength, but you choose."

The man squirmed himself down into the thin floor of dried grasses and closed his eyes. In a moment he was breathing softly. Carl propped himself up against the back of the lean-to and laid his sword across his thighs, hand on the pommel. He could hear sheep some way off and then a dog barking excitedly. A mourning dove announced its sorrow to the new day, and bees visited the flowers of the surrounding bushes.

Carl tried not to think of his father. It was how he had been trained. To let one's mind wander to distractions when one's life was in danger was to invite disaster.

"But when will I mourn you, Father?" he muttered. "When?"

Carl awoke to a hand on his shoulder. Jamm hovered before him, finger to his lips.

"Horsemen," he whispered.

Carl sat up, grabbing his blade, shaking the confusion from his brain.

He leaned forward, listening. A fragrant breeze whispered through the thornbushes, but over it he thought he heard the dull clop of horses' hooves and quiet voices.

They rode along by the old stone wall, tumbled down now and overgrown so that it was all but hidden. It was difficult to say how many there were—a few, he thought. No more than six. He could not hear dogs, and that was a good sign, but dogs were not likely. The road would have seen much traffic by dawn, as all the nearby landholders brought their produce and livestock to sell to the encamped army. Dogs would not track him among so many.

"Well, 'tisn't likely that the son was traitor without the father being in it as well," one rider said.

"The Prince don't need A'denné's army so badly that he'll put up with treachery," another answered. "A'denné's days are few, I'll wager you that."

" 'Tis not like the Prince is known for being just," one said, and they all laughed.

"We've only the son to worry about now," one man growled.

"Oh, someone met him with a horse and he's over the canal by now. We'll not find him."

And they were gone, voices fading into the warm afternoon.

"How long did I sleep?" Carl asked.

"Some hours. It's mid-afternoon. We should stay here till dark. There's a bit of cloud now. If there is no moon, it will make traveling hard."

"Nevertheless, I must do it. I must cross to the Isle by morning."

"The bridges have all been torn down, and any boats the Renné could find have been torched."

"I will swim if I must."

"It is a good long distance over the canal," the man said seriously.

Carl looked at him, trying not to smile. "You can all but toss a stone across it!"

"Oh, aye, but to swim so far. You would be taking a chance."

Carl laughed. He could not help it. "I have swum the River Wynnd. I think I shall manage the canal."

Jamm looked at him, certain that Carl was lying, which made Carl laugh more.

"Hush now, sir," Jamm said, and they fell silent.

A horse nickered nearby, and then they heard the measured plodding of its hooves. Twice it stopped, and then went on.

Jamm looked positively panicked. Taking hold of himself, he crawled down a low tunnel beneath the thorns, disappearing for a moment. Then he was back.

" 'Twas a man-at-arms, following behind the others. I could see a group of four going up the slope toward the wood. But this man lingered in the corner of the pasture."

"Do you think he heard us?"

"Mayhap he did. We should be silent now, in case he comes back on foot. If we're found we can pass through into the next field this way." He pointed to a small opening in the dense bush.

They were quiet then, straining to hear any sounds. Carl imagined that silent men-at-arms surrounded their thicket and waited only for them to put their heads out.

A little rain fell toward evening, and they set their jar out to fill, though it collected little. A wind came up from the north, chill and inconstant.

They waited until dusk before slipping out the back way into another overgrown pasture. They crouched down in the long grass and listened. Carl decided to take a chance and give Jamm back his blade. If they were found he might be of some help.

The sky was strewn with broken clouds, swept south by the wind. They dragged their shadows over the earth, bringing darkness with them as they flew. Stars appeared. The moon would rise later now, as it waned.

Just as Carl was about to rise a horse blew out, lips fluttering. He became still as stone. Jamm jerked a thumb back toward the thicket: whoever it was, they were on the other side.

A cloud shadow spread ominously across the field, and Jamm and Carl were off. Fearing men in the shadows of the overgrown wall, they crossed the field diagonally, keeping low, hoping the darkness and waist-high grass would hide them.

Halfway across the pasture the shadow passed on and starlight illuminated the wet grasses that glistened with new-fallen rain.

A shout sounded over the wind and Jamm ran like a hare, Carl close on his heels. The nobleman glanced back once to see men on horseback coming through a break in the hedge. He forced his legs to go faster but Jamm stayed ahead, fear seeming to give him speed.

They both stumbled over a log lying in the grass but were up and off again, gasping like bellows. Carl could see the far side of the pasture—a shadow line that seemed infinitely far away. The sound of galloping horses, however, grew louder, and a glance back told the truth of their hopes.

"They're almost upon us!" Carl shouted.

Jamm suddenly went down into the long grasses, disappearing. Carl thought he'd been hurt but then realized what he did and dove into the grass himself. On his hands and knees he crawled as he'd never done before, setting off to one side of their track.

In a moment the riders thundered past. Stopped and began riding randomly over the grass. Carl wormed down into the tall growth, pulled out his sword and lay still, letting the grasses bend over him in the wind.

A horse came so close he thought he would be trampled, massive feet pounding down not a foot from his head. He could hear the beast panting.

"Here!" someone shouted not far off, and Carl leapt to his knees, cutting at the leg of the passing horse. It went down in an awkward flailing of limbs and desperate whinnying. Before the rider found his feet Carl was on him: two quick blows aimed at his head and he lay still.

Four riders were converging on a small figure that darted this way and that, dodging the blows of a pursuing rider. Carl knew it was his chance to slip away, but instead he went for the nearest rider.

They were not men-at-arms but huntsmen or yeomen, Carl could see, and he took one from his saddle before any had seen him, severed another's leg at the knee, and hamstrung the next's mount. The last turned and spurred his horse to a gallop.

Jamm was on his hands and knees, gasping.

"Are you hurt?"

"No . . . I don't think so."

"We need those horses." Carl hauled the man up and they went after the riderless horses. It took them a precious quarter of an hour to catch hold of the skittish mounts, and then they were off, galloping across the field. Carl wondered how soon the man who escaped would take to find help.

Jamm knew the countryside well and led them by a confusing path, turning often and doubling back more than once. They would be hard to follow, but all of this took more time than riding a straight line toward the canal and gave their pursuers a chance to catch up.

Darkness had settled over the countryside, turning everything to shades of shadow. The prince's huntsmen could be anywhere, waiting quietly in the black pools that spread beneath the trees. Traveling by foot, one could go quietly, but horses . . . their heavy hooves were never silent. Jamm went on almost unerringly; having navigated these lands by darkness before, Carl suspected. But even so, they were forced to a slow walk in many places and the horses balked at going blind along narrow paths. They stumbled here and there and became nervous and skittish.

Carl was near dizzy from hunger. He'd not had any food in a day and the sprint across the field and the fight had taken more out of him than he would have expected.

"How far to the canal?" he asked when they found themselves in a track wide enough to ride abreast.

"We'll be there before sunrise, but they'll be waiting for you, I expect."

"Can they watch the length of the canal?"

"There are guards there already, fearing the Renné will cross over and bring war to the Prince of Innes."

"We might go north, to the river. It would not be difficult to drift down the Wynnd to the Isle. We might even find a boat."

"Jamm does not know the lands there, and perhaps the Prince has set a watch on the river, too."

"Then I will have to find a way past the guards on the canal." He thought it likely that the Prince had established watch stations along the canal, but there would be men hidden along the bank as well, and these would be the danger.

Jamm led them down a small embankment onto a narrow track. He leaned near to Carl.

"I don't like this traveling by horse. Our passing is not quiet. I know a man we might sell our horses to. He will keep them out of sight for a few days until he can sell them elsewhere."

I'm sure you do, Carl thought. He did not much like the idea of being led into a den of Jamm's friends. He had chased off the other highwaymen because, despite their vocation, they were timid by nature and unwilling to risk injury over what was probably very little. But not all robbers were so made, Carl was sure.

Jamm drew up suddenly. "Riders!" he said. They turned quickly into the wood, dismounted and led their horses into the darkness. Carl tripped and was battered by unseen branches but he forced his way on, taking hold of the tail of Jamm's horse.

They stopped in dense bush. Carl could hear the horses now, and a moment latter a smudge of yellow light wavered across the ruts. Three riders bearing torches passed, followed by half a dozen more, the men in the rear bearing torches as well.

"The Prince's men-at-arms," Jamm said after a moment. "Lucky it was dark and no one noticed our tracks." He drew a long breath. "How large is this reward for helping you, your grace?"

"Ten silver A'denné eagles."

"I shouldn't want to be caught with those in my pocket. I'll have to melt them down or cross the river with them. The Prince's men know someone is helping you," Jamm said. "If I'm caught now, with A'denné coins, they will likely torture me before my hanging."

"Fifteen silver eagles."

"I think ten of gold would be more in keeping with the risks, your grace. I would think the reward for your capture is twice that."

"That's a steep price, Jamm."

"Not for your life, your grace. Unless you value it at less?"

"Ten gold eagles," Carl said, wondering if Jamm merely was trying to find out how much gold he carried, and therefore how much risk he was willing to take to steal it.

They mounted again and took to the track, the riders more skittish than their horses now. Carl thought he heard horses approaching over and over but it was only the breeze through the wood, or the echo of their own progress. They left the track for a farmer's lane that led them across open fields and over a low rise. The moon lit their way across a dew-drenched meadow, and Carl was sure they were visible for furlongs in every direction. All it would take would be a set of eyes to be turned their way.

The picked their way down a hillside into a small valley. Carl could see cottages and farm buildings in their stands of shade trees, and a small stream winding along the valley bottom. A road followed close by this, crossing once at a bridge.

"My friend dwells down here among the farmer folk. 'Tis the land of the Earl of Tildd, but the lord lives some distance away and leaves the folk hereabout alone but for tax time."

"And your friend makes a habit of buying horses with the Prince's brand on them?"

"I should not call it a habit, but these are good stock and he might take a chance if the price is right. He's a horse and cattle trader by day, and no more prone to larceny than any of his calling."

They made their way down to the road, letting their horses drink from the stream. Carl stood by apprehensively while his horse had its fill. He didn't like this place. He felt exposed and there were too many people dwelling nearby. A dog began to bark at a nearby cottage, and Carl wanted to get on their horses and flee.

They mounted and trotted along the road, turning up a poplar-lined lane. Coming through a gate, a trio of fierce dogs surrounded them, growling and baring their teeth in the moonlight. A shutter screeched open but no face appeared. From inside came the wary voice of an elderly man.

"What do you want here, lads?" the old man asked.

" 'Tis Jamm, Holdin. I've a pair of horses to sell."

A round face appeared now, the light too poor for Carl to make out more.

"Aye, lads; that'll do. Quit your show," he said to his dogs, who growled less but held their positions. "You've chosen a poor night to come here, Jamm. There are men-at-arms abroad on all the roads, looking for a deserter, they say—though I've never seen them make such a fuss over a common deserter. They've been to every dwelling up and down the valley, some more than once, and have been none too polite in their inquiries, bullying and threatening everyone and looking through houses and outbuildings. Now tell me quick where these horses are from."

"We found them wandering over on the west-going road. They're as good a saddle horse as you'll find, with tack and all."

"Some of the Prince's men were killed over there, Jamm. You've not been fool enough to buy their horses, have you? Have they a brand?'

"Not that I've noticed, Holdin," Jamm said with perfect innocence, "but we found them after dark."

A moment of hesitation, and then the old man cursed. "Wait where you are."

He appeared in a long sleeping gown, a brawny silent youth bearing an axe in his wake. The old man cupped a hand around a candle, bidding the riders get down.

"Jamm, you damn fool!" he said almost immediately. "Get these horses out of my yard before you get us all hung! That's the Prince's mark on their flank. Get you off before I set my dogs on you."

Carl kept himself half hidden behind his horse, never letting the candlelight fall upon his face. He turned his horse away and mounted so his back was to Holdin and the boy.

"Be you careful, Jamm," the old man said as the thief put a foot in his stirrup. "If you're smart you'll get rid of those nags and slip back into the wood and keep your head down until this has all passed. It's not like you to take chances. You won't get enough gold for these to pay for your burial. Get rid of them somewhere. Cut their throats out in the wood. Otherwise they'll be found and you'll have huntsmen and hounds on you."

They went out the gate, the old man latching it behind them.

"You listen to old Holdin, Jamm. Get shut of those horses this night."

The thief and the fugitive nobleman rode down the lane in silence.

"That old man made sense to me," Carl said as they reached the road.

"Yes. Holdin's no fool. There's a wood not far off where people seldom go. I've laid up there days at a time and seen no one. There are some low hills there where the soil is no good for farming. The odd time there's a shepherd with a flock—usually just a boy with a dog. We could let the horses go there and we'd be on the Isle before anyone would find them."

"Holdin said we should kill them so they won't wander into someone's field and be found."

"Aye, well Holdin has horses enough that he can kill a few and not care, perhaps, but I think it would be no risk to let these go."

Carl was surprised by this sudden show of sentiment. To stay alive he would have guessed Jamm would kill a hundred horses. But then this little man had been taking risks for who knew how many years? He must have learned to weigh them to a nicety or he would have met old judge noose before now.

They trotted down the road, the local dogs sending up a chorus, having been set to barking by Holdin's hounds.

"Damn dogs!" Jamm muttered, spurring his horse. "Best get out of here. We can leave the road just over the bridge."

They cantered down the dirt track by moonlight, riding between the wheel ruts. The road curved toward the river then, and Carl could just make out the silhouette of bridge timbers under the overarching trees. Jamm glanced back and set his horse to a gallop.

"Behind!" he called, and leaning over the neck of his mount, raced toward the bridge.

Carl glanced back once. Riders, several of them! He whipped his horse with the reins, and tried to see through the dirt Jamm's mount was throwing up. The hollow thunder of hooves on planking echoed along the stream as they reached the bridge, and horsemen emerged from the shadows to block their way.

Jamm cursed, pulling his horse up so that it slid on the bridge deck.

"Go on!" Carl shouted. "We've no choice."

Carl drew his sword as he rode, sizing up the men before him, his heart pounding like hooves on the bridge. There were four riders, but they wore no helms nor did they ride chargers. Yeomen or huntsmen, perhaps, and this gave him a little hope. They parted a little, two to each side, as though to funnel him between them.

Carl slowed his headlong charge a little. The bridge deck was smooth from traffic and treacherous underfoot. He couldn't have his horse fall. He changed his course and went directly at the rider farthest to the right, and when the men all moved to intercept, he altered course back to the left, causing the riders to collide and curse each other. Carl swept through the opening to the left, parrying a wild blow with the flat of his sword.

He didn't look back but hoped Jamm had the sense to follow him. Where to go now, he didn't know. There could be more riders on the road ahead, but Carl was at a loss for what to do but gallop on and hope his horse would outlast the mounts of the men behind.

"To your left! Left!" came Jamm's desperate call from behind.

Carl pulled up a little and let the thief go past him, then fell in behind. The men who hunted them were some distance back, having fouled each other up on the bridge. Whether they were gaining he could not tell.

They set off up a narrow cattle track that ran along beside a yard-wide brook. Carl could see a wood ahead, the dark shadow beneath the trees seeming a haven. For the first time he noticed that a horn sounded from behind, and a distant answer echoed down the wold.

They reached the wood, their horses in a lather, and plunged into the utter darkness that clung about the feet of the trees. Jamm slid to the ground as soon as he was in shadow. The nobleman did the same, and took hold of the tail of Jamm's horse, hoping it wouldn't decide to kick him in the dark. They stumbled on, crashing through the underwood, and then Jamm grabbed his shoulder.

"Let the horses go," he said, and led Carl off in another direction.

Soon they heard the huntsmen thrashing among the bushes and trees, trying to follow the sound of the horses before them. Jamm doubled back, and after bashing into many branches and smashing their feet and shins on invisible roots and stones, they came back out of the wood. They could see riders making their way along the road from both east and west.

"We'll skirt the wood here, but keep to the shadows. Don't let them see you from the road."

Carl followed close on his guide's heels, the visibility only marginally better here. But they made good time and were soon over the shoulder of the hill and out of sight of the road. They clung to the edges of shadow as best they could, sprinting across areas of open moonlight and stopping to listen fearfully now and then.

They went on, tending south and a little west. In an hour they had crossed into the next wold and trotted down a hedgerow, keeping to the darkness. They gave the dwellings of men a wide berth, not wanting to set the dogs to barking again. Neither spoke unless they must.

Carl was weak with hunger and was driven forward solely out of fear. Jamm never said a word about hunger or food, and Carl wondered if the little man went without more commonly than he ate.

Twice they saw riders in the distance and hunkered down or slipped into a shadow to let them pass. Then they were moving again, Jamm driving them on relentlessly. Fear clearly increased a man's endurance considerably.

Jamm led them by a small spring, cautioning Carl not to step in the soft ground.

"Drink your fill," the little man said. "There'll be no more till tonight."

Just as the sky showed signs of graying, Jamm led them into a wood that spread over a hilltop. Here he pulled a crudely made ladder out of a thick stand of wild roses and lay it up against an oak. They climbed into the lower branches, where Jamm bade Carl wait. He went farther up into the dark, ascending into the sky, Carl thought.

"Pass me up the ladder," came a whisper from above, and Carl did, though with some difficulty in the dark. He then climbed up, trying to go where he'd seen Jamm go, hoping no branch would break and send him plunging down.

High up among the thick branches Carl found his guide on a small platform, lightly built of poles and covered in old reed mats.

"You have the most comfortable homes, Jamm," Carl said as he stretched out on the uneven platform, exhausted as he'd never been before.

"Not all men were born to comfort," Jamm growled. "Most aren't and never gain it. We're well hid, and that's what matters."

"Hear hear. You've done well this day, Jamm. Have you had many such encounters with men hunting you?"

"Few as close as this. I'll not be able to stay around here after today. If Holdin doesn't give me away, someone will. There'll be a reward for me now. I'll be off to some other place to start over. 'Tis a pity, for I know the country around here like no other. 'Tisn't likely I'll ever know another land like I know my own."

The sky brightened slowly and a soft breeze rustled the leaves around them. Carl felt oddly safe and at peace up here, though if they were found there would be no escape.

"You were born here?"

"Aye, your grace. Not so far from here, though we moved about a great deal. My father labored for farmers here and there, when he could. His love of drink usually cut his employment short, for he weren't a man to take punctuality too serious. He thieved a little when times were hard. And we thieved along with him, my brother and me. We lived in old shacks when there weren't no work. My father knew the land hereabout like no one else. Well, mayhap I know it better now. It'll be a pity to leave it behind."

"You can come with me. I'll find you work to do. You can be my equerry, as I've not got one now. It pays better than what you've been doing, I'll warrant."

"Almost anything does! But it would mean living all regular, I suppose?"

"I'm afraid so."

"I'm not much good at that."

Carl was surprised by the hint of sadness he heard in the thief's voice. "I've not been much good at anything I've turned my hand to at first, Jamm. But one can learn."

"So they say. I would have to swim the canal, though, and I can't do that."

"I'll carry you over. It isn't difficult—not as difficult as what we've done this day. You have to be gone from this place for a while anyway. If you don't like being an equerry you'll be no further behind. You'll have a suit of clothes and some coins in your pocket."

"Will you still give me my reward for guiding you, or would that be part of my duties, so to speak?"

Here was shrewd trader, Carl thought. "No, no. Your reward will be paid upon our arrival at the canal. That was our bargain and I will stick to it no matter what you decide."

The thief was silent awhile. Carl could make out his gaunt little face now. He looked haunted or ill. "Well," he said. "It is a handsome offer and as good as I'll likely get in this world, but I don't know if I can be an equerry. There is an awful lot that I don't know, proper manners and such. I've heard some of these knight's men can read! I can't imagine I would do anything but disappoint."

"Well, think it over," Carl said. "You can let me know when we reach the canal."

The little man nodded, lay his head down on the hard surface and closed his eyes. Carl had a sense that Jamm wanted him to argue a little more. Cajole him into it. Reassure him that the work was within his ken. But it was too late now. Jamm was already asleep, his face drawn and sad in the poor light, as sad as Carl had ever seen.

Jamm woke him during the hours of daylight, once when he heard hounds far off, and once more when they heard voices and the slow thump of hooves upon the hard ground. These men laughed as they rode. A hissing wind rattled the branches together, like bones in a cup.

The voices faded slowly, but then just as Carl thought he would sleep again, they heard the measured *clop clop* of a horse. It stopped several times, as though the rider listened. Carl remembered the man-at-arms who had found them the previous day.

Suddenly their hiding place seemed a terrible trap. There was nowhere to go if they were found. But Carl fought down the panic. Even so, he lay awake the rest of the day, trying not dwell on his hunger or the blackache that pierced his head.

Riders passed within hearing twice more that day. Whether it was the same group or some other, Carl did not know. Toward dusk Jamm woke and stretched. Carl could see a smile on the man's face.

"You seem strangely pleased with things," Carl said quietly.

Jamm gave a little laugh. "I just had a most pleasant dream. I was about to lay my hands on a box of gleaming gold and gems when me old mother appeared and began to lecture me about where such thieving would land me. She were talking loud as loud and I had just slunk into this place trying to wake no one." He laughed again. "Me poor mother. She must not be lying easy in her grave knowing what her third son is up to."

"Perhaps she'd lie more easily if you were an equerry to a distinguished young nobleman."

Jamm sat up and put a finger to his lips. Voices drifted to them on the wind, so soft that Carl wondered if he imagined them.

"Did you hear that?" Jamm asked.

Carl nodded. "They're not near to hand."

"Not yet," Jamm whispered. He stood, parting the branches carefully to look out. "Horses," he whispered, and sank down onto the platform.

Leaning close to Carl, he whispered in his ear, "There are riderless horses over there—tethered."

Carl tried to control his breathing.

Jamm jerked his thumb down toward the ground. "They must lie waiting for us to climb down," he breathed.

"Trapped," Carl mouthed, but Jamm shook his head and held up a finger as though to say wait.

And wait they did. The night grew darker and the heat of the day blew off with the breeze. Stars emerged in the great black sea of the sky, but the waning moon would not rise till later. Here, in the wood, it was black as slate.

Once he judged it dark enough, Jamm got slowly to his feet, putting a hand on Carl's shoulder to tell him to stay.

It was hard to see what Jamm did in the darkness, and he was so stealthy that there was no noise above the breeze in the leaves, the swaying of branches. The ladder touched Carl, and he slid back to give Jamm room to move it. Certainly whoever waited would put men at the base of the tree. They could never climb down.

But Jamm did not seem to be sending the ladder down. He slid it slowly over the platform and out along a bough. After a moment he followed the ladder out, into the spreading branches. The thief's stealth left Carl in awe, who could not imagine doing anything so silently.

After what seemed like an hour Jamm climbed back onto the platform and put his mouth close to Carl's ear. "Follow me," he said.

They went out one of the oak's great branches, Carl making every effort to be as silent as his companion. Jamm's patience impressed him, for every move was slow and deliberate, and followed by several moments of stillness and silence.

Carl thought it must have been an hour before Jamm reached back and found his hand. He tugged Carl forward and put his fingers on the ladder, which was wedged into the crotch of the branch and seemed to go off into space at a slight downward angle.

It must go into a nearby tree, Carl realized. That is how desperate they were. He looked up at the sky and wondered if they would be visible from below. What a cruel joke that would be.

Jamm went on and Carl waited, certain this flimsy ladder would not hold them both. He worried that it might not even bear his weight, for certainly he was heavier than Jamm.

Carl began to wonder if the moon would not show its face soon, for the night was wearing on. He could not understand why the men who hunted them could have been so patient. Did they wait for darkness for fear that he and Jamm had bows? His own father would have found some woodsmen and had the tree down.

Finally, the slight movement of the branch ceased and he hoped that meant Jamm had crossed over. Carl tried to be as patient as his guide, taking every move slowly, pausing between. He was not as agile as the wiry Jamm, but he did everything he could to make no unnatural sound. Several times he stopped because his head pounded so that he thought he would lose his balance, but then he went on. He slid out on the ladder, not sure how stable it was, inching along the rungs, feeling it bend beneath his weight the farther he went. Once, it creaked so loudly that Carl was afraid to move for several minutes, but he decided it sounded like the branches of a tree and went on.

Jamm was not waiting at the other end, and Carl was forced to find his way, feeling for branches, trying not to make noise as he slipped through the leaves. He heard a footfall on the ground below. Was it Jamm, or the men who awaited them? Had Jamm abandoned him and run off? He would not blame him if so. The risks had become too great for any reward.

Through the leaves Carl caught a glimpse of a cloud, glowing on the western horizon. The moon was rising. He tried not to let panic overwhelm him but went on deliberately, still pausing and waiting, though perhaps not for so long.

A hand reached out and touched him, and Carl flinched. It was Jamm. The nimble little thief led him down then, placing his hands and feet on branches. Still, their progress was as slow as a stone moving down a river. A final reach with his foot, Jamm's hand on his heel, and Carl touched ground.

They slunk off almost immediately.

Someone cursed, and Jamm flew back against Carl. They were off like scared deer, crashing through the bush, whoever Jamm had bumped into right on their heels. Someone crashed to the ground behind them, and by the time he was up again they had gained a crucial few yards.

Carl could hear men all about now, shouting and flailing at noises in the bush. One man cried out that he'd been cut, and a strange silence followed in which Jamm had the sense to stop. He and Carl dropped to the ground and crawled forward, afraid of blind sword strokes.

And then they were at the horses Jamm had seen from their platform. In a moment they were in the saddles, sending the rest of the mounts running into the darkness. They sprinted out into the open then, forcing their horses to run over the hard ground, hoping they would not trip or step in a hole. The waning moon lifted free of the cloud then and dimly lit their way.

Across the field, along the edge of a wood, down into a valley bottom thick with bush. Here Jamm drew them up and dismounted. They sent the horses running, and Carl followed Jamm as he wormed into the bush.

A little stony-bottomed creek opened out before them and they stopped to drink, water substituting for food in their diet, Carl thought. Jamm then led them down the creek, splashing and slipping for over an hour. They waded out of the waters then and climbed up the low bank onto a narrow track. Jamm followed this through moonlight and shadow, never slowing his pace. They stumbled and swore through the darkness, but took the falls as they went, Carl hoping that neither sustained an injury that would hold them up.

It seemed to Carl that this was the longest night of the year, not one of the shortest. Sometime before dawn Jamm stopped and threw himself down on the ground. Carl did the same, his stomach cramps suddenly gripping him like a fist.

"We are but a short walk from the canal," Jamm whispered when he'd caught his breath. "Can you swim it as you are?"

"Anything to get free of these men who pursue us. We need only find a branch to float our blades. We'll not cross the river bearing steel."

"The trees will not begrudge us a limb, I think. Not after what we've been through."

"And what of you, Jamm? Will you cross over with me? You needn't take the place of my equerry but can go off. You shall have some gold in hand."

"I will cross the river. I would be mad to stay here. But you must promise to keep me afloat."

"I will not let you sink, Jamm. You've saved my life. I will not let you drown now."

But they did not rise for some time, and then only did so for fear of the approaching dawn. They cut a branch from a tree to float their blades and went on, careful now, watching for the riders and men posted along the canal. They hadn't gone far when they heard horses, and men talking.

Jamm left Carl and went forward. He was gone awhile, and Carl began to fear he'd been caught when the little man reappeared almost under his nose.

"There are men posted all along the canal and riders passing back and forth, but there is a little stream that goes down into the greater water nearby. It is thick with blackberry bramble and no one will go in there. We can slip into the water and slide along like otters until we are in the canal itself. Give your branch to me and stay close."

Carl went forward, bending down and using his hands like an animal, but he was almost too tired to stand. Jamm went from shadow to shadow—almost a shadow himself, he was so wary. Carl could hear men talking not far off and smell the smoke of someone's pipe. Jamm led him down a sharp slope and through a tiny gap in the bramble. Spines grabbed at his clothes and sprang free as he passed.

Let no one hear, he thought.

They slid beneath branches that tore at their faces, silent and slow. For a long time they were so close to the men standing guard above that Carl could listen to their conversation as though he were among them.

A rat brushed past his face but he was too tired to even flinch. He felt Jamm's boots ahead of him in the water, looking for purchase on the soft bottom. Over and over Carl snagged the pommel of his sword and had to work it free. He would have left it there had not unbuckling his scabbard seemed impossible under the circumstances.

Finally they came to the still canal, pausing in the mouth of the little stream, staring out at the dark water. It appeared wider than Carl remembered, and he was weak. *What happened if the stomach cramps came while he was in midstream?* He pressed these fears down. They had no choice now. It was go on or lie in this fetid little creak until they died.

Carl pushed himself out into the waters of the canal and stripped his scabbard and blade off, laying them over the branch in such a way that he hoped would keep them safe. Jamm did the same.

Carl took a look around and up at the sky to get his bearings. He realized then that there would be men guarding the bank opposite, watching for anyone trying to cross over. They could be shot by the men they hoped would save them.

Carl shoved the branch gently out into the water, then looped his arm around it, lying on his back. He tugged a frightened Jamm to him and turned him so Jamm's back was against his chest. Not waiting to see if Jamm would panic, the young nobleman pushed gently out into the black waters.

"Hear?" one of the men on the bank said.

Someone began walking through trampled grass, then a silhouette appeared on the bank.

"Otter, Malick?"

"Perhaps. String your bow, Ben. See if you can stick it."

Carl felt Jamm go rigid with fear. He was breathing too fast and too loud.

"The captain doesn't much like us amusing ourselves on duty," Ben said.

They were bored! That's all it was. And he and Jamm might be about to pay for it.

Carl began to kick furiously, careful not to let his feet break the surface and make noise.

"Well, give me your bow, then," Malick said. "Come. It's an easy shot. Even I might manage."

The man disappeared off the bank but returned a moment later. Carl could see the dark form raise a bow, but then hesitate.

"Where did that devil go?"

"She's too smart for you, Malick."

"No! There she is."

The hiss of an arrow and then the small splash where it hit the water not a foot away. This brought others to the bank.

"There he be, Malick. I can hit him with a stone."

An arrow hissed again, dashing into the water just beyond Carl's head. He was kicking like mad now. If he hadn't been dragging Jamm he would have gone under and swum for the far bank, but he had to keep the thief afloat.

The air was filled with the sounds of arrows, suddenly, and one of the men on the bank fell, the others scrambling back into the wood. Renné archers were lurking in the wood opposite. What was he to do now? They were as likely to shoot him as listen to him.

Carl changed his course and let the small current draw them slowly downstream. He angled toward the far side, searching for a place to land. Dawn must not be far off for he could make out roots spiraling down to the water and bushes leaning over here and there.

He heard some men talking low not far off.

Carl brought them up to the bank, but when he tried to stand found the bottom too steep and slippery. For a moment he hesitated, but one look at the graying sky made up his mind.

"You," he whispered. "On the bank. I'm a man-at-arms in the service of Lord Kel. Can you help us up?"

Silence. Some hushed whispering.

"Who are you, sir?" came a voice.

Carl hesitated. There would be no welcome for the name of A'denné here. But what lie would be believed?

"I am Lord Carl . . . A'denné, and I have been spying for the Renné."

An arrow struck the bank a foot away, spraying Carl with mud. He found a root, pulling Jamm with him. The two men grabbed their swords and went hand over hand up a tangle of thick roots. Better to take a chance these men-at-arms would ask a few questions before killing them than stay in the water until a lucky arrow found them in the dark.

But the men on the bank took hold of them and hauled them up behind a barricade of stacked logs. They were deposited on the ground, dripping, and could just make out a few men, swords in hand, standing over them.

"Are there any more?" one asked his companion, who took the chance of glancing over the barricade.

"Not that I can see."

The ranking man-at-arms crouched down in front of Carl. "My lord will want to talk to you."

"And who is your lord?"

"The Duke of Vast."

Carl opened his mouth and stifled a sob. "We are saved, Jamm. Do you hear? We are saved."

They were taken back through a narrow, dark wood. Carl found himself walking hunched down as though he still feared being seen. An encampment lay not far off, and there they were given food and dry clothing. They were under the eye of armed men at all times, but they were left their weapons, and treated with all kindness and respect.

When they had washed away the dirt of their escape, they were handed over to a mounted company, given horses, and taken inland under this light guard. Carl did not ask how far they might ride or where they were going, for in all truth it seemed unimportant. They had escaped the Prince's huntsmen and were on the land of his new allies. Nothing else mattered.

After an hour's ride they came into the walled yard of a large house, and here they were bid to dismount and wait, which they did, in the kind sun streaming over the roof. The day seemed especially fine and precious to Carl. He was prepared to merely drink it in, to feel the sun's caress on his face, listen to the songs of the birds.

There was a commotion at the main door and the Duke emerged, a host of attendants in his wake. "Carl? It is you! Carl, whatever has happened?" And then the Duke stopped a few paces off, the elation disappearing from his face. "Where is your father?"

"Still with the enemy, I fear, if he is alive. My rescue of Kel Renné did not go unseen, and I was accused by the Prince of treachery. Fortunately, his witness died of wounds before he could be brought to confront me. I slipped out of the Prince's keep, but my father refused to come. He believed he had a task to finish, though certainly he will be under terrible suspicion now."

The Duke shook his head, his face drawn and serious. "Come with me. You have a story to tell, I can see."

But as Carl rose to his feet he was suddenly dizzy and would have fallen had not a man-at-arms caught him.

"River save us," the Duke muttered. "What has happened to him?"

Carl felt other hands bear him up.

"Our escape was a near thing, your grace," Carl heard Jamm say, his voice seeming to come from very far away. "Our way was hard, and very roundabout. Thrice we were almost taken but fought our way out or slipped away by darkness. We'd naught to eat for most of three days, and were starting to grow weak of it."

"Take him up," the Duke said. "We'll empty a room for him."

What happened next Carl did not remember, but sometime later he awoke in a room lit with the warm glow of evening. Jamm sat in a chair at the bedside.

Carl gave him a weak smile. "Don't look so serious. I need a little rest and food. Or is it your reward you are worried about? I'll give you it now. Where are my belongings?"

But this promised gain did nothing to change the grim look that resided on the thief's face. He leaned forward, whispering. "That man—the Duke—I saw him once before."

"What do you mean?" Carl propped himself up to hear, for Jamm seemed afraid to speak above the faintest whisper.

"Two weeks before the battle. He came down the western road where we first met. I was watching for easy prey but armed men were not to my taste. It was dark, and he traveled with only a small company. They met one of the Prince's men—a nobleman whose name I don't know. They had a conversation in a clearing—I can't tell you what was said—and then this man you call the Duke went back toward the canal. It was all very friendly, your grace. Like a meeting of allies."

Carl let himself fall back into the soft bedding. "We are in more danger here, Jamm, than ever before. River save us, what game is the Duke playing?"

Forty-eight

Prince Michael could not sleep. A stone dug into his ribs but he was too exhausted to shift himself. His eyes burned even when he closed them, and felt as though they were being sucked back into his head. But sleep would not come.

Hafydd had divided his guards into three watches, adding Beld and Samul to one. But Michael's only duties were to nurse Alaan, who was slipping away; the Prince could feel it.

Night was upon the Stillwater, the ghostly night. A waning moon, awash in the blur, lay like a shell upon the ocean bottom. It cast a thin light down between the trees. The fire had burned down to coals, and he could not force himself to rise to rekindle it.

Get up and see to your charge, he ordered himself. But he did not move. The two guards that Hafydd detailed to watch Alaan stood by in their black robes like servants of death. This left five to guard the island. The rest were asleep. If Elise planned to take Alaan, the odds were in her favor. The Prince kept his own blade near at hand, which the guards no doubt thought was to aid them. He would kill them if he had the chance. The fewer guards Hafydd had, the better. Hafydd was formidable, Michael knew, but he also took few risks and kept his guards around him always. The man might be a sorcerer but he was certainly mortal.

One of the two guards stumbled forward, making guttural noises. He did not even extend his hands to break his fall. The second guard fell before he could turn. The Prince was on his feet, blade in hand, and so was Samul Renné.

Beldor stepped out of shadow holding a bloody sword. He had severed the guards' spines above their mail shirts.

"Get him up," Beldor said. "The boat lies unwatched."

"Beldor," Samul said, worried. "What is it you do?"

"We must get away," Beld hissed. "This sorcerer, Hafydd, is like no other. He will sweep the Renné and the Wills from the land between the mountains and put himself on a throne. There is no hope but that we join our efforts to resist him." He turned on Prince Michael. "Your father has been a fool to aid such a man. Does he not see? Do you not?"

"You're right," the Prince said, and bent down to lift his dying charge. "But we must have Alaan alive and conscious to escape, and even then I'm not sure he will lead us."

Samul and the Prince bore Alaan down to the boat. He seemed as light as a child and limp as a half-filled sack of oats. They laid him down on a few blankets and covered him. He stirred and muttered something softly then was silent. In the cool night air the water felt warm. The three waded out into the drowned wood, putting the glowing coals on the island behind them.

Tam shifted to try to get feeling back into his leg. He sat on the gunwale, his bow in hand, an arrow nocked. They could see the island in the faded moonlight, the dull glow of a dying fire casting light on two ominous dark figures—Hafydd's guards. There seemed to be four other guards walking the shoreline. Where the Renné or the young Prince was could not be ascertained. Certainly Alaan lay by the fire.

Tam hoped Alaan was not too ill to lead them out, or that Elise could heal him quickly, for Hafydd would be after them—or would he? Elise thought he would keep his distance, watching, waiting for them to make their escape from the Stillwater.

A bat flittered by in the night, and goatsuckers sailed overhead. Frogs were not as loud here as in the swamp, but still they sang. Tam tried to regulate his breathing so he might hear any noise that signified danger. The others were all strung equally tight, Fynnol worst of all.

There was a sudden movement in the dim glow of the dying fire. One of the dark figures toppled forward, followed immediately by the other: the servants of Death joined their master.

No one spoke, for they had all seen it.

Other men moved into the glow.

"Is that the Renné and the Knights?" Pwyll asked, but Elise motioned for silence. She nodded to Baore, who began to pole them quietly forward.

Dease was roused from a most pleasant dream of a faceless woman to Toren's hoarse whisper and a hand roughly shaking his shoulder.

"Something has happened on the island," his cousin said. "Rouse yourself."

Dease was on his feet in an instant, staggering from the agony this produced in his brain. The pain and confusion had been slowly returning—ever since his meeting with the river spirit, which he was still not sure had happened.

Renné men-at-arms and A'brgail's Knights were sloshing hurriedly into the waters. Dease tried to push aside the insistent torment, swept up his scabbard and followed quickly behind. He knew Toren would be at the fore, and he pressed himself through the company until his cousin's familiar silhouette appeared. A brief vision of Arden standing at Toren's doors, his argument with Beld . . .

"Toren? What has happened?"

"Someone has killed several of Hafydd's guards and stolen Alaan away. Our lookout said it seemed to be men who were on the island."

"Prince Michael!"

"Yes, but there was more than one. Would any of Hafydd's guards betray him?"

"Samul. You think it was Samul." Dease cursed under his breath.

"Perhaps. Quiet now, we are drawing near."

Trees loomed up in the poor light, and branches reached down to surprise men, causing them to start or even strike out. A glow from Hafydd's fire grew and then Dease could see men moving about, some throwing brush on the flames.

The men around Dease came to a silent halt.

"How will we find him now?" Dease said.

"Oh, we can follow Alaan," A'brgail said. "But so can Hafydd. Something is not right here." The knight stared at the growing blaze. "Why do they wait?"

"I don't see Beld among them," Dease said. Their cousin's silhouette was unmistakable.

"He is not there," Toren said certainly.

"Then Samul and Beld have aided the Prince in stealing Alaan away. That is a strange turn."

"Yes. Gilbert is right," Toren said. "Something is not right, here. Why would Samul and Beld do such a thing? Who is Alaan to them?"

"We will ask them when we find them," A'brgail said. "And we will find them soon enough."

"Shh," Elise cautioned.

They sat silently in their boat, drifting gently on. The Renné were not thirty feet away, or so Tam guessed. They could hear them speaking—far too loudly, he thought—for voices carried surprisingly far over water.

"They don't have Alaan," Pwyll whispered.

"Then who?" Fynnol wondered.

"Did you hear?" a man's voice asked, and the occupants of the boat fell silent. Elise plunged her blade into the water and signaled Baore to take them on.

★   ★   ★

Prince Michael stumbled over some water-logged branches and got quickly up. He was pulling the boat—Alaan's litter—with one hand, and parting branches with the other. Samul was doing the same on the other side, and Beldor brought up the rear, pushing the boat for a moment and then stopping to listen for pursuit.

"Perhaps it will be the end of the watch before we are missed," Samul panted.

"Perhaps. I should have brought the waterwillow bark. I don't know what else we have to fight Alaan's fever."

"You really don't think we can find our way out without Alaan?" Samul asked.

"I'm sure of it," the Prince said. "I accompanied Hafydd when he pursued Alaan once before. Alaan is a sorcerer of some kind. He travels on paths others cannot find. But this place he has brought us: it is like an eddy in the river. Things fetch up here and circle round and round until they sink."

"Then we are going to die here, for Alaan is beyond our powers to heal."

"That is true, Lord Samul, but fortunately it doesn't hold true for everyone."

"Well, that is cryptic."

"There is another sorcerer here. A sorceress, to be more exact. She is our last hope. Unlike Hafydd, she has the power to heal."

"I will not ask how you know this," Samul said, trying to hurry yet make no noise, failing at both. "No, I will ask. How in the world have you gotten mixed up with these . . . people?"

"Hafydd serves my father. He was the start of it all. It is as though he appeared and then these others came to oppose him. I don't understand it."

Alaan shifted in his blankets and muttered. Michael put a hand on his forehead. He was afire.

"How will we find this sorceress who has the powers of healing?" Samul asked.

"She will find us."

"Of course. Soon?"

"I don't know. Let us hope."

They went on in silence then, wondering if Hafydd was already in pursuit, driving his men on as only he could. Moonlight filtered down through the branches and lay like dulled silver on the calm water. Clouds of mist rolled in slow, ghostly procession. As they entered yet another such cloud, Michael raised his hand to protect his face from unseen branches, but as it thinned they found two men standing before them.

The Prince and the Renné had blades in their hands immediately, looking around them frantically, wondering if there were more men hidden in the mist.

"Who are you?" Samul said.

The big one pointed with a massive sword. "I was the companion of Sainth for many lives of men. I am called Orlem Slighthand."

"Sainth? Who is Sainth?"

Alaan shifted in his litter and muttered something. Then clearly he said, "Orlem . . . ? Have I passed through at last?"

"No, my old friend. You are among the living yet." He gestured at Michael. "Bring him now. We must keep him safe."

"But he is dying. We must find someone who can heal him."

He gestured to his companion. "Rabal might heal him, if it is not too late."

The big man turned to walk on, but looked back over his shoulder. "Come. The servants of Death are near. I hear their hounds baying."

Samul laid his sword on Alaan's breast in the narrow little boat and began to pull it on. Prince Michael hesitated for only a moment and then did the same. Dimly he could make out the two figures lumbering before them. Nets of mist, cast by a faint breeze, drifted across their backs.

It seemed to Michael that he had fallen into a kind of madness. A madness that had begun when Hafydd came to his father's castle, and had grown more strange with each passing day. Until he found himself wading through a drowned wood, bearing a dying sorcerer and following a man who called himself Orlem Slighthand. And if all that were not strange enough, his companions were Renné—the enemies of his family for generations.

They walked in silence for most of an hour, the Prince guessed, and then waded ashore on one of the myriad small islands. The two men awaited them there. Once upon dry land, Michael realized that the man's size was not an illusion. Orlem Slighthand was massive, broad through, with arms like enormous tree roots. He wore an ancient shirt of mail and a helm unlike any the Prince had seen. His sword was a two-hander, but he held it easily in one.

The other man was not small either—his face hidden behind a thick, black beard and long hair, so that little more than his mouth, eyes, and nose could be seen—as though he were being sucked down into tar. He was strangely dressed as well, in clothes no tailor had made.

As they brought the boat up to the shore, the strangers bent down and the two of them lifted the boat, bearing it easily up the slope with Alaan lying in it, still as the waters. They found the remains of a wooden structure there, a makeshift thatch roof over three poorly repaired walls. To either side were window openings, staring blindly out over the flooded wood. A fire, burned down to coals, smoked in a pit before the open side.

"Lay him down here," the man named Rabal said. They lifted Alaan out onto a thin pile of bedding. Rabal bent over the inert form lying in the log boat, Orlem crouched down opposite him, and the three noblemen stepped back.

"Death draws nigh, Rabal," Orlem said softly. "I feel his breath."

"Then we know what we must do: keep his servants at bay, no matter what the cost. Go down to the foot of the island. Cattails grow there. Bring back all you can bear. All of you." He got up then and went to the fire, stirring the ashes and laying kindling over the glow.

Orlem bade them follow, and they walked quickly down to the

island's end. Using their daggers, they cut cattails and piled them on the shore. The Prince wanted to ask why, but the strangeness of the situation kept him silent. Why had he just left Alaan alone with someone he did not know? Did Alaan really recognize this man or was he just raving?

When they had all the cattails they could carry, they went stumbling back to the ruin, raining a detritus of dried reeds behind them. Rabal was bent over the fire, stirring the contents of a black iron pot, flames licking up from its base. He looked up from his efforts and beckoned Samul. "Stir this quickly and do not stop or it will burn. If it grows too thick and begins to dry, add this." He lifted a small, long-necked bottle of blue glass. "No more than you absolutely must."

Rabal showed them how to tie the cattails into bundles, and he placed these in a rough circle around the crown of the island, where the structure stood. He then went to each bundle, speaking words the Prince could not hear and doing something he could not see. When this was complete, he led them back to the fire. There, he took four sticks he'd laid on the ground so their ends were in the flame, and gave one to each of the noblemen and one to Orlem.

"Take these and go stand down by the bundles of cattails. If you see shadows coming ashore and feel a sudden coldness, then light a bundle and drive the shadows off with your torch."

"But these will soon go out," Beld protested.

"They will not go out," Rabal said, "not before morning. Now leave me to my task." He turned away.

"Now *this* is madness," Beld said to his cousin and Prince Michael. "How do we know they won't murder Alaan?"

"We don't," the Prince said, "but I'm sure these two could easily have killed us all and taken Alaan away. I don't think that's their intention. Let's go down to the shore. Watch for shadows," he added, turning his gaze on the Renné, "and I should be very vigilant, if I were you."

They positioned themselves at the four points of the compass and stood staring out into the dark night. Orlem was to the Prince's left, Samul to his right. He could see the small flames of their torches wavering in the breeze. There seemed to be shadows everywhere, moving as the mist blew this way or that, or when clouds passed overhead. The Prince was frightened for a while, and then the absurdity of the situation struck him. How foolish this would seem to anyone who came upon them. Perhaps Hafydd would appear and actually laugh.

Michael started when Orlem suddenly shouted at the darkness, stuffed his torch into a bundle of reeds, setting them afire, and then lunged down the slope toward the shore, bellowing and brandishing his torch. Michael stared into the night where the giant stormed, trying to peel back the layers of mist. Was that something there? Something dark and quick?

But then there was movement before him. Not men, he thought, but no beast he knew either. Shapeless and swift, they appeared, bringing a cold breeze that seemed to blow right through him. He did as he had seen Orlem do, lighting his bundle of reeds and then moving down the slope, waving his small torch and shouting at the vast darkness.

The shadows did not withdraw, but as he reached the water, they seemed to hesitate, lying beneath the trees, their shape swelling and shifting. Fear washed through him and then the shadows struck. Michael swung his torch at the darkness, screaming at the top of his lungs, half from terror. Something pale flashed in the darkness—like claws. And then Orlem came to his aid, attacking fearlessly, and the dark shapes withdrew.

"Did you see them?" Michael asked. "There, beneath the trees?" He could barely catch his breath to speak.

"I saw them; Death's ravenous children. Run up, now, and bring more bundles of reeds. They've not finished with us yet."

Michael did as he was told, wondering what he had seen in this strange wood. Something more than shadows, he thought. He collected the last bundles of cattails and returned to his post.

Michael took to walking back and forth a few paces, staring out into the dark where he saw shadows flitting from tree to tree, or thought he did. Twice more the shadows pressed forward, so that Beldor and Samul were forced to fend them off, the second time needing both Orlem and Rabal to drive them back. The two strangers appeared to have no fear of Death.

And then a voice called out. A woman's voice. "Michael? Michael of Innes? Is that you?"

"It is," he said in relief. And then to Orlem, who strode over, his sword in one hand, torch in the other: "It's all right. She is a friend." But Orlem went quickly down the slope as a boat appeared in the faint moonlight. In the bow stood Elise, a blade in her hand.

"She is a friend!" Michael called out as the giant blundered into the water.

"My lady?" Orlem said, his voice thick with emotion. "Is that you? Can it be, after all these centuries?"

"*Orlem,*" Elise said. "*Orlem Slighthand.*" And she began to weep.

Forty-nine

The giant whom Elise called Orlem helped her ashore, his own eyes wet with tears.

"Look at you, Orlem Slighthand," Elise said. "You have not changed . . . in all these years." She was laughing and crying at once.

"But you have, my lady. You are light of hair now, though beautiful still."

Elise looked around, her laughter suddenly disappearing as though she had seen something that disturbed her. "What is it you do here, Orlem?"

"We came seeking Sainth and have been fending off the servants of Death who have come to carry him back to their dark kingdom."

All levity was gone. "Take me to him." She hurried up the bank, Orlem at her side.

Left behind on the shore, Tam and the others climbed out of the boat, drawing it up the bank a little.

"Come up," Orlem called back. "Give them flaming brands, someone, for we will need all their help."

"Run up to the fire," a young nobleman said to Tam, "and arm yourself with a torch. Be you ready, for strange things occur this night."

"Are you Prince Michael of Innes?" Cynddl asked the stranger, whose once-fine clothes were torn and soiled. Even his face was covered in wounds.

"I am but we have no time for introductions. If you want to live, heed Orlem and arm yourself with fire."

Pwyll and Baore led them quickly up the bank, where a dark-bearded man kindled brands for them. While they waited, Tam could see Elise bent over Alaan, a hand laid on his forehead.

"Oh, he is so near," she breathed. "We must be quick. Keep his servants at bay, Orlem, as long as you can."

"I will do my best, my lady," the giant said as he rose to his considerable height, "but they are gathering in force now, their master not far off. If he comes, there is naught we can do. Even if we sell all of our lives to him, it might not be enough."

Orlem stationed them in a circle around the crest of the island, instructing them in their defense. The giant was calm and deliberate in everything he said or did, and Tam was surprised at how much confidence he gained from this. Orlem took up a place by the fire, keeping it burning bright, assisting Elise and the bearded man when needed, but watching over those he had set to guard the island.

Fynnol stood thirty feet away, rocking from one foot to the other. Even in the poor light, Tam was sure there was no mocking smile on his face this night.

On the other side of the crest someone began to holler and shout. Tam glanced over his shoulder to see Orlem sweep up a torch and run to the man's aid, hollering and shouting as he went.

Tam stared out into the night, the drowned forest bathed in pale moonlight. Clouds of mist wandered and swirled in and out of the shadows of trees. The whole scene seemed a nightmare. He waited, with his torch held high and to one side, so that its light would not spoil his vision, and looked for . . . what? Shadows, he'd been told, as though the Stillwater had only a few of those.

But then he did see shadows, in places where he thought the

light must fall. They flowed like water, swift and difficult for the eye to follow. And then they were before him. Shouting defiance, he swung his torch, despite the chill that came over him, took his courage away and weakened his voice.

He drew the sword his grandfather had given him and held it high, waving his torch at the shadows, beating them back, though he touched nothing. Dark wings seemed to flail at him out of the night, and he swung his torch to meet them. Others appeared beside him: Orlem, who showed no hesitation, wading into the fray, and Fynnol. Orlem's torch fluttered as it cut the air, like a flight of bats.

The shadows swayed and lunged this way and that, but Tam and Orlem stood their ground, swinging their flaming brands and shouting like madmen. Fynnol lunged at the darkness with his torch, then twisted strangely, falling. But he did not hit the ground. He was being dragged into the air! Tam could see the horror on his cousin's face.

Orlem leapt forward with a curse and swung his great blade so close to Fynnol that Tam was sure he'd kill him. The little Valeman hit the ground and bounced. In an instant he was crawling up the bank, frantic and terrified.

Before Orlem's onslaught, the shadows withdrew, hissing and whispering like winter wind. Tam turned to find Fynnol on the ground still, trembling so badly he could not rise. He stared blindly ahead and muttered under his breath

"Did the claws touch you?" Orlem said, but when Fynnol did not seem to hear him, the giant bent down and tore open the back of the Valeman's jacket. Tam saw Orlem take a deep breath and let it out—almost a sigh

"Luck smiled on you this night," he said. "You've not a scratch. If the servants of Death dig their claws into you . . . well, you would not be sitting here frightened out of your senses." Orlem helped Fynnol rise—picked him up, really, and stood him on his feet. "Come up to the fire. You'll need more than a moment to recover from that. The servants of Death had hold of you, lad, and if not for old Orlem you'd be on your way to Death's kingdom this night."

Tam looked over at Prince Michael, who shook his head. Tam knew exactly what he saw in the Prince's face. They had been frightened before, but now they were shaken to their souls. These shadows were not figments of their imagination, but the hands of Death reaching out to snatch them away—away from this life they knew.

Tam didn't know how many more times they were tested, but at some point he realized that the attacks had become less frequent, and then they ceased altogether. Orlem walked around the island speaking quietly to each of them.

"I think they're gone," he said. "Lady Sianon must have found a way to bring Alaan back from the very gate of Death. Sit you down and rest a little but don't relax your vigil. We might be tested once more."

Tam collapsed but still stared out into the forest. Prince Michael came over and threw himself down beside Tam.

"I have fought my father's enemies," the Prince said, "and I thought that strange enough, but to fight the servants of Death . . ."

"You saw them? The shadows?"

The Prince laughed. "I asked the same thing of Orlem when they first appeared. He answered as though I were a particularly stupid child. But for those of us who've lived the quiet lives of mortals, to encounter Death incarnate is difficult to encompass. I am Prince Michael of Innes."

"I'm Tamlyn Loell. Call me Tam, Your Highness."

The Prince waved a hand and tried to smile. "Oh, I've been cast out by my family, or will be when my father learns what I have done. Call me Prince Michael, or Michael if you wish. I think noble titles will not be mine in the future."

Cynddl wandered over and sat down beside them.

"Well, Cynddl," Tam said, "this will give you a story to tell. How many of us can say we've fought Death and drove him off?"

"More than you know, Tam," the story finder said. "Every man, woman, and child who has lain close to Death from sickness or injury has fought a duel with Death or his servants. This was Alaan's fight, and we only helped him a little." He glanced into the misty wood, tired but surprisingly calm. "But soon we will have Hafydd to deal with."

Prince Michael sat up, looked as though he would speak, but then did not. An instant later he said, "I can't tell you how I regret my father's foolishness in taking up with this knight. I wonder sometimes if he was bespelled, so hard was it for him to see the man's intentions, his various sorceries."

Cynddl shrugged, his gray head bent from fatigue and fear. "These sorcerers can be terribly convincing when they have need. It seems you, however, were not fooled, nor were you bespelled. Your father must have heard many things that pleased him."

"The birds sing," Tam said. "Listen. I think Death must have withdrawn or found another victim for even the frogs fell silent while his servants were near."

The twitter of birds flitting through the foggy wood was like an elixir to Tam. It was such a common sound, a sound he heard outside his window each morning in the Vale. He shut his eyes a moment and listened. He could almost hear the sounds of his grandfather making his morning tea in the kitchen below.

"Dawn is not far off," Cynddl said, and he took a shaky breath.

"Will Hafydd dare come now with both Sianon and Sainth here to oppose him?" Tam said, feeling he should fill this moment with words.

"Alaan is ill," Cynddl said, "and will be weak for many days, even if Elise can bring him back from the gate of Death. These others I don't know." He turned to Prince Michael. "Who are they, your grace?"

The Prince seemed even more exhausted than they, Tam thought, though he did not take his eyes from the darkness beyond their island.

"I hardly know more about them than you. We met Orlem and Rabal in the Stillwater as we escaped with Alaan. Alaan recognized them—or one of them. Orlem claimed that he had served Al . . . Sainth some time in the distant past, a claim I would have dismissed as absurd a few weeks ago, but I have seen too many strange things since. We followed them here, where the shadows found us, and then you came with Sianon. I don't know that we would have survived without your aid."

"Orlem would have sacrificed himself to save Alaan," Elise said. They turned to find her approaching, looking as pale and tired as any in the early light of morning. "But you have all fought a most valiant fight. One that can stand alongside the great battles of song and story."

"Alaan is out of danger, I take it?" Cynddl said.

"For a moment. His wounds were left to fester too long, and he is sick beyond my present ability to heal. There is only one thing we can do for Alaan, and that is get him to the River Wyrr. Only the waters where his father sleeps will make him well again, and even that is not a certainty now."

Tam realized that none of them had even made an effort to rise to greet her—all too exhausted to care about manners. Elise, however, continued to stand. She had a hand on the pommel of her sword in its scabbard and stared out into the watery wood that was slowly turning to gray.

"How will we get Alaan to the River Wyrr if he is too ill to lead us?" Tam asked.

Elise only shook her head. "I don't know, Tam. We will see how Alaan is in a few hours. If he immediately begins to grow worse again, then we are in grave danger. There will be no way out for us."

Tam was so weary that he almost cried at this news.

"I think we must stand watches," the Prince said. "Surely Hafydd cannot be far behind."

"He is near but he will not appear this day." She looked down at the three nearly prostrate figures and smiled sadly. "He is waiting for me to heal Alaan and then hopes to follow us when we leave the Stillwater. No offense, Michael, but you would never have escaped so easily if Hafydd had not let you."

"But Beldor killed his guards unexpectedly. Even *I* did not expect it, for I thought Beld to be loyal to Hafydd, while Samul and I schemed to get Alaan away."

"I'm sure it looked like you escaped of your own wiles—Hafydd even sacrificed two of his guards to make it seem so—but Caibre has sacrificed entire armies when it suited him. If Hafydd does not appear by midday, then I will be proven right, for he cannot be that far behind." Elise sat down among them.

"Can we stand against him," Cynddl asked, "now that we have greater numbers and Orlem and his companion to aid us?"

Elise shook her head and looked down at her hand, which rested on the ground. She looked so sad that Tam wanted to take her in his arms. "I would have to be much stronger than I am. Hafydd . . . He made his bargain with Caibre some time ago—his memories have all come back and he has made some accommodation with them. He is equal to all of us, easily." She hung her head, her shoulders sagging. "Let us set watches so that some might rest. We will need all our strength."

"But what will we do now?" Tam asked, and wondered if he sounded as frightened as he felt. "We are condemned to this place without Alaan. That is what Cynddl thinks. Condemned here for the rest of our lives."

Elise looked up, meeting his eyes, her look unreadable. "If Alaan dies, Sainth will become nagar again and go into the Stillwater. Once this occurs, Hafydd will do everything in his power to kill me—and all of you as well. No one who might be a threat to him will be allowed to live. Being trapped here for the rest of our lives might not be such a burden, for our lives will be short."

Fifty

"They have found each other," A'brgail said. He held a dagger suspended over the waters by a cord. It swayed back and forth, pausing in the same place, finally coming to rest.

"Alaan and Hafydd?" Toren said.

"No, Hafydd is still hidden from me. It can only be Sianon. The presence is that strong. But they're all in the Stillwater. All the children of Wyrr."

"But Sianon is the enemy of Hafydd?"

A'brgail stared down at the dagger in the gloom, rubbing his beard with one hand. "Of Caibre, really, but what you say is true enough." He began coiling the cord around his hand, the dagger wobbling and rising in jerks.

Toren shifted on the bottom, his feet softened and badly blistered by the long hours in the water. He was tired and sore, and unsettled by A'brgail's claims—by matters he did not understand or control. "What goes on here, Gilbert? All these sorcerers, who you say have found hosts to bring them back to life; and now they are all in this same place. This can be no accident. What is it they hope to accomplish here?"

A'brgail pulled the dagger up into his hand and paused—thoughtful as ever. "I wish I knew, Lord Toren. My half brother seems to have come here first, with Sianon in pursuit and Hafydd, with your cousins in tow, not far behind. It is Alaan's hope to defeat Hafydd, to send him through Death's gate—and not just him, but Caibre also. Sianon was the enemy of Caibre, yes, but she was no less destructive, no less ruthless. The difference is that she loved Sainth. Loved him only. They might make a pact against Hafydd, though what would become of them after I don't know, for I will tell you that having any of Wyrr's children alive is a danger to the rest of us."

A'brgail untied the cord from his dagger and slipped the blade into a plain black sheath. "And I must make some hard decisions. My half brother Alaan broke the vows I have taken by making his bargain with Sainth. For this I am sworn to make him pay a terrible price. Yet without him I don't know how we will defeat Hafydd." He looked up at Toren. "I have not the knowledge to do it alone."

"Alaan was a member of your order?" Toren said.

A'brgail shook his head.

"Then he has broken vows that you took, Gilbert, not vows that he took."

"He has violated the laws of our order, stealing a smeagh and making his bargain with Sainth."

Toren moved a little to one side as the soft bottom seemed to recede beneath his weight. "But you have need of him now. Is that not what you're saying?"

A'brgail tucked the dagger inside his robe, his gaze falling to the water. "I don't know how I will defeat Hafydd without help," he said softly. "For all my pride, I don't know."

"In times of war, alliances are forced upon us, Gilbert. Alliances we might not make out of choice. But what can be more natural than an alliance with your own brother?"

"If my brother were only natural. But he is no longer quite my brother. Oh, he looks like him, and even talks much like him, but in his pride he believed he could best the nagar—and no one gets the better of these beings. The nagar will always win."

"You accuse both your brother and yourself of pride, Gilbert. Perhaps you have more in common than you like to admit."

"Perhaps."

Toren moved again as he sank slowly down into the silty bottom. "What will we do now, Gilbert? Have we followed Hafydd here without purpose?"

A'brgail looked up at him, his normally confident air gone. "Perhaps we have. I came hoping to learn something of him. Or perhaps to work up my nerve to stand against him. But I know I am not ready for that. He would send me through Death's gate and barely take notice. I must make peace with my brother, it seems. But if he is with Sianon . . . You don't understand, Lord Toren. Sianon lived for war. It was air to her. I cannot bring myself to ally myself with one monster against another." A look of terrible pain crossed A'brgail's face, as though an old wound suddenly let its presence be known.

"Perhaps you will have no choice. One enemy at a time, Gilbert. That is what I say. Hafydd first, then we will worry about his sister; and even his brother, if need be." Toren glanced off into the mist in the direction A'brgail's dagger had been pointing. "Do you think my cousins are with Sianon and Alaan?"

"It seems very likely. What will you do if you are to meet?"

"I don't know, Gilbert. I cannot forgive what they have done."

"You realize that you were suggesting I forgive my brother for what he'd done."

Toren glanced up at his companion, who seemed to have passed through his crises of confidence. "Yes, but we need your brother to fight Hafydd. We don't need Samul and Beld. No one needs them, not even Hafydd."

"Let's go find my brother. I have a peace to make."

With the coming of dawn, crows began to converge, dropping out of the mist like a dark rain. They clung to the branches overhead and sank into a strange, brooding silence.

Prince Michael looked unnerved by this dark host, and when asked why, told Tam that they had been attacked by crows, which was where his many wounds had come from.

"But you were with Hafydd then," Orlem said, coming up behind the two who stood sentry. "Rabal will not let them hurt you now."

"They obey Rabal?"

"Yes, they are his servants, his subjects, perhaps. Rabal Crowheart is how he is known—to those few who know him in this age." Orlem looked around once and then motioned for them to follow. "Come up for a moment. We must talk."

They followed the giant as he made his ponderous way up the hill. Orlem looked big even beside Baore, for he seemed to have twice the breadth of their companion.

Rabal and Elise sat by Alaan, who flickered in and out of what appeared to be sleep. Once, he took liquid from Elise, but hardly seemed to be aware of anyone. The Renné stood together, begrimed, their clothes in tatters, boots falling apart from slogging through the water. Tam thought that he must look the same. He glanced around at his silent companions. Every face looked haunted, wary. Everyone kept a hand near a sword or, like Cynddl and Tam, held a bow. They'd fought against the servants of Death that night, and in the pewter morning light they all looked like they'd learned more than they wanted to know of mortality. Fynnol still trembled from his encounter. His eyes kept losing focus, as though he relived the moment again and again.

"We have decisions to make," Elise said, rising stiffly to her feet. "And we must make them quickly. Alaan is dying—" Her voice broke, and for a moment she could not speak. "Without him we are trapped here. Hafydd is sure to come looking for Alaan soon, though now he is waiting, his blade in the water trying to sense the movement of either Alaan or me. He believes that we will lead him out of this place." She took two paces, gazing down at the ground, then back at Alaan, her face lined and careworn. "If Alaan passes over, Hafydd will try to destroy us all. How many men remain with him?"

"About twenty guards is all that remain to him," Beldor Renné said, "and we are but eleven—though fighting men all."

"Not all," Elise said quietly. "Had we a hundred, I should not be confident of victory. Hafydd is an army unto himself."

"What does it matter?" Fynnol said. He sprawled on the ground, too tired to even sit up. "We are trapped here without Alaan. Trapped, and we will die one way or another."

This brought a pall over the company.

"There is a way out," Rabal said softly.

Everyone turned on the stranger, though no one said a word, as though not sure they had heard right.

"Or there was, for I have traveled in and out of the Stillwater several times. I know the way, provided the path is still there."

"But Alaan told me he would rather die here than risk leading Hafydd back to the land between the mountains—at least so he spoke when he seemed lucid." Prince Michael stood gazing down at the stricken wanderer, lost in thought.

"Without Alaan, I cannot stand against Hafydd, Michael," Elise said. "He will hunt us down—all of us. And then we can't be sure he'll not find his way out of the Stillwater." She inclined her head toward Crowheart. "Rabal found a way out. Hafydd is a sorcerer. He has resources we cannot know—that I cannot know. I think he will find his way out in time. If not now, in ten years or in twenty." She looked down at Alaan. "With Alaan's help I will grow strong. We can face Hafydd then. But if Alaan and I are dead, who will be left to stand against him?"

"Can we escape and leave Hafydd behind?" Cynddl asked. "Can it not be done?"

"It will be difficult," Elise said. "Hafydd can't be far away, and I don't know what we can do to escape him other than make all haste. But it is worth trying." She looked forlorn, Tam thought. Whatever she had done to help preserve Alaan's life had left her drained. As though she had fought her own duel with Death that night.

"We must decide quickly," Orlem said. "If Alaan is to live, we must get out of the Stillwater and back to the Wyrr as quickly as we can." He looked over at Crowheart. "I don't know that we can keep Alaan alive another day."

"We can be out of the Stillwater by this time tomorrow," Crowheart said, "but we must all go without rest."

"I think we should do everything in our power to return Alaan to the Wynnd," Tam said. "We can't even part the mists of this day, so how can we know what will happen in the months and years to come? I say we take Alaan and race for the path out. I've met the servants of Death now. Let's expend our efforts to preserve life, not destroy it."

Fynnol nodded, as did Baore and Cynddl.

"I agree with this young man," Samul Renné said. "Let's find a way out of this swamp. If I am to die, I don't want to wander here for the rest of time." He waved a sword off into the mist. "Let us be gone."

Beldor, Orlem, and Rabal all agreed, leaving only Prince Michael.

"I can't claim to know what Alaan had planned," the Prince said, his reluctance obvious, "but certainly he wanted to lure Hafydd to this place. It seems foolish to lead him out, which we are likely to do."

"Whatever Alaan had planned for Hafydd will not come to pass now," Elise said. "And I agree with Tam. Let Hafydd be the servant of Death if he so chooses. We should try to preserve life. It is too precious."

Michael bowed his head to this and they quickly began to gather up their belongings.

With Orlem, they were too many to ride, even in two boats, so it was decided to break up Rabal's boat so it could not be used by their enemies.

"We should take turns in the boat," Elise said as they settled Alaan in Baore's boat as comfortably as they could make him. Her voice was a little shaky, Tam thought. "Wading through the waters soon tires one. Rabal, you will have to guide us."

Orlem insisted Elise ride, and she did not argue. It was obvious that her efforts to heal Alaan had left her weak and exhausted. Baore took up a pole and pushed them away from the small island. In a moment they were lost in the fog, a host of silent crows following from tree to tree like a shadow.

Dease sat with his back against a tree, fighting to stay awake, head pounding, his brain unable to hold a thought for more than an instant before it went flitting off down some other path. He felt nauseated each time he stood, or when he exerted himself, which it was difficult not to do here. Coupled with his guilt and fear of discovery, he could not remember having ever been so wretched. He wondered if this were some kind of netherworld where he was paying the price for his mortal actions, and would continue to do so for lifetime upon lifetime.

"Dease?"

He opened his dark eyes, which took a few seconds to focus.

"We have decided to speak with this sorceress," Toren said. "You should come so that there is at least one Renné witness to any agreements I make with Beld and Samul."

Dease nodded, hesitated a second, then forced himself up, leaning against the tree until his dizziness and nausea passed.

"Let me help you, Cousin," Toren said.

"No. No, I'll be all right in a moment. It's passing already." He forced himself to stand unaided and tried to smile at his cousin's look of concern. "Let us go treat with this sorceress, for I have always wanted to see one."

"Beware, Cousin. Gilbert tells me that in the past men fell under this sorceress' spell and would wither from despair and want of her."

"She is sounding more intriguing by the moment. How beautiful she must be," Dease said, thinking for the first time of the spirit he saw in the waters. "What does she look like, I wonder?"

Toren shrugged. "Samul and Beld will be there, I think. I don't want to grant them any kind of amnesty for what they have done, but see little choice in this matter. A'brgail says that we cannot hope to fight Hafydd without the help of this woman, and apparently Samul and Beld have joined her."

"Choices are often forced upon us by circumstances, Toren. We might not like them, but events conspire to leave us no alternatives—or so it seems at the time. Our present circumstances are remarkable, to say the least. If you believe these tales of sorcerers reborn, then Beld and Samul are suddenly of very little consequence in the larger stream of events. You need never forgive them personally—that is not required. Grant them amnesty, but tell them they are not welcome back among the Renné. They will accept that, I think."

Toren considered this, as solemn as a mourner. Finally he nodded, then looked at his cousin from the corner of his eye. "Dease, do you think there were any others in this conspiracy besides Arden, Samul, and Beld?"

Dease felt all the moisture suddenly drain from his mouth. "I don't know. What did Arden tell you?"

"Beld's arrow felled him before he finished."

"Well, then only Samul or Beld might know, Toren. Ask them."

"I hardly think they will answer now." He nodded in the direction they should go. "Let us go find A'brgail's brother and make an alliance against this sorcerer."

"Well, that at least makes sense to me. Hafydd is a danger to us."

"Sense? Things stopped making sense when we rode up into a range of hills that should not have been there. Come along, Dease, you have fallen into a tale of old and can't get out until the sorcerer has been defeated." Toren's engaging smile dispersed the cloud of worry for a second.

Dease felt himself almost smile in return. "Let's hope that's the course of this tale. I think it has too many twists to flow so straight. But lead on, Cousin. I'm anxious to see how it all comes out."

They found A'brgail and his followers, and the small group of bedraggled Renné retainers, all gathered by the water's edge. Dease took one wistful look back at the solid ground they were leaving, and stepped into the cool waters. He guessed the morning was still in its youth, but with the cloud and mist one could never be sure.

He had the feeling that he was walking to his own execution. He was certain that Samul and Beld would show no loyalty to him, and Toren would learn the truth. Dease didn't think he could bear the pain that Toren would feel. He was certain that he couldn't bear the shame.

They waded through the water, following A'brgail, who walked out ahead of his personal guards despite their efforts to keep up. They were all tired and hungry and in the lowest spirits from this gray, lightless place. It felt as though they were in the land of the dead already.

As they approached the island, Dease smelled smoke; not the kind of smoke one got from a blaze, but rather the bitter smoke of old coals. Daylight spread a thin, colorless light throughout the drowned wood, where mist moved among the trees in slow, tattered ribbons. It was a day like every other they had seen in this timeless place.

A'brgail held his hand up, and the company stammered to a halt. He motioned for Toren and Dease to come near, and then pointed, speaking softly.

"Do you see the outline of an island?"

Dease did not, but then the mist parted a little and he saw the dim line like a hill's crest. He nodded.

"That is where my brother and Sianon wait."

Toren and A'brgail signaled the others to stay and went forward into the mist. A'brgail called out, the words echoing through the fog. No one answered. He called again, and after a long wait, a third time. No voice spoke in return.

They motioned to the others, and they all went forward, crouching a little, apprehensive of arrows. But they reached the shore of the island and there was no movement or sound or any sign of aggression. They waded ashore, dripping, their boots squelching beneath their feet.

"Let me go first," A'brgail said. "Sorcerers can leave spells to harm the unwary."

On the crest of the island they found a crude wooden shelter among a stand of trees, and a fire, burned to coals, smoking fitfully before it. A'brgail waved everyone back and walked around, looking intently at the ground, crouching down here and there.

"Do you see these marks on the ground?" he said as he knelt by the fire. "They were made with ashes. A spell was cast here. Stay your distance from it."

No one wanted to go near the spot, but gave it the widest berth.

A'brgail gestured to Toren. "I will have to use my dagger to follow Sianon." He went off to one side of the shed to divine for sorcerers.

A moment later he appeared around the corner of the shabby building.

"Hafydd is almost upon us!" he hissed. "Run!"

Fifty-one

Hafydd crouched low on the island's shore. His blade was in the water, his eyes closed. He could feel Sianon, not far distant now. They had found each other, his brother and sister, and now he would see if Sainth glowed brighter or continued to fade. It would tell him something of how quickly Sianon's transformation took place.

"What is it you do, son of Wyrr?"

Hafydd's eyes flicked open but he did not move. A few yards off, in the mist, stood the old man they had met before.

"I seek my brother, Herald of Aillyn. He was taken away from me this night by treachery, after I had brought him back from the very foot of Death's gate. I am worried beyond measure for his safety."

The old man took a step closer, moonlit mist performing a slow swirl around him. "You saved his life, then?"

Hafydd nodded once. He still crouched by the water, sword in hand.

"I spoke with your brother—offered him a great treasure if he would aid my master, but he refused."

Hafydd was sure he could cut this old man down in a trice if he needed to—here, foolishly away from his guards.

"And why would Sainth not aid your master, Herald?"

The great shoulders shrugged. Hafydd realized for the first time that the man held an unsheathed sword in his left hand.

"His memory reached back into the dark days of Aillyn's reign, when many terrible things were done that later Aillyn deeply regretted and did much to atone for. Sainth did not believe that a man such as Aillyn could feel remorse and change his ways."

"Yes, that is Sainth. He does not believe in men's better instincts, as I do myself. What aid does your master require?"

The man continued to stare at Hafydd, his eyes dark as crows. "He wove a great spell long ago, and now that spell has begun to fail."

"The spell that shattered the One Kingdom."

The old man nodded.

"But the spell . . . it was unnatural. It should fail and the lands be joined again."

"Perhaps you are right, son of Wyrr. But the cost will be great. Are you prepared for you own lands to suffer this devastation? Only Aillyn can save us from this calamity, but he must have a willing ally—someone with knowledge of the arts, for what must be done will be difficult and require the knowledge and endurance of a sorcerer."

"But Aillyn is gone, Herald; unreachable to mortal men."

"Not so, Lord Caibre. I have a stone that he possessed that will allow its possessor to bring my master back enough that he might guide someone through the task."

"A smeagh," Hafydd said.

"The word means little to me. I think this jewel is something far more. It is said to contain the secret knowledge of Aillyn and Wyrr's father, who was a great sorcerer and trained his sons in the arts."

"There were rumors once of such a jewel. My father possessed it, but when he passed into the river it could not be found."

"It had come to Aillyn by then, and I have it now."

"I am not Sainth, Herald of Aillyn, but if there is some way I might aid your master in this endeavor, you have but to ask."

The old man came a step closer, almost within reach of Hafydd's sword. "Aiding my master might require more of you than you are willing to offer. This jewel is like everything in life—in some way, you will pay for the powers it will provide."

"It is always thus, Herald. I am well aware of it."

"Then you still pledge your aid to my master?"

"I do pledge it."

The old man walked out on the land then. He sheathed his sword and fingered the gold chain around his neck. As he pulled this over his head, a green gem the size of a fingernail came glittering into the frail light.

He took a step toward Hafydd, the chain strung over his fingers. Hafydd realized that the old man meant to put it around his neck and he stood up to stop him.

"I must examine it first," he said, stepping back, raising his sword a little. "It might have enchantments laid upon it."

"Which it certainly does, but they are beyond our power to understand." The old man paused. "If you don't want Aillyn's gift, tell me now."

"No. It was my father's and is therefore mine by right. I will have it." Hafydd bent his head and allowed the old man to settle the chain upon his shoulders.

The man stepped away, gazing at Hafydd, his eyes blinking rapidly. He looked as though he would weep, as though he would fall down upon the ground and offer up his thanks. How great a burden this must have been—to guard this jewel for a thousand years.

"I will lead you to Aillyn's chamber," the old man said.

Hafydd took hold of the chain upon which the jewel hung and for a moment stared into the stone. "But you misunderstand, old man, if I cannot put Aillyn to some use, as the Knights of the Vow did so long with me, then I will crush this jewel into dust and scatter it to the wind."

He looked up at the old man and smiled at the man's horror. But Hafydd had his sword in hand, and the herald's was sheathed.

Still, the old man was surprisingly quick, getting his sword free of the scabbard just as Hafydd's blade took him in the neck. He fell heavily, his limbs bouncing limply; dead. The old man worked his mouth a bit and his eyelids fluttered, but then he was still as only the dead can be. Still as stone and just as cold.

How pathetic he looks, Hafydd thought. He sat down on a stone, unable to take his eyes from the dead herald for some reason. Somewhere inside he felt something strange—almost a sadness, or shame—but he pushed it down and turned away, walking up the slope of the island, the vision of the old man falling to the ground stricken from his thoughts—almost.

Fifty-two

Lord Carl was on his feet, though he could not shake a deep sense of fatigue. It was late afternoon, almost dusk, and despite his concerns, he had slept most of the day away. He dressed himself in a suit of clothes that had been left out for him, and pulled on his boots, which were not yet completely dry.

Outside he could see the Duke's army camped in a pasture that sloped gently up to the south. Around the commandeered home, guards stood at their posts or patrolled the grounds. Lord Carl leaned out the window and made careful note of each guard's position, the number on patrol, and how frequently they passed.

"But what will the Duke do?" he whispered to himself. Certainly Vast didn't know that Jamm had seen him meeting with an emissary of Prince Neit of Innes. Had he known, they would likely have been dead by now, or imprisoned.

Carl shook his head and took several deep breaths of the fresh evening air, but this neither cleared his head nor forced everything into sensible order. The Prince of Innes had not seemed to be aware that he and his father worked against him. Perhaps Vast had not betrayed them—at least not yet. Was the Duke playing both sides, waiting to see which might win? Had he not swept down from the hill and turned the tide of the battle for the Isle? But perhaps he hadn't. Perhaps he could see that the Renné were going to win no matter what.

Was Vast giving false information to Innes? This seemed possible. But Carl realized that if Innes discovered his and his father's true purpose, he might also learn that their contact with the Renné had been the Duke of Vast. And then Prince Neit would know he'd been played for a fool. That seemed too obvious a risk for the Duke to take.

No, the Duke was either playing both sides or was secretly an ally of Innes, Carl decided, which meant that he was in grave danger. Likely the only reason he had not already been returned to the Prince was that a well-guarded canal stood in the way.

A knock sounded at his door and a servant came in bearing a tray of food. He was followed by an advisor of the Duke's—a man Carl had met before, though he could not remember the man's name.

"It is good to see you up, my lord," the man said, smiling. "I rejoice at your astonishing escape."

"Thank you. It was more miraculous than astonishing, I think."

"If there is anything that I might do, my lord, please call on me."

Carl nodded to the food. "You have anticipated my greatest need. Beyond that, you could send me my man, Jamm, and I would like to see Lord Kel Renné as soon as it can be arranged."

"I'm sure the Duke will do everything within his power to accommodate you. At the moment he is off, seeing to his duties. He does ask that you not venture beyond sight of the guards, as there are still companies of enemy men-at-arms abroad. And if you don't mind, he asks that you not leave the house by night. We are at war and it is dangerous here yet."

"I am touched by the Duke's concern, but I've known risks enough of late. I won't be taking any I don't have to."

The man bowed and led the servant out. He had made no mention of Jamm or his whereabouts, and this worried Carl. His hunger, however, overcame his worries, and he shoveled food into his mouth in a manner that would have embarrassed him had he witnessed it in another.

Darkness drifted over the fields like smoke, and campfires appeared beneath the stars. Carl finished a goblet of wine and went to the door of his room. It was open, but he found two guards standing in the hall. One of them bowed to him.

"For your protection, your grace, we have been detailed to accompany you."

Carl nodded. "Do you know where my attendant, Jamm, has gotten to?"

"Likely down in the kitchens, your grace. It's said he was a might hungry."

"Can you lead me there?"

"We can, sir."

The house was moderately large, elegantly appointed, and apparently full to capacity, for Carl passed no fewer than thirty people between his room on the third floor and the kitchens in the cellar. The staff were at table—those not engaged in their duties—but they came to their feet when the young nobleman appeared. Jamm had been there, they said, but some hours earlier. No one knew if he had been given a place to sleep, which is what Carl suspected he was doing, though he had a nagging concern—a feeling that something was amiss.

He wanted to go outside to take the air but his guards insisted that he was not to do so, by order of the Duke, and that they would certainly be found derelict of their duties if it was learned that he had been outside. Reluctantly, Carl acquiesced, and as there was nothing else to do, asked to be returned to his rooms.

For a while he sat by the window, listening to the men singing—joyous in their victory, no doubt. Everytime he heard footsteps in the hallway he sat up, hoping it was Jamm, but the sound always passed him by. Unable to bear it anymore, he stuck his head out into the hall, only to find two new guards stationed there.

"Do you know what's become of the man who accompanied me here?" he asked the man nearest the door.

"That little highwayman, your grace? The Duke had a little conversation with him out in the stables. You're lucky not to have had your throat cut by that one, your grace. The Duke was most disturbed after his discussion with the little thief, that's what's said. Most disturbed."

"And I am most disturbed to hear it."

Carl pulled his head back inside, closed the door and cursed under his breath. How had they seen through the highwayman so fast? And what had the Duke learned from Jamm?

He went to the window and looked out again. He was three floors from the ground. Too far to jump. He remembered Elise Wills appearing in his room that night. How delighted he had been! But there was no roof outside this casement. Only a drop of many feet.

He stood in the window and yawned, stretching his arms over his head. A moment later he put out the candle, and then waited without sound. When the old mansion began to fall quiet, he stripped the bed of its sheets and knotted them together. They wouldn't reach the ground but he could get in the window directly below. Doubling the sheet around the post between the casement windows, he took hold of both parts and swung out. In a moment he'd gone hand over hand down to the window below.

The shutters were thrown back and one casement opened. He hung there for a moment, listening, and when he was sure the room was empty, he swung awkwardly in. The sheets he pulled down after him, folded them as neatly as he could, considering their recent use, and placed them on a shelf in the wardrobe.

Carl was tempted to rummage the room and see what might be useful, but instead he peeked out into the hall. There were still many people about and he could hear music and laughter below. He went back to the window and looked carefully out. Below him there was yet another window, this one with a light in it. It would be foolish to go down here, though the guards posted outside were some distance off.

The door latch rattled behind him, and a line of light ran along the wall as the door swung slowly open. Carl was out the window and clinging to the sill before he'd thought about it.

He looked down to see if his escape had caught the distant guards' attention, but both stood quietly in their places. In the room, he could now hear voices and laughter—a man and a woman. With a little luck they would not be coming to the window. His arms would soon grow tired, he realized, and the couple showed no signs of leaving. Indeed, they sounded as though they would be occupied for some time, unless their strength failed before his—which seemed very unlikely.

The footsteps of a guard passed below. Carl craned his neck to look down. As he was deciding what to do, a door opened below and a group of drunken officers came out singing loudly. When they passed, Carl let himself drop, landing on his toes, knees bent. He hit the ground and rolled, coming up to his feet. Taking up the same tune, he went lurching after this group, buttoning his breeches as he went as though he had just relieved himself somewhere in the dark.

Approaching the guard, he expected to be asked where he'd come from, but the man said nothing, and in a moment Carl was away from the house. He found a path that ran along inside the garden wall and followed it. The stables were easily found by following the smell, and then he slowed, circling the building, staying to the shadows.

It was a stone building, one story tall with no hay storage above. The prudent owner would not risk his prize stock to fire. Ostlers, stable boys, and equerries loitered out front, tossing coins in the dirt by the light of a torch. Inside there was no light at the moment—the fear of fire again. The stable could be entered by three doors in the front, and at one of them a guard leaned against the wall. There were split doors into the stalls, the top halves latched open on this warm night.

Carl continued his circle. There was a double door in the end of the building, and though this was in darkness, it appeared to be closed and he guessed it would be latched from inside.

Around the back was a fenced paddock. There upper sections of the stall doors stood open as well. He could see light from the other side of the building in these openings. Climbing smoothly over the fence, he went looking for a nice quiet mare, which he found in short order. He took a moment to whisper to her and pat her neck and nose, before slipping over the lower door and into her stall. The stalls were divided from the inner hallways with wooden bars above, a precaution against the stallions that were kept here. Many a knight's mount was bad tempered and spirited, and would bite the unsuspecting or lunge at a passing horse.

Carl reached through the bars and undid the latch, letting himself out into the long corridor that ran the length of the stable, good-sized stalls to either side. He ran from side to side, peering into every stall until he finally found one that was closed to the outside, had stone walls on two sides, and was barred on the other.

Carl peered into the dark space. "Jamm?" he whispered. "Jamm?"

A noise and then a dark face appeared only a few inches from his own.

Carl reeled back. "What have they done to you?"

"Beaten me near to death," the little thief said with some difficulty. "I've lost a few teeth and am not quite so handsome now."

Carl cursed beneath his breath.

On the simple latch he found an armorer's bolt, which he could not turn by hand.

"There's some blacksmith tools down at t'other end," Jamm said. "Have a look there."

Carl slipped quietly away, sliding along in a crouch so as not to be seen from outside. In a moment he was back with a tool that quietly opened the latch. He replaced the bolt carefully, dropping the blacksmith's tool through the bars into the dark. The light was poor, but still Carl could see that Jamm had been badly beaten. He walked slowly and with a limp, and bent over as though in terrible pain.

"You won't get far like that," Carl said. "We'd better find some horses."

"I'm in no shape to ride."

"Well, I don't think we shall find a cart for you." Carl thought a moment. "You'll have to ride up with me. Come along."

He soon found an old bridle, but no saddles. They slipped the bridle on the quiet mare Carl had befriended. Looking out into the paddock, he thought it was still deserted, and they walked the horse quickly out, finding a gate in the fence.

Carl helped Jamm mount and then climbed up behind him, holding him between his arms like a child. They set off at a trot into the darkness, saw no patrols and were lost in the night in a few moments. Jamm swayed as they went, trying hard to hold himself upright. He would have fallen if not for Carl.

"Jamm?"

The thief started.

"What did the Duke want of you?"

"Someone near the Duke sorted out who I was."

"How in the world did they do that?'

"Well, I think you gave them my name, sir, and clearly I wasn't a real equerry. My notoriety caught up with me, as me mother always said it would. Whoever pointed the finger at me must have known quite a bit about the lands beyond the canal. They enticed me out here, and the Duke had a few ruffians give me a good going over. I told them how we met and how we managed to escape."

"But did you tell them you'd seen the Duke before, as you told me?"

"I'd not be such a fool as to tell him that. No, that would have seen the end of me, quick enough. As it was, they threw me in that stall and said they'd tell you I'd run off. I think they were going to have one more go at me once I'd recovered a little, for I was fair faint by the time they'd plied me with their persuasions."

"Well, Jamm, I'm more than sorry that this happened. If I'd suspected it for a moment I would have been more sure about where we crossed the canal."

"Where are we going now?"

"I don't know. We need to find Kel Renné. I'm afraid that anyone else might turn us back over to the Duke. He'll no doubt spread a rumor that some dangerous prisoners have escaped. Only Vast and a handful of Renné know that I secretly served the Renné. To anyone else I am the son of one of their principal enemies."

"So we are on the run again?"

"So it would seem."

"I've not the lay of the land over here, your grace," the thief said. "So I can't hide us away as I could before."

"Perhaps not, but you have years of avoiding the yeomen and hunters. That will serve us well, I think. And this time your reward shall be greater, for we will tell Lord Kel the truth about his ally, and that will earn you the gratitude of the Renné."

"Well, I shan't count that silver till it's in my hand. Until then we need to keep ourselves alive. The Duke will send men out searching for us at first light. He's got quite an army there, with little to do. We need to put as many furlongs between them and ourselves as we can. The moon will be up soon and will not set before sunrise. If this nag can bear us, we should not stop but to let her drink until she falls beneath us."

"That we can do, but what of you, Jamm? You're none too steady yourself."

"I'll bear up, sir. We've no choice. Have we?"

"No. We can go to ground, but they might well find us, and then they'll lock us away so we can't escape. This is our one chance. If we only knew which direction we should go. . . . To find Kel Renné we will have to ask questions of people, and once we do that, the Duke will hear of it. I don't know how we will survive this, Jamm. I really don't."

Fifty-three

It was an eerie sensation, Carral thought. He could not, of course, see the child, and as the boy did not speak, he couldn't hear him either. It was as though he were a ghost; like the ghost who first came to him in the tower and set in motion this terrible chain of events that had led him here. But this was a child like no other. A child who spoke with silence and knew things he had never been told—or so his father claimed. He was uncanny and his abilities disturbing.

The Fáel thought this too; he could tell by the way they spoke, by the questions they asked and the way they asked them. And the wanderers had much greater tolerance for such things than the other peoples in the land between the mountains. After all, they had story finders and vision weavers living among them. The story finders were even venerated. The vision weavers were not treated the same way, but then, they dealt with a different strand of the world—they often saw disaster and tragedy—and messengers who brought bad news were always feared and distrusted.

But what kind of news would this child bring?

The boy claimed to have come seeking three men: one who heard the smallest sounds, one older than old, and a third who watched himself from outside. Clearly himself, Kai, and Theason, who never said "I." Carral could not shake the feeling that a messenger from the netherworld had come seeking them—and this feeling caused a numbness deep in his heart and confused his thoughts.

The Fáel elder, Nann, was as distressed as any, but Carral felt that her unease arose from different sources. Each time she spoke, her tone seemed to say; "Who would use a child like this? Who could be so heartless?"

Eber's explanation of the boy's message sent a chill through the company.

"Wyrr does not speak," Kai said. "He cannot."

"But do not men speak in their sleep?" Eber asked.

"Wyrr does not sleep. The great enchanter has passed over," Kai said firmly. Carral could hear the tension in Kai's voice. The forced politeness. Now that he knew a little of Kai's story, he understood. No one here should question his knowledge or his judgment. He had lived a hundred times longer than anyone present. He had served two of the great sorcerers of a mythical age. His authority should have been beyond question.

"Then he has passed through Death's gate?" Eber persisted.

"No," Kai said curtly, "but neither does he live. Not in any way that we understand the word."

"Well, I am confused by this," Eber said. "Wyrr is neither alive nor dead. Then he is a ghost?"

"No, he does not wander lost and wretched. His spirit was joined with the spirit of the River Wynnd, as we now call it. He is no more conscious than a river or a tree, a blade of grass."

"He dreams," Eber said. "My son tells me that he dreams."

"It is not possible," Kai said. "Rivers do not dream. They do not speak. Not even a river as strange and enchanted as the Wynnd."

Carral could hear the awkwardness this assertion caused.

"Then, good Kai," Carral said, "how do we explain this child being here, searching for three men who very easily fit our description?"

"I haven't said that he's not had visions, Lord Carral. Clearly he has. But good Tuath here has visions and does not claim that they come from a sorcerer who passed from this life an age ago."

"Llya does not understand the concept of deception," Eber said. "As of yet his speech has been as pure and honest as a new-born's cry."

"I would never suggest that he is trying to deceive us," Kai said, attempting to moderate his tone, "but only that he is deceived himself."

There was an unexplained silence, and Carral realized that Llya must have begun making shapes with his hands. Carral could almost hear the fascination—the horror.

"What does he say?" Nann asked, a tremor in her voice.

"He says that there is no time for talk. Wyrr and his brother stir and even from their sleep have set things in motion that could see all the lands brought to ruin. Wyrr's second son must be saved, and the eldest brother sent through Death's gate, though this will be more difficult than we can imagine, for the eldest is Death's favorite."

"But what of us?" Carral asked. "What does he want of Kai and me?"

"The man with the heart of a crow and his companion, Quick Hand, are not strong enough," Eber translated.

"Who can he be speaking of?" Tuath asked.

"Rabal Crowheart and Orlem Slighthand," Kai said in a stunned whisper.

"But who are they?"

"Two men of a . . . a certain reputation. I sent Orlem into the Stillwater seeking Crowheart, and the two of them to find Alaan."

The odd silence again, and then Eber said, "Llya says that only you can save Wyrr's second son . . . if Death has not already taken him."

Fifty-four

Elise had fallen asleep, if sleep one would call it. Baore was so concerned by her state that his attention kept wandering from his task of polling the boat, and in a place where trees could loom up out of the fog at any moment this was disastrous.

Orlem was concerned, but less so.

"What she did for Alaan has left her spent," he said. "Let her sleep. She will recover."

"But she can't be roused," Baore said, glancing at the big man through his mow of hair.

"I can rouse her if it becomes necessary, but let her rest now. She is just asleep. Nothing worse."

Tam believed what Orlem said and waded on through the waters, mists swirling slowly as their procession passed.

Alaan had roused several times and taken some water and a mouthful of food, but still he was wasting away, and had not spoken once since they left the island. He looked as though he could not live out the day.

They took turns in the boat, resting there for an hour before a stint at the poles, and then going back into the water. Tam let Fynnol have his turn in the boat, knowing how much the little Valeman needed the rest. They all needed rest. Rest and respite. Tam was sick of this place and of the fear of Hafydd. He walked on with a nearly blank mind, concentrating on placing one foot in front of the other. Muscles in his legs ached from pressing constantly forward through water. The thought of escaping the swamp was all that kept him moving. Otherwise he would have found an island and laid down to sleep, come what may.

Rabal stopped and the boat drifted up to him, Tam laying a hand on the gunwale so it would not bump into their guide, though Crowheart was more concerned to not disturb Alaan.

"We should arrange ourselves in case of attack," Crowheart said. "Hafydd will be hard after us once he realizes we are trying to leave the Stillwater. My crows might warn us of some dangers but some things can hide even from them. Unsheath your swords. It would be best to have two archers in the boat. Arrange your numbers equally to either side and watch your side carefully. Someone must be the rear guard."

"That will be my place, Rabal," said Orlem, hefting his great sword, which had not been sheathed since they left the island.

"Then I will go to the fore with Rabal," Pwyll said, and the others arranged themselves along each side.

Through the mists Tam could only sometimes make out the shapes of Rabal and Pwyll wading beneath the trees. Baore propelled the boat forward; the inert form of Alaan, covered in sweat, lay at his feet. Fynnol and Cynddl sat on the boat's thwarts with arrows nocked. Samul walked to the left of the bow and his cousin to the right. Tam took up a position to the right of Alaan, and Prince Michael of Innes to his left. In the boat, Tam laid his bow with a small supply of arrows. Thus arranged, they made their way through the drowned wood, the crows flocking from tree to tree overhead, their wings battering branches and air.

Over the sounds of the crow army Tam found himself listening intently, wondering what Crowheart expected to find in the mist.

Not knowing almost made it worse, for Tam's imagination was fertile even if his brain was tired.

The trees closed in around them for a while, and then the space between them grew again. The fog was especially thick that day, and there was not a breath of air.

Tam heard only the calls of the crows, and the swish of his companions wading through the waters. Then fog poured in, whirling like a dancer's costume, gauzy and insubstantial. It strangled out the strands of light falling between the trees, and muffled the sounds of men passing. He could no longer see Beld walking before him. Instinctively, Tam reached out to take hold of the boat's wet gunwale and realized he couldn't see his hand at arm's length.

"Is everyone here?" Orlem asked. "Let me hear your names."

Each said his name, voices muted as though even words could barely penetrate the fog. None were lost.

"Take hold of the boat," Orlem said. "Do not wander off—not even a step."

They all did as he said, stumbling forward like the blind.

"Rabal?" Fynnol asked. "Do you know where we're going?"

"Yes. This will only slow us. Don't be concerned. Crowheart can never be lost—even in fog thickening to water."

But slow them it did. Trees seemed to grow up before them now, and they were always maneuvering the boat around, though the trees were not seen until Rabal all but walked into them. Even the crows seemed to be confused by the fog, their anxious-sounding cries coming from far off rather than overhead. Tam reached out and touched Alaan in the boat, reassuring himself that the servants of Death had not stolen him away under cover of mist.

He shuddered at the thought of Death's servants. Their battle of the previous night seemed like a dream now—a nightmare. And suddenly the dense mist seemed full of threats. He half raised his sword as though fending off a stroke.

Something black flashed out of the fog, and Tam raised his arm to protect himself, only to find that a crow had landed on the gun-wale by his hand. But it was not a crow! It was Alaan's bird, Jac. The whist shuffled its small feet on the glistening wood and peered at its master. Twice it cried *whist* and then it fell silent, cocking its dark head from side to side. It then began a long liquid peeling, a song so beautiful Tam thought it could hardly have come from something so plain.

"What is that?" Samul's voice sounded from out of the fog.

"It is a whist," Cynddl said, "singing its song of love."

No one spoke for a moment, half expecting Alaan to magically rise at his servant's calling—but he did not stir. With the song's end, the dark little bird still stared at its master, head twitching from side to side. And then, without another sound, it leapt from its place and swam into the foggy air.

Tam wondered if Alaan's familiar had come to bid farewell, for it had called *whist* not once but twice—as though both Alaan and Sainth must have a death knell.

"That bird has never appeared at times of peace and safety," Baore growled. He had ceased to pole as his companions surrounded the boat and pushed it forward. "And look at this fog. It is thicker than any I've seen before. Thick as water, almost."

Tam felt the same. The fog was eerie and unnatural, as though something tried to keep them from continuing on. He wondered even if Hafydd might have created such a fog to keep Elise and Alaan from escaping.

They blundered on, bashing into branches and tree trunks, stumbling through the shallow waters. At times the fog grew so thick and disorienting that Tam found it difficult to keep his balance.

A wind sprang out of the west, cool and damp as the new morning. It sent the fog winging past, giving Tam the impression that he fell through a cloud. Throwing itself on the hidden trees, the wind began to tear away leaves and bits of bark, whirling them through the air. Its voice rose like a painful moan, and a storm broke over them like a sea.

The companions hunched over, throwing up their arms to protect their faces. A branch spun down through the fog and shattered a piece of the gunwale. Elise woke with a start, sitting up and shaking her head.

Pwyll climbed into the boat and, with his own body, shielded Alaan as best he could. The Stillwater belied its name suddenly, as waves began to sweep across the drowned wood, breaking against trees and throwing spray into the air. The boat bucked, and Elise leapt awkwardly over the side to help pull it forward. Waves reached Tam's chest, breaking against him and trying to throw him back. The wind was full of spray now, as the dense fog washed away, but with the flying debris from trees, one could see no more than before. Then rain threw itself down upon them, pelting them like hail.

The trees creaked and moaned and flailed their branches at the sky. Tam was battered by leaves and branches and had now and then to close his mouth and jump to keep his head above the wave crests. Water slopped into the boat, and rain beat down upon poor Alaan so that even he was soon wet through.

Branches went spinning past and Tam was struck several times, as he was sure were the others. Short, steep little waves tried to drown them and tossed the boat about like a skittish colt. Tam thought his arm would be yanked out trying to hold it.

Crowheart led them into a grove of trees that offered some protection from the waves and wind. Branches lashed about them and the wind screamed like a soul in torture. Here they huddled, as homeless as wild beasts.

"We cannot stop!" Elise shouted to Crowheart, her words torn away and whipped past Tam. "Alaan is slipping away."

"How can we go forward in this?" Crowheart shouted.

"Those who can must come with us," Elise called. "The rest must follow when they can. Alaan will die if we stop for even a moment."

And so they set their shoulders against the storm again, pushing into the wind and dragging the tossing boat with them. They went blindly on, unable to look into the wind, but Crowheart never seemed to hesitate. He led surely on as though he could see the Stillwater perfectly in his mind and set his foot where he wanted, even in the dark.

After several hours the wind grew hoarse and the howl abated a little.

"The storm is passing," Orlem shouted, but no one answered. The rest were too exhausted, and the waves still battered them, pushing them about like dolls. Fynnol had gone into the boat and lay near Alaan, unable to move. His small frame had not been made to stand up to storms, though he had endured it as long as he could before retreating into the boat. His heart was great, Tam thought, but his frame was small.

Slowly the waves subsided and the wind passed to calm. The surface of the Stillwater was awash in leaves and branches, and brown with silt stirred up from the bottom.

"Is anyone hurt?" Elise asked.

"Samul," Prince Michael said.

"It is small. Nothing," the Renné protested.

"Into the boat," Elise ordered, and took Samul's place.

Cynddl bound the nobleman's wound, which came from a falling branch, while Fynnol stood guard over the two with his bow.

"It is not severe," Cynddl reported, "but it will weaken his sword arm."

"I had only begun to heal from my last wound," Samul said. "Fortunately I can fight with my left almost as well."

"He does not exaggerate," his cousin said, but Rabal told Samul to remain in the boat for now.

For a moment Elise stood, her sword in the water, then she shook her head and smacked the surface with the flat of her blade. "Hafydd has made his circle again," she said. "I cannot tell if he is far or almost upon us." She waved to Crowheart. "Lead us on. Hafydd has hidden himself from me again. Who knows where he might be or what he might do."

The fog, which had been blown off by the storm, rose up from the waters again, though not so thick as it had been. As they walked they ate a little food to fortify themselves. The forest became more dense, the branches of trees sweeping down nearer the water, so they were forced to push them aside. Pwyll and Crowheart fell to clearing a path. At least the waves were smaller here, where the density of trees offered some shelter.

The water grew more shallow as they went, first only as deep as their knees, and then it shoaled to mid-calf. Everyone emptied out of the boat so it would float higher, for here and there they had to lift it over fallen trees that lay waterlogged on the bottom.

And then Tam realized that Crowheart stood on solid ground. He heard Fynnol stifle a sob at this. They had come to what looked like a beach. Brown grasses grew in a tangle, flattened in places as though winds came there often. Crowheart looked out into the fog, where Tam could see no trees, but as the boat ground ashore, he went forward and found Rabal standing on a rocky beach, calm water stretching out before him.

"What is this?" Elise asked.

"It is a lake, or so I have always surmised. I crossed it in a log boat before—paddling for perhaps two hours."

Baore looked up into the watery sky, hardly distinguishable from the lake before them. "But there is no sun to steer by, nor any feature of land. Do we follow the shore?"

Rabal shook his head. A crow had come and settled on his shoulder, where it preened itself, apparently unnoticed.

"We're out of the Stillwater at last," Fynnol said, his voice quivering a little.

"No," Rabal said. "We're but in another part." He raised an arm to point, causing the bird to protest. "My crows will guide us, but there isn't enough room in the boat for us all. Some will have to swim. There is no current nor have I ever seen the wind raise anything more than a ripple—though I'm sure today that would not have been true. Still, we must chance it. If there are swimmers among us, we should try to cross."

"I will swim," Elise said. "Let us carry the boat over. Alaan is almost gone and we've not a moment to spare."

The boat was taken up, borne over the narrow isthmus, and placed into the waters of the lake. Tam and the others who would swim began piling their weapons and clothes into the boat. Elise did the same without any sign of self-consciousness. The men looked away, more embarrassed than she. Baore took up the oars, with Samul, Orlem, Crowheart, and Pwyll aboard. He pulled out into the mist and the others went into the water, some plunging in and others going more reluctantly.

Elise dove in and swam a distance under the surface, her head appearing far out in the mist.

"I don't swim that well," Beldor Renné said.

"Cling to the boat when you become tired," Prince Michael replied. "Strike out or Alaan will die."

A flock of crows passed overhead and were heard calling in the distance, and then one reappeared out of the mist. It landed on the bow of the boat and rasped its rough cry. Off in the distance the flock answered.

Dease looked at the trees taken down by the storm, the litter of green branches and floating leaves.

"It is like a nightmare," he said to Toren, who gazed silently at the devastated wood.

Toren reached down and swept up a branch with a lichen covered bird's nest almost intact, but with no eggs. Dease noticed that his cousin's thumb was purple and swollen. So much debris had battered them that they were all bruised and worse.

"Yes," Toren said. "This whole endeavor has seemed so. Life shall never look the same to me now, knowing that this other world exists but a few days ride away. What thin walls guard us from this place? The distance between dream and nightmare." Dease looked up. "Perhaps we shall find the shore of this place soon. I've come to no longer care if we find Beld and Samul and bring them to justice or even if we rescue Gilbert's poor brother. Let us wake from this nightmare in our own land—in our own beds, preferably—and I shall weep with gladness."

A'brgail waited for them ahead and the Renné went forward. The knight appeared a little stooped, as though even he could grow tired. "I've been dousing," he said. "I can feel Alaan's life force slipping away. We must do everything we can to catch them. If Alaan can't be saved, then I must be present when he passes over. The nagar must go with him. It cannot stay here in this world awaiting another victim."

Elise felt almost content in the water, as though she were really an otter masquerading as a human. It was strange to her, who had never swum . . . until the night she threw herself from the bridge. That had been only days ago, yet if felt like the distant past. The flood of memories had been so great, it was as though years passed every day.

Around her the mist seemed to cling to the waters—as smooth and foggy as an old man's eye. She was looking for Hafydd, and wanted to be sure that she saw him first. How near was he? How fatigued from making his circles—three now in fewer than two days. He must be exhausted.

Voices floated out, tendrils of mist wafting as though pushed aside by words. Elise stopped where she was, listening. Then went slowly a little closer. And a little closer yet.

But these voices she knew. It was the Renné, and their Knights of the Vow. A strange sensation passed through Elise, as though she should swim both forward and back. Delaying Hafydd by even a few hours might buy them time to get Alaan out of the Stillwater, to escape before Hafydd could find them.

And here were the Renné. If Hafydd were behind them—and she was almost certain he was—then they could serve this purpose. A little delay might even trap Hafydd in this place.

She hadn't forgotten how her companions responded when she had suggested this before. But now . . . how would they ever know?

A'brgail crouched down, gazing intently at the ground. They had come to a narrow isthmus separating the flooded wood from what looked like an open body of water, though in the fog it was difficult to be sure.

"They carried a boat over here," he said. "Here is the mark of a keel."

"Sianon came in a boat?" Toren asked.

"It must be. And look at the number of footprints. Their company has grown . . . to nine or ten, perhaps more. It is difficult to be sure."

Toren looked back into the fog-laden trees, the motion like a nervous tic. "And what of Hafydd?"

A'brgail's gaze didn't follow Toren's but went to the fog that lay gray and impenetrable upon the open waters. "I don't know. He has hidden himself from me—for the time being." He gestured over the water. "Is this a small lake that can be easily walked around? Or is it large? Is making rafts a waste of our efforts? The distance across might turn out to be a mere stone's throw."

Dease looked out into the mist, which seemed to him like the fog in his mind that hid the words he required, the memories. He heard an axe bite into the body of a tree, the sound like a blow to his head. A small breeze sighed through the wood like a sleeper muttering. Dease walked down the rocky beach to get away from the noise, out of sight of his cousin and the others. He found himself in a patch of fog so thick that his world was reduced to a circle of only a few feet. Beyond, all was featureless gray.

"Here is a vision of the netherworld," he said aloud. "Perhaps I am dead already."

"You live yet," a voice said. A woman's voice.

He turned and looked into the fog over the lake but could see nothing.

"Ah, my vision," he said quietly.

A dim form appeared, and at first he wasn't sure it was on the water or beneath it. But it was the head of a woman, emerging from the waters—the river spirit he had met before.

"Sianon," Dease said, and saw that this surprised her. "A'brgail said you would appear. He claims you are a sorceress."

"What did you tell him about me?"

"Nothing. I thought you to be a water spirit, and in my confused state it took me some time to realize you must be this daughter of Wyrr of whom he spoke."

"It is more complex than that, for I'm not quite who he believes me to be. But I have come with a warning: Hafydd is near. Take up your weapons and fortify what positions you can. He will try to frighten you with bits of magic at first, hoping not to have to exhaust himself. But if you do not falter he will have to attack you with his guards. I don't think he will have much strength left to make spells. That will be your chance to kill him. Have you a good archer among you?"

"We have no archer at all." Dease crouched down and the vision in the water came closer—a woman certainly, but not quite natural, he thought. "Why should we fight Hafydd alone? He is your enemy, or so A'brgail claims."

"Because he will do away with the Renné if he can. Is that not reason enough?" She bit her lower lip like a child: a gesture completely at odds with her appearance; slick as a fish and hair like kelp. She raised a delicate, dripping hand and pushed her hair back from her face.

"But why should we not step aside and leave this battle to you?"

She glanced up at him, jolted out of her musing. "Are you threatening me, Lord Dease Renné?"

"It was not meant so. I am only saying that we would be better standing together."

"I would gladly join the Renné in resisting Hafydd, but this man A'brgail I cannot trust. You don't know what bargains these Knights made in the past. The children of Wyrr have reason to hate them and trust them never. But you travel with this knight yourself. How do you judge his character?"

"I cannot give A'brgail my endorsement, my lady, for I have known him but a few days."

"I will give him mine." Toren stood a few paces off, aswirl in mist.

Sianon started back but Toren put out his hands. "Wait. Please. We have reason to talk, I think."

The creature retreated so that she was barely visible in the mist, but there she paused. "You are allied with someone who would burn me upon a pyre," she said slowly. "What is left to discuss?"

"I can't think that A'brgail would treat anyone so."

"No? Ask him to what fate he believes I should be put. He might even tell you the truth. His Knights have murdered one of my kind before."

"What do you mean, 'one of your kind'?"

"He will know what I mean," the woman said. "Ask him."

"But my lady, are there not greater matters at stake? I have agreed that I would stop my prosecution of Beldor and Samul Renné, whom I believe are in your company, and they tried to murder me; and did murder my cousin, whom I loved."

"Perhaps your cousins will trust you, for Toren Renné has a reputation for honorable dealings, but I will never trust a Knight of the Vow, for they have no honor at all. You don't know what lies and trickery they employed in the past."

"But Gilbert A'brgail believes it his duty to make up for the past mistakes made by the Knights of the Vow. He is as honorable a man as I have met—and I have met more than a few men in my short life."

"And in more than a millennium I have met only a handful—and not one of them was a Knight of the Vow. Beware, Toren Renné. Hafydd will topple you and your family and all of your allies, including this precious knight. Hafydd has no loyalties, no principles whatsoever but these—to make war and to conquer any who dare stand against him. He would cast his children into the fire to win a skirmish."

"And what of you, my lady?" Toren asked softly. "It is said that Sianon was little better, even if men obeyed her for other reasons. They went into the flames as well."

"I am not Sianon," she said firmly. "I am Elise Wills. And though my family has been at war with yours for generations, Toren Renné, I would not see you die . . ." She glanced at Dease. ". . . or any of your family. Changed I am, wiser now and less quick to judge. I am not she who sacrificed her lovers and her children in the wars against her brother."

Dease did not know who was more dumbfounded by this assertion that she was Elise Wills—he or his cousin.

She turned and would have swum into the mist but Dease called out, "Wait! Lady Elise, if that is who you truly are. You took away my pain and confusion once. . . ."

She hesitated, then turned back. Dease splashed out into the water, the bottom dropping away quickly.

"Cousin! Be wary!" Toren called.

The specter came close, a faint smile of compassion crossing her face. "Do you see how your cousin trusts me," she said quietly, then took Dease's head between her hands and kissed his brow. She moved away as she let go of him, still holding his gaze.

"You love her of the burned face," she said suddenly. "That is what's said of Dease Renné. I remember now." She paddled back into the fog, still staring at him. "Perhaps you are noble after all."

She looked from one cousin to the other. Dease could see her face change as though she struggled to make some decision.

"I will tell you this," she said at last. "Across the lake lies the path out of the Stillwater. Come as quickly as you can and I will leave you a track to follow. But you must outdistance Hafydd, whom we will leave in this place if we can. If you don't want to be trapped here, hurry! Build rafts and follow."

And then the mist fell over her like smoke, obscuring her features, a coal fading to ash.

★   ★   ★

Tam took hold of the stern of the boat to rest for a while, though he still kicked and paddled with one hand. Elise had disappeared sometime earlier and he had begun to wonder what happened to her. Not that she was in any danger—she was in her element, after all, and he suspected she was stronger than any two men.

Tam twisted around to look at Alaan, who lay ash pale and insensible. How he lived, Tam did not know. Any other man would have been dead days ago. At least Tam now knew that the bodies inhabited by the children of Wyrr could die, which gave him some hope. Hafydd was not like the ghouls in some stories who could never be killed.

"Here is land!" Pwyll sang out.

"And none too soon," Tam heard Fynnol say, though his cousin was obscured by the boat.

"We are not there yet," Crowheart said. The boat rocked beneath Tam's hand as someone shifted about. Tam pulled himself out to one side so he might see ahead. There, Fynnol and Prince Michael swam, but ahead of them he saw something large looming out of the watery air.

It looked like the prow of a ship but soon turned into a rock, three times the height of a man. It was steep-sided and broken into blocks, as though it were some ancient ruin of a fortification, though Tam was sure it was a natural formation.

They passed it by, Baore giving himself room for his oars but little more so that they might see it close to. The crow left the bow and flew up onto the rock, cawing at them incessantly, as though it thought them too stupid to understand such plain speech.

"What say you, Crowheart?" Orlem asked. "Is it much farther?"

"No, not far compared to what we've traveled. My crows have led us directly. Go forward, Baore, and we will find the shore by and by."

Cynddl came and took hold of the transom beside Tam, the story finder taking his turn to rest, as had all the others but Elise.

"We have not had a story in some time, Cynddl," Tam said, half in jest.

"I have been so overcome by stories, Tam, that I haven't felt much like telling them. They've battered me like rain in a hurricane. I've been drowning in stories." He fell silent then. "But I will have many to tell when we have the chance."

More rocks rose up from the waters, in appearance much the same as the first, though some were crumbling away, the blocks fallen into the water. Dusk began to settle over the shadowless land, and Tam feared they would not find the shore before it grew dark. Then what would they do? Certainly they could not all rest in the boat. Perhaps they would find a rock they could scale, but that would best be done while there was still light.

Another stone tower appeared before them, water slopping gently about its base. Baore turned the boat, following along, but it appeared to be unbroken. Upon a ledge, a line of crows called down at them; mocking, Tam thought.

"Perhaps they've brought us here to drown," Fynnol said, spitting out a mouthful of water.

"We might find a place to scale these cliffs," Cynddl offered. "But we will never bring Alaan up unharmed."

"These cliffs are higher than you think," Crowheart said, "for the tops are lost in cloud. Do not fear. My crows are smarter than you know—smarter than many a man, I will tell you. They are not lost. Follow on," he said firmly. "Follow on."

"Why did you not speak of her before?"

"I was not sure she was anything but a specter of my confused brain." Dease looked from A'brgail to his cousin. "Perhaps I didn't think anyone would believe me, as my brain was clearly addled."

"But how stands your confusion now?" Toren asked. He gazed at his cousin oddly, as though measuring him.

"It is gone. I feel entirely myself."

A'brgail had become very still. He placed his splayed fingers tip to tip, in an almost reverential pose, and then touched these to his chin. "She began by telling you that Hafydd was upon us," the knight said, "and then changed this warning, saying make haste or we would be left behind in this place?"

"Those were her words, more or less. Is it possible? Could we be trapped in this netherworld?"

A'brgail seemed not to have heard, so lost in thought was he. "Perhaps. But the nagar were always known for their cunning and their lies."

"She claimed to be Elise Wills," Toren said, "but Lady Elise was believed to have drowned the night of the ball. How can she be alive now?"

"It might be another lie, but it is not impossible, my lord. The nagar prey upon those who come before Death's gate. Someone carrying a smeagh as they die draws them, and they offer sweet blandishments and seductions. But bargains with nagar always go awry. She may have been Elise Wills once but she is Sianon now. Sianon, who confounded the brains of all those around her, for everyone loved her and tried to please her, as you hope to please her now, Lord Dease."

A tree fell, crashing and splintering into the Stillwater. Dease could hear the axes taking off the limbs, though the blows did not cause him pain now.

Toren looked out over the flat waters where the specter had disappeared. "If that was cunning, it was magnificently so, Gilbert. She seemed at odds with herself, telling us first about Hafydd, and then warning us to make all haste, so that we would not be trapped. Perhaps there is a conflict between the person she was and Sianon. If that is so, then it was the second warning that was true. I say we make all speed."

"We might be rushing headlong into a trap."

"If she wanted to trap us, why appear at all? There were a thousand places to lay a trap in the Stillwater." Toren caught A'brgail's gaze. "If your brother can lead them out, it is possible that those close to Sianon will find the path, while those who are not so near will be left behind. If that is so it would be to her advantage to have us detain Hafydd. The way might close before him. But something inside her could not treat us so foul, and she bid us make haste. I think that is the truth and we should press on."

"You are too willing to read good into people's intentions, Lord Toren. If she was Lady Elise then she is a Wills and the traditional enemy of your family. Sianon hates the Knights of the Vow. She could destroy us both. Do not put it past her—the children of Wyrr were more vengeful than any Wills. You cannot imagine."

"You would rather stay here and fight Hafydd?"

"No, but we needn't do either. We can step aside and let Hafydd pass us by, then follow."

"It is a gamble, Gilbert."

"Toren is right in this," Dease said. "The trees are already falling. Let's build our rafts and go on."

A'brgail stood very still for a moment, his eyes fixed on nothing, and then he nodded. "I will give way, as you are both so adamant, but never trust Sianon. She has led tens of thousands to their deaths. Tens of thousands."

Fifty-five

A path of bubbles, delicate stepping-stones, stretched out into the mist. Dease dipped the branch he used as a paddle and pulled it through the water. Between the rough logs of their rafts, water welled up, slopping over occasionally to soak his breeches. His knees were wet and pained him where he knelt on the rough wood.

"If Alaan and Sianon escape the Stillwater, we will wander here forever," A'brgail said. He was a few feet away on a separate raft, his angular form softened by the mist. No one answered him. A'brgail was not in favor of following the advice of Elise Wills—or Sianon, as he referred to her.

Dease, however, had met this specter twice now and felt there was something about her . . . He'd seen the look of compassion in her face as she'd taken away the pain and confusion in his head— if only temporarily. She was hardly the ruthless, cunning nagar of the old songs. A'brgail had warned that she would bewitch him, but Dease felt that, on the contrary, she had revealed some part of her- self; the part that was Elise Wills, he suspected.

If anything, he wondered if she was not giving in to this com- passion too much. What if it were necessary for someone to delay Hafydd? The man was a monster. Would it not be worth their lives to trap him in this place where he could not bring destruction to the land between the mountains?

What concerned Dease was not that Sianon had tricked them for her own benefit, but that Elise Wills had not used them as she should.

The unchanging day wore on, unmarked by any movement of light or shadow. The massive cliff seemed to have coalesced out of the fog: fog turned to harsh stone. The top was lost in mist and low cloud.

"How will we ever scale that?" Tam asked.

"We shall not," Rabal said. "On such a cliff you would be but an ant on a castle wall."

Tam rested in the boat, where he sat wrapped in a blanket, shivering from his time in the water. Orlem was at the oars, driving them on, untiring, uncomplaining. Alaan lay upon damp blankets on the floorboards, rocking softly on the waters. How limply he moved to the boat's motion, his head swaying as though he had no strength left at all. Tam reached down and rearranged his blankets, afraid to feel his brow. Afraid that Alaan would be as cold as the waters.

Elise was somewhere in the lake, and the others swam close by or clung to the boat to rest. Orlem and Crowheart had stayed in the boat, taking turns at the oars, which they handled with all the mastery of Baore or Tam.

Tam despaired of ever finding his way out of this place, and he was certain now that Alaan would die before they escaped. How futile this whole journey was. They might all die in this place, though Sianon and Caibre would live on, no doubt finding their way out one day. He hoped only that a generation would be spared the sorcerers' war.

Tam looked at the giant rowing. The oars were so flimsy compared to his massive arms that he thought it a wonder the oars didn't snap like twigs.

"You knew Sianon . . . before," Tam said, wondering now if he wandered into very private lands. "What was she like? As she is now?"

Orlem shook his head, and for a moment Tam thought that was all the answer he would receive. The man narrowed his clear eyes, a thousand lines appearing in the corners. Had Orlem Slighthand laughed much in his younger days? There was no laughter in the man now, as though once you had seen as much life as he, there was no humor in it. Laughter was for the foolish, the ignorant.

And then the giant said softly, "No, she was not then as she is now. Raven-haired, to begin with, and more proud, though she always had a way of carrying herself so that even the most lowly pikesman felt that she noticed him. She did not spend the lives of her men needlessly, but when required she would send her own children into battle without regret. People said that she was heartless, and she was, but she lamented it and knew that she should have feelings that she did not. It was the price of her gift—Sianon was loved by all she encountered, but she could love none in return. Try as she might, the feelings were never there. But now, Lady Elise . . . she is not quite the same. She is compassion itself, though perhaps in time that will be worn away. Perhaps the price she will pay for this is that not everyone will love her. A small price to keep one's heart."

"Not if you want to build an army," Crowheart offered from his place. "Or a kingdom."

"And what of you, Tam? What has brought you to this place with Sianon?"

"Chance, Orlem. Chance. We met Alaan far in the north, near our own home. He was being hunted by some of Hafydd's guards, who then chased us down the length of the River Wynnd. We met Elise there, and fled together down the river to Westbrook. It is a wonder we survived."

Still swinging the oars, Orlem tilted his great head toward Tam. "And where did you get such a blade?"

"It is my grandfather's."

Orlem considered this a moment. "Well, it is as fine a sword as you will find in the land between the mountains, for it came almost certainly from the forge of Blendal Wennt. If you have ever unwrapped the hilt you will have seen his mark, for it was always made there. It is an ancient blade, Tam, made before much of the art was lost. There will be a story of how your grandfather came by that, for such swords have histories that their owners keep more carefully than their own family's."

Tam glanced down at his sword, the pommel glinting dully in the gray light. "He said nothing to me about it. It has lived all my life in a trunk in our attic."

This almost gained a smile from the big man.

The crow that still crouched on the bow began to call, strutting about in its place as though alarmed.

"Smoke," Crowheart said "Do you smell it?"

Rabal drew his sword, sitting up and sniffing the air. Tam took up his bow and nocked an arrow. The swimmers hung back, feeling vulnerable in the water. The smell of smoke became stronger, and then Tam heard the crackle of burning wood.

A smudge of red and orange appeared in the fog, and as they approached, a small figure could be seen crouched near. Crowheart stood in the bow, his sword ready, and Tam pointed his arrow at the apparition.

The man raised his head, abruptly, as though he'd been napping. He rose; weaponless, Tam could see.

"Theason!" Crowheart called out, and Tam realized he was right. Here was the little gatherer of herbs they had met far up the River Wynnd, bearing a warning from Eber son of Eiresit.

"Here you are at last," the small man said. "Theason had begun to despair that you would ever arrive. Does Alaan live yet? Tell Theason that he does."

"He clings to life, friend Theason, hardly more," Cynddl answered.

In a moment the swimmers crawled ashore, cold and tired from the crossing. A smooth tongue of rock lapped into the water there, the only break they had seen in the massive cliff.

Crowheart stepped stiffly ashore and looked around. There were crows perched on the barren branches of leafless trees and on ledges in the rock walls.

"How is it you are awaiting us?" Rabal waved a hand at his traveling companions. "And you know these men?"

"Theason was sent to meet you," the little man said, as though worried that he'd done wrong.

"By whom?" Cynddl asked.

"It is difficult for Theason to say. Kai drew the map, but it was a small boy named Llya who knew where you would be found."

"Llya?" Tam said, pulling on his clothes. "Eber's son? But he cannot speak."

"He has no voice, but he has speech all the same. He told Kai of this place, and here you are, just as he said. Theason has brought you a gift."

Elise appeared then, surfacing next to the boat, where Pwyll stood looking down at Alaan, close to tears.

"What gift?" Elise said sadly.

"Water," Theason said. "As many skins as this small frame would bear. Water from the River Wynnd."

No one answered for a moment, confused by this news, but then Elise came out of the Stillwater, no thought of clothing.

"*Give it to me,*" she said, snatching a water skin from Theason's hand. Alaan was lifted from the boat and carried quickly up the slope. Elise dropped to her knees by Alaan's side, pulling the stopper from the vessel. She poured a stream of water across Alaan's pale face, whispering gently as she did. A shiver ran through him, but then he was still again. Still as death.

"Please . . ." Elise whispered. "Please, Alaan."

His mouth opened a little and she poured the liquid in, hardly more than a drop, but Tam could see that he swallowed it. Then a little more.

Elise then directed the stream of water onto Alaan's wound. "Bring another skin," she said to Pwyll.

The tourneyer was given another by Theason, and from this he gave Alaan more water. The wanderer opened his eyes for a moment, then gagged and choked.

"How many skins have you?" Elise asked.

"Theason has six," the little man said.

"And how distant is the Wynnd?" she asked.

"Almost a day's journey, but you'll not leave here this night. The way is steep and too treacherous to pass. Climbing here by daylight was all that Theason could manage, and he has spent his life wandering such places."

"He is right," Crowheart said. "The path from here is too dangerous to risk by night. It will be all we can do to bear Alaan along it by daylight."

Alaan coughed again just as the skins were emptied, but Tam could hear him breathing now, see his chest rise and fall. It was as though some life flowed back into him.

Elise looked around. Her hand rested upon Alaan's chest with great familiarity. "Then we'll spend the night here, and set out at dawn. But how we will get away without Hafydd following, I don't know."

"The way will close after we've passed through," Crowheart said.

Elise had begun to don clothes Baore brought her, but she stopped buttoning her shirt to stare at Crowheart. "Then you can find the hidden paths, as Alaan does."

"No one can find them as Alaan does, but I can travel them." Crowheart seemed prepared to offer no more.

Elise glanced at Orlem as though he would provide the answer, but the big man shrugged.

"Kai can draw his maps because he spent many lives of men

traveling with Sainth," Elise said. "Orlem did not spend nearly so long in Sainth's service and he is much less adept. But you, Rabal Crowheart, what is the explanation for your skill?"

"There is none, my lady," he said simply. "I was born with this."

"And who were your parents?"

"They were unremarkable, I tell you honestly. A smith my father was by trade. My mother was from a family of weavers."

Tam thought Elise looked exceptionally skeptical of this, but she smiled. "It is a wonder, then," she said, "though there is something about your eyes that reminds me of someone I once knew." She turned back to Alaan.

Tam found Theason bent over the fire, where he was tending some steaming fish. How long ago it seemed that they had met on the Wyrr, Theason waking him from his sleep to bring him a warning from Eber—a warning about the nagar. He glanced over at Elise.

"Theason thought you might arrive hungry from your journey." The small man raked his coals out to find some more heat. The scars on his face were pink in the fire's glow—scars from a lion, Theason had said, and for some reason, Tam didn't doubt him.

"Hungry!" Fynnol said. "I could eat all of those fish myself and cry for more. Did you catch them here?"

Theason nodded.

In a moment Fynnol, Baore, and Cynddl had lines in the water. And before long they were adding bass to the prospective dinner. Elise came down to the water's edge, but instead of a fishing line she held her sword. Crouching down, she put the blade in the water, closing her eyes a moment. She was dressed in Fynnol's clothes again, her mass of yellow hair wet and carelessly tied back. Tam thought how clear her skin, how perfect the line of her jaw.

"He is still hidden," she murmured, then shook her head, and rose more gracefully than a woman dressed in a man's clothing had a right to do. "We must set guards and remain wary. Hafydd is not far off. He waits for us to lead him out. I don't know how we will slip away without him following. But eat," she said, turning to the others, "the first watch will be mine."

No one argued, but all set to the fish dinner, spirits high at the thought that they had only one more night in this place and then they would escape.

As they ate, Elise took a moment to give Alaan water from the Wynnd, and this time he drank thirstily. His eyes opened and he muttered something Tam could not understand, though he thought he heard the name "Sianon."

Wandering over toward the wall as though he had some private business, Samul removed Hafydd's gift from his jacket. He opened the small box and gently removed the egg, muffled in moss. Surely he had fallen under the spell of Hafydd's words—all of his talk of Hafydd ruling and of he playing some part in his kingdom. But Beld had seen most clearly. Hafydd would sweep everyone aside. Even if he had recognized Samul's talents, and spoken to his most secret desires, Hafydd could not be trusted. Samul knew he wouldn't betray his own kind to Hafydd, for it was a battle now between men and sorcerers. Men brought ruin enough, Samul thought, what unimagined destruction could sorcerers bring?

He wondered if there was some way to destroy the egg so that it would not perform its function of drawing Hafydd. He might burn it, perhaps. He held it in the palm of his hand a moment, staring at the fine sky-blue pigment. How innocent it looked.

"What have you found, Cousin?"

Samul started. Beld stood a few paces off in the languid mist, staring at him. Samul slipped the box into a pocket. "Only an egg," he said.

"Let me see it, Samul. Is it a thrush's egg?"

Samul moved his hand away as Beld reached out.

Beld smiled at him oddly. "Is it precious? Are you so ravenous?"

"Almost, Cousin," Samul said.

Beld snatched the egg from his hand, examining it in the poor light. "I don't know that I've seen another like it." The egg cracked in his fingers, and he rolled the spoon of his thumb over it. Out of the delicate wreckage crawled something black. *A wasp!*

Before Samul thought to crush it, the wasp was gone, flying off into the fog as though upon an errand of the utmost importance. Samul watched in dismay as it was swallowed by the mist. When he looked back, Beld was staring at him.

"This is a strange land where crows attack like wolves and wasps hatch from eggs," Beld said. "Have you ever heard of such things?"

Samul shook his head.

"Best say nothing to the others," Beld cautioned. "Who would ever trust you again?" Without saying more, he turned and went back toward the fire.

Darkness was not yet complete when Tam walked up the draw, wondering about the path out. Theason had said they descended, but certainly he meant they would climb up. Up those cliffs that disappeared into the clouds.

At the end of the draw Tam found almost a dozen narrow openings crowded close together, the stone between looking for all the world like massive tree roots. He stood for a moment, regarding the dark, irregular fissures, wondering which one might lead out.

"It appears to be a labyrinth," he whispered. "What a strange place."

He thought a fire might once have swept over this small oasis of vegetation among a desert of rock. Along the shore lay a strip of green, but beyond that the grasses were coarse and brown, and the shrubs that lived had many dried, dead branches. The few strands of trees were leafless skeletons, gray and weathered, their bark long peeled away. It was a forlorn place and affected Tam's spirits, even with the thought of escape so near.

A noise from behind caused him to turn. Cynddl came striding quickly up.

"Do I interrupt your meditation?" the story finder asked.

"No. I only wondered where the path out might be. I think I needed to see it for myself. I hope Crowheart knows which of these will lead us out."

"So do I," Cynddl said. He looked around, his face tired and pale, his dark Fáel eyes sunken and lusterless. "This is not a . . . peaceful place, Tam. . . ."

"It does have a sadness about it. I feel that."

"You are aware of such things, Tam," Cynddl said. "The stories here . . . well, I have only begun to hear whispers of them, but they are filled with regret and mourning. This is an entrance to the Stillwater. A place where it lies near our own lands. Men have found their way in here, and perhaps women too; wandered into the Stillwater only to be lost in its labyrinth. Some few found their way to this place again, only to discover the path out existed no more. I think you would find bones lying not too far beneath the surface here."

Tam nodded. Cynddl's words seemed true to him. He didn't know why. "Crowheart can pass through, though," he said.

"So it seems. And did you see how Elise reacted to that news? Crowheart has done nothing to earn anything but gratitude from me, but . . . One wonders who he is, what he is doing in such a place, and where he comes from."

"Yes. And Orlem Slighthand. Who is he, Cynddl?" Tam turned to look at the story finder as though he would have an answer. "Elise knew him—or more truthfully, Sianon knew him. He spoke of her to me—not Elise, Sianon. How old must he be?"

"Orlem Slighthand I know something of," Cynddl said. Tam looked closely at his friend to see if he jested.

"There are stories about a man by that name, Tam. Very, very old stories. Orlem was a warrior of great fame, a near giant who was unmatched in battle. But it was said that he suffered a wound to his spirit—though I can't tell you more. The stories I know are only fragments, but Slighthand was said to have wandered all over the world seeking a cure for his sorrow and torment. He was a fig-

ure of romance and tragedy, Tam, for he lived on and on, his sorrow unabated."

"And that is our Orlem?"

"Unless he is someone who has taken the name or had it given
him."

"He loved Sianon, you think?"

"It was said that none were immune, save her own brother."

"Brothers, I would say, for Caibre hated her."

"Do not be so sure of that."

This surprised Tam. "What do you mean?"

"Well, think of the depth of Caibre's passion. Does it not suggest
that he loved her once, or grew to hate her because he loved her, or
because he showed this one weakness and she was the cause?"

A shout brought them both up short, and then they were sprinting down the slope, stumbling in the growing darkness, cursing
themselves for leaving their bows behind.

Fifty-six

"**I** led them here," Elise was saying as Tam and Cynddl arrived. Both Orlem and Crowheart turned to look at her in surprise.

"I would not see Toren Renné trapped in this place, for he did everything he could to make peace with my family, and would have, had my father been the head of the Wills."

"What of these Knights you've been cursing?" Crowheart asked.

"I don't trust them yet, but they travel with the Renné and have their trust. I'll accept their presence if Lord Toren will vouch for them."

"My lady," Orlem said solemnly, "there is something about these Knights—" But he didn't finish, for then the unmistakeable sound of voices came out of the mist.

Elise dried her blade on the tail of her shirt. "I believe that Toren Renné wishes us no harm, but let us take up arms to be safe."

"What of us?" Samul said, glancing at his cousin almost as though he feared him.

"I think you will find your cousins ready to come to some ac-commodation," she said. "We all need one another here."

Tam thought they looked a ragtag band of mercenaries, their clothes torn and soiled, faces dirty and grim. Had there ever been a more ill-assorted company of travelers?

A dark mass appeared to coalesce in the fog, and this became a raft with men paddling and one standing in the bow, sword in hand.

"Stay your distance!" Elise called out, surprising Tam with the authority in her voice.

The paddlers ceased, but the raft carried its way, slowly. A second raft appeared and then another, until there were four in all.

"Lord Toren?" Elise called. "You were right. We must speak."

"I am here." One of the paddlers stood. As the raft drifted closer, Tam could see the tall nobleman—the man who had refused the laurels the last day of the fair, when Pwyll's only horse had gone lame.

"We have led you to the path out of the Stillwater, but we will have you vouch for your companions before we lead you farther."

"What will you have of me?" the man asked who stood on the raft's bow.

Elise gazed at him a moment and then took a deep breath before going on. "Only you and I know the history that lies between us, Gilbert A'brgail."

"It does not lie between us, but between other Knights of another time. I have done nothing to earn your enmity."

"Perhaps, but nor have you done anything to earn my trust. The Knights of the Vow tormented Sianon."

"And I renounce them for it. The Knights were corrupt and forsook their vows."

"Then tell Toren Renné what you think should be done with me." She turned and gestured. "Or with Alaan. Would you let us live, or would you see us burned?"

"Alaan . . ." he said. "Alaan is my brother, my mother's son. As much as I deplore what he has done, I cannot harm him for it." He looked evenly at Elise. "You are here, all three of you, for good or ill. If the part of you that was Elise Wills can help us destroy Caibre, then I will have peace between us."

Elise considered this, glaring at the man as though she might at any moment strike him down. "If Toren Renné will vouch for you I will accept this."

"I will," Lord Toren said quickly. "Without reservation."

Elise nodded, then pointed up the shallow draw. "This is the way out of the Stillwater, but it is not a path such as you have seen before. After we have passed through it will close behind us. We believe Hafydd lies waiting somewhere out in the mist, waiting for us to show him the way out of this place. We will try to slip away at first light and hope he does not follow. If we can trap him here, war might be avoided for many years, perhaps generations."

The Renné and the Knights of the Vow came ashore, A'brgail asking to see his brother, Alaan.

Elise, Orlem, and Pwyll all hovered near as the knight in his gray cloak went and stood over the sleeping form of Alaan, his face filled with sadness and concern and anger. Tam thought this knight a noble and tragic-looking figure, his bearing proud and sad.

Elise regarded A'brgail. "Is he really your brother?"

"My half brother, yes. Impetuous he has always been, troublesome as a child. Now look what he's done."

"Trapped Hafydd in the Stillwater. Thousands might thank him for that."

"If he has actually trapped him," A'brgail said bitterly. "Hafydd is no fool. He will find his way out yet."

A'brgail started at the sight of Orlem, noticing him for the first time.

"Orlem Slighthand," Elise said.

"But I know that name," the knight said quietly.

Orlem made a slight bow, as though he'd been paid a compliment.

They all crept away then, leaving Pwyll to stand guard over his master.

Before the Knight of the Vow said anything more, his eye was drawn elsewhere. Tam turned to see what had attracted his attention and saw the Renné gathered: Toren, arms folded, Dease at his side; Samul and Beld, standing quietly defiant before them.

"We are allies of necessity," Toren said, "but I will not grant you pardons for what you've done. Arden Renné lies in his grave, and that cannot be forgotten. This I offer: I will leave off hunting you, and you may go where you will, but never show yourselves on Renné lands for then your crime will find justice. Heed me in this, Cousins, for though I give you freedom, I forgive you not." For a moment Toren said nothing but only stared down at his two cousins. "Look at all you accomplished," he said. "Arden dead and nothing changed, nor would it have changed had you succeeded in murdering me. The war you wanted is upon us and would have come no matter what."

"We never wanted war," Samul said evenly. "We did not want to see the Isle of Battle given over to our enemies, who we believed were plotting against us. And in this we have been proven right."

"Well, I have arranged to cede the Isle to the Wills anyway. To Lord Carral Wills, who has become our ally and who we will recognize as the legitimate head of the Wills family. Could you not have trusted my judgment a little longer? Samul? Beld? Was Arden's life not worth you living with a little doubt?"

Beld was about to answer angrily, but Samul put a hand on his arm and he held his peace.

"We have one enemy, now," Samul said. "Let us concentrate our efforts on him and have peace between us."

"Peace, Cousin," Toren said, "but nothing more." And he turned and walked away. Dease hesitated a second, as though he would say something, but then followed Toren.

"Well," Elise said quietly to Tam. "It is amazing that Renné pride would allow even that. . . . Oh, my own family are no better. Pride, Tam, it is a terrible weakness."

"But did you hear? The Renné have ceded the Isle of Battle to your father and recognized his claim."

Elise smiled. "Well, I shall let myself feel a little pride at that—though it is pride of my father, who has seen at last."

★   ★   ★

The wasp swooped down and hovered before Hafydd. The sorcerer held out his hand and the insect settled on his fingers, where it walked about, agitated.

"And who sent you, my little friend?" the sorcerer said. "Ah, but of course, you are entirely black. Samul Renné. It seems that even I can be surprised."

He lifted his hand up to his mouth and blew upon the wasp. For a moment it braced itself against this wind, its wings blown back, but then it released its hold and flew into the air, circling the sorcerer once, then disappeared into the gloom.

Hafydd thrust his sword into the water and pointed. His guards took up their makeshift paddles and propelled the raft on, over the calm of the fog-washed lake.

"I don't know if it's wise for Toren to see us together," Dease said. "Unless you want to make him suspicious."

"No," Samul said, "I have come to tell you that even Beldor has agreed to keep your secret."

Dease was not sure he believed this: oh, Beld might have said it, but Dease was deeply suspicious of anything his cousin did—especially anything that did not provide some immediate benefit to Beldor. He looked around but in the growing darkness and fog they were hidden.

"Why would Beld agree to that? He hates me almost as much as Toren. He always has."

"Beldor owes you, Cousin. It was he who shot Arden by mistake. He who knocked you senseless and left you to be found. What could he expect you to do but what you've done? No, Cousin, you have not to fear from Beld. It is I who must fear him."

"You?"

Samul nodded, his shoulders hunching up, deep wrinkles appearing at the corners of his eyes. "Yes. Despite his apparent change of heart, I fear he serves Hafydd still. Even Elise suggested that our escape from Hafydd, which Beld managed, was too easily accomplished. Warn Toren that Beld is a danger still. If I die in circumstances you deem questionable, will you kill him for me?"

"You ask a great deal," Dease said.

"Not really. His death would benefit you as well. Warn Toren. Beld's treachery is not done."

Surprisingly, Samul reached out and pulled Dease to him, embracing him, and then he went back into the gathering night. Dease stood for a moment, dumbfounded. He had dreaded this meeting more than any other—facing his coconspirators—but the fear that they would unmask him had come to nothing. Instead there was only more talk of treachery, more promises of revenge, as though the Renné could never escape this. Arden had once said it was in their blood, like madness in other families. Or it was the Renné madness, and they would never be free of it.

Tam had stood his watch, and now relaxed by the fire. Baore, Fynnol, and Elise were making a kind of sling that would allow Baore to carry Alaan on his back, which Theason assured them was the only way they could possibly get Alaan out of the Stillwater. They had already sorted through their belongings, choosing the few they would carry. Baore's tools had been distributed among the various bags, as he would not leave those behind unless forced to. Tam and Cynddl had hauled the bundles up to the end of the draw, where the tall openings waited like dark mouths. The waters of the swamp must have once run out here, when they were much higher or in flood seasons.

Now Tam sat by the fire making a few arrows from wood he'd collected up the draw, and crow feathers that Rabal's army had lost upon the ground. He had only a few arrowheads left but thought they might be needed.

Samul Renné lounged some distance from the fire by Beld, who slept, apparently. The other Renné kept their distance from these cousins—the assassins of Arden Renné. They mingled with the few

Knights of the Vow, though these men were hardly sociable. They were a sober, quiet group, polite in their manner, but so reserved that Tam thought of them as being without personality—one interchangeable with another.

Orlem and Crowheart stood guard, their swords in hand. These two, who seemed to have appeared out of an old ballad, left Tam wondering. He feared that he stared at them too much, but they were such a mystery. Orlem had to be ancient beyond counting. The oldest man that Tam had heard of had lived one hundred and fifty-two years. Orlem must be many times that age.

Sorcery, Tam thought. Sorcerers were said to have lived great spans of years—many lives of men. And here he was, walking beside them. Speaking with them. They even listened when he offered his opinion. Listened to *him.*

He looked up into the foggy dark. This night seemed endless. They stood watches by no system, for there were no stars to set, barely a hint of the waning moon. His sense of time lay in ruins. Dawn might be almost upon them or hours away—he no longer knew.

Prince Michael came and threw himself down beside Tam.

"Here is a skill I have never learned," the young nobleman said. "Will you teach it to me?"

"Fletching arrows is quickly learned yet takes years to master. You begin—" But he did not finish. Tam heard the unmistakable sound of an arrow, then the thud of it burying in flesh.

"Out of the firelight!" Orlem shouted.

Everyone was on their feet and scrambling up the slope. Men shouting to wake their sleeping fellows.

A hail of arrows landed among them, though neither Tam nor the Prince were struck. They bore up a hobbling Renné man-at-arms who had an arrow in his calf. Nearby, Orlem carried Alaan and Pwyll guarded the giant's back.

Halfway up the draw the group came to a halt and turned back. There was a fearful silence, as everyone peered at the bleary fire, trying to see through the mist and darkness.

"*Sianon!*" came Hafydd's voice echoing eerily up the draw. "You cannot escape me, now. Surrender, you and Sainth, and I will let your followers go unharmed. Refuse me, and they will share your pyre."

Elise stared into the darkness, her sword raised. She turned to Pwyll and Toren Renné. "He is testing me to learn how far the transformation has progressed, and whether Alaan is strong enough to lead us on. Sianon would not give herself up to save any-one, as he well knows. Better he thinks me stronger than I am." She drew herself up and took a deep breath.

"Come, Brother," she shouted. "Bring your silent guards, but warn them first of what occurred when last you challenged me. You shall not leave this place, Caibre, son of Wyrr. I do not care what the cost to me will be. You shall not leave."

Elise's declaration was met by silence. A breeze moaned up the draw. A crow called once.

"What will he do?" A'brgail whispered. "What should we ex-pect?" The knight appeared to brace himself, sword in hand.

"He will attack, and soon," Elise said. "Caibre was capable of many things. Fear was always his greatest weapon, but fire was his particular element, as water was Sianon's. Do not be deceived by his appearance. Hafydd is not old. He would cut down any man here who dared face him alone. No matter how many you number, do not think to engage him without me. He is a sorcerer. Armies of men have fallen before him. Armies."

Elise did not take her eyes from the slope down to the lake, dimly lit by the fire below. Beside her Orlem and Crowheart were rigid with tension. In the poor light, Tam thought he saw a glimmer upon Elise's cheek as she gazed out over the lake.

"Is it true, Rabal, that we cannot pass through by darkness?" she asked.

"We could pass through, my lady, but the climb down cannot be managed without daylight. It is so treacherous that dampened by only a little rain it is impassable."

"Then we are in a fight to the death—all of us. If I fall you will have to take your chances and pass through the caves."

"The caves are a labyrinth, my lady," Crowheart said. "Passages leading every way, joining and splitting. Most who enter there without knowing the way never see the sun again—in this land or in the land beyond."

"Then Theason will have to guide you. I wish you all luck."

A gust came up the draw then, warm and dry like a wind off the desert. The fire they'd abandoned below seemed to grow, glowing red. The flames bent toward them and fluttered like torn banners.

The fire leapt to the long grass, and caught by a gust, came raging up the draw, flames blazing like blades from the forge. The bushes went up like torches, the skeletal trees writhing in the wind as though trying to shake fire from their limbs.

Pwyll and Theason lifted Alaan and retreated into the cut, where there was only stone to fuel the fire.

"Beware!" Elise shouted above the din. "Fire is Hafydd's sword."

The entire company retreated to a tiny island of shattered rock that had broken off the wall above. The flame came squalling up the slope, leaping from tree to bush to tree. It was upon them in an instant, like a wave washing up from a lake of fire. Through the dancing flames Tam could see the black-clad forms of Hafydd's guards charging up the grade.

Tam's companions were all at work employing shirts and jackets to beat away the flames that leapt about them, catching here a person's pant leg or pouncing into their hair. Tam's vest caught fire, and Cynddl reached out and tore it off him. And then the flames around them fell to nothing, the grass consumed, though the bushes and trees still burned. Smoke and ash ground into their eyes.

Tam raised his bow and shot at something moving, for the burning trees did them this one service—Hafydd's guards were not invisible. Tam nocked an arrow and shot again. His own company spread out to give themselves fighting room, stepping onto the still warm grass, burned black and brittle.

Hafydd's guards were upon them, crying strange words and driving them back. Tam saw men falling, though who he could not tell. He shot three more arrows before he was forced to cast his bow aside and draw his blade. But Orlem took down his attacker with one vicious blow, the man falling at Tam's feet, still as stone. The fight spread out then, there being no line of battle but only skirmishes here and there. Orlem ran from one place to another, his great sword driving the black guards back wherever he met them. Elise, too, cut men down or threw them back, Baore beside her, knocking men senseless with his shod staff.

And then Tam saw Orlem stumble, falling awkwardly to one knee. A man aimed a savage two-handed stroke at the giant's head, but a Knight of the Vow threw himself into the path and was cut nearly in two.

Hafydd had come.

Before Tam could move, Elise and A'brgail leapt to Orlem's aid, the two of them feinting and slashing at Hafydd by turns. The dark-clad knight was forced back, but only a step. Long enough for Orlem to get stiffly to his feet. With these three ranged against him, Hafydd should have been forced to retreat, but he stood his ground, forcing the others to leap aside to avoid his blade, which would dart at one only to be aimed at another.

But then Hafydd did jump back, and thrust his sword into a burning bush. He pulled it free, the length of the blade now awash with flame.

"Beware!" Elise shouted, but it was at she Hafydd aimed his next blow, and Elise lost her footing and fell awkwardly.

Hafydd would have cut her in two, but Orlem leaped in with his great long sword, slashing at Hafydd's head and forcing him to dodge back. The flaming blade was elusive, a wavering sheet of fire trailing its every movement, which fooled the eye. Tam, not sure which was blade and which was fire, dropped to his knees and searched for his bow in the blackened grass.

Elise began to struggle up, but Hafydd stamped his foot and shouted and the ground shook beneath them, throwing Elise down again and staggering Orlem and A'brgail.

Hafydd's sword flashed down, but Elise rolled aside. Tam nocked an arrow and fired, and saw Hafydd hesitate a second before slashing at Elise again. In that instant A'brgail recovered and thrust at Hafydd, who staggered back, then drove the pommel of his sword into A'brgail's face, knocking him to the ground.

Hafydd stamped his foot again and the ground shuddered beneath them, a sound like thunder reverberating up the draw. Tam fell to his knees but in an instant had nocked another arrow. The problem now was that his own companions leapt about, and he feared shooting them instead of Hafydd.

A'brgail regained his feet somehow, though unsteadily. Tam saw Hafydd's blade flicker, and A'brgail was suddenly aflame, his surcoat burning like a torch. Neither Orlem nor Elise wavered from their task. Still they went at Hafydd, forcing him to dodge and parry, his flaming blade forcing them back now that there were only two. A'brgail stumbled blindly away, tearing at his cloak.

Tam dropped his bow and went to the Knight's aid, tearing his flaming surcoat off and casting it down onto the blackened grass. A'brgail rubbed fists into his eyes and then, squinting and blinking, went back to the aid of Orlem and Elise. But they were being driven back now, Hafydd's sword swinging with renewed speed, first at one, then the other.

Tam searched for his bow in the dark, realizing now that even the three warriors were no match for Hafydd, who was wily beyond measure and never tired.

Fynnol barred the mouth of one passage, sword in hand. Beyond him he could see silhouettes of struggling men falling. Pwyll and Cynddl stayed near, protecting the passage and Alaan, but Fynnol was the last line of defense and knew he couldn't fail. Flames still erupted up from the grass, sending human torches flailing and rolling on the ground. Trees looked like flaming runes, and everywhere there was fighting and men screaming in pain.

Behind him, Theason grunted as he tried to drag Alaan farther into the cleft in the stone. Fynnol wondered if the little man would survive after all he had done for them. He wondered if any of them would survive.

In the murk, Fynnol thought Orlem staggered and fell, then three men broke through and engaged Pwyll and Cynddl. Fynnol leapt out and cut off a black-clad guard who circled to the Fáel's right, but then he was in a fight with a much more skilled opponent. He leapt this way and that, dodging and twisting to stay alive. Then Pwyll came to his aid, driving the man back, cutting his arm with a stoke so quick Fynnol's eye could not follow.

And then the cry went up. *"The shadows! The shadows!"*

For an instant Fynnol didn't know what was meant, and then a surge of fear rocked him, and he dove for the opening in the rocks.

Samul Renné was fighting for his life. Two black-clad guards were upon him, skilled fighters, cunning and quick. They did not tire but feinted and lunged, driving him back toward the wall. Once there, Samul knew it was only a matter of time.

"Renné!" he called in desperation. "Renné!" But there was no response—the treacherous would be left to die. His foot came up against hard stone as he dodged back yet again. Here he would make his end, so near to the gate out of this netherworld.

But then someone loomed out of the fog and smoke, engaging one of Samul's attackers and dispatching him in a few strokes. *Toren!* His cousin rounded on the second man, the odds suddenly turning against Hafydd's guard. Samul lunged forward and cut the guard's leg out from under him. As the man fell, Samul slashed at his throat, the blow cruel and true.

Before he could turn to thank Toren, his cousin toppled forward, someone on his back, swinging at his head and screaming. It was

Beldor, his blade broken, smashing at Toren with the pommel. Samul leapt at Beld, driving him off Toren, the two grappling and rolling in the blackened grass.

Beld came up on top, a dagger at Samul's throat.

"So you agreed to kill me, did you, Cousin? You of all the proud words and noble principles."

Samul could feel the point of the dagger press into his skin, see Beld's rage-filled face hovering over him in the garish light.

"Well, it is I who will reap Hafydd's rewards, now. And you who will rot in this pit."

Someone was shouting not far off, but Beld would cut his throat before he could call out. And then Samul realized what they were shouting. *"The shadows! The shadows!"*

Samul saw the words register on Beld, but even as his cousin looked up, a dark wing seemed to fall on him from above, claws tearing into his back and shoulder, hissing like rain on a fire. And Beld was yanked up into the air, into the endless night, his scream echoing off the walls, calling over and over down the valley, until it echoed only in Samul's mind.

Samul staggered up, rolling Toren over. A moan escaped Toren's bloody mouth. Samul hauled him up so that he sat and leaned heavily on his cousin.

"What happened?"

"It was Beldor. He jumped you from behind."

"Where is he now?"

"Dead," Samul said. "Gone. Come, get up. We're in danger."

Samul found both their swords, then helped his cousin stand. He could see Orlem and Crowheart not far off, waving flaming brands at shadows that swept out of the night and then were gone again.

Toren bent over and retched, leaning heavily on his cousin.

"Come, Toren. It isn't far. I'll get you to the passage out. You'll be safe."

"Safe? What are these black wings that come out of the night?"

"Some kind of sorcery. Make haste, Toren, or they will have us next."

But Toren thrust him away, swaying as though he would fall. "I will walk on my own," he said disdainfully. "First you would kill me, now you save me. What manner of man are you, Samul? Have you loyalty to nothing at all?"

"Loyalty to Beld? Is that what you would have liked to have seen? He was going to kill you, Cousin, and when I stopped him he tried to kill me. He was treacherous to the center of his soul. Get you on, then. You cannot fight as you are. Go, before a servant of Death takes you and your damnable pride off into the endless darkness."

Toren did not answer, but staggered on, one hand braced against the stone wall, his sword hanging loosely in his hand, too proud to take help from a traitor like Samul—who had just saved his life.

A flaming brand was thrust into Tam's hand by Elise, and nearby he could see Orlem waving his torch at the sky and shouting like a madman. In a moment he was doing the same, shadows hissing and lunging at him. He saw men dragged screaming into the sky, but had no time to worry about who they might be. Staying alive took every bit of his attention. Where Hafydd had gone he did not know.

"Fall back to the cleft," Elise called, but there was no quick re-treat. Men who turned to run were snatched from behind, disap-pearing into the dark and fog.

A shadow dove from above, and Tam thrust his brand into it, hewing at the dark wing with his blade, and screaming so that his throat seemed to tear. A hand grabbed him from behind, dragging him, stumbling, into a cleft in the stone.

"Get up, Tam!" Cynddl shouted. "We have to go farther in." The Fáel hauled Tam up.

A shadow blotted out the dim light of the opening, like a giant bat coming home to roost. Tam swung his makeshift torch at it, shouting and threatening with his sword. Cynddl still pulled him back by the collar of his shirt, steadying him as they went, for Tam dared not look away.

The cleft they had entered was tall, the light of Tam's torch unable to find the ceiling. Above them, the shadow flowed into the darkness, hissing like a viper.

"This way," Cynddl said, and pulled Tam into a side passage.

They were back to back, now, shuffling awkwardly down the narrow tunnel. Waving his brand overhead, Tam tried to pitch the light into corners and penetrate the high shadows. The shuffling of their feet and the scuffing of their shoulders along the stone were not as loud as Tam's heart, his ragged breathing. He had been frightened before—too many times—but this night was different. He had not really understood when the shadows had come before. But now he realized if they could not escape, that was his death slithering among the shadows overhead. And it would find him in time.

"It is up there. I can hear it," Cynddl hissed.

Tam waved his torch, his arm growing stiff and tired.

"Cynddl? Can you take the brand for a while? I must rest my arm."

Cynddl's hand closed around the brand just above Tam's. A stab of pain ran through his shoulder as he lowered his arm.

"There!" Cynddl shouted.

The shadow fell upon them, hissing and flapping as though it had wings. The claws darted at their faces, and they dodged this way and that, screaming in fear and defiance. Tam slashed at the claws and the darkness, his sword sparking off stone. Cynddl brandished their torch, then stumbled, bouncing off the rock. As he did so he threw the brand to Tam who slashed at the shadow with it.

And then it was gone, up into the darkness, a long hiss echoing down the passage.

Cynddl struggled up and took the torch from Tam. "Beware, Tam," the Fáel said, "it might be above us yet."

They continued down the passage, back to back, gasping from exertion and fear.

"It is gone, I think," Cynddl whispered. "I can't feel the cold in my heart that these servants bring."

"Perhaps, but I for one will not relax my vigil."

Shouts echoed distantly, the words distorted, almost inhuman.

"Where are we?" Tam wondered aloud. "Crowheart said it was a maze from which men never escaped."

"We are alive, that is all I know. Had we stayed out in the open the shadows would have snatched us into the air, as they did so many."

"Alive and lost. This won't burn forever—not even with Elise's magic upon it."

"We haven't gone far, Tam. I think we can find our way back to the Stillwater, if we must."

"And who will we find waiting for us? Hafydd? The servants of Death?"

Cynddl fell silent. They scuttled along like a single beast, leaning against each other. Another garbled shout; not so far off this time. Then a long wailing scream, which turned into a hiss.

Cynddl reached up as high as he could with their torch, trying to drive back the darkness above. "The shadows have not given up," he whispered.

"No," Tam answered. "Nor will they ever."

Samul Renné tripped and stumbled forward, bracing himself on the rock wall. He could not see far, the light from his brand reflecting dully off the undulating walls of the passage. He cursed under his breath.

"Which way?" he muttered.

The tunnel seemed to fork every twenty paces, and there were numerous side passages, some of which seemed to climb up, and others that wormed down into the earth.

He heard a long, drawn-out hiss, and felt a chill like a cold wind blowing through him, and then it was quiet again. The chill passed.

Samul tried to swallow, but his mouth was dry. "They will have me yet," he whispered. "Damn their dark hearts!"

Voices! He heard voices! But from which direction? He jogged along as best he could in the narrow passage, stopping to listen at each opening. He could not make out words, or who might be speaking but to find any of his allies in here would be a relief.

A mumbling sound rumbled down one passage, and Samul followed it as it went down and around, turning to the right, then back under itself like a winding stair. It went left then, sharply, and leveled out. With each step the voice grew louder, though no more clear.

Samul went carefully now, trying to make no sound. Anyone could have run into these passages to escape the shadows.

The rumble almost divided itself into words. Samul stepped gingerly around a corner and there he found Hafydd in a small chamber, the boy known as Fynnol upon his knees before him. They both looked up as Samul appeared, Hafydd awkwardly holding aloft a torch, a sword in his other hand.

He has an arrow in his shoulder! Samul realized.

"Samul Renné!" Hafydd said. "You never cease to surprise me. You cannot know how uncommon that is. And what have you done with your cousin?"

"He is dead."

"Ah, I'm so happy to hear it." Hafydd glanced back at the miserable Fynnol. "I was just questioning this whelp about the woman who has become Sianon. He was trying with all his wit to deflect my questions, to tell me half-truths and even outright lies—but he actually told me a great deal more than he meant to. I don't suppose I need him, now that you have arrived." Hafydd raised his sword.

"He knows more of her than I do," Samul said. "They traveled together for some time. He also knows much of this man you call your whist. You could kill him, but there is likely more to be learned from him." Samul strolled into the chamber, trying to hide his reluctance.

Hafydd hesitated, his sword raised. "You think so, truly? You are not just moved by pity?"

"Pity? I will kill him myself when the time comes, if that will re-assure you."

Hafydd considered this. "Do you hear that, Fynnol of the Vale? Your executioner has gained you a stay of sentence. It will not be long though. We will feed you to the shadows soon enough."

"Sooner than you know," came a hiss, and Hafydd whirled around.

In the corner of the chamber a shadow lingered, where light from their torches did not—or *would not*—penetrate. It moved like black smoke, oozing and roiling. Samul felt himself recoil, and he could not catch his breath. Fynnol Loell hid his face in his hands.

At the center of the darkness was a form—man-like and tall—but the roiling shadow fooled the eye.

"Even sorcerers do not stand before me," the voice snarled, and Hafydd dropped to his knees before Fynnol, his sword held limply, now. Samul felt his own knees strike the stone, his torch clattering down on the floor of the chamber, almost setting Fynnol afire.

"You have come for me at last," Hafydd whispered

"Perhaps, but it is not you I seek." The shadow moved, smoke drifting along the chamber wall. "You have sent many to my Master's realm, son of Wyrr, and long you have eluded him."

"If you are not Death, who are you?" Hafydd asked.

"I am the Hand of Death. I sit upon the step at the foot of his throne. I speak when he wishes to be heard. And now he has sent me forth to find you, son of Wyrr. There are two who have eluded Death for many lives of men."

"My sister and brother."

"No, my Master shall have them soon enough."

Samul saw Hafydd's gaze drop from the shadow to the floor. "My Father and his brother."

The shadow was silent a moment, then said, "Bring them to Death's gate and you shall not pass through—not for many hundreds of lives of men."

Hafydd did not answer, but he nodded his head, tightening his grip on his sword.

"These others serve you?" the shadow whispered. Samul thought he heard an insatiable hunger in those words.

Hafydd nodded.

"Do not fail, son of Wyrr." And the shadow flowed into a passage, darker than the darkness, silent as a thought.

For a moment they all stayed as they were, then Hafydd rose to his feet. He turned and stared down the passage where the Hand of Death had disappeared. Samul collected his torch from the floor and lurched to his feet, only to find his knees still weak from fear. He put out a hand and leaned against the wall. Even Hafydd was unsteady and shaken. Fynnol snatched up the brand Samul had dropped, and was on his feet and diving into the mouth of another passage before Hafydd noticed. Samul could have stopped him, perhaps, but didn't try.

"Let him go," Hafydd said. "He is but a minnow in the waters where we swim."

"Yes," Samul said. "Whether Fynnol Loell lives or dies this day hardly seems to matter after what I've just witnessed."

Hafydd stared at him a moment. "You saw that the Hand of Death did not touch you because you served me?"

Samul nodded.

"Never forget that." Hafydd struck the stone with the flat of his blade so that it rang, and moaned. "This way."

An arrow glanced off stone and shattered on the opposite wall. Orlem pressed Elise back with his arm, flattening her against the cool rock. Behind her, Baore pushed back against the curving wall, his staff in hand.

"How many are they?" Elise asked.

"I cannot say," Orlem answered. "But they're before us and behind, now. If we could only do without light." He nodded at an opening across the narrow tunnel. "We must go there."

"That will give the archers their chance."

"That cannot be helped. Be quick. I am armored—stay behind me."

Elise held the flaming brand aloft, her sword in the other hand. "Are you both ready, then? When I count three."

They leapt across the passage, colliding in the narrow opening. An arrow exploded on the rock behind them, a spray of splinters catching in Elise's hair.

"Go quickly!" Orlem pushed them both ahead.

Their footsteps rumbled down the passage. The tunnel angled down, the sculpted walls curving in and out. Unlike the other tunnels they had been in, this one was low-ceilinged—only a few feet taller than Orlem.

Elise and Baore were quicker than Slighthand, and rounded the corner before him. They met a blind end, a small chamber opening up around them, a light rain of water dribbling down from somewhere high above.

"We're trapped here!" Baore said, his words echoing several times.

Elise looked desperately around. "Can you climb up Baore? The water comes from somewhere."

Baore threw down his shod staff and scrambled up the smooth rock, bridging across a corner of the chamber. They heard the sounds of men behind; a scurrying of footsteps, like rats.

"If only I had a bow," Elise said.

Orlem stood by the opening to the chamber. "We shall be forced to fight our way out, my lady—"

A strange ringing came down the passage then, vibrating the air so violently that it pressed on Elise's ears, as though she were deep under water.

"What is that?" Orlem asked.

"Hafydd. He's found me." She looked up. "Baore?"

He was trying to move across from the corner now, looking for footing. "There is something," he called down, "but I can't quite see."

Elise handed the flaming brand to Orlem who could hold it much higher than she.

"There is . . . a small opening. We might squeeze through."

"You go up, my lady," Orlem said.

"We will all go, but not for a moment. Guard the passage."

The water that fell collected in a shallow pool and then disappeared into an small opening in the stone.

"Water . . ." Elise said. "Sianon could do much with water." She closed her eyes and opened herself to the memories—the memories she had been struggling to keep at bay.

They seemed to surge through her, the power of them, of all the emotions, buckling her knees. But she staggered forward, splashing the water over her, onto her face and neck. Without opening her eyes she made water marks on the wall, characters Elise did not know, words she had never heard. A voice chanted . . . her own voice, though it sounded strange in her ears. Vaguely she heard the clatter of swords, Orlem shouting. She stood in the middle of a pattern marked in water on the floor, her body almost shaking with the power of the enchantment.

And then she collapsed to the rock. Strong hands lifted her high up, and then another took hold of her wrists and dragged her over a lip of coarse stone. She could not even lift her face and felt her cheek scrape along the rock.

"Elise? Elise?" It was Baore, sounding more worried than she could remember.

"Orlem," she gasped. "We cannot leave him behind. He'll be drowned."

Elise opened her eyes to see Baore on his knees, silhouetted in a small opening. The flaming brand came into view, thrown from below, and Baore caught it, setting it on the ground behind. Next his shod staff came to hand, and she watched him brace himself, rigid with the effort.

Orlem's face appeared as he came up Baore's staff hand over hand. How Baore had held the giant she did not know.

She forced herself up, dragging herself up the stone wall until she was standing. "Make haste," she whispered. "The waves will sweep all before them."

"Take her on, Baore," Orlem said. "I can hold this opening for some time, even against Caibre."

"No!" Elise said. "You must come. Don't argue with me now."

Reluctantly the old warrior followed. Baore helped her, bearing much of her weight.

A thundering echoed in their ears, and a wind blew from behind. "Brace yourself," Elise said.

Water jetted down their small passage with such force that it took their legs from under them and battered them against the walls. Baore rose first, coughing, then dragged Elise up.

"What is this?" Baore shouted.

"I've raised up the Stillwater in great waves. Let them break Hafydd against stone."

"But what of the others?"

She did not answer. Orlem was on his feet and pressing them forward. The next wave announced itself with the same thundering roar, water shooting down their tunnel and throwing them against the walls.

When Elise stood they were in darkness, their light snuffed out. "Baore?"

But the Valeman did not answer.

"My lady?"

"Here, Orlem. Cast about and see if you can find Baore. If he's been knocked senseless he will drown."

She sloshed through the water, searching with her hands and feet. They could not find him, and after a time they went on, feeling their way in the dark. The roaring of the next wave rumbled somewhere deep in the cave.

"I didn't know what I was doing, Orlem. The enchantment is greater than I intended."

"Press on, my lady. If this passage fills . . . , " but he did not finish. He would drown, but she would not. That was the truth of it. Sianon would live on.

*   *   *

The servants of Death seemed to have gone, but Tam and Cynddl were lost.

"We have made so many turns," Tam said, "I can't begin to remember them all."

"Nor can I. We can only go on and hope we discover a way through or find Theason."

"What's that sound? Do you hear?"

Cynddl stopped and Tam bumped into him.

"Listen," Tam said. "It comes from behind."

The thundering roar reached them, and then a river of water rushed around the corner of the passage and struck them like a running bull. Tam kept his feet, but Cynddl was thrown down and washed along the tunnel. Almost as quickly as it came the water began to subside.

"Theason said nothing about water!" Tam said as he helped Cynddl to his feet. The water, waist high, ran quickly by.

"It is sorcery!" Cynddl called over the noise. Then the thundering came again.

"Up!" Tam yelled.

Bridging their feet across the narrow passage they clambered up, a wave of water shooting by below. A dozen feet up they found a narrow ledge, wide enough to stand on. The light from their torch showed it snaking off along the wall.

"The water once ran at this level," Cynddl said. "Let's press on quickly."

They'd not gone fifty feet when they heard coughing and splashing below. Tam took the brand from Cynddl and held it out over the passage.

"That's Fynnol!"

Tam thrust the brand into the Fáel's hands and went climbing quickly down. Beneath Fynnol he found Baore bearing him up. Tam grabbed the little Valeman.

"Fynnol. Up! You must climb up or you'll be drowned." The water was now neck deep on Baore.

With his help the cousins managed to reach the high ledge before the next wave came washing through. They collapsed against the sloping wall, gasping and choking.

"Hafydd must have done this," Cynddl said.

Baore shook his head, fighting for breath. "Elise . . ." he said. "We were trapped by Hafydd and she created an enchantment."

"She might drown us all!" Cynddl said.

"Where is she now?" Tam asked.

"I don't know," Baore said, straightening up. "I was washed down a narrow little tunnel in the dark. I don't even know how I survived."

Another wave crashed through the tunnel below, soaking them in spray.

"We won't stay above the waves for long," Tam shouted over the roar. "Look how high the water is now. We have to find a way out, or passages that lead up."

They set off down the passage on their narrow ledge, the water surging and crashing below, like surf against a cliff.

Elise had lost Orlem in the dark and crashing waves, and now she could not find him. Even she was thrown against the stone each time a wave washed through the caves. She would dive to the bottom and try to find some handhold but the rock was too smooth.

As the wave subsided she fought to the surface and called out, but no one answered in the darkness.

"Oh, Orlem," she sobbed. "Look what I've done."

And then she heard an echoing response to her call. She shouted again and again heard an answer. She swam in the direction of the sound, cautiously though, for Hafydd might still lurk here, somewhere.

"Who is there?" a muffled voice said in the darkness.

Elise scooped up water and blew into her hands, whispering an incantation. The water she held coalesced and glowed a soft opalescent green, like luminescence in the surf. In the frail light a man appeared.

"A'brgail? Is that you?"

He'd shed his surcoat and mail and clung to the rock, half out of the water, his bare arms white in the pale light. Elise could see his face was bruised and bleeding, as were his hands.

"Barely," he growled, his voice hoarse. "This sorcery has all but drowned me and has drowned many others. I have felt their bodies float by, some my own brethren, I fear."

He appeared gaunt and haunted, as though sure of his end yet clinging to life till the last.

"Come with me," Elise said. "I will try to get you out if I can."

The roar of another wave came to them and Elise reached out and took hold of A'brgail. They were torn off the rock and rolled down the passage, crashing over and over against the stone. When the wave subsided Elise still held the knight in her arms. He was almost limp. She carried him to the surface and made her light again.

"A'brgail? Come, you must climb up. I think I see an opening."

A shadowed oblong in the stone lay not far above them, though she could not be sure whether it was an opening. With Elise helping, A'brgail struggled up, pulling himself over the lip as the next wave washed through. The water only reached their knees, here. Elise held up her soft green light, looking around.

"You have your sword still!"

"Miraculously, yes."

"May I have it a moment?"

A'brgail handed it to her and she thrust the blade into the water.

"This way," she said.

"How do you know?"

"In the water I can sense many things. This will lead us out, though it is a good distance yet."

They limped along the tunnel, both injured and frightened.

"Hafydd has almost drowned us all," the knight said.

Elise did not answer.

"Will these waves ever stop?" he asked.

"Soon," Elise said softly, and cursed her foolishness again. She didn't remember enough to perform enchantments, not of such complexity and power. If she had killed Tam and his friends and Toren Renné she would curse herself forever.

The passage sloped down eventually, and the water became deeper. It surged up toward them with the passing of each wave, but the power was diminished and they made good progress.

At last they came to a place where the passage dipped down and was all but filled with water. When a wave poured in there was no air at all.

"Well," A'brgail said calmly, "it seems I can go no farther."

Elise had to admire the man's equanimity. "I will swim on and see if you can pass this way." She reached out to give A'brgail the light, but he hesitated.

"It won't hurt you," she said. "It's only water."

"Will you not need it?" Still, he held his hands back.

"No, and I don't know if I have the strength to make it again. Take it, unless you prefer the dark."

The knight reached out, but flinched as though someone were about to pour boiling water into his cupped hands.

"It is like a jellyfish!" he said.

"And so will we be if we don't escape this place soon. We'll be battered to a soft pulp and drifting with the currents."

Elise dove into the water and swam, feeling the width of the passage, testing the water's depth. There was just enough air space for A'brgail to pass, but when the waves surged the passage filled to the ceiling. She emerged into an airy passage and waited there, listening, hoping still to find some of the others, but there were no sounds of men.

She swam back to A'brgail, a surge carrying her through.

"There is air all the way through, though not when the waves come. If we manage it just right you might make it through without having to hold your breath."

She could see that this unnerved A'brgail. He might be able to swim a bit but he did not like the water. He was not confident in it.

Elise went out into the passage, where the ceiling dipped down until it almost touched the water. She let the surge come in and just when it was about to reverse she called out. A'brgail dove in without hesitation, swimming clumsily, but with determination.

They were almost through when the water surged again, checking A'brgail's progress. Elise reached out and grabbed him, hauling him forward.

They surfaced, the knight choking and coughing, spitting up water. Elise supported him until he could breathe again.

"You have courage, Gilbert A'brgail. I will give you that."

"Staying here and drowning seems a poor alternative."

"Then let us go on."

They scrambled forward, the walls reflecting Elise's light. The waves did not roar through this passage as they had earlier, but the water seemed to rise around them and then to subside almost gently.

"How much farther?" A'brgail asked.

"Some distance. We need to go down into the labyrinth, yet, and there will be more water as we descend."

A'brgail stopped, leaning heavily against the wall. "Can we not just wait here until the waters subside?"

"We might, yes, though I don't know when that might be. But Hafydd seeks me still. I sense him, searching."

A'brgail pushed himself upright. "Then on we must go," he said faintly.

Around a bend they found a drowned Knight of the Vow, and A'brgail paused over the body. He reached down and gently brushed the man's dark, wet hair back from his eyes. "So young," he said softly. "A whole life to live. I brought him here to this end."

"It is the lot of those who lead," Elise said. "Men die, no matter how careful you are. Sometimes being careful leads to more deaths. I have seen it."

A'brgail nodded, and they went on, the knight glancing back only once.

*   *   *

They were in water up to their necks, Fynnol struggling to keep his face above the surface, Baore bearing him up as he could.

"I don't think I can do this much longer," Fynnol said, spitting out a mouthful of water.

Tam worried that *Baore* might not be able to keep it up. Cynddl and he were doing what they could, but when the waves came it took all the strength they had just to survive. They held onto each other in the dark, frightened of being separated. The lone swimmer would be lost, and they knew it.

A wave swept in, lifting and driving them down the passage. Tam was scraped painfully along the wall, and then slammed into a corner of stone. For a moment he could not move, and then he realized the others were not there and he swam desperately on, calling out. In a moment they were together again, hands taking hold of him in the dark.

"All here?" Cynddl said.

They answered weakly.

"I hit my head on the ceiling that time," Cynddl said. He did not need to say more. The water level had reached the point where they would soon lose their air. They would be in a drowned passage.

None of them spoke, saving their strength. Tam knew that a few more waves and they would be done, but they would go down together, he was sure. They'd stood by one another down all the length of the River Wynnd—they wouldn't forsake each other now.

The next wave threw them all up against the ceiling so that they were forced to dive down as best they could. When the water subsided again they all came up choking and gasping for air.

"Let's make a wager," Fynnol said. "One more wave, I think, will do for us."

The water surged around them like surf, lifting them and dropping them down again. They clung together, frightened and without hope.

"Tam . . ." Fynnol began, but then the water took hold of them again.

"Here it comes!" Tam shouted.

The water dipped low, then rose, casting them down the passage, slamming them into stone. Fynnol's hand was torn out of his and Tam was driven against the stone ceiling and dragged along.

This is the end, he thought. And then he felt as though he were falling, falling. Falling through the air.

He heard Fynnol shout, and then Tam splashed hard into water, knocking the last air from his lungs. But this water was cool and still. He fought to the surface and there was light. Star- and moonlight!

"Here!" a voice called. "Over here!"

Tam heard someone surface a few feet away.

"Baore! Where is Fynnol?"

"I don't know," Baore wailed. "I lost him. . . ."

Cynddl broke the surface.

"We've lost Fynnol!" Tam called out.

"He is here," Cynddl gasped, "but I can't bear him up."

Baore and Tam flailed through the water to their cousin's aid. They took hold of him and with the story finder's help made their way toward the voice.

"Who is there?" Tam called.

" 'Tis Theason and Prince Michael."

"Have you Alaan with you?"

Silence.

"He-He did not surface when we fell into the river. I think he was dead even then."

They found Theason and the Prince on a large, flat rock in the shadow of a high cliff. The two helped them crawl onto the stone, where they collapsed, unable to move. Tam heard a muffled sobbing from one of his companions.

"Theason," Cynddl said. "Where are we?"

"On the River Wynnd," the traveler said. "That is what Theason thinks. Daylight is not far off, though it will be a day without joy. I—I could not keep Alaan afloat. I was not strong enough."

"At least we are back in the land between the mountains," Fynnol said. "Thank all the spirits of the river for that!"

Tam propped himself up on one bruised elbow, water still running from his hair, his clothes sodden. "What has become of all the others?" Tam wondered. "Pwyll and Elise, Crowheart, Orlem, the Renné, and Gilbert A'brgail?"

He saw Theason shake his head in the dark. "Theason doesn't know. I don't understand how we came to be here. This was not the path I traveled to the Stillwater."

"Elise will not drown," Cynddl said, sitting up, but appearing bent and huddled in the starlight. "She is of the river, now. I think the same of Alaan, if he was not dead when you reached the Wyrr. The nagar were preserved by the river. It is almost more their home than the land."

"Then Hafydd will live as well," Tam said, and felt a sudden overwhelming urge to weep. "All we have been through, and we accomplished nothing. Alaan is dead. Hafydd alive." He sat, drew up his knees, and buried his face in his arms.

"It is worse than you know, Cousin," Fynnol whispered. "I met Hafydd in the tunnels. He tried to get me to tell him of Elise and Alaan, though I told him as little as I could, given that he held a sword over my head. Samul Renné arrived, and was greeted like an ally. And then, when I thought Hafydd would cut my throat, a dark presence appeared. I couldn't see it, for the light of our torches would not penetrate the shadow surrounding it. 'I am the Hand of Death,' it said, and even Hafydd fell to his knees before it. I heard it offer him a bargain. If he could bring Wyrr and Aillyn to Death's Gate then he would be granted a span many hundreds of lives of men. As it disappeared, with Hafydd and Samul watching, I snatched up a torch and ran. I don't think they even tried to follow, so shaken were they by what had happened."

"How do you kill someone who has made a bargain with Death?" Tam wondered.

"Well," Cynddl said softly. "There is an ancient story about just such a man. . . ."

Elise raised her dim light, as water flooded around her waist. She and A'brgail were crawling along a low, narrow tunnel, half filled with water. In her other hand she carried A'brgail's sword, her knuckles all bloody and battered.

"How much farther?" A'brgail asked.

She could make out his haunted face a few feet behind. "I don't know. Not far."

"Do you sense him still?"

"Yes. Hafydd pursues me, yet."

A'brgail grunted and they crawled on. Elise's knees were now numb to the beating they were taking on the rock. The water surged around them so that only their heads were above water. Elise could hear A'brgail gulping down air, breathing fast. He was terrified, yet there was no panic, even here where he could surely die.

She was scrambling now, pounding her one hand and knees down on the stone, half afloat, trying to keep her light aloft to guide them.

"Lady Elise?" A'brgail said as the water rushed away again, giving them air. "You tried to get me out, even though you believed I was your enemy, you tried. Sianon would never have done that."

Elise was about to answer but stopped, shielding the faint light with her hand. A'brgail almost blundered into her from behind.

"Do you see?" she asked. "Is that light?"

"It . . . perhaps it is!" A'brgail pushed past her, in the narrow tunnel, and thrashed through the water. There seemed to be an opening ahead, though it was low and small.

They scrambled desperately forward. Another wave was coming. She could hear it. And then it broke upon her, driving her forward, the walls of the tunnel tearing past. It subsided, and she lay still. Near at hand someone was coughing or retching, she could not be sure which.

Overhead, between the branches of trees, she could see the pale sky of early morning. Tears welled up and for a moment she could not speak or even move. She lay looking up at the branches and the sky through a blur of tears.

An odd splashing sound echoed from the opening and then water gushed around her. She sat up shakily. A'brgail lay half in the pool of water and half on land. It was a stream, she saw, with a small cave opening into the bank. A last small surge of water washed out, and then it was quiet.

"Where are we?" A'brgail asked.

Elise gazed around her. "In the land between the mountains, but where, I don't know. Did Theason not claim the way was treacherous and could not be passed in the dark?"

She crawled out onto the bank and sat cross-legged, her brain too addled by the battering she had received to even begin to consider what had happened.

"What's become of the others?" A'brgail wondered aloud.

"I don't know." She forced herself up and looked around the banks of the stream. "No one has been here," she said.

"Did no others survive, then?" A'brgail was sitting up now, still coughing sporadically.

Elise thought a moment. "Clearly there is more than one way out. Let us hope Crowheart or Theason led the others to safety."

A'brgail did not look like he believed this. Very gingerly he employed a finger to explore a purple wound on his brow. "And Hafydd?"

She thrust his blade into the trickle of water that emerged from the opening. Elise shrugged, the motion causing her pain. "Get up, A'brgail," she said going over and dragging him to his feet. "He is not far."

The knight swayed, but then gained his balance. "Will he never give up?"

"Caibre? He can never let a thing go. You must know that. He will not rest until I am destroyed. And you, A'brgail. When he learns that Knights of the Vow exist still. . . ."

"Then let us be off."

They hobbled up the bank supporting each other, the soft light of a new day falling through the forest. They walked among the rays that slanted through the green, clutching each other's arms. A sorcerer thrush called once, its flute-like notes drifting like a falling leaf. Elise pointed. There, on a branch, perched a nondescript little bird, its dun crest and golden eye visible in the clear light. It bobbed its tail once, flicked its head, and was gone into the shadows and green as though it had never been there at all.

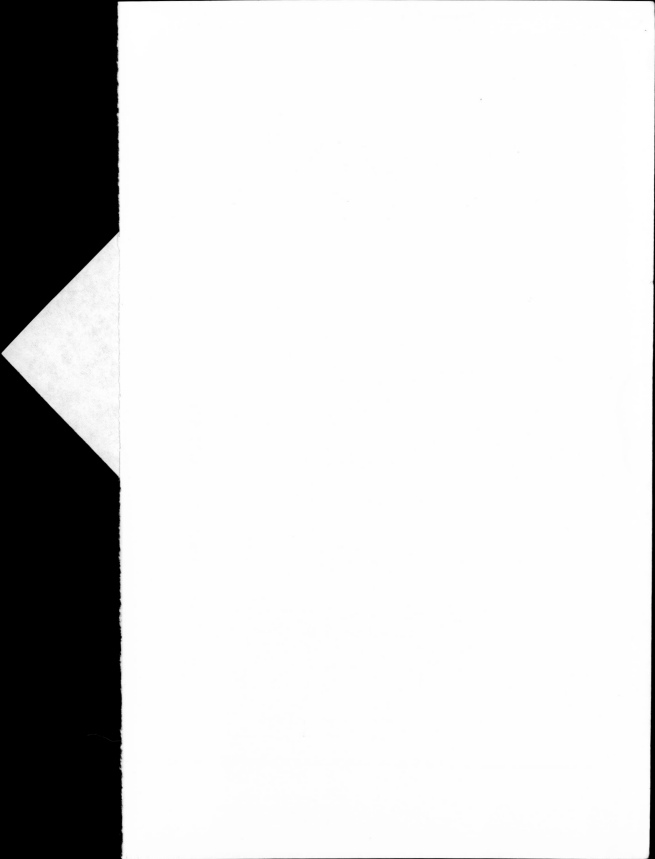

READER'S VIEWS
Initial and/or write
your comm